After Mag

Mirei wasn't sure if she wa
muffling effect of the softly [...] snow.

The air was clear of summoned power. The landscape was a wreck. Pine trees behind Mirei had been reduced to kindling. Debris from the slope on the other side of the path was strewn everywhere. A boulder blocked part of the path downhill; the blood crusted on it was rapidly freezing. In its wake lay the shattered remains of a red-haired woman.

Not much was left of the witches or their horses. The skinny witch had been singing Fire; that had been the catalyst and shaping force for the power that annihilated her. Mirei stumbled past the bloody pulp that had been a horse. Ashin wasn't hard to find; her clothes made a blackened stain in the white of the snow.

Ashin smiled weakly at her. "Next time, give a little warning."

Acclaim for *Doppelganger*

Also by Marie Brennan

Doppelganger

Warrior and Witch

MARIE BRENNAN

WARNER BOOKS

NEW YORK   BOSTON

Cover design by Don Puckey
Book design by Stratford Publishing Services, Inc.

Warner Books and the Warner Books logo are trademarks of Time Warner Inc. or an affiliated company. Used under license by Hachette Book Group, which is not affiliated with Time Warner Inc.

Warner Books
Hachette Book Group USA
1271 Avenue of the Americas
New York, NY 10020
Visit our Website at www.HachetteBookGroupUSA.com

Printed in the United States of America

First Printing: October 2006

10 9 8 7 6 5 4 3 2 1

To Kyle, for putting up with
a summer full of
inconvenient working hours.

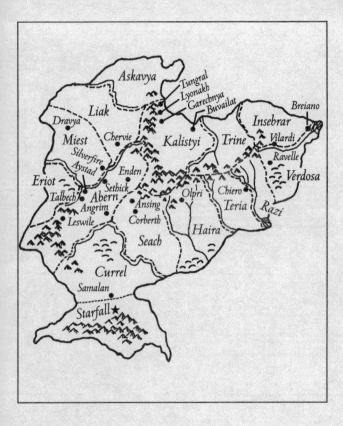

PART ONE

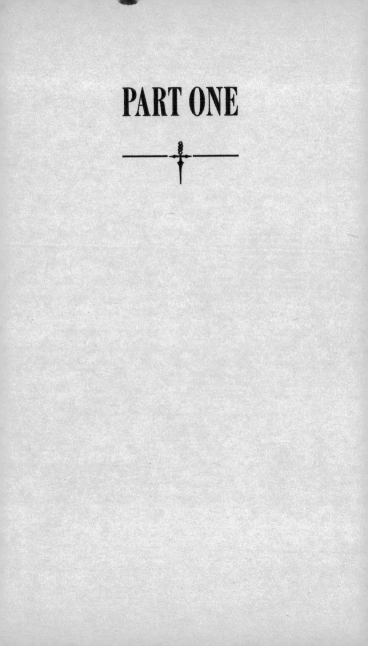

Chapter One

FOR EIGHT DAYS, Mirei thought she could relax.

Those days weren't empty of stress; her very presence at Starfall was a source of tension for the witches around her. Her life was no longer in danger, though. Her magic was under control and the Primes were no longer planning to execute her; on the whole, her situation had improved. And so Mirei began to relax.

But on the ninth day, a Cousin woke her with a message that she was needed in Satomi's office. That alone was a sign of trouble. Mirei had gone to that office every morning since coming back to Starfall, and given that she didn't sleep in, she was always there by First at the latest. If Satomi had sent a servant to wake her early, then there was trouble bad enough that it couldn't wait.

Mirei sent the Cousin away and dressed as quickly as she could, throwing on the first thing that came to hand. It was a lightweight blue dress, on loan from some witch, or perhaps another Cousin. Miryo's clothing, left behind when she went in search of Mirage, didn't fit her muscled shoulders, and the only clothing of Mirage's she had was her Hunter uniform. Wearing that only stirred people up even more. As did going armed; Mirei had to stop herself short of taking the sword that leaned against the wall by her bed. There might be trouble, but she sincerely hoped it wasn't bad enough that she would have to kill anyone.

And you'd look like an idiot, wearing a sword over a dress.

Unarmed, she left the New House, the residence for newly tested witches who had not yet established homes elsewhere. It was only a short walk from there to the main structure of Starfall, a rambling complex filled with offices, libraries, and classrooms. The hour was early enough that few people were about, for which she was grateful. They still stared at her, and it brought back surreal memories of her childhood as Mirage. People had stared at her then, too, for the fiery red hair that made her look like a witch. She'd snarled about it for years, only to find out that she *was,* in a sense, a witch—or rather, the other half of one. Getting over *that* revelation had taken a while.

Ruriko was waiting in the outer office, surrounded as always by piles of paper. She exchanged one look with Mirei; Ruriko could say more with one look than most women could with a speech. Then the secretary waved her through, into the Void Prime's office, and turned back to her work.

The interior room was one Mirei had never seen before eight days ago, yet it had become familiar with startling speed. As a witch-student who had not yet been tested, Miryo had never been summoned to this inner sanctum, with its elegantly tiled floor, shelves of books, and tidy sheaves of paper. She'd spoken instead with the unranked witches who taught her classes, or occasionally the Keys who served the Primes and ran much of Starfall's business. Since returning as Mirei, though, she'd spent much of every day here, sitting in one of the high-backed chairs, trying to help quell the trouble she'd caused.

Satomi was alone inside—another worrisome note. Usually other people were present for these meetings. The Void Prime stood next to the window, gazing out over the predawn landscape. She, too, was much more familiar than she had been—enough so that Mirei could read the tension in her body, even though she was trying to hide it. Satomi had the kind of face that registered age by acquiring more dignity, rather than lines, but today she looked old and tired.

The door closed softly behind Mirei; she waited, then ventured to speak. "Satomi-aken. What's happened?"

Satomi's voice was quiet, flat, despite its richly trained tones. "Shimi is gone."

"Gone?"

"From Starfall. She left in the night." Satomi turned away from the window. The lamps in her office, lit against the early morning darkness of the sky, made her look even paler than usual, and painted her delicate features with shadows. The unrelieved black of her dress only accentuated it. Black was her Elemental color, and she'd always worn it on ceremonial occasions, but she hadn't put it off since Mirei came to Starfall. Mirei suspected it was in mourning for all the doppelgangers who had died. Or, perhaps, for her own.

The Void Prime crossed to her desk and picked up the single sheet of parchment that lay on it. She scanned it, not appearing to really read the words, and then handed it to Mirei.

> *I have left, and will not return. I refuse to remain in company with that abomination. The doppelganger is taken out of us for a reason; to bring it back in is*

rankest heresy. It must be destroyed. To state that it is the Warrior and the Void is no argument in its favor—on the contrary, that is exactly why we must get rid of it. It is the destruction of life, the destruction of magic, the antithesis of everything that is this world, and if we welcome it back in, we will have committed a terrible sin. It will not be enough for that monster to leave. We must destroy it, and remove this horror from the world.

Mirei shook her head in disbelief, putting the sheet back down. "She almost sounds like a Nalochkan."

"She was raised in Kalistyi," Satomi said grimly. "The Nalochkan sect was as strong in Kalistyi when Shimi was a child as they are now. Clergy never come into our halls, of course—Nalochkan or otherwise—but the influence still penetrates."

"You mean . . ." Mirei fumbled for words. She wasn't awake enough yet to handle this rupture to the tenuous peace. "She can't actually *share* their beliefs—can she? To disavow the Warrior, to say she's not even part of the *Goddess*—" It would be radical enough in an unranked witch; though the witches didn't call themselves a sect, they had their own approach to religion, and rarely strayed from it. For no less a woman than the Air Prime, one of the five women who ruled Starfall and its people, to show such allegiance to an outside sect—

Satomi turned back to the window, placing her slender hands on the sill. When she spoke, her voice was low, betraying her tension. "No. I would not say she shares their beliefs, not to that extent. But the influence is there. And we of Starfall have never given as much attention to the

Warrior as we do to the other four Aspects of the Goddess; the Void has, for us, been as much practical as theological. We neglect it, as we neglect the Warrior. And for someone like Shimi, who needs a reason to believe you are anathema . . . it would be easy to magnify that divide. Especially when she grew up surrounded by Nalochkan beliefs."

Mirei sank into a chair. When other witches were there, she behaved more formally, but in private Satomi allowed her some liberties. "I don't get it. You had doubts, sure, but you killed your own doppelganger. I can understand why you didn't want to believe that I was right—it meant that you were wrong to kill her. But what's Shimi's reason? Why won't she believe?"

"Because she *didn't* kill her doppelganger." Satomi bowed her head. The two of them had never addressed this issue directly, not since the Void Prime told Miryo of her own doppelganger's death. Mirei had only come to understand it fully when she and Satomi fought in Star Hall. Then she had realized the cause of the Void Prime's reluctance to accept what Mirei had to say. "I remember looking at her, and I remember recognizing her as the other half of myself. In the end I convinced myself that she was a threat I must eliminate—a threat to all of us, not just myself—but that memory came back to me when you told us what you had done. Shimi has no such memory. It is easier for her to believe that doppelgangers are anathema, when the alternative is such a radical change."

"But what does leaving accomplish, except to openly declare her opposition? If she's so worried about what's going to happen, then she should stay and try to minimize the chaos. She's one of the five most powerful women here—"

Mirei stopped mid-sentence, because Satomi had turned around, and her pale green eyes were full of fear she had not shown before.

"Ashin sent us the list," the Void Prime said.

The words didn't register. "The list?"

"Of the other doppelgangers. Who they are. And where."

Mirei's heart skipped a beat, painfully. The list. The Void-damned list. There were other doppelgangers out there, alive—the nonmagical halves of witch-daughters. A group of conspirators among the witches had arranged in secret for them to survive the ritual where they were supposed to die, because the conspirators were convinced they *shouldn't* die. And they were right; Mirei had proved it. But prior to that, Starfall had branded those witches as heretics, had even assassinated their leader. One of Mirei's tasks in the last eight days had been to communicate with Ashin, the Key of the Air Hand, and the only one of the conspirators she knew personally. She had been trying to convince the woman that it was safe, finally, to admit where the doppelgangers were.

It seemed she'd finally succeeded.

"Shimi has it," Mirei said softly.

"Ashin wrote to us last night, after we sent you away. Shimi had no chance to make a copy of the list, but she wouldn't need to; we spent hours discussing it. She knows where they are."

Suddenly Mirei couldn't bear to be sitting; she rose to her feet and moved a few steps away with quick, tight strides that barely helped to ease her tension. Her boot heels clicked on the tiled floor with shocking loudness. "She'll go after them. But no—she can't kill them. Not without the other half of each pair, the witch-daughter. She'd have to kill both at once, for them both to stay dead." Her gaze snapped up to meet the Prime's. "You have to protect them."

"I've already taken steps," Satomi said. "And will take more, after I speak to the other Primes, which will be soon. As for the doppelgangers themselves, we'll write to the witches that are nearest to them, send them after the children. If they move quickly enough, we should be there ahead of Shimi, or whomever she has sent in her stead."

For a moment that seemed like an ideal solution, heading the Air Prime off at the pass. Then Mirei had a brief, vivid memory of standing on the balcony of a tower at the Hunter school of Silverfire, watching two young girls train below, listening to the Grandmaster of the school say, *"There's another at Windblade, and one at Thornblood."*

"Bad idea," she said.

Satomi paused on her way to her desk, shoulders stiff with affront. "I beg your pardon?"

"No way in the *Void* is that going to work. Not for all of them. You're going to send a witch into a Hunter school and have her say, 'Sorry, I need to walk off with some of your trainees'?" Mirei shook her head, knowing her fear was making her be rude. "They'll throw her out on her ear. *If* she's lucky."

"They will not have a choice," Satomi said crisply. "We will use magic if necessary."

"Oh, even better. You send witches into three different Hunter schools and have them throw spells about before they run off with trainees. Aken, you'll start a *war.*"

The Void Prime raised her eyebrows in startlement. "They would be that angry?"

"We do *not* like witches interfering with us," Mirei said. The word "we" came out reflexively, and she saw Satomi notice it. But Mirei was as much a Hunter as she was a witch, the Mirage part of her had lived that life, as the Miryo part had lived here in Starfall. "They might not be able to stop you. But trainees belong to their schools, just as much as our daughters belong to Starfall. Stealing them away—you're talking about offending not one but *several* groups of trained assassins, mercenaries, and spies who already don't like you very much. You do *not* want them angry at you."

Satomi's hands clenched on empty air, a gesture of frustration and impotence. "Then what do *you* suggest? We can't just leave them there for Shimi to take."

The answer was obvious. "I'll go after them."

"No. It would take too long for you to get there."

"It would take me no time at all."

Mirei saw the heartbeat of incomprehension in the Void Prime's face, before Satomi realized what she meant. It was an understandable blindness; translocating living things was supposed to be impossible. And so it *had* been, until Mirei recreated herself out of Miryo and Mirage. That rejoining gave her access to the magic of the Void, believed untouchable until then. Satomi was not yet accustomed to allowing for that in her plans.

"You could bring them right back here!" the Prime said, hope lighting her eyes. "We wouldn't even have to wait!"

Mirei almost agreed. Then instinct murmured in the back of her head. She was still learning what she could and could not do with Void magic, but one thing she had learned was how exhausting it was, especially translocation.

She had to shake her head. "No. I don't think I can move more than just myself."

The hope in Satomi's eyes withered.

"Maybe I'll be able to someday," Mirei said. "But I'd rather not experiment with something that tricky yet. I can take myself to Silverfire now, though. There are two there, right?" Satomi nodded, not that Mirei needed the confirmation. "I need to talk to Jaguar anyway. He knows he's got two of them, and that they're like me—that is, like Mirage was. If he'd hand them over to anybody, it would be me. So I can get them to safety, and then go after the other ones." She thought it over, grimacing. "Windblade, I can probably manage; we're friendly with them. Thornblood will be a different story. Their people hate my people's guts. But I'll figure something out."

Satomi pulled herself up, spine straightening from its momentary slump. "The rest are fostered with farmers, tradesmen, the like. We can take care of those."

"Fine." Mirei's mind was already racing, thinking ahead to what she would need. Translocate to Silverfire, then ride to Angrim—that would take about four days. Fortunately, both Thornblood and Windblade were just outside of Angrim, so she could kill two birds with one stone. Then—assuming she found a way to steal a girl out of the hostile territory of Thornblood—the long ride back south to Starfall, where the doppelgangers could be protected. Once she got away from Angrim with the other pair, they could pick up an escort of Cousins, or even other witches. Just in case Shimi, or anyone else, tried something. There could well be Thornbloods on her tail at that point, and who knew how many witches out there might agree with the Air Prime about the new situation?

But her experiences as Mirage told her how well plans survived actual testing. Better to stay adaptable. "Give me a sheet to communicate with you," Mirei said. The written word was slower, but on the road, it would be an easier spell to manage than bringing Satomi's image up in a mirror. "I may have to play things by ear. And you can get in touch with me if anything else happens here."

Satomi nodded. "Very well. Bring them back to us, as quickly as you can."

PACKING DIDN'T TAKE LONG, once it dawned on her that she didn't need supplies for a ride. She would have to get a horse from Silverfire anyway, and she could get food at the same time. Assuming Jaguar let her kidnap two trainees in the first place.

Well, if he didn't, she could translocate back to Starfall. No food necessary.

She changed into uniform: the loose pants, shirt, short jacket, and sash that identified her not just as a Hunter, but as a Silverfire. The silver pendant she wore, the triskele knot that was the witches' symbol, she tucked out of sight inside the shirt. Then, putting on the jacket, she froze in the act of flipping her hair out from under the collar.

It was a reflexive action—for the part of her that remembered being Miryo. For the Mirage half, it was something she hadn't done in over a decade.

Long hair. Void it.

From the hard calluses on her knuckles to the scar on her left hip, the body she had was Mirage's—except for the hair. Mirage had been the Void half, the Warrior half, the physical counterpart to Miryo's magic, and so when the Goddess put them back together as one person, most of the qualities she had picked up from her life as Hunter had stayed. But the hair, for whatever reason, was Miryo's, and long. Mirage's hair had been cropped short.

And if Mirei showed up at Silverfire with hair past her shoulders, they'd *know* something was off.

She looked around her room and sighed in frustration. Not a pair of scissors in sight, and if she tried to hack off her hair with a dagger, it would look even more bizarre. She could create an illusion, but she wanted to avoid magic as much as possible while around Hunters.

She went in search of help instead.

Eikyo had not yet taken her test, and so was still living in the students' hall. Mirei received some startled looks and bows as she went through the corridors and up the stairs; her notoriety in Starfall was unmatched. But she was getting used to that. Arriving at Eikyo's door, she knocked crisply, and hoped her friend was home.

She was. Still wrapped in a dressing robe, Eikyo answered the knock. Her round face showed her surprise. "Miryo. What—" She caught herself, and grimaced. "Mirei, I mean. What are you doing here so early?"

Mirei generally spent her mornings talking with the Primes and her afternoons demonstrating her new abilities to a variety of other witches, but she'd managed to arrange things such that she and Eikyo saw each other most days. It was a deliberate move on her part. Miryo and Eikyo had been close friends; she didn't want the other woman thinking of Mirei as a stranger. Mostly she had succeeded. The slipup with her name was the exception now, not the rule.

She gave her friend a crooked smile. "I need my hair cut."

Soon she was seated in a chair, listening to Eikyo's scissors snip around her head. The long strands of her hair fell to the floor in a fiery drift. "I wish you'd tell me why you want this done," the witch-student said dubiously, for the third time.

"Satomi has a job for me, that's all. And people won't think a witch with short hair looks nearly as odd as a Hunter with long hair." Mirei turned slightly, as if that would let her see the back of her own head. "Are you done yet?"

"Nearly. I don't know how good it'll look, though."

"Better than if I did it myself, I can promise you that." Mirei ran her hand over her scalp when Eikyo finally stepped back, and felt the familiar-but-strange sensation of short hair ruffling against her fingers. How much time would it take before her own body stopped feeling half alien to her? "Thanks."

"You look weird."

Mirei grinned wryly. "Thanks. Look, I've got to go."

Eikyo stopped her with one hand on her arm. The look in her blue-gray eyes was worried, as if she'd guessed there was more to the situation than Mirei was telling. Satomi would have to announce Shimi's departure soon; Mirei wondered how people would take it. "Is there anything I can do to help?" Eikyo asked.

Mirei shook her head. "For me, no. But I'm sure there will be things for you to do here."

Her friend's mouth twisted. "That's not what I meant."

"That's not what *I* meant, either," Mirei said, sobering. "The trouble hasn't ended, Eikyo. I may have found an answer to the doppelganger problem, but it's going to take a while for people to adjust to it, and we're going to hit a lot more potholes in the road before that's over. Satomi's going to need help. Even after I get back."

Eikyo nodded reluctantly. "Goddess go with you, Mirei."

Mirei had already gotten more direct help from the Goddess than she could ever have expected, with the miracle that brought her back together. She wasn't going to count on more. The sentiment, though, was appreciated. "You too, Eikyo. And be careful."

FINALLY SHE STOOD in her own room, dressed, shorn, ready to go.

Her final act was to belt a sword onto her hip, and as she did so, she remembered that the blade was not her own. It belonged to Eclipse, her Hunter partner, who also had most of her other belongings—those that she hadn't left behind in Angrim when she translocated out of the city.

I should get those back from him, Mirei thought, and did some calculations in her head. *He ought to be at Silverfire by now.*

The thought brought a spark of pleasure, but also of nervousness. *Why in the Void am I nervous?* It didn't make any sense. Eclipse had been Mirage's closest friend, her year-mate at Silverfire—practically a brother. And though Miryo hadn't known him for as long, the two of them had gotten along quite well.

That was it. Eclipse was effectively the only person in the world that Mirei had known as both halves of herself. Ashin she'd met only briefly, and everyone else had belonged to one half of her life or the other. Mirage knew

Hunters. Miryo knew witches. Both of them knew Eclipse, and he knew both of them.

She'd seen him very fleetingly after rejoining, before she left for Starfall. Her thoughts had been so fixated on what had happened to her, and what she was planning, that she hadn't had much time to wonder what Eclipse thought of her now.

And what she thought of him. The rejoining meant she had layered and somewhat contradictory memories of him. Quasi-brother and friend; known for years and known for mere days. She couldn't predict which version might win out in her mind, and that made her nervous.

But standing in her room wouldn't make the problem go away, and she was wasting time. Mirei took a deep breath and exhaled slowly, banishing such scattered thoughts from her mind. The spell she was about to attempt was a tricky one, and she did *not* want to find out what would happen if she screwed it up.

Mirei rotated her shoulders to loosen them. Large spells often required foci, Elementally-linked objects that helped the caster juggle more power than she would be able to handle otherwise. One of the first questions the magical theorists at Starfall had asked her when they heard about Void magic was, what were its foci? The answer she'd given them had set off a storm of philosophical speculation that left her head spinning. As near as Mirei could tell, the main focus of Void magic—perhaps the only focus—was movement.

She began to sing, her voice calling power from the world around her and shaping it to her will, and as she sang, her body flowed into motion. Mirage, the doppelganger, the Void-linked part of herself, had grown up in environments that centered on movement. Temple Dancer. Hunter. It wasn't an accident. She'd possessed special gifts for those things before rejoining with Miryo, strength and speed beyond what her body should have had, because the Void belonged to the Warrior. Those advantages had gone away with the rejoining, but the affinity for movement remained, imprinted on her through years of training.

So she sang and she danced, and the spell built around her. She reveled in the feeling. Miryo had spent weeks avoiding the use of her magic, for fear it would destroy her. Now it was safe, and wondrous. She shaped the strands about her body, and blinked out of sight.

There was a shattering moment of nothingness—then she was in the wood behind Silverfire.

The effect left her breathless. She wasn't sure she'd ever get over that. The concept that translocation moved its target through the Void had always been an unsubstantiated theory; living creatures died if you tried it on them, and you couldn't ask an object where it had been. Mirei now had confirmation. She didn't know how long the transit lasted—an instant? an eternity?—and she prayed to all five Aspects of the Goddess that no theorist ever tried to extend the time. She'd fling *them* through the Void. Let them study it that way.

A foot slammed into her lower back and threw her into a tree.

Mirei caught herself and spun to face her attacker. She blocked, not fast enough; a fist clipped her cheek—

"Mirage?"

She blinked her vision clear in the dim shade of the

wood. The Hunter in front of her was familiar. "Shit, Viper. Yes, Void damn you, it's me."

He backed up a step, but did not drop his guard. "Prove it."

"*Prove* it?" She stared at him. "Did somebody hit you in the head since the last time I was here? Don't you remember my face?"

"Prove this isn't some illusion."

His words turned Mirei cold. Hunters liked to keep witches from meddling in their business, yes, and were paranoid about them as a result, but there was no reason for Viper to expect a witch to show up in the woods of Silverfire.

Or was there?

"Warrior's blood, Viper, you know me." Mirei straightened up slowly. She roughened her tone subtly; if he noticed how trained she sounded, he'd be sure she was a witch. "I was here, what, two weeks ago? With Eclipse. You'd bet ten silver on me showing up sooner. Your leg was injured—well, if that kick's anything to go on, you're feeling better. You were playing guard for the infants, so they could try to sneak past you on the front wall." He still didn't look persuaded. "You make a weird snorting noise if somebody grabs your hair during a fight. We used to go for that in sparring, just to hear you do it."

That last bit finally sold him on it. Viper relaxed. "Okay. Sorry. It's just— I attacked before I really saw you. Seemed like you came from nowhere. Slowing down, aren't you?"

"Or you're getting faster," she said lightly, but inside she winced. She *was* slower, and hadn't yet learned to shift her tactics to compensate.

"What in the Void are you doing back here, anyway?" Viper asked.

"Came to see Jaguar. Got to talk to him about something."

Her fellow Hunter gave her a sidelong look as they began to walk toward the Silverfire compound. Mirei had chosen a familiar clearing in the woods as her target; the better she knew a place, the easier it was to aim for. She still shivered to remember how she'd jumped completely blind to Eclipse's room at an inn, after she rejoined. That had been the tail end of the miracle that made her whole again. She wasn't about to try it again without divine help.

But Viper was speaking, and his words reminded her that there was more going on here than she'd suspected. "Does this have anything to do with our two, shall we say, special cases?"

"Does your paranoia have anything to do with them?"

Viper groaned. "Four ways from feast day. Some of the first-years jumped one of them the other night, for being such a brat."

"It's a time-honored way of resolving differences among trainees."

"Yeah, but it didn't solve the brattiness, and next time it might be worse. Traditional-sized bloodbaths are fine, but I don't want a real mess on my hands."

"The joys of babysitting duty."

"My leg's nearly solid again, and you'd better believe I'm getting back on the road the minute I can."

They were in the compound by now, and Mirei kept Viper chatting about less important matters as they headed for the tower that stood at the center. Or rather, he let her do it. Silverfire Hunters took investigative jobs often enough that neither one of them could miss the fact that there was a subject they were both edgy about. Mirei didn't want to tell Viper anything before she told Jaguar, and Viper . . . he was holding something back, too. Like, perhaps, why he was afraid of a witch showing up under an illusion. Mirei was glad she hadn't put one up.

"You staying long?" Viper asked as they arrived at the door to the building that stood at the tower's base.

"Not sure."

"Well, catch me before you leave. You and Eclipse vanished awfully fast last time."

Because they'd found out about the doppelgangers. Mirei nodded at him. "Right. I'll see what I can do."

He walked off. She closed her eyes to let them adjust from the growing morning sunlight, then stepped into the dim closeness of the office.

For the first time the rail-thin man behind the desk looked startled. "I didn't get word you were coming."

"Guess I've learned to sneak better, Slip," Mirei lied. "I need to talk to Jaguar."

"He's busy."

"I don't care."

Slip had his expression mostly under control again; his eyes only widened fractionally at her flat declaration. "You the reason we've had witches skulking around lately?"

No wonder Viper was paranoid. "Did Eclipse not bloody explain anything? Or has Jaguar just not let you in on it?"

Slip cocked his head to one side. "We haven't seen Eclipse since you were here with him last time."

His words jolted her. "Haven't *seen* him?" She did her mental arithmetic over again. Ten days, since she left her year-mate and erstwhile partner with instructions to return to Silverfire. Either he'd found some good reason to disobey her . . .

. . . or he'd run into trouble.

Slip answered the question before she could ask it. "We haven't heard about anything happening. But that doesn't mean it hasn't."

She could find him; the spell wasn't hard when you knew the target as well as she knew Eclipse. But she could hardly resort to magic in front of a former Hunter, especially Jaguar's aide. Mirei swallowed her curse and snapped, "Right. I don't care who Jaguar's with, or what he's doing. He and I talk *now.*"

"Go on up. In the meantime, I'll kick some people in the asses, and try to get you more information."

Eclipse might just be in hiding, Mirei thought as she climbed the creaking staircase. When she last saw him, there had been Cousins out looking for them both. Those had all been called off after she went to Starfall, but did *he* know that? Still, a search wouldn't halt Eclipse, just slow him down. Something else was going on.

Mirei knocked on the Grandmaster's door, then went in when Jaguar responded.

He was at his desk with a stack of papers he covered before she came in. The Grandmaster of Silverfire was a man gone hard with age, like wood weathered by a storm. His gray hair was trimmed meticulously short, and like many Hunters, he was always clean-shaven. The irritated look in his light blue eyes smoothed out into careful blankness at the sight of her. She saluted him, and he considered her for a moment before saying anything. "Mirage. Wisp told me you'd vanished from Angrim. Have you come back to give me the explanation you promised?"

Mirei had forgotten that Wisp would wonder where she had gone, after taking refuge in the temple. "Yes," she said. "You were supposed to get it from Eclipse, but Slip tells me he never arrived. So I guess I have extra problems to deal with."

"*Extra* problems?"

"I'm afraid I came here with one already in hand."

Jaguar held up one hand to stop her. "I see. Come here a moment. I want to show you something."

He rose and beckoned her over to a tall wooden cabinet that stood against one wall. She'd never seen it open; as far as she knew, that was where he kept sensitive papers about the doings of Silverfire's people. Mirei approached, and Jaguar reached out for her shoulder, looking almost companionable—

And then he spun her violently and slammed her back against the cabinet, a knife at her throat.

"Make one sound before I tell you to and I'll slit your throat before you finish it," he said, in a terrifyingly level voice. "*You're not Mirage.* Your voice is different, and you're too damned slow."

Mirei kept her curse safely behind her teeth. Jaguar did not make idle threats.

"Your voice sounds trained," he said. "Which tells me you're a witch. Tell me, *briefly,* who you are."

Briefly. Mirei answered him as best she could, and stopped trying to disguise her voice. "Half Mirage."

The Grandmaster's eyes narrowed. "Explain. Level tone."

Which was to say, without the variation in pitch that might disguise a spell. Magic used a different language in addition to its music, but some spells were short; she could attempt one mid-sentence and pretend it was a name. But Mirei wasn't about to try it. "Half of me is Mirage. The other half is—was—a witch named Miryo."

He processed this. "Why? Level tone, still." And the knife hadn't moved.

"Because they—I—started out as one person. Split apart in infancy—the witches always do that. It's part of how they get their magic. The half that's like Mirage is normally a soulless shell, just a body. They kill it. But Mirage survived. Shared a soul with Miryo. Miryo's magic was going to kill them both. She was supposed to kill Mirage. Tradition, but wrong way to solve the problem. They—I—found a better one. Back into one person. Lost the edge off my reflexes, though, and my voice is different." Her shoulders were tense with the effort of keeping her tone as flat and expressionless as possible.

"Then the two girls training here," Jaguar said, "are the same."

"Yes."

He'd known they were like Mirage in their physicality, their knack for the art of fighting, but not what it had meant. Jaguar looked intently into her eyes. "Why are you here? Just to explain?"

"They're in danger."

Finally, slowly, he backed off. The knife left her throat, and he lowered the arm that had her pinned. He did not put the blade away, though, and Mirei knew he still practiced knife-throwing every day.

"I thought they might be," Jaguar said. "Tell me more."

Chapter Two

◦◦◦—┼——┼—◦◦◦

AFTER MIREI WAS GONE, Satomi leaned her forehead against the cool glass of her window and let her breath out slowly.

She prayed to the Goddess that this was not the start of new, worse trouble—but she feared otherwise.

Lifting her head, she could see out across Starfall, both the sprawl of buildings too loose to call a town and the domain that went by that name. Pale gray granite blocks quarried from these mountains, the multihued greenery of the trees beyond. Her office faced north, toward the rest of the world. She'd chosen the view deliberately. Her predecessor as Void Prime had used a room on the south side of the main building; her predecessor had believed the outside world was not her concern as Void Prime.

To some extent, the woman had been right. The Void Ray dealt with the internal affairs of the witches; the world outside their own people was the responsibility of the other Rays. But for a long time the Void Prime had also been the linchpin of the Primes as a whole, and that meant, in Satomi's opinion, that she could not afford to ignore the rest of the world.

She gazed out at Starfall, breathing slowly to center herself. This was her home, and had been for nearly as long as she could remember. She'd spent the first ten years of her life in Haira, but then, like all witch-students, she had come here for her real training. Since then, she had hardly left. Fifteen years of studying, before being tested as a witch. Then the hunt for her doppelganger. Finding it at last in Liak.

Not it. Her. *Her name was Orezha.*

Then returning here after Orezha's death, and entering the Path of the Head in the Void Ray, dedicating her life to research and recordkeeping. Advancement to the position of Key of her Path, overseeing all the Head witches of her Ray. And finally, promotion to Void Prime, the leader of an entire fifth of Starfall—and, in a sense, the leader of all witches, whatever their affiliation.

For the first time, Satomi felt old.

Her health was still good, and her hair showed no strands of white yet, but she wasn't sure she had the energy to cope with the upheaval Mirei had brought. But what other choice did she have? Not retirement; the last thing the community of witches needed right now was to lose a Prime. And Satomi had no illusions about the prevailing attitudes about this situation; she was far and away Mirei's strongest supporter. The confrontation in Star Hall had staggered everyone, and to varying degrees it had convinced them—but not entirely. Satomi had to make sure that conviction grew, instead of fading. Starting with her fellow Primes.

Satomi stepped away from the window and straightened the plain black silk of her dress. They would not like that she had sent Mirei off without consulting them, not least of all because it meant she had told the young witch before she told *them.* But she could not let the discussion get bogged down in that. The real issue at hand was not what to do with the doppelgangers, but what to do with Shimi.

She left her office and went through the hallways to their council room. Unlike the ruling hall, where the Primes settled disputes and pronounced judgments, this place was not meant to impress; it was a working space, and practical. A large table dominated the room, with five comfortable chairs spaced around it, and a wealth of lamps provided light. The chairs might be carved with the Elemental symbols of the five Rays, but that was the only decoration, and the cushions were worn besides. The room itself was layered in permanent spells, protecting it against eavesdropping or anything that might disrupt the Primes' meetings.

Satomi put down the books she was carrying and settled into her own chair to wait. She was reading Shimi's letter yet again when the other Primes began to come in.

Rana arrived first, looking sleepy. Oldest of the Primes, her wispy bun of hair had gone solidly white. People had been murmuring for years now about the possibility of her retirement, but she'd been in the position of Water Prime for so long that few could imagine her gone, and besides, she still did her job well. Ministration to the common people of other lands, the province of her Ray, was not the most glamorous of Starfall's work, but it did require a diligent hand.

Not long after that, Koika showed up, her stocky form dressed in simple breeches and shirt as always. She gave Satomi one of her usual broad smiles, but it faltered when Satomi failed to return it in kind. "What's wrong?"

Satomi shook her head at the Earth Prime's question. "We'll wait for everyone to arrive."

Arinei came last, and Satomi wondered if she had timed it that way, because the Fire Prime entered in a well-staged fury.

"Why did you not tell us?"

Most Primes came from the Heart, the Path dedicated to organization and administration, but Arinei had been a Hand. Advising the Lord of Insebrar, she had learned to play her emotions like a lyre, manipulating those around her with carefully calculated extremes. Satomi did not disapprove; it was a useful trick. But she had also learned not to be cowed by it.

"About Shimi? By the time I finished with my necessary tasks, it was time for this meeting anyway."

"Necessary *tasks*? This isn't the yearly accounting, Satomi."

Calm was its own kind of weapon, as much as Arinei's crafted volatility. "No. It is, however, the disobedience of a witch to the wishes of Starfall. Which makes it first and foremost my responsibility."

Koika was frowning; Arinei was seething. "So you've already dealt with it, I hear," the Fire Prime said. "Sent Miryo off, dispatched Cousins and witches—is there anything left for us to do?"

"Mirei," Satomi said coldly, pronouncing the name with edged clarity. "You might do well to remember her name, since her existence is the source of our current complications. And yes, there is much yet to be done." She passed Shimi's letter to Koika, who sat at her left. "For those whose unofficial spy networks haven't already informed them of what's happened.

"Shimi is gone, and by her words, we have to assume she poses a threat to a dozen students, both here and at our regional halls—and also to the doppelganger halves of those students. That threat is what I've been dealing with this morning. The students have been made safe, and the doppelgangers are being gathered in."

Now Rana was reading the letter, her eyes widening with shock at the harshness of the words. Satomi went on. "That, however, is treating the symptoms, rather than the problem. We must mend this breach with Shimi."

"I assume we can't find her," Rana said, offering the letter to Arinei, who ignored it.

Satomi shook her head. "She's warded herself against it." Which was, in itself, a serious violation of her duties as the Air Prime. The witches of her Ray were itinerant, serving anyone they found in need, which made it all the more imperative that they be able to locate and communicate with their Prime when they needed her.

"She might go back to Kalistyi," Koika said.

Arinei snorted. "Or anywhere *but* Kalistyi, since she knows we'll look for her there."

The lines in Rana's brow furrowed even more deeply. "If she's warded, she might be under a disguise spell, too. If she goes to ground, we'll never find her."

Satomi shook her head again. "She won't go to ground. Think of what kind of woman Shimi is. Do you really think she would be content to register her disagreement with us, and then simply retire from the situation?" No woman that passive would ever have risen to the rank of Prime.

"So what do we do?" Koika asked. "Put out word for all witches and Cousins across the fifteen domains to look for her?" She grimaced at her own words. "We might as well hire Hunters to chase her down like a criminal."

The statement produced an unpleasant silence in the

room. They'd done that once before, and not long ago, hiring a Wolfstar assassin to murder one of the Fire Keys. For, ironically enough, believing that doppelgangers should not die.

Satomi steered them away from the memory, before it could spark new arguments. "Shimi is in dereliction of her duty, and in rebellion against the will of Starfall. We agreed days ago on the message we sent out to all of our people—"

"Shimi disagreed," Arinei pointed out, her expressive mouth settling into a hard line.

"But the consensus was in favor of the message. Four against one; she was overruled, and that means she's bound to abide by our decision. We agreed to support Mirei's new way, and to instruct all witches to do the same. If Shimi wanted to register her continued disagreement, there were acceptable ways for her to do so. This is not one of them." Satomi flicked the letter Rana had returned to her. "Therefore, we must temporarily suspend her authority over her Ray."

Arinei's eyes narrowed. "What do you mean, *suspend*? We can do that?"

Satomi picked up one of the books on the table before her. Her own experience as a member of the Path of the Head had been useful this morning. "There's precedent. Most recently—though by normal standards it's not recent at all—was Dotoku, Prime of the Fire Ray, just over three hundred years ago. Her political activities became, well, suspect; you can read about them if you'd like. Censure and suspension of authority requires the agreement of the other four Primes. Reinstatement—and Dotoku *was* reinstated—requires three."

She passed the book to Arinei, who had held out a peremptory hand for it. The Fire Prime scanned the pages quickly, obviously not attending much to the details of her predecessor's machinations. "Oh. I remember this. Her Ray was run by her Keys in the interim."

"Under the supervision of the remaining Primes," Satomi said. "Which is what we would do, as well. We have to make certain Shimi won't begin trying to use her subordinates as tools for her personal crusade, and also to ensure that the rest of the world won't see her actions as sanctioned by Starfall."

Arinei's head shot up at the words. "We'd make this *public*?"

"How can we not?" Koika asked. "We can't be sure what Shimi might do, so we've got to take steps to keep it from reflecting badly on us. At the very least we ought to tell the Lords."

"The Lords," Arinei said icily, "are *my* concern, last time I checked."

Territorial squabbles were something they could not afford right now. "No one's arguing that, Arinei," Satomi said, spreading her hands in a conciliatory gesture. "But in your position, surely you can see the necessity. The information need not go past the Lords at present, and I'm confident you can convince them of that. It seems apparent, though, that Shimi might decide to take radical action, and that will *not* be the time to begin telling the rest of the world that we didn't sanction it. We'd look like we were trying to cover our mistakes."

"Fine," Arinei said, biting the word off. She snapped the book shut for emphasis. "We suspend her, then."

"If the suspension should prove *not* to be temporary," Koika said. "Then what?"

Satomi had another book in front of her with the answer to that, but she deemed it better not to trot it out just yet. She didn't want Arinei accusing her of anticipating just that outcome, and judging by the tense muscles in the woman's neck, she was in that kind of mood. "The precedents for that are even older," she said, leaving it deliberately vague. "But aside from the formality of removal, the process is as it always is, for choosing a new Prime."

"Out of the Keys," Rana said thoughtfully, leaning forward and propping her chin on one hand. "Naji, Hassei, or Ashin."

Koika had been glancing at the remaining books; Satomi wondered if she suspected the relevant volume was in the stack. "Naji was the presumed successor," she said, turning her attention back to the circle of her fellow Primes. "But we might want to consider Ashin now, given that she's one of the ones who wanted the doppelgangers to live in the first place."

"I see we're condemning Shimi in advance," Arinei said acidly.

"That *wasn't* what I meant—"

"We need," Satomi cut in, before Koika could further feed Arinei's desire for an argument, "to have a conference with the Air Keys as soon as possible. In person, that is. Ashin is traveling back to Starfall; she should be here in about five days."

Koika considered it. "We can't wait that long on the censure, though."

"No. We should carry *that* out this afternoon. We'll gather the Keys of all Rays and any Air witches currently at Starfall in the ruling hall, make the declaration—there's a script for it; I'll give you copies—and the Air Keys can send word out to all the witches of their respective Paths. The end of the declaration is a spell that will suspend Shimi's power and authority as Prime. We will meet to perform that when the bells chime Light." It was now an hour shy of Mid; that would allow them seven hours to prepare. She did not expect to need that much, but Arinei was prickly already; Satomi wanted to avoid indecent rush.

When the other Primes had nodded their agreement—grudgingly, in Arinei's case, but she did nod—Satomi turned to Rana. "On to other matters, then. Have you spoken with Obura?"

The Water Prime nodded, her lined face showing relief at the change of subject. "She's—well, not confused, exactly, but this will be her third daughter. She's very used to the old way of doing things."

"She'll just have to adjust," Koika said, not sounding at all sympathetic. The Earth Prime lacked Satomi's zeal for the new way, but once she had decided to accept it, her mind was quite set.

"Make certain she understands what to do," Satomi said to Rana. "It isn't very complicated. She simply needs to present her daughter to the Goddess *before* beginning the ritual to create the channel for magic. As I understand it, everything after that will be the same."

"Except the bit where she kills the doppelganger," Koika added. Her light tone offset the bluntness of her words.

Satomi smiled ruefully. "Except that. Both children will live, the witch-child with the capacity for magic and the doppelganger-child without. They will share one soul, since she's exposed them to starlight and the Goddess's eyes, and we will raise them both until it's time for them to come back together."

Rana sighed and brushed her hair from her eyes with one knobbly hand. It trembled slightly, and Satomi realized that Obura was not the only one with fear. "Yes, but try to see it from her point of view. She's been told all her life that under no circumstances should she allow her daughter anywhere near starlight until *after* the ritual. She feels like we're telling her to throw her daughter into the fire, it's all right, fire isn't hot like everyone always said it was."

"Just keep reassuring her. Everything will be all right. She will see. And she will be the first witch since Misetsu with the opportunity to know both of her daughters—both halves of her daughter." Satomi clicked her tongue in exasperation. "However you want to say it. This is an honor for Obura." Pregnant witches throughout the domains would soon follow in her footsteps. Change would be slow—these children had to grow to adulthood before the difference would really be felt—but it would happen.

Standing, the Water Prime nodded. "Are we finished?"

"Let's meet an hour after High, to make sure we're prepared for the ritual. But yes, other than that, we can adjourn."

Arinei was gone almost before Satomi's words were finished, the heavy wooden door thunking back into place behind her with unnecessary force. Rana followed her, still looking concerned for Obura. Koika gathered her notes, and spoke quietly to Satomi as she did.

"You'll want to keep an eye on Arinei."

"Yes." Satomi sighed, trying to release her frustration. "She's afraid we're being unfair to Shimi."

"I think there may be more to it than that." Notes tucked into the crook of one arm, Koika looked at the door as if seeing through it to where Arinei strode through the halls. "I'm not sure what else, but I'm certain there *is* something." She shrugged apologetically to Satomi. "I don't read human body language as well as deer."

Satomi stood and gripped the Earth Prime's arm. "Deer and other things of nature are your province."

"But we can't afford to ignore each other's provinces. As you knew when you took the north office."

The Void Prime nodded. "Let me know if you hear anything—from witches of your Ray or others, or even Cousins—that seems important."

"I will," Koika said.

WHEN WORD CAME, however, it came not from Koika, but from Naji, the Key of the Air Heart. And it was not good.

Naji stood on the tiled floor before Satomi's desk not long after the bells chimed Mid, her normally serene face animated by distress. "I didn't know who else to tell. You're not my Prime, Aken, but—" Her hands spread, helplessly. "It's an internal matter. Therefore Void business. And I thought it best to come straight to you."

Satomi stood up from her chair and came around to guide Naji into a seat. "You're sure it was a sending to the *entire* Air Ray?"

"Yes," Naji said, and the implication—unintended on Satomi's part, but useful for its effect—that she might not know her own business well enough to tell the difference had the benefit of focusing her. "She sent to us all, just before Mid."

"Let me get pen and paper," Satomi said, and returned briefly to her desk. "All right. Now tell me, as precisely as you can recall, what Shimi said."

Naji let out a slow breath, eyes closed, to center herself. Her memory was excellent, once she calmed down enough to use it; it served her well, as head of the administrative Path of her Ray. " 'I send this to you, my daughters, so that at least one-fifth of Starfall may know the truth. The creature calling itself Mirei is an abomination. Misetsu, our holy ancestor, blessed of the Goddess, learned through painful experience the truth of the doppelgangers, and in her wisdom she established the tradition we follow to this day. The abomination among us has performed feats that may dazzle, but they cannot last. If we join our daughters to the dross they were meant to discard, who knows what misfortunes they will suffer? We must not follow this dangerous path. I beg you, my daughters, to trust in the wisdom of our predecessors. Do not fall into this trap. My fellow Primes, blinded by these tricks, will tell you not to heed me, but I hold fast to what we know to be true.' "

Satomi listened to the recitation with detached, bitter admiration. *Well played, Shimi. You kept your Nalochkan sympathies in check, and stressed themes that will strike a chord with a wider audience. I might wish you were less competent at your job.*

"Thank you," she said to Naji. "You were very right to bring this to my attention. I was about to send you a message myself, you and Hassei both, and Ashin on the road. You have heard that Shimi is gone from Starfall, and why?" The Heart Key nodded. "The Primes decided this morning to suspend Shimi's authority over your Ray, pending a resolution of this issue. Unfortunately, it seems we haven't moved fast enough. This sending is exactly the kind of problem we wished to prevent."

Naji had regained most of her composure, although her fingers still twisted in her skirt. "What should I tell my Path?"

"That we will be addressing them in the ruling hall at High." They could move up the preparations for the ritual. "Every Air witch currently at Starfall is required to attend. Absence will be treated harshly." And it might not be a bad idea to send immediate word to the Cousins who watched the roads out of Starfall, to detain any witch who attempted to leave. No sense allowing Shimi any more supporters than necessary.

"Would you like me to tell Hassei?"

"No, I'll tell her myself. And Ashin. Just inform your Path." Only Shimi could deliver a sending to all Air witches at once, as a function of her authority as Prime, but the three Keys together could achieve the same effect, by sending to each of their Paths. That would be useful, once the Air Prime was suspended.

Naji nodded, rose, bowed, and left, and Satomi went instantly to work, notifying everyone involved that they would be stripping Shimi of her authority sooner than expected, before she could do more harm.

BY THE TIME THE BELLS CHIMED HIGH, everyone had gathered. Outside, the noon sun beat down on the buildings of Starfall, but little of that warmth and light penetrated the ruling hall. Five heavy thrones sat in a row on a dais, each dominated by the banner that hung above and behind, stitched in the colors and symbols of each Elemental Ray. They faced rows of benches divided by an aisle; the aisle itself was paved with the worn, nearly illegible grave slabs of early Primes.

Four of the thrones were filled; the last, under its white and silver Air banner, was conspicuously empty.

The benches were well populated, and at the front of their ranks were chairs for the fifteen Keys, eleven of which were filled. Not all of the figures seated in those chairs were physically present, though. A few Keys, Ashin among them, were away from Starfall, but had been notified in time to perform the complex spell that sent projections of their images here. Had they waited until Light, as originally planned, they would likely have had all fifteen. Satomi wondered if her decision for haste had been the right one.

All of the Air witches currently at Starfall were present. None of them had tried to leave, but three others had—one each from the Void, Water, and Fire Rays. Word had spread rapidly from the Air witches to the rest of Starfall. No doubt it was doing the same out in the other fourteen domains of the land. But they could do nothing about that at present, save what they were already carrying out.

Satomi addressed the gathered witches, outlining the situation in clear, bare terms. Hardly anyone even shifted in her seat as she detailed Shimi's actions. When done, she rose to stand in front of her throne, black banner at her back, and spoke into the tense silence of the hall.

"What affects one branch of our people affects all," she said. "From the Earth to the Void, the Elements interrelate, and so, too, do the realms of our concern. The actions taken by one witch have repercussions for her sister.

"On this day, we gather to consider the actions of Shimi."

The other Primes stood up from their seats. Koika went first, as protocol dictated. "Shimi has undermined the foundations of Starfall, at a time when we need them to be strong. For this, we censure her."

Then Rana. This was not the spell itself, but it was just as ritualized as if it had been. "Shimi has refused to bend to the consensus of the Primes, who have agreed upon the best path for Starfall. For this, we censure her."

Finally Arinei. It felt awkward and off; there should have been another voice between Water and Fire. Satomi had not realized how accustomed she was to the rhythms of their rituals until it was disrupted. Always it was five Primes, five Elements, five components to everything they said. Even raising a new Prime involved five, the four incumbents and the newcomer. The imbalance created by the loss of one was palpable.

"Shimi has spread confusion among the witches in her care," Arinei said. This much, at least, Satomi granted her: in public, in ritual, she showed no sign of her own doubts and dissension. "She has failed in her duty to lead them. For this, we censure her."

And now it was Satomi's time to speak, too soon, last in a series of four instead of a series of five. "For her actions, we hereby censure Shimi. Let it be known to all the witches of her Ray and of others that from this time onward, we suspend her authorities, privileges, and powers as the Prime of the Ray of Air, until such time as a majority of three Primes in agreement see fit to reinstate her in her position."

Ruriko brought a small table forward and set it on the dais before Satomi. On the table were the foci for the spell. Though not as complex by half as the ritual that installed a witch as Prime, suspension was difficult enough to require aids.

Their four voices blending together, the Primes took up the foci and sang the spell that made their words into reality. Some of the powers granted to a Prime were magical; others were tradition and law. The ability to send to the Ray as a whole, to raise or dismiss Keys, to admit a new witch into the Ray. These things and more they took from Shimi, by the power of the spell they sang. Satomi took the part of Air in the chorus; the Void Prime always sang the missing Element, unless she was the one suspended, because there was no role in it for Void power. She wondered, briefly, if it would be rewritten some day, when witches like Mirei ruled.

The closing declaration did not take long, and then the Primes exited through a side door. Arinei immediately began stripping off the ceremonial robe of gold and red that she wore over her dress, with stiff, tight motions that communicated her mood better than angry words could. Koika and Rana did the same, more slowly, not looking at Arinei.

Satomi herself stayed by the door, listening to the snatches of conversation that emerged into audibility as the assembled witches filed out of the hall.

Among them she heard murmurs of discontent, and she was afraid.

Chapter Three

JAGUAR BACKED AWAY from the cabinet, allowing
Mirei to move out into the room again. At a nod from the
Grandmaster, she sat down in one of the chairs set before
his desk. He remained standing, knife still in hand.

She let out a slow breath and laid her hands flat on her
knees, stilling her nerves. "This is . . . delicate information. There are problems among the witches right now,
and some people wouldn't be happy that I'm telling you
about them. But I owe allegiance as much to Silverfire as
to Starfall, and besides—I need your help."

"There have been witches here," he said, after a moment's pause. "Outside Silverfire, that is—not in the compound. We don't *think*. Witches, or Cousins. They haven't
done anything yet, but it has us nervous. Indera's hair has
red in it, and many people know that Amas dyes hers. We
suspected this had to do with them."

"How long have they been watching, do you think?"

"Six days."

Shimi hadn't known where the doppelgangers were that
long ago. It had to be Ashin's fellow conspirators, following through on the instructions Mirei had given them right
after her transformation, to keep the doppelgangers safe.
*Best not to explain that to Jaguar, though; too compli-
cated. Stick with the current problem.*

She ran one hand over her cropped hair, then made herself stop. "There's at least one witch who is probably going to try and kidnap those two. Kidnap them, and later kill them. So, in short, I've come to ask you to let me take them away."

"For what purpose?"

Protection did not need to be named. "Eventually, they'll be like me. They'll rejoin with their witch halves."

"Or die."

"Not if we can prevent it."

Jaguar paced, wariness lining his body with tension. He was old, but still hard. "I knew when they came here that the past was repeating itself in some fashion. Not exactly, of course—Tari-nakana bought your training here, while these girls were both brought by their parents. But still, to see two more, with the kinds of gifts you have— you *had*—I wondered if there was Starfall influence I was not seeing."

"Yes and no," Mirei said. Certain witches would no doubt cheerfully beat her for airing their dirty laundry in front of an outsider. Then again, other witches—Ashin's "heretics"—had paid her, an outsider, to investigate Tari-nakana's assassination, to confirm their suspicions. Or were supposed to have paid her. She wondered if she would ever see the money, or the boons she and Eclipse were owed.

"Tari-nakana," she said, leaning forward. "She paid for me to come here, yes, and talked you into taking me even though I was thirteen. She knew what I was. After that, she went and arranged for others like me to survive. They're called doppelgangers. She got them fostered with false parents, and probably made sure the children would be sent to Hunter schools when they were old enough. But it wasn't a Starfall thing. Remember how I was hired to Hunt her assassin, and whoever hired *him*? He was working for the Primes."

Jaguar stared at her. "But you were hired by witches yourself."

"Renegades. That's why they turned to outsiders for help; they couldn't trust their own. The Primes had Tari-nakana killed because of what she was doing with the doppelgangers. It's a metaphysical thing; they thought doppelgangers were a threat to the existence of magic itself. Which turns out not to be true, and I've convinced them of that." *Sort of,* her mind whispered caustically. "It doesn't bring Tari-nakana back, though." She had never thought of it before now, but Tari-nakana had died because of her. Mirei regretted that she had never had a chance to speak to the woman.

"So who are they in danger from?"

"Well, not everybody agrees with me yet. It's going to mean some big upheavals in the way they do things, and of course you're going to get resistance to that. That's a general problem, though, not the specific one. There's this one witch from Kalistyi who has fairly Nalochkan attitudes about the Warrior—" Mirei stopped, momentarily frustrated by the tangle of concepts packed behind her words, which she couldn't find a simple way to explain. She had never expected to sit in the office of the Grandmaster of Silverfire and talk metaphysics.

But Jaguar was not a stupid man. He had risen to his position partly by virtue of his ability to take scattered pieces of information and link them together by intuitive leaps. Nodding, he said, "So these girls, these doppelgangers, are associated with the Warrior. Which is why they're stronger and faster. Why they understand fighting, and learn it so well."

Mirei nodded in reply. "Dancing, too—anything physical. Anything based on *movement,* I should say. Which is something I still don't quite get yet; the Warrior's Element is the Void, so why are they associated with the physical? But whatever it is, the doppelgangers are that part of the self, while the witch-halves are the rest of it. The four concrete Elements, the four Aspects of the Goddess that are stages of life."

"And they used to kill doppelgangers. So this one witch believes they should still do so, and will attempt to follow through." Jaguar walked to the window and gazed out over the compound. Mirei could hear the sounds, faintly, of Silverfire's daily life, adolescents being trained to spy and kill for those who could pay them. The noise was as familiar as the ever-present singing at Starfall.

Jaguar nodded to himself, still looking out the window. "We can defend them."

"No offense, sir, but I don't think so."

Now he turned to face her, and he did not look amused. "You don't think we're a match for a single witch?"

Void it, Mirei thought wearily. *Why did I ever think I could get away without telling him everything? We're bloody well trained to investigate. I'll be lucky if I keep the decorations on the walls of Satomi's office a secret.*

Hanged for a fleece, hanged for a sheep. If she didn't convince Jaguar, no way in the Void was she taking those two doppelgangers without resorting to serious magic. "It might not be just a single witch. You see, the one we're worried about is the Air Prime."

Of all the Rays to be in danger from, that might be the worst. Like Silverfire Hunters, Air witches were itinerant. They did different work and served out of charity, rather than for money, but the similarities were enough that Jaguar could visualize the situation without her coloring it in for him. Air witches were *everywhere.* They weren't tied to specific places. They were mobile, adaptable, and therefore highly dangerous. They lacked the resources of other Rays, but anyone who had ever worked as a Silverfire Hunter knew how far you could still get without those, if you were creative enough. The real question was how many of them would follow Shimi, if she told them to cause trouble.

"The ones we've been seeing around," Jaguar began.

"*Probably* not hers, though I can't say for sure. I think they belong to the renegades I mentioned, the ones who hired me. They've been worried about coming out into the open, and what might happen to the other doppelgangers. I can find out. Silverfire's not going to be safe, though; she knows your two are here. The Void Prime was all set to send witches in after these girls herself, to get them to safety. I talked her out of it because I know what response that would get. But Shimi, the Air Prime, may not have such compunctions. She gets a couple of witches to help her out, and she could burn this place to the ground."

It wouldn't solve the problem of the doppelgangers; they would just come back to life, as long as their doubles were still alive. Sharing a soul was an odd business. Mirage had died twice, Miryo once. Mirei remembered all three, and shuddered to imagine what burning to death would be like.

Then, with a chill as if someone had poured cold water

down her back, she thought, very distinctly: *I can't let Jaguar know that. He finds out his best trainees are also unkillable—and why—then he won't give them up, not for anything.*

"When this business is done," Jaguar said. "Will you bring them back?"

Mirei hesitated. Eventually, the girls would have to rejoin with their witch-halves. That wouldn't be for years, though, given the way Starfall trained its daughters; there would be time for the Hunters to finish their own educations. But that assumed Starfall would let them go.

She had waited too long. Jaguar's face was settling into hard lines, reading her answer in her silence.

"Maybe," she said, before he could tie himself too strongly to that conclusion. "I can't give you a better answer than that; I'd be lying if I did. I want to bring them back. I will if I can. But I don't know how long this trouble will last, and what will happen along the way, and what the other witches will want to do."

"Those girls belong to us as much as to them."

Did they? The two here had less than a year of Silverfire training under their belts, while they owed their entire existence to the magic of Starfall. But once you entered a Hunter school, you belonged to them, until—unless—they chose to let you go.

She looked up into Jaguar's cold, light eyes. "See it this way, if you can," she said quietly. "They're still in Silverfire hands. Because I'm one of your own. And I'll take care of them."

He met her gaze, unblinking. Mirei knew she had always held a special position in Jaguar's regard. It was not necessarily a privileged one, not in the sense of lenience;

he'd held her to the highest standards when she was in training here. But he had allowed her into Silverfire years late because of the promise he saw in her. That promise was gone now, lost in the merging with Miryo. Would he still trust her as he once had?

Would he still see her as a Silverfire?

"Train them," he said at last. "They are born of the Warrior, as you were. That may not last, but while it is there, it should not be wasted."

She nodded. "I will."

"Then you may take them," Jaguar said, and went to the door to tell Slip, while Mirei prayed to the Goddess that she would be able to keep her promise.

THE RUNNER SPOKE quietly to Briar, but the first-year trainees were already learning the fine art of eavesdropping. "You're in trouble," Tanich hissed at Indera, leaning under his horse's neck. "You're getting hauled in before the Grandmaster. He's going to rake you over the coals for being such a snot."

"Idiot," Indera whispered back at him, looking superior. "The Grandmaster doesn't bother himself with stuff like that. It's a *privilege* to go see him." But inside, her guts twisted. A group of her year-mates had jumped her the other night; had the Grandmaster heard about that? Scuffling in public was an offense, but private fights like the one in their dormitory were common, and ignored. Surely she couldn't be in trouble for that.

"You're just jealous," she added, mostly to see Tanich glare at her, but also because it was true. They all hated her, every one of them, because she was better. Stronger and faster and a better fighter; she'd taken Lesya down in two heartbeats the other day. They *needed* to jump her in a group, or she would win. And she didn't bother to suck up to them the way that stupid cow Amas did.

"Indera." The runner had gone, and now the elderly Hunter who was supervising their tack lesson in the stable was looking at her. "Amas. Grandmaster's office, now. Leave your horses as they are."

Indera's heart thrilled when he called her name, but her enthusiasm faded when she heard Amas being added. Was this a good thing, or not? Couldn't be about the scuffle the other night, or they wouldn't be calling that prig along with her. So what *was* it about?

She didn't have time to stop and consider it. No one kept the Grandmaster waiting. The two trainees left the stables immediately, side by side, and crossed the compound in the growing heat of the morning.

"I bet he has something special for us," Indera said, to cover up her nervousness. She had to scurry to keep up with her long-legged year-mate, and it irritated her. "We're being promoted to the second year. Or even the third. Because we're better than everybody else."

"We're stronger," Amas said in her soft voice. She never spoke loudly, or sounded angry. It drove Indera up the wall, like everything else about her. "We're faster. We're good at fighting. That doesn't make us *better.*"

"We're Hunters. Stronger and faster is all that matters."

"We're *trainees,* and you're wrong."

Indera slowed enough to glare at Amas's back. What she wouldn't give to beat the spit out of the other girl— but she couldn't. The masters used to put the two of them together for sparring, and Indera knew firsthand the knack Amas had for kick attacks. With the other girl's long legs, it meant that Indera couldn't get inside her reach. A real fight between them . . . Indera wanted to believe she would win, but she couldn't be sure. Not like she could with the others.

If she wants to act like she's the same as everybody else, that's her problem, Indera thought spitefully. *She can be a dog. I'm a wolf. I'm going to be the best Hunter Silverfire's ever had. Better than Mirage, even.*

They reached the building, were waved up the stairs by Slip, and walked into the Grandmaster's office.

"Mirage!" Indera blurted, forgetting even to salute the Grandmaster behind his desk.

Amas didn't forget. Indera hastily copied her, flushing in embarrassment, and hoping that her idol didn't notice.

It *was* Mirage. No other Hunter in the world had hair like that, flame-colored and cropped short in a Hunter's practical cut. She was in a Hunter's uniform, much like the trainee uniform Indera herself wore, and the body inside was lean and hard. Indera envied her long-fingered, capable hands, with their calluses and strong tendons, and wondered how soon she would look like that herself. This woman was the epitome of everything Indera wanted to be. Indera had never thought she would actually *meet* her, not this soon. Not until she was older, mostly trained, ready to claim a new name as a full Hunter.

Mirage was eyeing her—*eyeing both of you,* a corner of Indera's mind murmured, but nevermind that—with cool gray eyes that betrayed nothing of what she was thinking. Indera stood bolt upright, hoping the woman noticed her own hair. Amas dyed hers, to hide the color that made people whisper about witches, but Indera's was its natural red-brown.

The Hunter glanced away from them without saying anything and nodded to the Grandmaster. "All right. I'll keep you informed, as best as I can." Her voice was melodious and polite. The sound of it made Indera shiver.

"Very well," Jaguar said. He had not told the trainees to stand at ease; they stood rigidly just inside the door. The Grandmaster rose and came to stand before them.

"You're going to go with Mirage," he said. "You both know who she is. Do what she says, when she says, without hesitation or argument. Treat her like she's one of your training-masters. If either of you disobeys her in the slightest, she has the authority to punish you however she sees fit. And when you return, you'll be punished for it a second time. So don't disobey."

Indera waited, hardly breathing, trying to figure out what he meant by this. *We're going with her? Where? And why?*

"You may be young," the Grandmaster said at last, "but you are of Silverfire. Don't dishonor that."

"Yes, sir," Amas murmured, and Indera echoed her blindly. Could this mean what she thought it did?

Mirage stood and saluted Jaguar. He nodded to her, then turned back to his desk. "Come with me," the Hunter said. Indera sketched a hasty salute and followed her out, dizzy with joy.

AS SHE WENT AROUND the Silverfire compound, gathering the supplies she needed, Mirei wondered what she had gotten herself into.

Two doppelgangers, in the abstract, were a simple enough idea. She could manage two doppelgangers. Somehow, though, she'd failed to realize that what she was really taking on board were two eleven-year-old girls, one of whom very clearly had a bad case of hero worship. It was flattering, in a way, but also unnerving. The last time she'd dealt with trainees for any real length of time, she'd been one herself, and then they'd been more occupied with giving her nasty looks than idolizing her.

Mirei left the two girls outside while she spoke to the quartermaster and the armorer. The latter stop was, as far as she was concerned, the more important one. She could keep herself fed through scrounging if she had to, but her pack of useful supplies had vanished with Eclipse, and things like sleeping oil and flash powder were not to be found by the side of the road.

The quartermaster promised to send her requirements to the stables. Mirei carried the special supplies herself, and found the rations already there. Slip must have sent a runner, too, because Briar had three horses waiting to be saddled.

"Where's Mist?" he demanded of Mirei, suspicion chiseled into every line of his old face. Mirage had accused him once of caring more about the mare than about her, and he'd agreed.

"In Angrim," Mirei said. *Assuming Wisp hasn't sold her off, out of irritation for me vanishing like that.* "Resting. She needs it."

"Where's the horse you came in on?"

"Didn't come on a horse. Why do you think I need one now?" Mirei didn't want him continuing that line of questioning, so she turned to the trainees and nodded at the tack. "Saddle them."

The last bags of supplies came while the girls were fumbling their way through the task. Mirei took them from the quartermaster's assistant and dumped their contents out onto the ground, sorting through them and tossing various pieces to the trainees. "Put those on when you're done."

She realized, halfway through stripping off her own uniform, that while she was long since used to the communal bathing of Silverfire, the other two were new enough to be self-conscious. Mirei suppressed the urge to grin at their expense, and then lost all amusement when she realized her silver pendant had swung free. She caught it quickly and tucked it back into the shirt the quartermaster had provided. *I hope no one noticed that.*

The girls didn't seem to have, and Briar was checking their work on the horses. The taller girl—must be Amas; she had the dyed hair—brushed at the long vest she wore over a pair of wide-legged trousers, expression puzzled. The stockier girl, Indera, was looking dubiously at a head scarf. "Askavyan *peasant women*?" she said.

Good on her for recognizing it. "That's the idea," Mirei said. She covered her own hair and tied the scarf in a tight knot. "Put your old clothes in the saddlebags, and get them lashed on." Briar had finished checking the horses; as he turned to her, Mirei said, "I know, I know. I lame these horses, and you'll lame me. Permanently. They'll be fine."

He cracked a brief grin. "Get you going, then."

Disguised as Askavyan peasant women, the three of them rode out through the gates of the Silverfire compound, and Mirei wondered what she had just let herself in for.

THEY HADN'T GONE FAR before Mirei caught sight of someone lurking among the trees, watching them.

"Wait here," Mirei said, and heeled her gelding off the road.

The woman she'd spotted tried to run, which she should have expected. Mirei pulled the scarf off her head, hoping it would help; if the woman was Shimi's spy, then it probably wouldn't make matters worse, and if she was Ashin's, then she might stop.

She stopped. Mirei didn't press her luck, but halted the gelding well back, holding her hands out unthreateningly. They were concealed from the road by a fold in the land at this point, so she didn't have to worry about the girls watching.

"I'm Mirei," she said, and drew out the pendant as evidence.

The woman nodded nervously. She didn't look like a witch, but Mirei would have laid money on her being under a disguise spell. "Gichara," she said. "Water Hand. Ashin sent me to watch the girls here."

"So I guessed," Mirei said dryly. "You've been seen. More than once, or do you have friends here?"

Gichara shook her head. "No, just me. Never been much good at sneaking. I told Ashin, but she said I was closest—my town's in central Miest—and we needed the girls kept safe."

"They will be," Mirei said. "Ashin told the Primes where to find them, and so we're bringing them all in. The one who isn't safe is *you.* Get out of here before the Hunters decide to chase you down. It's all being taken care of."

Looking relieved, Gichara nodded. When she'd moved off through the trees, Mirei didn't return immediately to the road. As long as she had privacy, there were a few things she should do.

First and foremost was the spell that would block any

attempt to find her magically. She didn't need to protect Amas or Indera; spells of that kind couldn't locate doppelgangers or their witch-halves. From a magical standpoint, they were one person in two places at once. But now that she was a single person again, Mirei could be found, and she didn't want Shimi tracking her to the doppelgangers.

When that spell was finished, she sang another one—to find Eclipse.

The resounding silence in her mind was almost painful.

Shaking her head to clear it, she cast the spell again, this time on Viper, just to be sure she wasn't making a mistake; this was the first time she'd tried something like this. The spell returned a resonance that read as Silverfire in her mind.

Another try for Eclipse gave her the painful silence again.

So that, she thought grimly, *is what the blocking spell feels like from the other side.*

Which meant that Eclipse was the prisoner of a witch.

She sat on a tree stump near the gelding and stared at the grass in front of her. She needed to get back to the road—the girls would be wondering where she had gone—but she couldn't move just yet.

Who could have taken him? She could see only three possibilities: Ashin's conspirators, Satomi's people, or Shimi. The former might have done it to keep him safe, but if so, why hadn't Ashin said something about it already? Why hadn't she let him go? He had to have gone missing before Shimi left, but she might have sent allies to capture him, once the Cousins were called off.

That, or Satomi had him prisoner, and hadn't told her.

Mirei chewed on her knuckle for a moment more, then pulled out the parchment Satomi had sent with her. She scrawled a quick note, explaining his disappearance and concealment under a spell, then sang the quick phrase that would send it to Satomi's matching sheet. If the Void Prime had kidnapped her year-mate, then pretending she didn't know would not help anything.

But, after a moment's consideration, she sent the message to Jaguar as well. He had no enchanted page, no mirror she could speak through, but she knew exactly where he was; she wrote out her message in Silverfire's code on another scrap of paper and dropped it out of the air onto his desk. With no way for him to reply, she had no idea what he was going to do with the information, but at least he had it.

Then she rode back to where she had left the girls.

They were still there, looking horribly confused. Indera said cautiously, "If you please—Mirage—what's going on? Why did Jaguar send us with you? Are you going to give us special training?"

The name gave her a pang; she didn't like lying. On the other hand, she had very good reasons for not explaining her transformation just yet. It was going to be hard enough as it was, and she didn't want to do it more than once.

"No," Mirei said, in answer to the girl's question. "That is— Well, Jaguar told me to train you while you're with me. But it won't be like you get at Silverfire, practically every waking minute spent on lessons. You'll just have to pick up what you can, and then I'll work on combat in the evenings, if we have time. But no, you weren't sent with me for training."

"Then what *are* we here for?" Indera asked, a plaintive note in her voice.

How much do they know? Mirei gave Indera a measuring look, then asked, as a test, "Who were your parents?"

"Um?" Indera had clearly not been prepared for that. "My father's a carpenter in Gatarha. That's in Liak. My mother's an herb-woman. I used to help her, sometimes."

"Farmers," Amas said, when Mirei looked at her. "Rice, some oats, and a few sheep. In northern Miest."

They don't know a blessed thing. I don't know if that makes my life easier, or not.

"Right," Mirei said. "Well, I don't want to have to explain things multiple times, so you're going to have to live with curiosity for a while. Short form is, we're going to Angrim, and while we're on the way there we don't want anybody noticing that we're Hunters if we can avoid it. Hence the disguises."

"Are we in danger?" Indera asked. She seemed excited by the prospect.

"Just don't draw attention to yourself. Once we're done with our business in Angrim, I'll be able to tell you more." And Mirei just hoped that, sometime between now and then, she would figure out a way to steal the Thornblood trainee.

Chapter Four

AN UNEASY PEACE reigned over Starfall for the next few days. No one else tried to leave in a manner that blatantly suggested they were fleeing to join Shimi; witches did leave, but they had to. Satomi could not bring the business of Starfall to a halt.

Ruriko came into Satomi's office one morning, where the Void Prime sat dealing with the backlog of correspondence that had built up in the wake of Mirei's dramatic arrival. "Aken, there's someone who wishes to speak with you."

"Who is it?" Satomi asked, signing off on a revenue report. Misetsu and Menukyo, but she hated dealing with the tedious economic work of keeping this place running. There were witches in the Path of the Head who handled most of it for her, but she still needed to stay informed—however boring she found it.

"Eikyo."

The name didn't ring a bell. "Path and Ray?"

"None. She's a student. A friend of Miryo's, I'm told, and she and Mirei were spending time together before Mirei left."

The use of both names caught Satomi's attention. She paused and looked up at Ruriko. "What does she want?"

"To help, Aken."

Interesting. She had a meeting with Ashin in less than half an hour; the Hand Key had arrived that morning. Satomi could put off the revenue reports for a while longer, though, to meet with this friend of Miryo's, and perhaps of Mirei's, who wanted to help.

"Send her in," Satomi said, and pushed the reports to one side.

The woman who entered looked faintly familiar. She was a student, yes, but one of the oldest; in fact, Satomi now recognized her as the one next in line for testing. Short, with a compact build that gave her an air of solidity even though she was plainly nervous about a private audience with the Void Prime.

"Aken," the student said, and sank into a bow.

"You're a friend of Mirei's, I'm told," Satomi said, choosing the name very deliberately.

The slight hesitation before Eikyo's response illustrated the woman's carefully chosen words. "In a manner of speaking, Aken. I was a friend of Miryo's, and Miryo is a part of Mirei. I'm still getting to know Mirei. But I think we could be friends."

Satomi smiled at the shift in tone at the end. "If I weren't hauling her into meetings and sending her off on errands, you mean."

"Not at all, Aken."

Of course not; Eikyo was clearly too discreet to be so cheeky to the Void Prime. "Ruriko tells me you'd like to help."

"Yes, Aken. With the . . . the situation."

Ah yes. "The situation." How obliquely we all refer to it. "Why?"

Eikyo was keeping her eyes on the floor; it looked

more like deference and nerves than a desire to hide anything. "Because Mirei asked me to."

Satomi raised her eyebrows, but Eikyo did not look up to see, so she spoke into the silence. "Oh?"

"Before she left." Eikyo took a deep breath. "She came to my room to have me cut her hair short like a Hunter's. She wouldn't tell me what she was going to do."

Good, Satomi thought. *The fewer who know, the better.*

"—but she told me there would be things to do here, and that you would—" Eikyo cut off suddenly.

"I would what?" Satomi said.

"That you would need help, Aken."

Which is true enough, and I suppose I can't begrudge Mirei for sending me aid. Goddess knows I do need it. "What do you have to offer in the way of help? I don't mean that in an accusing fashion. I'd like to know what you can provide."

Eikyo shrugged uncomfortably. "Not a whole lot, I fear, Aken. I mean, I'm not a witch yet. And there's only so much I can do without magic."

But she might be useful among the students, if only Satomi could figure out how. "What are your inclinations? Do you know what Ray and Path you'd like to take?"

"Earth Heart, Aken. I get along very well with animals."

Which was possibly the least useful answer the student could have made. Satomi didn't let that show, though. No sense discouraging the woman, even if wildlife was the *one* group she didn't expect to have problems with. "Well, Eikyo, thank you for coming to me. I'll have to think about this, and consider what you might be able to do." Satomi allowed herself a deprecating smile. "I fear I'll only know what kind of help I need as more problems present themselves. But I'll contact you if something arises."

"Thank you, Aken," Eikyo said, and sank into another bow before leaving.

Satomi sat back in her chair and considered this, tapping her lips with one finger. She hadn't been politely turning Eikyo off, although the student might have taken it that way. She really *didn't* know what to do with her at present.

But Satomi was sure she would think of something.

A SHORT WHILE LATER, Ashin stood on the carpet before Satomi's desk in an uncomfortable silence.

Satomi broke it by rising from behind her desk and gesturing at a chair to one side. "Please, sit." She came around and joined the Air Hand Key, deliberately lowering the formality of this meeting.

"It's good to have you safely back at Starfall," Satomi began when they were settled.

Ashin's dark eyes showed wry amusement. "Seeing as how I ran out of here in fear for my life?"

It was true. Ashin had left because of a strong suspicion that the Primes had ordered Tari's death over the issue of the doppelgangers, and if one renegade Key could die, so could another. No one had known at the time that Ashin was involved, but still, the danger had been real. Satomi winced at the blunt words and said, "There were . . . misunderstandings."

"You don't need to mince words, Aken. I know you called me and Tari and all the rest heretics. I don't hold a grudge for that. I'm just glad that you've seen the truth."

Which led inescapably into the current situation with

Ashin's erstwhile Prime. Satomi sidestepped it for the moment, though, in favor of making something else clear. "I fought against it, I admit that. A large part of me did not want to accept what Mirei had to say."

Ashin nodded. "I heard about your own doppel-ganger."

"Orezha," Satomi said quietly. "I want people to know her name."

"She's the last one that will happen to."

I hope so.

Satomi brushed that fear aside. She had a specific matter she wanted to address, before this afternoon's meeting with the other Primes and Ashin's fellow Air Keys. "You were right to leave Starfall when you did. If we'd known about your connection with Mirage, we would have taken . . . harsh steps."

"You would have killed me. After using any means necessary to get me to talk about the rest of them."

Sometimes Ashin's bluntness was refreshing; other times, it was a bit much. Still, Satomi couldn't deny the accusation. And she'd brought this subject up herself. "It would have been a mistake to do so. I'm glad we avoided it, though we can hardly take credit for that—Mirei was the one who stopped us. I just wish that we could undo some of our other mistakes."

A faint, bitter smile touched the corner of Ashin's mouth. "Like Tari."

"Like Tari," Satomi agreed.

The uncomfortable silence returned.

"How many people know about that?" Ashin asked at last.

"That Tari's death was not an accident?"

"That she was assassinated by a Hunter you hired, because she was doing things you didn't like and didn't want made public with a trial."

More than a bit much, this time. Satomi forced herself to answer the question. "The five Primes. Mirei. Yourself, and anyone else you've told. The Wolfstar we hired."

"He's dead."

Satomi's eyes widened. "You killed him?"

"Mirage killed him. I would have thought you'd know about that by now. Yes, he's dead. You've forgotten to list Mirage's partner, Eclipse."

She had forgotten him completely. Satomi's stomach lurched. Bride's tears—Mirei had sent her a note, saying he was missing, and in the struggle to deal with problems closer to home she had not given him a second thought. Which she *should*—because he was one of the few outsiders aware of their problems.

Satomi hoped Ashin had not read that shock in her face. "Not many, then."

Ashin leaned back in her chair, regarding her steadily. "Let me guess. You'd like to keep it that way."

She couldn't do this sitting down. Satomi rose from her chair and crossed the room to the window, looking out over the daily life of Starfall. Several Cousins were in the courtyard in front of the students' hall, unloading a shipment of grain. "We erred in how we dealt with her, and should atone for that in some fashion. But not by making it public knowledge. Not right now."

"More lies?" Ashin asked softly.

Satomi turned back to face her. "Yes," she said. "Which will sit poorly with your nature, I'm sure; you're a straightforward woman. But if I have to lie in order to prevent more strife, I will. The Goddess may judge me for that at her leisure."

Ashin stood up, too, and wandered over to run one finger thoughtfully along the front edge of Satomi's desk. "What are you going to do about Shimi?"

Not as much of a non sequitur as it might seem. "Looking ahead to the future?" Satomi asked, trying to keep the cynical note out of her voice. "To the prospect of replacing her?"

The Hand Key heard the cynicism anyway. Her dark eyes grew hard. "Not exactly. More looking to the question of whether she'll *need* replacing."

Satomi realized her misstep, too late to take it back. The best she could do was reassure Ashin, as much as possible. "We're not planning to have her killed."

"Not *planning* to." Ashin did not blink. "But you won't rule out the possibility."

Three quick strides brought Satomi close to her. "I am afraid of revolution," the Void Prime said in a quiet, intense voice. "I am afraid of a war among us that might end with many dead. There are those who would follow Shimi. If they win, then doppelgangers will continue to die, as they have since the beginning. Those are deaths others may not count, because doppelgangers are not yet quite real to them—but they're real to me. I do not want Shimi's arguments to prevail. But I don't know what kinds of lengths we will have to go to, in order to stop her. *I don't know* whether I should accept the deaths of living witches as the price to pay for that. And if so, how many. At the moment, I'm not planning for anyone to die. But if you want the truth—" Satomi felt a terrible urge to laugh, but not because it was amusing. "I don't know what I'll have to do tomorrow."

Ashin met her eyes steadily throughout this unexpected speech. Satomi could have lied; like many honest people, Ashin was not always adept at picking up the falsehoods of others. But Ashin valued honesty, and so Satomi was gambling by giving it to her.

"She may expose what you did to Tari," Ashin said at last.

Satomi's shoulders were still tight; Ashin had not said what she thought of Satomi's words. "I doubt it. She still approves of that choice. She can't condemn it publicly, because it would make no sense with her declared stance, but neither can she support it; she'd alienate too many of her potential supporters." And the carefully worded tenor of the message to the witches of her Ray showed that Shimi was very deeply concerned with the image she presented of herself. "She won't say anything. Not at the moment."

"Then I'm your only potential leak," Ashin said.

And Eclipse, the missing Hunter. And the other witches Ashin might or might not have told. Satomi kept silent and held Ashin's gaze.

"All right," the Hand Key said at last. "For now."

Which would have to be enough.

A COUSIN WOKE Satomi in the small hours of the night.

She swam with difficulty back up into consciousness; the Cousin had caught her in deep sleep. "Wha—" the Void Prime mumbled, pushing herself up in bed.

"Aken, I apologize. Rana-meri is here, and needs to speak with you urgently."

In the middle of the night? "What time is it?"

"Not quite Dark, Aken."

What could be happening at such a late hour? Satomi rolled out of bed and pulled on a dressing gown. The Cousin vanished discreetly as she went out into her sitting room, where the Water Prime was waiting.

Rana looked like she had not gone to bed. Her snowy hair formed a disheveled cloud around a face white and strained.

"She killed it."

The words made no sense to Satomi's sleep-fuddled mind. "What? Who killed what?"

"Obura. She killed the doppelganger."

Obura. Pregnant witch. No, not pregnant—she'd given birth a few days ago. Five days ago. Yes, of course; tonight she was slated to perform the ritual on her daughter, which would create the channel for magic. And, in the process, the doppelganger.

Who was dead.

Rana had started talking again, a low stream of words without much force behind them, as if she couldn't muster the energy. She had been old for years, but now it was like some part of her had simply crumbled away. "She did it the old way. Kept her daughter out of starlight— I thought she'd presented her to the Goddess, the way we told her to. But she lied. And the midwife tending her lied. They said she had, but she hadn't, and then when she did the ritual she killed the double. Said *her* daughter would be pure."

Satomi had gone very still, one hand still holding the front of her dressing robe closed. She looked around blankly in the dim lamplight, found a chair, sank into it.

A child had just died.

Not a child. A shell. A soulless body, because Obura had done it the old way, the way everyone else had done for centuries. Until the light of the stars, the Goddess's eyes, touched an infant, that infant had no soul. It wasn't a person yet. What Obura had killed was nothing more than a body.

But it could have been more.

"Where is she?" Satomi asked into the silence left by Rana running out of words.

"In her quarters," Rana said. "With Cousins guarding the door. I didn't know what you would want done with her."

Satomi herself didn't know. But she would have to think of something. She was the Void Prime, the linchpin of the circle of Primes, the ruler of the Ray whose dominating concern was the affairs of Starfall, the actions of its people.

In these dark hours after midnight, in this room so faintly lit by a single lamp, with her mind off-balance by the suddenness of her waking, she felt old. And she didn't want to deal with this problem.

But I have no choice. No one else will take this responsibility.

And to abdicate it would only make problems worse.

Satomi rose, put one hand on Rana's shoulder. "Have you slept?" The Water Prime shook her head. "Then go to bed. I'll handle this for now."

BUT SHE DID NOT GET A CHANCE to, because she arrived outside Obura's door to find the two Cousins in an unconscious heap on the floor, and the rooms behind them empty.

She tried a finding spell, but knew before she cast it

that it would do no good. Obura had a blocking spell up. So did the absent midwife. Blocking spells, hardly ever used because they were only useful against fellow witches, but now they were springing up like a cancer, everywhere she turned.

Satomi sent Cousins and witches in search. Rinshu, the Key of Obura's Path, made a stiff-faced apology. Rana awoke and took up her own duties, looking as though the sleep had done her no good at all. The searchers came back with nothing.

They still had Obura's daughter, for what good it did them. Satomi knew, as Obura had no doubt known, that they would raise her as usual. Children belonged to all of Starfall, not just to their mothers; Obura would not have been with her daughter long regardless. And Satomi could not simply refuse to educate the girl as a witch, as a revenge upon her mother; what would that accomplish? The child would study, and grow, and someday face the traditional test, and be yet another witch missing a part of who she could have been.

Satomi sat at her desk, head propped on one hand, and stared at the list Ashin had given them, of other doppelgangers in the world. Twelve, not counting Mirage. Four old enough to enter training as Hunters; eight of varying ages below that. All spirited out of Starfall in secret after the ritual.

But how, exactly? Ashin's daughter was one of them. Sharyo, the witch-half, was here in Starfall, under close guard; the doppelganger, Indera, was in Mirei's care. That one was easy to explain. Ashin had been one of the first witches Tari recruited to her rebellion, and she had volunteered her child to the cause. Cold-blooded of her, perhaps, when she didn't know there even *was* a better way of handling doppelgangers than killing them, but Ashin was in her own way as much of a zealot as Shimi: She believed in Tari's cause, and gave everything she had to it.

What about the others, though? Not every doppelganger of the twelve was the daughter of a witch in the conspiracy. Some of them belonged to witches who had no idea of what had happened. They had carried out the ritual in the usual way, killing the doppelganger with a dagger to the heart, not realizing that the infant would come back to life shortly after. It worked because the child had a soul before the ritual began; then the two bodies shared that one soul. The witch could kill the doppelganger, or the doppelganger could kill the witch, but anyone else would have to kill them both.

So the infant doppelgangers came back and, with the help of some allied Cousins, the heretics took them away from Starfall to be raised by false parents. But at some point before the ritual, the rebels must have arranged for the babies to be exposed to starlight.

Plausible, certainly; there were ways to do it, if you were determined. Even if the child was not your own.

But that didn't explain Mirage. And it didn't explain Orezha.

There was no conspiracy of heretics, when those two survived. Discovering Mirage was the catalyst that made Tari begin her subversive campaign. The thirteen-year-old girl had been a Temple Dancer in Eriot; Tari saw her perform, realized what she was, and arranged for her to be transferred to the Hunter school of Silverfire, because of a doppelganger's gifts for fighting.

How did Mirage get there in the first place?

How did Orezha?

Kasane, Miryo and Mirage's mother, would not have done it deliberately. And Tsurike Hall in Insebrar was, like Starfall, built with special rooms for newborns where the child was at no risk of seeing starlight until after the ritual. The same was true of Satomi's own mother and Kanishin Hall, where she had been born. It was true of *every* hall the witches built.

But still, from time to time, doppelgangers survived.

Someone had to do it on purpose. Someone with opinions like Tari's, but who, unlike her, never tried to take it further. Unless their attempts were so deeply buried that no history gave any sign of them.

Someone. A witch? Possibly, though it took special madwomen like Tari and Ashin to gamble innocent lives on the hope that the current way was wrong.

Even if it was a witch, though, she would need help. The bodies of the doppelgangers were given to the Cousins to dispose of.

The Cousins, who served the witches in all kinds of mundane tasks, from cooking to cleaning to guarding them with steel. The Cousins, whose numbers were made up of descendants of witches who failed their final test, and who occasionally took new women of that kind into their ranks.

The Cousins, who hardly ever opened their mouths around a witch for something that was not absolutely related to business.

Satomi rose abruptly from her desk and strode to her office door, to the outer room where Ruriko sat amid her own piles of paper. "Ruriko."

The secretary looked up. "Aken?"

"When is Eikyo scheduled to be tested?"

Ruriko kept her files obsessively organized; even the stacks of paper were tidy. She turned without hesitation to a ledger on the shelf, opened it, and flipped swiftly to a page, no searching. Only then did she pause.

"In two days, Aken," she said, looking up at last.

Satomi cursed softly. That soon. She should have remembered—and would have, were it not for the chaos. She wagered she was not the only one who had forgotten. "Thank you. Please notify Eikyo that I would like to speak to her. And—" She hesitated. "Keep it discreet."

That had to make Ruriko curious, but the secretary simply nodded. "Of course, Aken. When do you want to see her?"

"As soon as possible," Satomi said grimly.

EIKYO WAS IN HER OFFICE less than an hour later, clearly startled by the summons, but doing her best to hide it. "You called for me, Aken?"

Satomi was pacing along the windowed north wall of her office. To the Void with looking like the self-assured Prime; despite spending the last hour debating with herself, she still wasn't entirely certain this was a good idea. She would see what this student thought of it, though, eager as she was to help. "I have thought of something you might do for me."

"You have but to tell me, Aken, and I will—"

The Void Prime held up one hand to stop her. "Wait until I've told you what it is, before you agree to anything. I know you said you wanted to help, but I'm sure you didn't have *this* in mind."

Eikyo's blue-gray eyes widened in apprehension.

"You *don't* have to do this," Satomi said clearly. "I mean that. I know that a suggestion from a Prime might as well be an order, but I won't have you doing this of anything less than your own free will. Understand?"

"Yes," Eikyo whispered.

Satomi took a deep breath. "So. Ruriko tells me you're due to be tested in two days."

Eikyo nodded.

"We can still go through with that. In fact, we *should*—show everyone that the business of Starfall hasn't been disrupted."

"Aken—" Eikyo's head had come up in surprise. "But with Shimi-kane gone—"

"Just Shimi," Satomi reminded her. "While she's suspended, you need not use the honorific."

"But—can you even do it, without her?"

"Of course," Satomi said. "It even happens more often than you might think. There have been times—not many, but a few—when a Prime couldn't attend, for one reason or another. Critical business elsewhere, or sometimes illness." She smiled at the student's clear confusion. "You've never heard about it, of course. We bring in one of the Keys in her place, with an illusion to make her look like her Prime. Even the witches whose tests were conducted by a Key don't know it happened to them." Arinei had been one such, though Satomi would never tell her.

"Shimi's departure will not stop our work," Satomi continued, putting more confidence into her tone than she felt. Half of keeping life normal was convincing people it *was* normal. Though that would be a lost cause with Eikyo, in a minute. "We'll appoint one of her Keys to stand for her—without an illusion, though, since everyone's well aware that Shimi's not here. You'll be tested in two days." She smiled at the student. "I hope you've been studying."

Eikyo turned pale, but she nodded.

The smile faded from Satomi's face almost immediately. "This, then, is where the chance for you to help comes in.

"You said to me yesterday that you're a student, and not as much use as a witch. Well, I have witches who support me—not enough, but some. And one new witch, her pendant still warm from the silversmith's workshop, won't tip the balance much. But you stand at a crossroads where—if you are willing—you may take a path that no one else can."

Eikyo's lips went suddenly white as she pressed them together.

"I am asking you," Satomi said quietly, "to participate in a lie . . . and become a Cousin."

She thought she saw Eikyo sway. What were the odds that the girl would agree to it? Satomi hastened to offer an explanation. She did not expect it to do much good, but she offered it anyway. "The Cousins are a vital part of Starfall, yet we know terrifyingly little about them. They do not confide in us. They do their jobs; they clean our rooms and halls, prepare our food, defend us when we need it. Such has been their lot nearly since our line began.

"It was a few generations after Misetsu that the first woman lost her memory and her chance at magic in the test. One by one, others followed. What should be done with such women? We must either send them out into the world, or keep them among us. In the world, they would be alone, with no kin or friends to help them. Among us, at least, they need not start from scratch."

Eikyo *was* swaying on her feet. Satomi took her by the arm and guided her to a chair; the student sat without any sign of awareness that she was moving. The Void Prime went on, softly. "We don't mistreat them. You know that. The ones who fail their tests pick what jobs interest them, and learn their trades; how many people in other domains have that much choice? Many of them have children, and then those children either follow their mothers' trades, or choose something else. They stay here because we are their people."

At her own words, she laughed softly. "Or so we tell ourselves. We don't really *know* why they stay.

"And there are more things we don't know. Doppelgangers have survived in the past; they *had* to have had a Cousin's help. The Cousins themselves claim not to know anything about that—but can we believe them?" Satomi cast a glance at one of the books on a shelf behind her desk. It was a history she had read shortly after her ascension to the position of Head Key in the Void Ray gave her access to it; she had never touched it again until Miryo's test showed that her doppelganger was alive. It detailed the efforts Tokaga, Void Prime in those days, had made to discover how Orezha had survived.

"We have ways of determining whether someone is telling the truth," Satomi said. "You've studied those spells. But we can't place every Cousin under the lens like that; there are too many of them. And taking such extreme actions . . . does not help our relations with them." There had been some unpleasant repercussions to Tokaga's efforts.

Eikyo showed some sign of life at last; she turned and looked at Satomi, eyes still very wide.

Satomi spoke quietly, meeting her gaze. "We *must* know more about the Cousins. About what they do, and how, and why, when we are not watching them. There's a whole society around us we know almost nothing about. They won't talk if we ask them to; the only way I can think of to learn about them is to place someone among them who *will* talk. But no current witch could do that. Even with an illusion to hide who she is, they'd wonder who this newcomer is, when there's no word of anyone failing her test. It has to be a student, ready for the test— but who has *not* failed. Someone who retains her memory, who knows she has a task. And you are in a perfect position to do that."

And then she fell silent, because she could think of nothing else to say. She simply had to wait.

Finally Eikyo stirred, and spoke. "I . . . would not be tested?"

"You would go through the questioning of the Keys. But for the ritual itself—no. Everyone else would believe it had happened, but it would not have."

"Then I wouldn't be a witch."

Satomi had considered testing the girl, and then simply lying about the result. The odds of passing were substantially in Eikyo's favor; those who died or became Cousins for real were in the minority. But magic was hard to resist, once you had it; the masquerade would be far more plausible without it. "Not yet," she told the girl reassuringly. "Afterward, we would test you for real. I would not leave you among the Cousins forever."

The young woman's hands were trembling in her lap. She looked down and clasped them hard together. "I . . ." Her voice trailed off, and for a moment she was silent.

Then she turned back up to face Satomi, and her eyes were full of tears. "Aken, I—I've been afraid of this for years. Afraid that I would be a Cousin. I'd rather *die* than have that happen to me. If I'm not going to be a witch, then I'd rather the Goddess kill me, than take away my mind."

Satomi reached out and took the student's hands in her own. "You *won't* lose your mind. That's the point. You'll know exactly who you are, and why you're there."

"But—" Eikyo's breath was coming rapidly, though she was clearly fighting to maintain her composure. "Why now? If this is so important, why haven't you done anything about it before?"

The Void Prime pressed her lips together. The young woman had a point. She *should* have worried about this before now. *But Cousins are Cousins; they've always been there, since the day you were born, keeping your world in good working order. Who ever stops to think about what they do when out of sight?*

"I suppose," she said at last, her words coming slowly, "that it's because of Mirei. Her arrival here was like an earthquake, and this is one of its many aftershocks. I find myself questioning many things I took for granted, and wondering what else we have missed. What else has become habit, that should be changed. The way we relate to the Cousins may be one of those things."

"And—you can't just *ask* them?"

Satomi's breath came out in a short, soundless laugh. "My rank carries a certain amount of weight with them, and no more. They do what I tell them to, and politely stonewall anything else. I cannot get more out of them except by force—or subterfuge."

Eikyo took her hands out of Satomi's, picking at the cotton of her skirt. Satomi let her sit in silence for several long moments and tried not to show how desperately she waited for an answer.

"You need me to do this," Eikyo said, almost inaudibly.

"I need someone to. You're the best candidate."

Another silence.

"All right," Eikyo whispered. "I will do it, Aken."

Chapter Five

❖━━━◆━━━❖

MIREI FORGOT to allow for saddle sores.

She'd spent the last five years of her life on the road, moving from place to place as an itinerant Hunter, usually alone. So she made her usual calculations of travel time: four days to Angrim from Silverfire, and then nine days or so to Starfall, barring weather.

She forgot to allow for eleven-year-old girls.

To be fair, Amas and Indera did their best, and didn't complain. But what Mirei thought of as a solid traveling pace was brutal to them, and they simply couldn't last an entire day on horseback. Their training included daily trail-riding to toughen them up, but they weren't anywhere near ready for Mirei's pace. She had to slow down, take breaks, stop early, and try not to worry about how long it was taking them to reach Angrim.

Mindful of her promise to Jaguar, Mirei worked on teaching them things as they rode. Unfortunately, she hadn't the faintest idea what first-year trainees were supposed to learn.

Jaguar had decided, back when Tari-nakana convinced him to take Mirage in at the ripe old age of thirteen, to throw her in with the trainees who were of an age to be her year-mates, rather than putting her with the first-years. It had been a grueling experience for her, trying to

catch up on everything she had not learned in her appren-
ticeship as a Temple Dancer, but that had been the point:
the way Jaguar saw it, if she survived *that*, she was tough
enough that she deserved to stay.

But at the age Amas and Indera were now, Mirei had
been in the Great Temple in Eriot, spending her days in
far different lessons. Now she had no idea what to do with
her miniature doppelganger flock.

Horse care, certainly, because she wasn't going to
handle all three mounts herself. How to sleep outside as
comfortably as could be arranged; Mirei had some coin,
but Askavyan peasant women did not, and she wasn't
about to abandon the disguise that so usefully hid their
red heads and cropped hair. Edible wildlife, coupled with
the things that one would not want to eat oneself, but
which might be useful against others. Indera already
knew some of those from helping her mother. Other elements of surviving the traveling life.

And, of course, fighting.

Even raw from riding, Indera was wild to learn from her
hero. Her young face showed echoes of her true mother's
high-boned features; when she set herself to practice,
some of Ashin's intensity came through. Amas was less
vocal than her year-mate, but the wiry girl took everything Mirei cared to give her without a hint of reluctance.
Which left Mirei having to figure out just how to teach
something that had always come very naturally to her.

It came naturally to the doppelgangers, as well. That
was part of *being* a doppelganger, being the Warrior aspect of a soul. But that didn't mean they wouldn't benefit
from a systematic method of learning. Mirei had to delve

back into her memories of her earliest days at Silverfire to figure out what they should do.

She gave them this much credit: they didn't complain. Much. *"Slowly,"* Mirei said late one afternoon, in the daisy-strewn meadow where she'd taken them to practice. If they couldn't use all the hours riding, then she would use them for something else. "Slow makes you work on your balance as well as your form. Start in stance— pivot—tuck your leg—*slow!*" she barked as Indera began to kick outward at speed. Amas had a talent for kicks, with her long legs, but Indera needed work. "Slow extension means you'll think about your line, your aim, whether or not you're keeping your guard up. Again. Pivot—tuck— extend—now bring your leg back in, your body back up. Now the other side."

Indera lurched slightly on the next kick. Out of stance, she scuffed at the grass with one toe. "Sorry. The ground's rough here."

"You think you're going to be doing all your fights on the practice room floor?"

The trainee flinched at the snap in Mirei's voice. "No." Without another word, she went back to the exercise.

It was good for them, making them think about form and precision, even when their butts and thighs had been pounded into jelly by hours in the saddle. And it saved Mirei from having to do anything other than watch and critique, which meant they had no chance to find out that their reflexes were better than hers. Mirei could beat them easily, even both together, but her reflexes had been legend; she didn't want the questions that would arise from her slower movements.

So many pitfalls she had to avoid. And so many things

she would rather be doing—like finding out what had happened to Eclipse.

When she wasn't teaching, she asked questions about them both. Subtle ones, wandering to many side topics she didn't much care about, but she got the information she wanted in the end. Neither of the girls had the slightest real clue that their supposed parents were not their own. However Tari and Ashin and the rest had gone about placing the doppelgangers with false families, they'd done a much more delicate job of it than whoever had spirited the infant Mirage out of Starfall. Seniade, as her foster parents had named her, had known from a very young age that she was a foundling, and not just because of her flaming red hair. Amas and Indera believed in the lies they'd lived.

She was not looking forward to destroying those lies.

She couldn't put it off forever, of course. She would tell them the truth as soon as the two doppelgangers in Angrim were secured. And then she could get an escort of witches and Cousins, take them to Starfall, and go back to helping Satomi figure out how Void magic worked and what repercussions this would have on the witches' way of life. While Amas and Indera and the other two met, for the first time, the other halves of their souls.

Once she was done in Angrim.

TAKING THE DOPPELGANGERS into Angrim would be idiocy. There were two Hunter schools on the outskirts of Abern's capital, Windblade and Thornblood, and they didn't like each other much; the city, lying between them as it did, was a hornet's nest of spies. They kept an eye on each other—several legions of eyes, actually—and then others kept eyes on *them*. Other Hunter schools; Lady Linea, Abern's ruler; even the witches had some people there.

Mirei met with substantial resistance, though, when she tried to tell Amas and Indera to stay behind.

"We're Hunters, too," Indera said stubbornly. "We know how to be subtle. We won't cause trouble."

"You're *trainees,* and you're staying here." Mirei silenced further protests with a glare. "This isn't negotiable. You do what I tell you to, when I tell you, or you regret it. Understand?"

Indera nodded unwillingly. Amas merely watched the whole exchange. *I'm going to have to be careful of that one,* Mirei thought, casting a swift glance at the silent trainee. *She's been watching me this whole trip, all seven Void-damned days of it. Keeping her own counsel. Weighing what I say. Got to be careful of her, when I finally tell them what's going on. She may not take it well.*

She stashed the two girls in a Silverfire bolt-hole east of the sprawling edge of Angrim. It wasn't exactly a secret place—she had no doubt both Windblade and Thornblood knew of its existence—but for a short stay, it should be all right. She had every intention of getting in and getting out as fast as humanly possible.

Nevermind that she still hadn't decided what to do about kidnapping someone out of Thornblood.

Mirei got Amas and Indera settled, then went out to where her borrowed gelding was tethered. "Don't even think about it," she said as she checked over her tack, not bothering to look back at the door of the "abandoned" farmhouse. The startled scuffling noise she heard was answer enough. "Follow me, and I'll flay the skin off your back. Understand me?"

"Yes," Indera called back, half-meekly, half-sullenly.

"If I'm not back by nightfall, feed yourselves. Bread and jerky only. Don't go scrounging, don't light a fire. If I'm not back by morning—" Mirei hesitated. What *should* they do, if this went wrong? "Then ride back to Silverfire, as hard as you can. I don't care if your legs are bleeding pieces of meat by the end, just get there as fast as possible. Got it?"

"Yes," came the answer again, this time in a chorus of Amas and Indera.

Mirei mounted up and rode west without another word.

The day was barely half spent, and alone, Mirei could set as hard a pace as she wanted. She didn't gallop; that would only draw attention. But she rode fast, wanting to finish this and get back to the bolt-hole before her charges found something stupid to do.

Windblade was on the southern side of the city. Mirei went there first. Jaguar had promised to send pigeons ahead; Silverfire and Windblade were friendly with each other, as Hunter schools went, and in particular he had a good relationship with the Grandmaster of Windblade, with whom he had once cooperated on a major commission. If all had gone well, he had smoothed the way for her.

Unlike Silverfire, half a day's ride from the small town of Elensk and therefore protected by isolation, Windblade was heavily fortified. Jaguar had guaranteed that he could at least get them to let her in. Which was good, since Mirei was *not* going to attempt to translocate blindly into an unfamiliar place. If she ended up needing to sneak into Thornblood, she'd have to do it more slowly.

The main gate of the compound was a massive thing,

two iron-banded oak doors wide enough to allow a large cart through. The guard kept watch from the allure above, and challenged Mirei as she rode close. "Halt. State your name and business."

Mirei pulled off her head scarf. She wore her Hunter's uniform underneath the disguise, and she was sweltering in the heat; a part of her hoped the guard would demand more evidence, so she could remove a few layers. "Mirage of Silverfire," she said, remembering at the last instant not to give the wrong name, and to disguise her trained witch's tones. "My Grandmaster should have sent a message in advance. I have business with *your* Grandmaster."

Red hair came in handy for once. To his credit, though, the guard didn't take it as sufficient proof. He delved about for a moment in a case clipped to his belt, then produced a piece of thin rice paper that looked, from what Mirei could see of it, like a sketch. Clearly they, like Silverfire, kept information on other Hunters, and had informed the gate guards she would be coming. After a moment of comparing the sketch to her face, he nodded. "Right. Wait there."

He turned and gestured to someone on the other side of the wall, then took up his post again, eyes on the road, but keeping peripheral watch on Mirei. A few minutes later, a small side gate swung open. The opening ran at an awkward angle through the wall, and was narrow and low enough that Mirei had to dismount and lead her reluctant horse through. If it ever came to an outright attack against Windblade's compound, no one would find this a convenient entrance.

Two people awaited her on the far side. One, a young trainee, took her horse to a nearby stable. The other was an adult Hunter, who checked Mirei swiftly but thoroughly for weapons, then indicated she should follow him.

Never before had she set foot in another school's compound. She kept her eyes mostly on her guide's back, so as not to seem unduly curious, but noted down details out of her peripheral vision. Windblade's buildings were packed more closely together than Silverfire's, limited by the walls that demarcated the compound; she saw few open spaces, and surmised those must be toward the back. After all, the trainees would need somewhere to ride, and to practice the archery their school was famous for. The structures, though, were built more of wood than of stone, and had larger windows with shutters thrown open in hopes of a cooling breeze. Winters were kinder here.

The building she was led to looked more defensible. The Hunter leading her knocked on the outside door in what sounded like a specific pattern, waited for a call from within, and then opened it with a wave for Mirei to precede him.

There were three people inside, two men and a woman, all in Hunter clothes. Both of the men stared at Mirei in startlement. "What are you doing here?" the younger of the two snapped, voice harsh with suspicion.

Mirei saluted the whole group. The older man, wide as a barn door and twice as thick, was probably the Grandmaster, but she wasn't sure. Better to be polite, in a situation like this. "I'm Mirage of Silverfire. Jaguar, I believe, has sent a message about one of your trainees."

The younger man dropped the papers he was holding and walked up to her where she stood, just inside the room. Her guide had closed the door and was standing behind her; without looking, Mirei knew his posture had shifted to readiness. *This might be about to go very bad.*

The man spoke with sharp, hostile clarity. "You took her with you yesterday."

Damn it. I hate being right.

Mirei made an instant decision *not* to try and control her expression. It helped; the clear shock and dismay on her face sent some of the tension out of the man's shoulders. "A witch," she whispered through her clenched teeth. Shimi, or an ally of hers? "Damn it to *Void!*"

"How do we know *you're* not the witch?" the woman said, rising from her seat. She did not come near, and her hand hovered in a way that told Mirei there was a knife sheathed at the small of her back.

"Did the other one mention Jaguar's note?" Mirei asked.

The Windblades exchanged glances. "No," the woman said softly. "And we should have been suspicious of that."

"But we weren't," the younger man said, and that told Mirei everything she needed to know about what had happened the previous day.

"I have to go," she said into the silence. She fixed her eyes on the older man, the one who hadn't spoken yet, but whose manner as he listened to the others identified him as the one in charge. Which would make him Wall, the Grandmaster of the school. "Sir, I'm sorry. If I'd been here sooner—" She tried not to curse the softness of her two charges, and only partially succeeded. "I'll get her back, I swear. But right now, I need to go and make sure someone else is safe." *She probably isn't.*

The older man spoke at last, and his deep, resonant voice confirmed his identity. "Why does a witch want

Naspeth? And why did Jaguar send *you* to take her to safety?"

Mirei did *not* have the time to give him the explanation. Not with one doppelganger stolen, two others vulnerable in a bolt-hole east of the city, and a fourth yet to be secured. She went for the quick and dirty version, hoping it would divert their anger away from Starfall. "There's a religious fanatic among the witches, a renegade who's gone off on her own. She thinks people like Naspeth are an abomination."

"People like *you*," the younger man said.

Wall spoke again before Mirei had to decide how to answer that. "So she's going to kill Naspeth."

"Not yet," Mirei said. "She thinks it has to be done in a special way, and setting that up will take a while. I told you: I'll get Naspeth back."

"Who is this fanatic?"

Mirei looked the Grandmaster of Windblade in the eye and lied with every fiber of her being. "I don't know. The Primes who warned me about her didn't say."

Wall approached her at last, and the others melted out of his path, all except the Hunter still standing guard at her back. Up close, he was truly enormous. "That's not good enough."

"I'll tell you more as soon as I know anything," Mirei said, not betraying her deception with so much as a flicker of eyelash. She'd tell him more as soon as she thought it was safe to do so. Which might be never. "Now I *have* to leave."

"The Thornblood," the woman Hunter said.

The two schools hated each other, but it was too obvious to lie about. They would know there was a girl there like Naspeth. "Yes. I'd rather chase down one missing trainee, not two."

After a moment in which the only sound Mirei could hear was her own pulse, Wall nodded. "Then go."

SHE RODE HARD for the city, knowing her progress was being noted, and not caring.

Mirei didn't know if the last doppelganger was still within Thornblood's walls, and had no idea what to do if she was. There was no friendly introduction smoothing her way there. Nothing but a compound full of people who would kill her on sight. But she had to try.

She got to Angrim's walls and had to slow. Mounted traffic was only permitted on a few of the major streets; the rest were too narrow and twisted. *If I ride straight for Thornblood, I'll never make it; someone will get nervous and take me down. Warrior's teeth and toenails. Got to move more subtly, but be ready to run like fire if I have to, and get back to the other two.* There were Silverfire agents in Angrim, but she couldn't stop long enough to contact one. She had to improvise.

She left her horse in a hostelry toward the eastern side of the city and took to the streets on foot. Avoiding the places where she *knew* there were spies, she made her way through alleys, courtyards, shops with doors on multiple streets. Soon the Askavyan peasant disguise was gone, replaced by shirt, trousers, and cap that probably belonged to a clerk. Her Hunter uniform went into a bundle on her back. She also swiped a knife. Mirei melded in with the crowds, then slipped out again and nicked a cleaning woman's drab rags. She was nearly to the north edge of the city now, and paused to find a good place to hide and change a second time. The neighborhood here was more run-down; with a change of clothes, she could be a servant returning home at the end of the day. Then she'd have to decide what to do about breaking into the school.

Or I could bypass that bit entirely, because she's not in the bloody school.

Mirei faded back into the evening shadows, rags forgotten in her hands, as two figures emerged from a side street. In the dim light, the woman's pale, short hair glimmered, almost ghostly, and her rangy silhouette was unpleasantly familiar. The smaller figure behind her had her head covered, but it didn't take a genius to guess who it was.

Mirei had not seen Ice since the Thornblood had smashed her head into the floor of an Angrim inn, knocking her out for transportation to Miryo—well, she sort of had, when Miryo watched the arrival of the Hunters through an enchanted mirror. The overlap of the two memories was briefly disorienting. *Nevermind, that's not the point,* Mirei growled at herself. *Stop picking daisies and follow her.*

Ice had vanished into another alleyway, girl in tow. Mirei sauntered across the street, doing her best to look like an ordinary clerk, no one to be suspicious of. How many spies would there be, in this quarter? *Ah, Void it, just get the girl and worry about the spies later.* The only attention that mattered right now was Ice's, and once again, Mirei had cause to be glad that the Thornblood was not as good a Hunter as she liked to believe.

They were headed toward the northeastern edge of the city. Should she jump Ice now? No, because the trainee would probably run at the first sign of trouble, and then

Mirei would never chase her down. Besides, she wanted to know where Ice was going. Judging by the Hunter's furtiveness, this trip was not one she was supposed to be taking.

The shadows were deepening into twilight, making the two figures harder to follow. Mirei closed up the gap, afraid of losing them. And then, blessedly, Ice stopped at a building, and pushed the trainee through the door ahead of her.

Mirei slipped up to the door the moment it closed. Ear to the wood, she heard footsteps, the creak of stairs, Ice saying "Go on up." *Two sets of feet; good.* Mirei forced herself to wait a few heartbeats more, until the sounds had faded, before she tried the handle.

The door was unlocked, and she glided through.

She found herself in what looked like a clerk's small office. *Pity,* she thought wryly, *that disguises won't do much good now.* There was a desk, a wall of cubbies filled with paper, a staircase. And from the floor above, voices.

Mirei eyed the staircase. She'd heard it creak under the weight of the others. Getting up it silently would take forever, if it was even possible. The flash powder she'd brought from Silverfire was uselessly safe with her supplies in the bolt-hole. Was it worth the risk to just charge?

Ice, according to one of Silverfire's agents in town, had sold information about Mirage to the Primes. The animosity between them went above even the standard rivalry between their two schools. Ice had hated Mirage before they even met, because of Mirage's inborn talents.

Would that hatred go away just because this time the one with the gifts was a Thornblood?

Can I apologize after the fact if whoever's up there isn't on Shimi's side?

Yes.

Mirei threw herself up the staircase.

They heard her coming; a deaf man would have heard her coming. Mirei had a heartbeat, when she reached the top, to thank the Goddess and all her stars that there were only three people in the room: Ice, the trainee, and a witch. A heartbeat only: Ice had drawn a blade, and the witch was singing a spell.

Mirei cleared the remainder of the steps in a dive-roll that took her straight past Ice and into the room. Behind her, there was an explosion of splinters as the spell hit where she had been. *Okay, so we're not playing nice.* Ice swore in shock and flinched back from the detonation, and then Mirei was on her feet, knife in hand.

The witch was closer, standing next to a small desk and chair that were nearly the only furniture in the room. She was about to begin another spell. Mirei didn't give her time. She bull-rushed the woman, knocking her to the floor, and vaulted on top of the desk as Ice lunged for her. A kick sent the Hunter reeling backward. The trainee dodged out of Ice's path with snakelike grace, even while staring in confusion at the scene that had erupted with so little warning.

Mirei spun down off the desk. Ice had recovered and was coming for her; Mirei had to retreat, cursing the disguises that put her here with only a knife against the Thornblood's sword. The witch was singing again, voice ragged with stress, but she maintained her tone well enough that the spell was going to work. Mirei dodged inside Ice's guard, slammed her elbow into the Hunter's face, and in the brief space she bought for herself gasped out the syllables and pitches that would cancel the witch's spell dead.

Both of her opponents stopped and stared. *The witch has never seen magic canceled. Ice . . . Ice just saw me cast a spell.*

Then the trainee tackled her from the side.

Mirei crashed to the floor, the girl tangled around her legs. Ice was moving in to attack. Mirei had no time to be gentle; she kicked the girl solidly in the head, then pivoted and swept Ice's feet out from under her. But the witch's voice was filling the air again—

She didn't even think about it. She just threw.

Her knife took the witch in the throat. The woman's spell died into choking silence; the energy it had built hovered, on the edge of manifesting but cut off before completion. One more syllable, and it would be done— but the witch collapsed to her knees, hands clawing weakly at the blade, unable to finish.

Ice hurled herself on top of Mirei, hands scrabbling for *her* throat. Mirei dug her fingers into the other Hunter's wrists, seeking pressure points, her legs fighting for leverage beneath Ice's weight. Finally she got a lock around one leg, and applied force; Ice gasped with pain as her knee tried to bend the wrong way. Her grip slackened. Mirei forced Ice's hands back, took a good breath, and sang a holding spell.

It almost didn't work. Her tone was rough with the strain of the physical struggle; there had to be a way to make her fighting work as a focus, but she had yet to figure it out. The unevenness of her voice almost sent the spell awry, especially with the unfinished remnants of the other witch's spell still hanging in the air. But it worked, just barely, and Ice went rigid and still.

Mirei shoved her off and climbed to her feet. She went first to the witch, but it was far too late; the woman lay unmoving on the bare floorboards in a pool of blood. Mirei pulled the knife from her throat and laid her out on her back. "I'm sorry," she murmured.

A rustle behind her made her turn. Ice had not broken the spell; the trainee was stirring where *she* lay. Mirei tried to remember how hard she'd kicked. Weirdly, she almost hoped it had been *very* hard. Judging by her own experience, if the girl had died of it, then she would come back without the headache she'd have otherwise.

Assuming this was the Thornblood doppelganger.

She stepped over Ice's frozen body. The Hunter snarled as she did, and thereby discovered that she could still make noise; the spell held her jaw in place, but it didn't stop her vocal cords. A stream of badly enunciated invective was delivered at Mirei's back as she knelt to examine the girl on the floor.

The trainee seemed roughly the right age—eleven, or twelve at the most. Her oval face and delicate features didn't remind Mirei of any particular witch, but that didn't mean anything. The hair would be the telling point. When Mirei slipped off the kerchief tied to her head, though, the scalp beneath was shaven bald.

Standard procedure for Thornbloods? Mirei wondered. *Or special treatment for a red-haired girl? If her hair even is red. Won't necessarily be. Is this the doppelganger, or not? Misetsu and Menukyo, I hope so.*

The girl was alive, at least. Mirei turned her attention to Ice, and could not keep the anger out of her voice. "This is her, isn't it? How much were you being paid, Ice? To betray someone of your *own damned school* to a witch?"

Ice mumbled something virtually unintelligible; the only word Mirei picked out was "hypocrite." "Slowly and clearly, Ice," Mirei said mockingly. "Otherwise I won't be able to understand all your finely crafted insults."

"Void-damned witch," Ice snarled, with admirable clarity.

Mirei had never been more aware of the newfound irony of using the Void for cursing. She couldn't deny the words, though; she *was* a witch. After years of hating Ice for calling her that. "They were going to *kill* her, Ice," she said, gesturing at the girl. "Did you know that? Or didn't you bother to ask? Was the chance to get rid of someone like me too good a bargain to pass up?" Fury made her tremble. "She could have been the pride of your school. Surely that means something to you, even if you don't care that she's *an eleven-year-old girl.* Hate me, fine; I'm a Silverfire. But she's one of your *own.*"

Ice said something that came out mostly vowels. She growled in frustration, then tried a different word. "Freak."

Mirei regarded her in silence, wondering what to do. She'd used magic in front of Ice. Given the chance, the Thornblood would tell the world. Witches had long neglected the Aspect of the Warrior in their theology; Hunter schools were descended from Warrior cults. The two groups had never gotten along. And now she—a Silverfire, and a witch—was about to steal a Thornblood trainee.

She had the knife in her hand, still wet with the witch's blood.

If she killed Ice, someone would find the bodies of a

murdered Hunter and witch in this room. There would be an investigation. Someone might remember seeing Mirei; this was Angrim, after all. The Thornbloods, and Shimi, might learn what she had done.

If she left Ice alive, they'd *know* who killed the witch. And Ice would put the worst spin on it she could.

Mirage would have killed Ice. It was the logical solution. But the part of her that had been Miryo could not be so cold-blooded about it. The woman was a Thornblood, but also a human being. Could Mirei just pass judgment on her, here and now, and end her life?

Her hand tensed on the knife—and then a small foot hit her in the kidneys.

"Mother's *tits*," Mirei swore, and spun around just in time to grab the fist headed for her face.

The trainee struggled, and the contact with her was enough to tell Mirei she did indeed have the Thornblood doppelganger on her hands. Fortunately, even Warrior-blessed strength wasn't enough to overpower her, not when the body it rested in was a mere eleven years old. Mirei got the girl pinned, then snapped, "Will you bloody well stop that? I'm on your side."

"Silverfire," the girl hissed, as if the word were the foulest insult she could think of.

Great. So they've indoctrinated her already. "Try to forget about that for a moment, and concentrate on the fact that I'm the only woman in this room who didn't want you dead."

"Don't listen to her," Ice said, and went on from there, her clarity rapidly degenerating into unintelligible mush.

"Ice, for the love of the Warrior, shut up before I cut your throat."

Mirei's careless threat hit the girl she held like a blow. The doppelganger froze, staring at her, then began to fight all the more wildly. "Murdering witch! You touch her and I'll—"

"Look," Mirei said, and hauled the girl to her feet. "You'll get more of an explanation later. For now, what you get is this. That witch"—she pointed at the body on the floor—"wanted to kill you. Ice"—she pointed at the Thornblood, who had ignored the order to shut up—"sold you out to the witch who wanted to kill you. They both think you're an unnatural abomination who should be destroyed. Or something like that: I won't go so far as to assume Ice thought much past the 'jealousy' stage. The point is, you've probably noticed that you're faster and stronger and better at fighting than any of your yearmates. As it happens, that's why certain people want you dead. I, by contrast, want you to live a long happy life with flowers and puppies, and can—as a side benefit—tell you *why* you are the way you are."

And I don't give a damn which way you choose, really, because if I have to stab you and cart your dead body out of Angrim tonight, I will. You'll recover.

The girl had, for a wonder, stopped struggling. She was staring at Mirei's hair. "Am . . . am I a witch?"

"Witches cast spells with music. You couldn't carry a tune if I gave you a bucket to put it in." Mirei was guessing, but it had been true of Mirage. Sense of pitch appeared to be the property of the witch-half. Still, she didn't want to start off by lying to this girl. "But there *is* a connection there. Like I said, I can explain everything. I just don't want to do it here."

"Why not?" the girl demanded.

"Notice how Ice has finally shut up? She wants to hear what I have to say. I don't feel like telling her, since she's a mercenary with the ethics of a dead rat. We've also just had a noisy fight in a city full of spies. Explanations can come when I don't have to worry about being arrested."

"Don't trust her," Ice half shouted, still frozen on the floor.

Mirei didn't answer that. Instead, she let go of the doppelganger and stepped back, hands relaxed at her sides. The knife lay on the floor next to them where she'd dropped it; she saw the girl's eyes flick toward it, once.

Six heartbeats later—Mirei counted—the doppelganger dove for the blade.

Mirei kicked it across the floor before her hand touched it and leapt back, singing. The doppelganger crumpled to the floor in a sleeping heap.

Ice was swearing at Mirei again, or at least Mirei assumed that's what the smear of noise was. She spoke over it. "Count yourself lucky, Ice. I recently became a new woman who's less pragmatic than the one you knew. Because of that, I'm going to leave you alive. On the other hand, you're going to be the first person I've tried this on, so you'd better hope nothing goes wrong with it."

Then, ignoring the mounting yells of the paralyzed Thornblood, Mirei began gathering suitable foci for a spell to change Ice's memory.

Chapter Six

THE FOUR REMAINING PRIMES stood in a hallway and conversed in low voices.

"It will be ironic," Koika said wryly, "if the Keys don't pass her."

Satomi smiled, though her face didn't much want to bend. "I doubt it. Ruriko says her memory is excellent."

"But with this much pressure on her? Perfectly intelligent girls have failed the questioning before, because of nerves."

Satomi sighed at Koika. "Thank you for the comforting words."

Arinei was pacing nearby; the heavy blue silk of her skirt cracked with her quick, tight strides. "I still don't know what you hope to gain by this charade."

"Come, Arinei," Rana said. "Surely you learned this, serving in Insebrar. The servants often know far more about the Lords' affairs than those Lords realize. It's past time we had a care for that, ourselves."

"I pay more attention than a Lord does," Arinei snapped. "The Cousins do their work and go home, like ordinary people. What little they know about our affairs, they do nothing with. We have nothing to be concerned about."

"Then Eikyo will find nothing, we'll bring her home

and test her properly, and all will be well." Rana's expression belied her carefree tone, though. In the meeting where they had argued this plan, Rana had been forced to play mediator between Satomi and Koika on one side and Arinei on the other. She, unlike Satomi and Arinei, had come from the Heart Path. The Hands of her Ray spent plenty of time adjudicating village squabbles, but Rana had little experience with it, and no liking.

Koika held up a hand to stop them all before the argument could begin again. "It's time."

Wordlessly, they arranged themselves into a line, spacing out so as not to leave an obvious gap where Shimi should have been. The double doors in front of them swung open in well-oiled silence, pulled by two Cousins on the other side, and together they entered the room.

Eikyo sat in a chair with her back to them, facing the array of the fifteen Keys. The cotton of her dress between her shoulder blades was dark with sweat, and the water glass at her side was empty. The questioning was not an afternoon stroll.

The Keys stood, and after a moment of startled paralysis, so did Eikyo. She turned and saw the women behind her, bowed to them and to the Keys, and stepped aside.

"This one has brought her mind to you for testing," Satomi said, repeating the traditional words she had uttered countless times. "How do you find it?"

As Key for the Void Head, Hyoka answered her. That, too, was a part Satomi had played many times in past years. "Her mind is sound and well-prepared. We commend her to your trial."

Which will not be the trial everyone expects.

Eikyo bowed again to the Primes, her knees visibly unsteady. Satomi could not blame her. But neither could she say anything to comfort the young woman; they had to carry out the outward trappings of this ritual, at least.

The four Primes led her from the room, with Naji following them. There had been disagreement over which of the Air Keys should stand in Shimi's place. Koika had argued in favor of Ashin, and Arinei had argued even more vehemently against her. Naji was a safer choice, politically; before this trouble began, the presumption had been that she would succeed Shimi as Prime.

The outside air was uncomfortably still and hot. Satomi waited, Eikyo at her side, while the Primes and Naji dispersed to their doors around the outside of Star Hall; then she brought the young woman to the northern arm of the structure, the one dedicated to Earth. Koika broke protocol just a tiny amount, to smile at Eikyo in reassurance.

The others remained outside as Satomi led Eikyo inside, down the hall of Earth. Their quiet footsteps echoed against the pale silver marble of the walls, fading upward into the lofty spaces above. Here, in this branch, the stained-glass windows were greens and rich ambers, lit by permanent spells that allowed them to cast colored light down inside the building even when outside was black night. The other three arms showed the colors of their Elements, and as many times as she had been in here, Satomi never tired of its beauty.

In the center, where the four arms converged, was a dais, and the place of the Void.

It no longer looked as it once had. Formerly, the pillars and vaulting of the Hall had leapt upward farther yet, into an untouchable blackness thick with spells that had given the center of Star Hall a disquieting feel. It was the best the architects had been able to do, to represent the Void.

Mirei's arrival had changed that, like so many other things. It was here that she had confronted the Primes, with the rest of Starfall watching, in an attempt to show them what she had achieved. The Primes, off balance and fearing what she might destroy, had attacked her. The conclusion of the ensuing battle had taken out the roof.

Now, the upper reaches of Star Hall were gone. The vaults of the center crossing were shattered; the rubble had been cleared away, but no rebuilding had happened yet. Satomi wasn't sure what to *do* about rebuilding. Their understanding of the Void was changing; their representation of it should, as well. And a part of her liked the starlight now visible above the jagged stumps of the walls. The stars were the eyes of the Goddess; they had come down and danced about Misetsu, the first witch, when the Goddess gave her the gift of magic, here in the mountains now called Starfall. For all Misetsu's later flaws, that had been an unsurpassed miracle.

They had arrived at the dais. There were ritual words for this, too, but Satomi did not use them.

"Are you sure you want to do this?" she asked the young woman gently.

Eikyo swallowed hard, and then nodded.

She wouldn't insult Eikyo's courage by asking again. "We'll be back later. I suggest you meditate; it's what you're expected to do anyway."

"I hear and obey, Aken," Eikyo whispered. Satomi had to fight not to flinch at the words. They were the traditional response, spoken in answer to the words she herself had not said. Eikyo had prepared too much for this not to reflexively come out with her memorized responses, even when they were not necessary.

Satomi touched her on the shoulder, then exited out the south, through the hall of Air.

Naji was waiting outside, looking both apprehensive and excited. She had never done this before, and no one had told her what they had planned. "Now we wait?" she asked Satomi quietly.

"Inside," Satomi told her. "We return at midnight."

THEY HAD TO MAINTAIN the appearance of the thing. One aspect of this affair everyone had agreed on, without quibble: As few people as possible should realize that Eikyo had not really been tested.

The Primes and Naji met again shortly before midnight, and Koika, who had the best knack for it, cast a spell over them all that would keep Eikyo from noticing them until they were in position. Anyone watching from the facing windows of the main building should see her doing so. To a student, it always looked like the Primes appeared out of nowhere. Someday, Satomi hoped, they *would*, with Void magic translocating them to their places.

Then they dispersed to their doors again. Satomi entered through Earth again, with Koika.

"Here we go," the Earth Prime whispered, and they went inside.

Eikyo was kneeling on the dais, hands clasped in meditative prayer. The tension on her face had smoothed out in her trance, Satomi was glad to see. At least the girl had not spent all this time worrying.

When the other women were all gathered around, with

Satomi on the dais next to Eikyo, Koika sang a short spell to make them visible again.

At which point they diverged from ritual.

Satomi touched Eikyo on the shoulder again. "We're ready."

Out of the corner of her eye, she saw Naji move in startlement. As Eikyo surfaced from her trance and stood up, Satomi turned to face the Heart Key. "I'm sorry to have misled you," Satomi told her, but with her body language she communicated a different message. She was not sorry at all; she was the Void Prime, and Naji should not even think to question her.

"I don't understand, Aken," Naji said, but her tone was confused rather than challenging.

"We will not be carrying out Eikyo's test tonight," Satomi told her. "Though everyone must think we have, which is why we've carried out this deception." She gave the Key a coolly reassuring smile. "It's no fault of yours, don't worry. In fact, I don't doubt you'll have your chance to test students; there are others besides Eikyo who will need assistance before Shimi returns."

"*If* Shimi returns," Koika said. Arinei glared at her. A stickler for protocol, the Fire Prime would defend to the last moment the distinction between suspending and removing Shimi from authority, and Satomi could have kicked Koika for raising that issue now.

Instead she turned to the others, pretending she did not see Arinei's anger. "We'll need to stay in here for a while. Eikyo, please come with me; I have a few last things to say to you."

She drew the girl aside, back down the arm of Earth. It didn't matter which way they went, but the student had long shown an affinity for that Ray; the least Satomi could do was to put her in the place where she would feel most comfortable.

"Do the students still use the code of five?" she asked Eikyo, keeping her voice low. In the crossing, the three other Primes and Naji were trying to settle down to wait; unfortunately, Star Hall was a space for ritual, not relaxation. There wasn't even anywhere to sit.

Eikyo's blue-gray eyes went wide. "Aken?"

"The code of five," Satomi repeated. "For passing secret messages. It's an ancient tradition—if by 'ancient' I mean that it predates *my* youth, at least. Do you know it?"

"Y-yes, Aken."

"Good. I want you to use it whenever you communicate with me."

Understanding dawned on Eikyo's face. Then she frowned. "But—won't the Cousins know?"

"I don't think so. Those few of them who were once students won't recall it, and the others have had limited opportunity to pick it up. Besides, you have to know to look for it, to see that a message is buried within, and they'll have no reason to suspect you. It seems the most reliable way to communicate. Understand?"

Eikyo nodded wordlessly.

"Good. Notify me if anyone says *anything* about the doppelgangers; that's the main thing. But also pay attention to what they say about us, the witches. Anything that seems to be more than routine talk." Satomi sighed in frustration. "I wish I could give you something more specific. I want to know how they live, how they think—what lives are being lived, out of our sight, and whether we need to be concerned about them. Or even how those lives could be improved—do they feel mistreated? Questions like that. Trust your judgment."

"I will, Aken."

Satomi reached out and squeezed her shoulder. "You will do fine, Eikyo. And we *will* bring you back. I swear that, before the five faces of the Goddess." Here in Star Hall, the words carried extra force. Satomi did not make vows lightly, and even less would she do so in this ritual space, with the light of the Goddess's eyes shining down through the shattered roof.

When she judged that enough time had passed, Satomi called everyone together into the center of the Hall. The Primes raised up columns of coruscating light from the Elemental symbols marked into the floor; Satomi, from where she stood on the dais with Eikyo, raised Naji's for her. It was one of the authorities they had stripped from Shimi, a minor, showy sign of a Prime's power.

Eikyo lay down on the floor, trembling, so that everyone would be where she would have been, had the ritual gone on as usual. They had to maintain appearances, after all. Especially now, at the end. Satomi sang, quietly, the words of a spell to render her unconscious. With one last sigh, the student—soon to be a Cousin—passed out.

The Primes and the Key stood around her in a ring, poised on the columns of light. Now was when Satomi would discover whether her authority and presence were enough to keep Naji silent for these next, crucial moments.

She looked the Key in the eye and said, "What I do now is necessary. Do not interfere."

And without waiting for a nod, she began the spell that would overlay Naji's memory of this time with the ritual that should have happened.

Because as few people as possible should know that Eikyo's failure was a lie.

Naji realized what the spell was before Satomi was far into it. Her face went white, but her obedience held; with the other Primes there, saying nothing in protest, she bowed to the will of Starfall.

They had come in as usual, according to the words Satomi sang. They put Eikyo through the tests. First the verbal challenge; then the trials of the Elements themselves. The young woman had seemed to do well. Failure came, as it always did for Cousins, at the end. When they opened her to power.

Her mind broken by the onslaught of force, Eikyo had begun to speak incoherently. Satomi strung together an appropriately muddled set of sentence fragments. There were volumes and volumes in the archives of Starfall, recording the words spoken by new Cousins; no one knew if they had any importance. Witches had tried, from time to time, to extract meaning from them, but they'd met with little success. They seemed to have no more significance than the rantings of ordinary madwomen.

Eikyo had broken in this manner. And then, when the flood of words stopped, she had fallen to the dais, unconscious, her memory and self lost forever.

The intricate net of power built, drawn through the focusing structure of Star Hall, shaped by Satomi's words and voice. Eikyo had failed. Tragic, but true. Any other memories that contradicted those events were to be forgotten; any details Satomi had neglected to supply were to be filled in.

Finally, the names of those the spell should affect.

"Naji," Satomi sang, and then before anyone could re-alize what she was doing, "Arinei, Koika, Rana."

The spell flared outward, to the four women around her, and settled into place.

Because as few people as possible should know the truth.

Now only two did.

SATOMI WAITED in one of the smaller outbuildings of Starfall for Nae to come.

On the bed behind her, Eikyo slept. It was a small kind-ness given to those witches who failed, who became Cousins; they were given drugs, to keep them asleep until they reached their new homes. There would be as little re-minder as possible of what they had lost.

Nae entered without knocking.

Old without being elderly, thin without being frail, the woman was the closest thing the Cousins had to their own leader. Nae's face had weathered and hardened until the lines on it seemed carved by a knife. She looked impas-sively down on the figure in the bed. "What was her name?"

Nae alone, of all the Cousins, would know for certain who this young woman had been. "Eikyo."

The Cousin thought it over. "Kyou, then. Where was she raised?"

The loss of memory was thorough, but it helped for the new names of failed witches to be at least close to what they had once held. "She grew up in Abern. Seshiki Hall. Insebrar would be good, I think."

She was treading on the older woman's toes by making the suggestion, but Satomi wanted Eikyo somewhere spe-cific. Tsurike Hall in Insebrar was where Kasane had given birth to the daughter now called Mirei; it was from there that the infant doppelganger had somehow been spirited across the land to Eriot. One of those two domains might contain clues as to how that had happened, and Tsurike Hall seemed a good place to start.

Fortunately, tradition dictated placing new Cousins as far from familiar places as possible, to minimize the risk of anyone recognizing them. Nae nodded in acceptance of the suggestion. "What talents did she have?"

"She's very organized," Satomi said. Traits like that didn't always survive the transition, but—with a jolt of startlement she hoped Nae did not see, Satomi remembered that Eikyo was *not* a Cousin, and would retain everything of who she had been. It was easy to forget that this was a charade.

All the better. I'm less likely to give the truth away.

"Very organized," Satomi went on, gathering her wits. "And she has a good memory—that is, she will learn things easily. Some kind of administrative position, perhaps." She conveniently left out Eikyo's talent with plants and animals. If the young woman was to tell her anything useful about the Cousins, she'd have to be among them, not out in the wilderness.

Nae gazed down at the sleeping girl, expression unreadable. Satomi wondered how *she* felt about these occasions, when she took charge of someone Starfall would no longer keep. Did she mourn their failure? Rejoice at the addition? Was she bitter at the witches, and glad to see one of their number fail?

Questions like these were why Eikyo was asleep on the bed.

Satomi drew herself together, putting speculation

aside. "I'll have a cart waiting outside before dawn," she said. "Notify me if there's anything you need."

She said it every time and, every time, she heard not another word from Nae on the subject. Just a brief message from wherever the new Cousin was sent, informing her that the woman had arrived safely. The former students vanished into their ranks without a ripple.

But not this time.

Satomi left Nae there, and returned back to the main building—but not to her room, nor her office.

THE PRIMES' OFFICES were all within a short distance of a high, open-air patio that extended across the roof of one of the lower parts of the building. The door to this space was not locked, but ironclad protocol meant that only the Primes ever spent time outside on its flagstones; others came there just to deliver messages, and then only when the messages were important.

There had to be one place in Starfall where the Primes could have some peace and quiet.

Satomi went there now to pray. There were chapels for that, but tonight she preferred to be beneath the stars. She felt the witches had done wrong to lock themselves farther and farther away from the Goddess's eyes, behind stone walls. When she stepped out onto the patio, though, she found herself not alone. Arinei was there.

The other Prime's expressive face was drawn and weary. Satomi came up to her, but did not reach out; the two had been colleagues for years, but never close. She would have touched Rana, or Koika. But Arinei's pride was too sensitive.

"I wonder if we made a mistake," Arinei said. She had

her arms braced against the carved stone of the railing. Her eyes roved restlessly across the late-night landscape of Starfall, the treetops rustling softly in the breeze.

"Mistake?"

"Testing Eikyo the way we did. Without Shimi. With Naji in her place."

Satomi's apprehension faded. Arinei was not referring to what they'd actually done. "It's hardly the first time. Primes have been sick or absent before."

"But what if that caused her failure?"

This was very much a conversation Satomi did not want to be having, with the knowledge bottled up behind the false front she had constructed. "Other students have failed, Arinei, and we've never known why. But they've failed with all five Primes there, and students tested with a Key present have passed. It was simply coincidence this time."

Arinei did not seem reassured. Bickering with her since Mirei's arrival had made Satomi's patience with the volatile Prime wear thin, but the woman's expression now reminded her that, for all her faults, Arinei was dedicated to Starfall and the well-being of its people. Her heart was in the right place, even if she did not always agree with Satomi on the right course of action.

"I do wonder, though," Satomi went on before she could stop herself, "why those failures happen."

The Fire Prime looked toward her for the first time. The starlight was not strong enough to show her expression. "The question has been asked before."

"And never answered. But Mirei has me wondering about all manner of things that we take for granted, or have stopped asking about. Why do some students lose their memories? Why do others die?"

"Because the Goddess judges them," Arinei said, her tone taking on a harsh edge. Or was that just tiredness? "The qualities necessary to be a witch are not in them."

Satomi sighed. Now she looked away, at the shadowed flanks of the mountains. "It wouldn't concern me as much if this was something our daughters all chose. But it *isn't*. We choose it for them. We train them from the cradle for this life."

"We can't afford to delay it. Preparation requires years of study."

"And yet still some of them fail, even with study." And they hadn't always done it this way, though Satomi kept that thought to herself. The elaborate, codified course of study their daughters followed hadn't been some divine revelation from the Goddess to Misetsu. It had been built up over centuries of work. Yet she remembered, from her days in the Path of the Head, how small a difference it had made in the number of women who passed the final test. Some, but not enough. As long as women failed, it was not enough.

A faint breeze flowed across the patio, briefly ruffling her hair. "How *did* we begin doing things this way?" Satomi murmured, half to herself. "And what might happen if we did them differently?"

"What do you mean?" Arinei asked, warily.

"If a witch didn't conduct the connection ritual, then her daughter would be ordinary. Yes? The ability to touch power is not inborn. But we always choose to pass it on." Satomi pondered this. "I wonder what would happen if we conducted that ritual on a child who *wasn't* one of ours."

No response from the Fire Prime. Misetsu had only done it to her own daughters, and had taught them to do the same; from that decision had come their tradition, their people. But Misetsu had made errors out of pride; they knew that now. What if this was one of them?

"Or an adult," Satomi added, as the thought came to her. "We've always performed it on infants because we had to do it before they had souls. But if the soul is no longer a problem, then why infants? Would it work the same on an adult? Our daughters don't touch power until the test; they could study just as well *without* the channel inside them. Of course, then you wouldn't have the doppelgangers to raise separately. The witches who resulted wouldn't be like Mirei, with both magic and battle in her background." There might be reasons for working the ritual on infants. Benefits to be gained by seeing yourself from the outside for a time.

"I wonder, too, what will happen when Mirei has children." A faint smile touched Satomi's lips as she said that, the first real one in a while. "I suspect some of our Heads may order her to take up with some man, just to see if she has sons. And if she does—what about them? Can they learn to use magic, too? Misetsu only ever had daughters, but that could be chance. And her descendants, the ones who survived, lacked a part of themselves. We've never had an opportunity to see if men might be part of this."

Continued silence from Arinei. Satomi sighed. Too many questions with too few answers, and she was not at all sure she wanted to experiment with such things. "I doubt I would live to see the full result, even if I started trying out these ideas. I think the only reason we test our daughters at twenty-five is because it's five fives, a sacred number; we *could* do it at a different point. But you're right: They do need study. Quite a lot of it. And I am old enough that I don't expect to see Obura's daughter tested, much less any children Mirei might have."

Smiling at that thought, Satomi turned back to face the other woman. "Especially since I doubt we could pin her down to *have* children just yet." Would Mirei consider taking that year-mate of hers for a father? She seemed very close to him. Of course, they would have to find him first.

Arinei did not seem amused. The Fire Prime's face was closed and unreadable; she presented certain emotions to the world when it suited her purpose, but she could also lock them away. Satomi wondered what was going on behind the mask.

"It's late," the other woman said. "And I am weary. I believe it's time for me to seek my bed."

Satomi nodded, but didn't move toward the door. "As you will. I'm going to stay out here for a while longer yet. I'd like to pray for Eikyo—Kyou, as she'll be known from now on."

Walking away, the Fire Prime answered under her breath. "If you think the Goddess will hear you."

Chapter Seven

❧——————❦——————❧

GETTING OUT OF ANGRIM unseen could be done. Getting out of Angrim unseen with an unconscious body could also be done, but it was harder.

Mirei thought she had managed it, but she wasn't sure. She missed surety. Hadn't there been a time when things seemed clear and she didn't have a lot to worry about? It couldn't have been that long ago, but it felt like ages.

The comatose doppelganger jounced in the saddle in front of her as they rode through the darkness toward the bolt-hole. Mirei hadn't the faintest idea what to do with her once she woke up. Herding two eleven-year-old girls was hassle enough; adding in a third with no reason to like her didn't appeal.

And what about Naspeth?

Mirei hadn't the first damn clue what to do about the missing Windblade doppelganger. If the witch in that room had been behind that disappearance, Mirei had lost her chance to find out when she put a knife in the woman's throat. Naspeth might be somewhere in Angrim right now, tied up, waiting for a kidnapper who would never return. It was probably the best-case scenario: if that were true, then sooner or later someone would find her or she would get loose.

Pretty sad, when that's your best-case scenario. Do

*you think the Windblades will be nice enough to notify you
if she comes back?*

And a corner of her mind wondered with sick curiosity
just how a doppelganger's ability to come back to life
would work in the event of death by dehydration. How
many times might it happen, before Naspeth got free?
What would an experience like that do to a young girl's
mind?

Mirei growled such thoughts away. She would do
something about Naspeth. She didn't know what, but
she'd do it. Just as soon as she dealt with the three she currently had.

Once she got them moved from their current hiding
spot—she wasn't about to believe the Silverfire bolt-hole
was safe anymore, not after today's adventures—she
would contact Satomi. Through the paper or, if possible,
through a mirror. The Void Prime could direct her to
witches or Cousins who could be trusted. The loyalty of
the witches in Angrim was a dangerous unknown.

So. It was a simple plan, partly because complicated
plans tended to fail more, and partly because she couldn't
think of anything brilliant to do. Get to the bolt-hole,
bring Amas and Indera somewhere safer, contact Satomi.
Explain things to them. Get them back to Starfall.

Find Naspeth. Somehow.

Because she'd meant that promise to the Windblades.

She reached the abandoned farmhouse. Mirei pulled
her gelding to a halt, slid off carefully with her burden.
No sense beating the girl up any more than necessary. She
whistled a soft birdcall to announce her presence, then
carried the doppelganger through the doorway and laid
her on the uneven floor.

The house was quiet. Mirei put her face close to the trapdoor that led beneath the house and said softly, "Amas? Indera?"

No answer.

Please tell me they're just being careful.

Mirei pulled open the trapdoor and dropped into the cramped space below the house. The bags were there, but otherwise it was sickeningly empty.

She was out into the main room again faster than thought, knife in hand, checking on the Thornblood. Not awake yet, and not likely to wake in the near future. Mirei pulled her to one side, out of sight of the door, and risked leaving her there as she slipped around back to where the other horses were tethered, in the faint hope that they were just seeing to their mounts.

No such luck—though the horses were there—and she felt a rising panic in her throat.

She went at a half jog back toward the front of the house, and nearly put her blade into a nearby tree when a voice said from it, "So who's *she*?"

Mirei kept hold of the knife—though she nearly dropped it on her own foot, aborting the throw—and let out a lengthy, vicious curse. When it was done, she said, "Where's Amas?"

"Over here," a soft voice said, and the taller doppelganger dropped from a tree to the ground.

"We just wanted to see if we could hide well enough that you wouldn't see us there," Indera said, climbing down from her own perch. "I guess we did." She looked disgustingly proud of herself.

Mirei fought the urge to plant a fist right on that self-satisfied expression. "I told you to stay *inside*," she snarled. Her jaw creaked with barely contained fury.

"We were hidden," Indera said, as if that justified everything.

"You were *outside*, in a place that isn't nearly as bloody safe as I'd like it to be, within spitting distance of a city crawling with spies who certainly know this bolt-hole is here. I'm riding myself to rags trying to keep you children *safe*, and one of you's missing, and another one tried to kill me, and I get back here to find *you* two playing *training games*?" Mirei cut herself off, not because she'd run out of things to say, but because her own voice was rising dangerously high. When it was back under control, she growled, "Get the horses saddled. *Now.*"

Indera had the sense not to say anything; she was no doubt the one who had suggested the exercise. Amas, though, spoke quietly from the side. "Where are we going?"

"I'll tell you when I'm damned well ready. *Get the horses.*"

But Amas stood her ground. "There's more than the two of us. You just said so. The girl in there is one, I guess, and there's another one missing. But those two weren't at Silverfire; they must have been at Thornblood or Wind-blade. Why are you collecting all of us? *Is* this all of us?"

Two swift strides brought Mirei up to Amas's face. The girl flinched back—she could hardly do otherwise—but she met Mirei's eyes in the darkness.

"What are we?" Amas whispered.

Mirei clenched her jaw, trying to keep herself from saying something she might regret. Finally she snapped, voice low, "I will tell you *later.*"

"You keep promising answers *later*," Amas said. "Do

you *mean* those promises? Or are you just putting us off until you can herd us safely into whatever it is you have planned for us?"

In a moment of unexpected honesty, Mirei admitted to herself that she wouldn't be nearly so irritated by Amas's insistent questions if they hadn't been the kind of thing *she* would have asked, in the trainee's place. That realization allowed her to swallow down her anger and respond levelly. She spoke both to Amas, still fighting not to retreat in front of her, and Indera, watching from behind.

"I mean them," she said. "I'm not going to lead you blindfolded into this. But I wanted to have all of you— there's only four—so I could explain it just the once, and now that I have all it looks like I'm going to get, I want to wait at least until we're somewhere that I don't have to worry quite so much about Thornbloods or city guards breathing down our necks. There was trouble in Angrim, and I'd like to get away from it right about now."

Amas accepted that, after a moment, with a cool nod that reinforced Mirei's wariness of her. She didn't accept *anything* just because someone in authority told it to her; she had to weigh it, consider it, and then decide how best to respond to it. Mirei turned to Indera, and found her nodding, too. But she probably hadn't taken the time to think before doing so.

"For the last time, then," Mirei said, "get the horses."

THE RIDING WENT FINE for about an hour, and then the Thornblood woke up.

Mirei, engrossed in mental calculations of where to go and how long it would take to get there and what the best course of action would be once they did, didn't notice as quickly as she should have. By the time she realized the movement in the body she held wasn't just caused by the horse's stride, the girl was wrenching herself out of Mirei's grip and crashing hard to the ground below.

Amas's horse nearly trampled her. The Thornblood rolled to her feet, disoriented, but alert enough to set off at a lurching run for the nearest trees, as if she could somehow escape three mounted pursuers. She might have, had it just been the trainees; their horses were spooked by the sudden commotion, and the girls were having trouble getting them back under control. Mirei, though, brought her gelding around, and was soon alongside the running girl. A quick stunt brought her out of her saddle and took the girl down in one clean move.

The Thornblood was screaming again and flailing wildly; the flailing turned out to be less panic and more a cover for a sudden, snakelike blow at Mirei's throat. Mirei knocked it aside, cursed the fading of her own reflexes, and finally got the trainee pinned.

"Bloody witch!" the Thornblood was screaming. She'd caught sight of Amas and Indera, now, and seemed to recognize them as fellow Hunter trainees, though not Silverfires. They had taken off the scarves while hiding at the bolt-hole; uncovered, their cropped hair was visible in the light of the newly risen moon. Both had dismounted, and were watching in startlement. "Don't trust her! She's a witch! She's going to take us and kill us—"

"I already told you, I'm the one who *doesn't* want to kill you," Mirei snapped, tightening her grip on the girl's wrists. "Will you shut up already, or will I have to spell you to sleep again?"

And then she heard her own words, and looked up, and saw the other two staring at her.

The Thornblood saw it, too. "I told you! She's a witch! She killed a Hunter, she casts spells—"

"I didn't kill Ice," Mirei said reflexively, and saw the Silverfires notice that she *hadn't* denied the rest.

Amas backed a step away. "You—"

Mirei stood, hauling the third doppelganger with her; both Amas and Indera backed up this time, as if open air would shield them from her.

She cast a quick glance around. They weren't on one of the Great Roads, the major routes that had been in place since Three Kingdoms times; she'd chosen to take a smaller lane, leading southward toward the hills of northern Currel, precisely because it was less well-traveled. Unfortunately, she didn't know it as well as she did the Great Road to the east of them. Mirei wracked her memory. Up ahead—she had no clear image of what was up ahead. But there had been a forested dell just a short distance back where they had watered their horses. It was a little shielded, at least.

"Come with me," she said, dragging the Thornblood back toward her horse, which had stopped nearby.

"You're going to kill us!" the doppelganger shouted.

Her paranoia was growing tiresome. "If I was going to kill you, I could have done that in Angrim, and not hauled your carcass around like this," Mirei pointed out. She glanced at the others. "You, too. And no, I haven't held off because I need you three for some evil ritual where I'm going to nail you to trees and—and—" Her imagination failed. "And do whatever you're supposed to do in an evil ritual. Damn it to *Void*, doesn't anybody believe I'm trying to help?"

"Funny way you have of helping," Amas said.

"Should I have waited until you *were* in trouble, just so you'd trust me?" Fat lot of good that had done, with the Thornblood. Mirei pulled a coil of rope out of her saddle-bag one-handed, while the girl struggled ineffectually to hook her feet out from under her. She tied the doppelganger up, Amas and Indera watching silently with their reins in their hands, then threw her captive over the saddle, with a rag stuffed in her mouth for good measure. "To the Void with waiting. You want explanations? Come with me. Take it while I'm still in a mood to offer." Mirei rode off down the road, back the way they'd come, and didn't look to see if the other two followed.

AMAS GLANCED OVER at Indera, but didn't say anything.

She didn't have to. They were a pair of eleven-year-old girls in an unfamiliar domain, in the middle of the night, with few supplies and no money. Even trying to calculate how they would get back to Silverfire on their own made Indera shudder.

But that wasn't even the point. The point was that Mirage had dangled bait in front of them, and neither of them could pass it up.

They remounted and followed the Hunter. She didn't ride far; soon she turned off the road to a dell that Indera remembered stopping in. When they arrived back at the tiny spring, they found Mirage waiting, the other girl still tied up and gagged, but leaning against a tree.

"You're staying gagged because I don't want to have to shout over you," Mirage was saying to her. She glanced up as the other two arrived. "Glad you came. Tether your horses over there, find a place to sit, and the show will begin."

They obeyed her orders silently. Amas perched on a rock. Indera put her back against an elm, where she could watch both Mirage and the stranger. Her nerves were jumping with anticipation. This, clearly, was what they had been brought from Silverfire for.

She was about to understand.

Mirage let her air out in an audible gust. "I've only done this once before, you know. Strangely, it is *not* easier when the people involved aren't holding knives."

This made no sense, but no one braved the silence to point that out.

The red-haired Hunter looked around at the three of them. "You three share something," she said. "You probably noticed it long before they sent you to Hunter schools to train. You're faster than the people around you. Stronger than you should be for your size. You love to move, pick it up easily, and when it comes to fighting, it's like you're *born* to it. You're young, so you don't know much yet; a trained fighter could take you down. But you'd be learning from him while he did it."

And it was true of Mirage as well, Indera thought, although she had not said so. That was why she was such a great Hunter.

"People may have used the phrase around you," Mirage said. " 'Blessed by the Warrior.' " She paused, meeting each girl's eyes in turn. "It's more true than you know.

"The Goddess has five faces. Four of them form the stages of life: Maiden, Bride, Mother, Crone. The fifth, the Warrior, is outside that cycle. She ends life. Where they are the four Elements that make up the world, she is the Void, nonexistence. And—for whatever theological, metaphysical reason, I couldn't tell you—the movement of the body is her domain. Especially when the body moves to kill."

Here among the trees, where the light summer breeze could not penetrate, the air was stiflingly close and still. Indera felt a trickle of sweat slide down the side of her face, but didn't even move to brush it away. She didn't want to break—

Break the spell she's creating? she thought, chilled by the phrase that had reflexively come to mind. *The other one called her a witch. And Mirage . . . she didn't deny it.*

But this couldn't be an actual spell; Mirage was speaking normal language, with no singing. Still, the thought wouldn't quite leave Indera alone. Mirage was her hero, but how well did she know the woman? How much could she trust her?

Mirage had gone on. "They say the human soul has the same five parts to it. Four for life, and one that's separate from that set.

"You three—in simple terms—are that fifth part."

The stranger kicked suddenly against her bonds, a startling sound in the quiet of the night. It looked like surprise, not an attempt to escape.

"The reasons for this," Mirage said, "are complicated. So bear with me."

She exhaled again, slowly. "Two of you have red hair— I know you dye yours, Amas. I don't know about you—" She nodded to the shaven-headed girl tied up before her. "But I'll bet it's true of you, too. So I'm sure people have said that you're witches.

"You aren't. But you *do* have a connection to them."

Indera, listening to this speech, began to wonder. Mirage was talking *to* the three of them. She kept saying "you." Never "we." It might be mere chance. But she'd said *they* weren't witches. She hadn't said that *she* wasn't.

But Mirage was like they were. Wasn't she?

"Witches aren't born with magical power," the Hunter said. "The power is out there, in the world; they have a channel, a connection, that allows them to take it and manipulate it. That channel's created when they're five days old. The ritual that does it splits the child into two bodies. One of them has the channel; the other doesn't.

"The witches used to do this ritual before the infant was presented to the Goddess. They disposed of the body that didn't have the ability for magic, and took the other one out into starlight." Mirage grinned and ran one hand over her short hair. "I could now go into a very long and complicated story—and I will someday, if you want me to—but let's keep it simple for now. As simple as this can be, anyway. Basically, the witches have found out that they way they were doing things wasn't a very good one. There's a better alternative, and that's the one I'm here to tell you about.

"The two halves are connected no matter what. You'd have to ask one of the theorists at Starfall to get an explanation of how that works. But this part, I know: If the child has a soul when the ritual happens, then the two bodies *share* that soul. The witch-half, the one with the channel, basically gets the four parts that are about life. The other one gets the Warrior part. They call that one the doppelganger."

Mirage glanced at them, one by one, meeting each of

their eyes. Then she spoke again, softly. "As you might have guessed by now—that's what *you* are."

Indera found her voice at last, though it came out small and timid. "And—you, too, right? You're like us."

Mirage sighed and looked down at her hands, not meeting Indera's eyes. The silence stretched out, painfully.

"I . . . was," she said finally, her voice very quiet. "But I'm not anymore."

The bottom dropped out of Indera's stomach. Not like them. Not like *her*. When she'd been so sure that Mirage, more than anyone else in the world, would understand.

"My name," the Hunter said, "isn't Mirage anymore, because I'm not exactly the woman who had that name. That's the rest of what I need to tell you.

"You can't just leave the doppelgangers alive. There was a reason the witches used to kill them off. If a witch's double is alive, then when she tries to use magic, she can't control it. The doppelganger is a part of herself that's not concentrating on the spell, that doesn't know how to channel the power. And unstable magic like that is *very* dangerous. It'll kill the witch, sooner or later, *and* the doppelganger, and anybody else unlucky enough to be caught in a spell gone wild.

"Some witches still think we should be doing things that way." Mirage's eyes—*no, not Mirage's,* a corner of Indera's mind whispered in betrayal, *she's someone else*—flicked toward the third trainee, where she lay bound and gagged. "One of them was in Angrim tonight. She would have taken you prisoner, and eventually killed you. But there's a new way, now—one that I found."

The woman began to pace, still talking. *Such a smooth voice; she sounds so much like a witch, how did I not notice it before* . . . "The doppelganger and the witch start out as a single person. They're meant to go back to that, when the time comes. Part of me is Mirage, the Hunter you all have heard of." She turned and faced them again. "The other part is Miryo, a witch you never met."

The third girl yelped something Indera couldn't make out through the gag.

"I am," the woman admitted quietly, "a witch."

She reached into her shirt and brought out a silver pendant Indera had glimpsed once before, when they were dressing in Silverfire's stable. There was little light beneath the trees, but enough for them all to make it out: the triskele knot of Starfall.

"My name is Mirei," the woman said. "I'm a witch, *and* I'm a Hunter, because I'm both Miryo and Mirage. The Goddess gave me a new name when she made me whole again. There's some other stuff that went with it—you'll hear about that eventually. It has to do with a kind of magic that didn't used to exist, because it draws on the Void, and without the Void part of their nature—the doppelgangers—the witches couldn't touch it. But that's metaphysics, and it can wait for later.

"The point is, you are all like I was—the Mirage part of me. There are girls out there, your age, who look *exactly* like you. They have the channel for magic, and will be witches when they're old enough. When that happens, you'll rejoin with them. There's a ritual for it. Then neither one of you dies."

Indera climbed unsteadily to her feet, Mirage's words—Mirei's—buzzing in her ears. "Hang on," she said. "Let me get this straight. You're telling me that when we get old enough, we're going to be super-fast, super-strong Hunters *with magic*?" The possibilities made her head spin.

And then it came to a crashing halt.

"No," Mirei said.

Indera stared at her. "What do you mean?"

Mirei sighed again. "You'll have magic. And you'll be strong, and fast, because if I have my way you all will keep training as Hunters, learning to use the gifts you have. You're the Warrior part, and should honor that. But the reason you've got those gifts is that you're . . . distilled. You're the Warrior, without the rest. Once you rejoin your witch-halves, though, you'll be complete souls again."

"And?" Indera demanded, heart racing.

"And you'll be physically normal. As normal as Hunters are, anyway. You'll be faster and stronger than people who don't have your training, but not supernaturally so." Mirei shrugged. "It's a trade-off."

Indera had no words. Her pulse pounded in her ears as she stared at the woman before her, the *stranger* masquerading in a skin Indera thought she knew. To lose her gifts—to not be the Warrior-blessed person she was now—to give all that up, and stop being herself, to be somebody else instead, some *witch*—

Mirei wasn't even looking at her. The woman's eyes were on the other two girls, the gagged stranger and Amas watching with her usual impassive silence. "Like I said," she went on, as if she didn't see Indera's fury, "there are people who don't like that idea. Their solution to it is to kill you. I've taken you all from your schools because they know you're there; they've already kidnapped the fourth one, a Windblade trainee named Naspeth. They won't have killed her yet—it's complicated, and I'll tell

you why later, when your heads have stopped spinning—
but that's their plan, ultimately. And since these women
who want you dead are witches, your schools aren't
enough to protect you. Naspeth's disappearance proved
that. I'm taking you somewhere you'll be safe, with
witches to guard you."

"But you said witches want us *dead*," Amas said,
speaking for the first time since they came to this dell.

"Some do." Mirei grimaced. "Witches don't all get
along. There's a dissident faction that wants to go on killing
doppelgangers. We're still working out how many of them
there are, but there are some we *know* are loyal. They'll
protect you."

"For how long?"

The blunt question produced a momentary silence. "I
don't know," Mirei admitted at last. "I hope we get this
cleared up quickly, but I can't promise that we will." She
rubbed both hands over her scalp, looking tired. "I *did*
make a promise to Jaguar, though, that I would train you
two, for as long as I had you away from Silverfire. I'll do
what I can about that. Your reflexes may be better than
mine, but I still know ten times as much as you do."

Her grin faded as she looked to the other girl. "For you,
the situation might be different. Here—I'm going to take
your gag off, and untie you. Just don't bite me, or start
screaming again, or run away, okay?" Mirei knelt in front
of the girl, received a wary nod, and began work on the
knots. "You've already been taught to hate me because
I'm a Silverfire, and now I'm a witch, too, which Hunters
don't like as a general rule. But I really am trying to help
you, and I'll train you if you'll let me."

The bonds were off, and the gag was gone. Mirei

looked into the eyes of the shaven-headed girl. "What's your name?"

The girl licked her lips, back still against the tree, and considered the question as if unsure whether it was some kind of trap. Finally she said, "Lehant."

"Lehant. We . . . got off on the wrong foot. And for all I know, you don't believe a word I say." Mirei turned to eye all of them, finally noticing Indera again, but paying no particular attention to her. "Maybe none of you does. But I promised you an explanation, and I've given it to you, and I swear on the Warrior's blade that it's the truth."

Looking back at Lehant, she added, "And I'll train you with the other two, if you're willing to learn. It won't be the same as what you were getting at Thornblood, since our styles are different, and no doubt I'll pay when people find out I taught a trainee of another school. But I'll do it."

Her words were one last blow to Indera's already bruised heart. This bald stranger was a *Thornblood*. A trainee of the school Silverfires hated most. And Mirei was offering to *teach* her.

This was what Indera had been dragged out of Silverfire for. Away from where she was meant to be.

Mirei stood up from where she crouched by Lehant and cracked her back with a sigh. "Right. I've talked myself out, and it's been a *really* long day for me. We'll camp here for the night. Indera, you're in charge of food. Amas, Lehant, take care of the horses and the bedrolls."

"And you?" Amas asked, her tone cynical at the division.

Mirei smiled ruefully. "Well, since you know what I am, now, I don't have to make up excuses to wander off while I cast a few spells. But don't worry," she added, as the others tensed at her words. "I won't do them here."

She went a few steps away from the spring, paused, and looked back at them all. "Don't think this means you can wander off, though. I'll be watching."

Then she vanished into the shadows under the trees, leaving the three girls to their tasks.

INDERA COOKED a quick broth, the other two settled them all for the night, and then everyone bedded down, Lehant with Mirei's blankets.

Mirei set herself to sleep very lightly, because she wasn't an idiot. Lehant clearly didn't have much liking for her, especially after the way they had gotten started. Amas was a harder read, and questionable because of that; there was no way to tell which way the girl might jump. Mirei wanted to make sure neither of them tried to sneak away.

She set herself to sleep lightly, and with her bedroll under Lehant, it shouldn't have been hard.

She slept like a rock, and woke late in the morning with a mouth that felt packed full of cotton.

Blearily, reflexes fighting against a pervasive lethargy, she rolled over and scanned the camp. Two horses, not three. Two doppelgangers—not three.

Lehant and Amas were still there.

But Indera was gone.

Chapter Eight

━━━◆━━━◆━━━

WHETHER ARINEI WAS the source of the murmurs, Satomi could not discover. But they spread through Starfall like wildfire in the wake of Eikyo's test.

She failed because Shimi wasn't there.

They shouldn't have broken tradition.

It made Satomi want to scream. She had perfectly solid answers to those murmurs, but she couldn't use a one of them. She couldn't tell them that Eikyo hadn't failed; that would negate the entire purpose of the exercise. And she couldn't tell them that other witches had been tested by a Key, because no one below the rank of Key was allowed to know that.

The unrest came at a bad time. Mirei hadn't reported in; Satomi had sent three separate queries to her through her counterpart to the sheet of enchanted paper the woman had taken with her, but none of them had been answered. She couldn't send anything more directly, because she didn't know where Mirei was, and she couldn't find Mirei because the woman—understandably—had a blocking spell up.

The young witch had effectively vanished, and Satomi was afraid of what that might mean.

Other witches had been sent to collect the doppelgangers not at Hunter schools, and not all had met with success.

Three of the other eight were now missing. So was one of the witch-children who'd been at a regional hall—Chanka, barely two years old. Her doppelganger Anness was safe, after a pitched battle; Shimi had sent someone after her, too. Satomi had a difficult time smoothing that incident over and convincing the Lord of Trine, who knew about the situation with Shimi, that this was not going to mean magical battles breaking out all over.

And she could only hope she'd told him the truth.

Five doppelgangers safely on their way to Starfall; seven witch-students young enough to still be at domain halls also coming south under escort; four witch-students here; four more doppelgangers traveling with Mirei. Hopefully.

But Starfall itself was becoming more and more restless.

People knew when a witch-student failed; success was celebrated, and its absence was noted. Traditionally, though, the incident was not spoken of openly, and was not spread beyond the domain of Starfall itself, so that the new Cousin could take up a position elsewhere without fuss. But tradition was breaking down in so many other places, Satomi didn't know why she had bothered to think this one would hold.

Because I wanted it to, she thought bitterly. *Because I needed it to.* Luck had not obliged her. People knew Eikyo had failed, and were talking about it, and the news had spread rapidly to many other parts of the land.

If I find out Arinei fostered this deliberately, I will flay the skin from that woman's back.

She couldn't afford to, though, and Arinei knew that quite well. One Prime had been suspended; they couldn't lose another. Satomi didn't know of a single time since the institution of the office of Prime that two of them had been gone at once.

So she had to fight by every means necessary to hold things together, as rumors slipped through the halls and grew daily more outrageous. Little had actually changed in the witches' lives, but that didn't matter. The fear of change was enough. Satomi issued a few declarations intended to reassure her people, but mostly she was relying on subtler means; witches in her Ray, women she knew to be loyal to the new order, spread counter-rumors where they could. But Satomi couldn't stop everything.

The Primes, who formerly had met as a group rarely more often than once a week, were now having daily conferences in their council room, and sometimes more than daily. They had to work together, not separately. Reports came in of witches abandoning their postings, and not just in Air; there were those in other Rays who feared the consequences of Mirei's existence, or simply preferred Shimi's promise of normalcy. And never mind that their actions were contributing to the disorder.

The ones Satomi feared, though, were the ones who stayed where they were. Stayed, and planned action.

How good a rebellion was Shimi capable of building?

She tried to shake this thought off as she strode through the hallways, on her way to yet another meeting. Shimi was one woman. A Prime, yes, with an aura of authority no ritual could strip her of, and intelligent, but one woman. A strict proportion would put only a fifth of the witches behind her, and that was assuming that she alone could be as effective as the other four together. No, she would not be able to muster more than a small fraction of their people. Enough to cause trouble, yes—*How much trouble did Tari start, with a bare handful of allies?* her mind whispered treacherously—but nothing they could not overcome.

Satomi reassured herself with this logic, arrived at the council room, and found Koika and Rana already there.

They waited to begin their business, because no one wanted to alienate Arinei further, and a good half hour passed before they became impatient enough to search for her. First by runner, then by magic.

They met the painfully resounding silence of a blocking spell.

Arinei was gone.

THEY DID NOT LOOK for her first in the ruling hall, and so they missed their chance to find the message before the rest of Starfall did.

> *The proper traditions and authorities of our people and our way have been corrupted by Satomi, who dishonors her office as Prime of the Void Ray.*
>
> *The fate of Eikyo, daughter of Dairai, is only one sign of many. Satomi would bring such change to Starfall as would destroy it forever, robbing us of the gifts passed down from Misetsu in ancient times. She would risk the lives of innocents in reckless experimentation, testing her questions of magic on the bodies of children not of our people, endangering our daughters by depriving them of the teachings they need to survive the Goddess's test. The fate of Eikyo is a warning to us all.*
>
> *I cannot in good conscience stand by a woman who would throw so many of our established tradi-*

tions away on the appearance of one woman of dubious loyalties. This Mirei owes allegiance to the Hunter school of Silverfire, and cannot be trusted to keep our secrets. She has vanished from Starfall and has not reported back. We must ask ourselves what she is doing in her absence.

Thus it is that, with a heavy heart, I, Arinei, raised Prime of the Fire Ray, have departed from Starfall in protest. With me have gone others who are loyal servants of Starfall. We shall not return until Satomi steps down from power, is removed from her position, or shows sufficient proof that she has seen her error and will not continue in it.

In the names of Misetsu and Menukyo, and the Goddess who watches over us all.

At the bottom were five signatures. Not just Arinei's, but those of four Keys: Mejiki and Kekkai from Fire, Goyoi of the Earth Hand, and Rinshu of the Water Head.

It was posted on the doors to the ruling hall, in plain sight. At least half the witches at Starfall had seen it by the time Satomi got there. She took it down, but knew the gesture was futile. Arinei's damage could not be undone.

"So now we suspend her, too," Koika said grimly.

The Earth Prime was leaning against the wall in the council room, too tense to sit. Her blunt fingers picked at a loose thread hanging from one sleeve. Rana was slumped in a chair across the table from her, staring at the wood's polished surface, hardly blinking. Satomi sat in her own chair, and could not stop looking at the two empty chairs that made this room seem so deserted.

"We can't," she said into the silence.

Koika glared at her. "The time for dancing around Arinei's tender sensibilities is over, Satomi. We *have* to suspend her."

"But we *can't*," Satomi snapped back, sitting upright. "Suspension requires the consensus of four Primes. We have three."

An awful silence followed her words, as everyone looked at the empty chairs.

Satomi bent her head and ran her fingers into her hair, gripping the strands as if to pull her mind out. "It's my fault," she said to the table. "I spoke with her, after . . . after I took Eikyo to Nae. I . . . I was tired. I was speculating. I didn't mean half of what I said, not seriously, but I asked questions . . . things about our traditions. Why we do certain things, and not others, and what might happen if we did them differently. I should have thought. Arinei's a traditionalist, and I knew she was on edge . . . but I said them, and she took them seriously, and now she's gone."

Rana's voice was hardly more than a whisper. "Then write to her. Tell her you didn't mean it. She'll come back."

Satomi laughed bitterly. "After posting her self-righteous diatribe on the doors of the ruling hall, for all to see? Arinei will not back down from that. She *cannot*. Her position as Fire Prime would be damaged beyond repair."

"Look," Koika said, coming forward to touch her hand, still buried in her hair. "It isn't your fault. I'm not saying what you said to Arinei didn't hurt," she went on, when Satomi looked up to dispute that, "but it was merely the last flakes of snow that broke the branch. Something else would have done it, if you hadn't."

Satomi wished she could believe that. After days of fighting a diplomatic war to keep Arinei mollified, though, she couldn't forgive her lapse that easily.

A timid knock at the door made them all jump.

"What now?" Rana said, voice heavy with dread, as Satomi went to the door.

Onomita was outside. Key of the Fire Head, the only ranking witch of her Ray remaining at Starfall, her round face was pale with nerves. Everyone was looking at her askance since the departure of her fellow Keys and Prime. Some of them were wondering whether she was truly loyal to the people she had stayed with; the rest, no doubt, despised her for not having the courage to go with them. Satomi had no illusions that everyone still here was loyal.

The Key had a folded piece of paper clutched in one shaking hand. "Aken—I found this—You asked me to look in her office—"

Satomi took the paper, unfolded it, and read.

> *Eikyo is not truly a Cousin. This was a plan of Satomi's. She wishes to place a spy among them. If I do not remember this, then someone has altered my memory.*

The handwriting was Arinei's.

Satomi's eyes shot to Onomita's, and found them wide with fear. Onomita had read the note, certainly. She would not have brought it here, otherwise.

And now she was terrified of what Satomi would do to her.

Satomi didn't even feel herself pulling in power until she heard her own voice, singing a short phrase in a snarl barely clear enough to effectively shape the spell. The note in her hand burst into flame; she released it, and glowing ash drifted to the floor.

Behind her, Koika and Rana were crowding close. "What in the Void *was that?*" Koika demanded, staring at the vestiges of the note. "What did she find?"

Arinei didn't trust me. And the worst part is, she was right not to.

All three women were still staring at her. What in the Void was she supposed to do about this? Wipe everyone's memories of the note? How much more was she going to compound this problem, that had seemed like such a good idea at the time?

Oh, Maiden's mercy, Satomi thought with sudden fear. *What will Arinei do to Eikyo?*

She needed breathing space to find out. Satomi turned first to Onomita. "Thank you," she said to the Key, keeping her tone as unthreatening as possible. "Come to me if you find anything else that looks relevant. But I hardly need tell you, I hope, that every bit of this must remain *completely* secret." She'd explain later that by "completely," she meant that not even Rana and Koika should know.

Onomita nodded, her head bobbing more times than necessary before she gathered her wits and stopped.

"This is an extremely delicate time," Satomi went on, just to reinforce it. "The last thing we need is more rumor and suspicion flying around. We mustn't jump to conclusions. Understand?" If Onomita *didn't* understand, then soon Arinei might have all three of her Keys on her side.

The woman nodded, bowed to the three Primes, and left. Satomi closed the door and turned back into the room, facing her other two immediate problems. Their eyes were still wide with worry. With sudden startlement, Satomi realized what this must look like from their perspective. They didn't know what the note had said, and their imaginations were no doubt supplying all kinds of possibilities even worse than the truth.

She could use that.

I even manipulate my friends, now, Satomi thought grimly. She didn't like it, but that didn't mean she was going to stop.

I just hope that I truly am doing what's best for my people.

"Arinei is in a position to do us far more damage than Shimi ever was," the Void Prime said, crossing the room with brisk strides and resuming her seat at the table. "Her note was a listing of Lords and Ladies that might be sympathetic to their cause—I say 'they,' because we must assume that she will join forces with Shimi. Arinei is practical enough to see the advantages of that, even though she doesn't share Shimi's Nalochkan zeal. And Arinei has the influence necessary to get the Lords to listen to her, especially with both her Heart and Hand Keys on her side."

Satomi would have been happier if her words had been more of a lie. The only part of it that was false for certain was the part about this being in the note. Satomi had every confidence—every fear—that the rest of it was true, if not written down anywhere.

The other two Primes had seated themselves again, as well. Satomi went on. "Topping the list, of course, was Lady Chaha of Kalistyi. Her religious beliefs mean she will be open to Shimi's arguments."

"But what can they *do*?" Koika broke in, putting her interlaced hands on the table and leaning forward. "If we can't suspend Arinei, then they can't suspend any of us. We're at a deadlock, in terms of authority."

"Here in Starfall, yes." Satomi wished for the first time that her chief ally among the Primes had been someone more politically savvy than the Earth Prime. Koika was intelligent, but she spent much of her time monitoring and modifying the weather patterns of the land, and other matters that had little to do with people. When humans came into Koika's sphere, it was through questions of physical survival. "But we must worry about the world outside our domain."

Rana knew where she was going. "The Lords all have advisers," she reminded Koika.

"I know that," the Earth Prime snapped, nettled by the older Prime's patronizing tone.

"So think about what Arinei can do through that," Rana said. "If Lady Chaha's Fire adviser happens to be on our side, then Arinei and Shimi will likely convince the Lady to abandon her for someone else. Someone allied to them. If the advisers agree and the Lords don't, then those advisers can work on convincing them."

"Soon enough," Satomi said, taking up the thread when Rana faltered, "we find ourselves locked out of the governance of those domains. Our influence wanes. What percentage of our income does the Fire Ray contribute?" No need to answer that one out loud; Koika, as the Prime of the Ray tied with Air for the smallest contribution, was well aware of how much money the Fire Ray possessed. "Without that income, we're crippled. Soon the ordinary witches will become dissatisfied with us. Under those conditions, questions of morality and ideology give way to practicality. We'll find ourselves facing a true revolution for the control of Starfall."

Koika, as always, thought in brutally practical terms. "Why not just assassinate us?"

Rana's knobbly hands began visibly trembling at the question. Satomi, though, had thought of it already. "There's no guarantee they won't try that, too."

It would be hard. The Primes were always guarded, and by now they had made doubly sure those guards were trustworthy. No witch was likely to catch one of them unaware enough to take them down with a spell, and an outsider wouldn't stand a chance. Other witches, though, would be far more vulnerable. And assassinating their allies could do almost as much damage as killing the Primes themselves.

Koika slumped back in her chair, shaking her head. "So what do we *do*? I don't know politics; that was always Arinei's job. How do we fight this kind of war?"

Satomi looked from the Earth Prime to the Water Prime. Rana did not meet her gaze. There would be no relying on her. Harsh as it was to say, Rana was too old; you had only to look at her lined face to see that she was not prepared to face these kinds of challenges. She was a good Prime, but not for times like these.

Which left only Satomi to answer Koika's question.

She lifted her chin and made her voice as level, pragmatic, and confident as she could. "Well. If this is a war— and we must consider it as such, now—then we must think like generals. We must disrupt their communications, counteract their offensives—and send spies among them, if we can."

* * *

MOST OF THE WOMEN gathered in the room came from the Void Head. They, more than anyone else, were inclined to ask questions of theory, about how spells worked and why. Inventing new ones was outside their purview—that was a religious matter, driven by faith, not research—but they could and did modify existing spells, adapting them to new purposes.

And also counteracting them. Mirei was the only woman in the world capable of canceling spells outright, with the power of the Void, but centuries of women had worked on the matter of how to oppose spells, and thereby negate their effect.

"We have several tasks at hand," Satomi said to the assembled group. Mostly Void Heads, but not all; there was always the occasional witch who engaged in this study as a hobby. And Satomi saw distinct value in getting women of different Rays to cooperate. If she could not cancel the fragmentation plaguing them, she could counteract it. "Hyoka, I leave it to you to decide how best to divide your time and effort."

The Key of the Void Head nodded. She had collected this group, along with Kimeko, the Heart Key; Hyoka knew who was qualified, while Kimeko knew who was loyal. Or at least likely to be. Of Hyoka's loyalty, Satomi had no doubt; the woman was a theorist down to her bones, and she saw Mirei's existence as a fascinating and so far inscrutable puzzle. If she could have recombined all the other pairs on the spot, just for more examples to study, she probably would have.

Satomi passed a sheaf of paper to Hyoka. "First, the

ritual of suspension. As it currently exists, it requires the participation of four Primes. The ritual of reinstation, however, requires only three. This suggests to me that it may be possible to work the suspension with three. I want to know if it can be done, and if so, how."

A few of the listening witches shifted at her words, but no one looked surprised. They'd known, when Hyoka recruited them, that they were here to work against Shimi, Arinei, and all the other witches in revolt. And they'd just come from the public session where Koika and Rana had demoted their errant Keys.

"Second," Satomi went on, "the ritual that creates a Prime. It instills the participant with certain authorities and abilities that are exclusive—only one woman can have them for a given Ray at a time. I want to know what the effect would be of performing this ritual when the previous recipient of those qualities has been suspended of them, but not removed from her position. What metaphysical repercussions is that likely to create?"

More rustling, although much of it was coming from women who looked avidly curious instead of offended. Hyoka had chosen the group well; Satomi was offering them theoretical challenges the likes of which they did not often get to handle. They would do it, just to see if it could be done.

Arinei should have feared these women, not me, Satomi thought wryly. *They're the ones who want to experiment.*

"Third, our message papers." She held one up; it was the top sheet off a stack she had brought for them to tinker with. "I want to know everything you can figure out to do to one of these. Intercepting messages, sending false messages, preventing them from working, finding out where the people using them are. Destroying them at a distance, even. Anything that would make them less useful to others." This was a more dangerous inquiry; the first two were things only the Primes could do, with limited applications. This, however, could seriously disrupt *everyone's* communications, if it fell into the hands of the other side. Witches all over the land depended on these sheets to send information. They were easier to manage when traveling than mirror-sendings, they didn't require the writer to know the location of the recipient the way sending objects did, and even nonwitches could use them, if they knew the proper musical trigger. It would severely hamper the dissidents, if the papers became unreliable. But what could be done to others, could be done to Satomi's people as well. Satomi made a mental note to tell Hyoka only to place the most reliable women on that project.

She didn't let that worry show. "These projects take precedence over whatever other work you may have been doing," she said. "I know some of you have been working on the study of Mirei's new magic, but until she returns to Starfall"— *Which had better be soon,* she thought savagely—"then there is little you can do on that matter. Hyoka, make up a list for me of any work that needs to be reassigned to other women." And she would just have to hope she could find people to cover it. Enough witches had slipped out of Starfall that they were decidedly shorthanded. The corridors felt half empty when she walked down them.

Gazing out over the women, sitting at their tables, many with books and paper already laid out before them,

Satomi had the sudden, disquieting feeling that this was the first stages of an army.

I hope it doesn't come to that, she thought. *But I'm afraid that it may.*

SATOMI LOOKED UP from the sheet of paper Hyoka had given her. The Key stood on the other side of her desk, tension forming a skin over her excitement that did not completely hide it. Hyoka knew full well what she had just handed to her Prime, but the part of her that loved theoretical puzzles could not help but be giddy over what she and her assistants had put together, so soon after being given their task.

"This isn't what I asked you to research," Satomi said.

"I know, Aken. That is, you didn't ask for this *specifically*. But I was thinking about the questions you *did* ask—not the questions themselves, but why you asked them. What purpose you're trying to reach by those paths. And whether there might be another way to approach it, one you didn't think of, but which might accomplish the same end." Hyoka nodded at the paper, and bounced on the balls of her feet as she did so. "This is what we found."

Satomi's eyes dropped back to the tidy notation there. Too arcane for her to fully understand it at a glance—Hyoka had not given her the proposed ritual, as that hadn't been worked out yet; instead, she had a thicket of metaphysical logic to read—but she grasped enough to know that this would not exactly accomplish what she had in mind. It would get her there, yes, but with a number of side effects she was not entirely sure she wanted.

Her silence made Hyoka garrulous. "I went looking

back to the accounts of how the Prime offices were insti-
tuted," she said. "To examine the things you asked—how to
suspend a Prime with three, or what would happen if you
put in a new one without fully removing her predecessor—
you have to look at how things began, to answer questions
like that. And, well, we've all been thinking so much
about our traditional practices, thanks to Mirei. So I went
back and looked, and then I started to think about this as a
solution. It *should* work."

"Removing *all* the Primes," Satomi said, her voice flat
with skepticism.

"And then reinstituting the ones you want to keep."

One had to admire the sheer brass of it. Even while
reeling at the potential problems. "You would have to
raise the Primes without any other Primes playing a part
in it, though—at least the first one."

"Which is where the histories come in. They had to do
that in the first place." Hyoka twisted her hands together,
now looking a little more nervous, a little less elated. "I'm
not *quite* sure yet how they did it. The records aren't clear.
But we know it can be done—it must be possible—
because it *was* done."

Against her will, Satomi found herself plotting out the
order and the timing, looking for ways the dissidents
might be able to interfere. Disband the entire circle of
Primes: Arinei would lose her authority. Then raise new
Primes. They were traditionally taken from the ranks of the
Keys; had any Prime ever *not* been a Key first? Something
for Hyoka to research. If the Primes had to be Keys, then
she, Koika, and Rana would have to demote some of their
people to make room. But no, that didn't work; you
needed a Prime's authority to make someone a Key. They

could not make themselves Keys while also Primes, and once they weren't Primes, they wouldn't be able to do it then, either.

So it would *have* to be possible to make ordinary witches Primes, or this wouldn't work. Reinstate herself, and Koika, and Rana, and then choose successors for the other two. Naji for Shimi, and for Arinei . . . well, it would have to be Onomita, as she was the only Fire Key remaining at Starfall. Satomi would need to talk to her about the note she'd read, then—or else change *her* memory, too. Could Onomita handle that responsibility, dropped on her so suddenly? Or should they look to the unranked witches for possible successors? Was there anyone ready to take up that burden?

As for how the others might interfere, she saw remarkably few opportunities, at least at the moment. They could prevent the disbanding from happening, perhaps, which would return them all to stalemate. They could try to slip in their own replacements, before the Primes could reinstate themselves—but that would require them knowing they were about to be disbanded, and having the rituals necessary to raise new Primes out of nothing. With luck—and good security—Satomi could see to it that this would take them completely by surprise. They wouldn't have time to put in their own people.

Three Primes reinstated, two Primes replaced. Then strip the rebellious Keys of their authority and replace them, and find a new Air Heart to replace Naji.

It *could* work.

Assuming that Hyoka could turn theory into application, and Satomi had the nerve to try such a radical move.

She handed the sheet back to Hyoka. "Look into it. Tell

me what you find out. Keep this under the *strictest* security; your people are not to speak to anyone other than each other, you, or me."

"And Koika and Rana?"

Satomi met her gaze coldly. "Themselves, you, or me. No one else."

Hyoka moved in startlement, then bowed. "Yes, Aken."

Chapter Nine

MIREI STUMBLED to her feet, off balance, head thick and slow. Her eyes kept going over the scene, not quite processing it yet. Two horses: hers and Amas's. Two trainees: Amas and Lehant.

No Indera.

No Indera's horse.

The foul taste in her mouth stopped her where she stood. Mirei raised one hand to her lips, then swore. Ferraleaf. Someone had drugged her. Drugged her and taken Indera.

Taken only one? a more alert part of her asked. *Taken one, and left the others here?*

And how would they have fed her the drug, anyway?

Mirei's eyes went, inexorably, to the pot the previous night's broth had been cooked in. It had been washed in the spring and set upside-down against a rock to dry. No evidence left.

But Indera had cooked the broth.

Ferraleaf. One of the herbs she had pointed out to Amas and Indera on the long ride from Silverfire to Angrim.

Mirei swore again, louder. "Void-damned idiot," she added. It was easier to keep her thoughts going around the aftereffects of the drug when they were said out loud. "Watching the wrong bloody two. Left your eyes off her.

Ferraleaf likes damp—let's see—yes, there it is, right by the spring, how clever of you to spot what's left of it *now,* when she's fed you most of the plant. Didn't drink the broth last night, did she? Weren't watching for that. And didn't taste it, either, because she put salt in, like you told her to. Good job, Mirei, you're a wonderful teacher."

Her rambling, venomous monologue broke off as she turned and found Amas and Lehant had stirred into wakefulness.

"She's gone," Mirei said. No point in trying to hide it. "Drugged us and ran. Don't know how long ago."

She began to cast about on the ground as the other two struggled upright. Her body was stiff from her unnaturally deep sleep on the ground with only her cloak to protect her, but she disregarded it, working the stiffness out as she looked for tracks. Indera had taken a horse; that would be hard to hide—yes, there, leading back toward the road. Mirei followed the marks, leaving the trainees and the horses behind for the moment, and emerged out from under the trees into the sunlight of late morning. If Indera had left as soon as they were soundly asleep, then she could have quite a head start.

The hoofprints went to the road, and vanished into the hard-packed dirt.

Mirei straightened from her crouch and began cursing once more in a low, unbroken monotone. The lane was smaller than a Great Road, yes, and less heavily traveled, but there was enough traffic on it, and enough time had passed since the last rainfall, that the surface was an unreadable carpet of dust. No way to distinguish one set of hoofprints from another. Indera could have gone in either direction, and could have left the road at any point.

Bad enough to lose Naspeth because she didn't reach Angrim in time. How was she supposed to justify losing Indera when the girl had been *right there*?

A rustle in the dry grass made her spin. She staggered a step, equilibrium still not recovered, and found Amas behind her.

"Why in the Void aren't *you* gone, too?" Mirei demanded, saying the first thing that came to mind. "I thought you'd be the one to run. You, or the Thornblood."

Amas gave her that same infuriatingly level look as always. "Why me?"

"Because you treat everything I say like I'm a marketplace vendor trying to cheat you, and you just haven't figured out how. I expected *you* to question the things I said last night."

"But not Indera." Amas shook her head. Red-gold roots were appearing in her dyed hair, glimmering in the morning sunlight. Her expression almost pitied Mirei's lack of understanding. "She worships you. Worshiped, I guess. Wanted to be just like you. She *loves* being who she is, being this—doppelganger thing. Then you come along and tell her you're going to take that away."

"I'm saving her life."

Amas shrugged, sardonic. "I guess she's not very grateful."

"So why didn't you run away with her? Are you more grateful?"

"She didn't ask me to come," Amas said. Then she smiled, with a cool edge to it. "And I haven't finished thinking about what you told us." The smile faded; she grimaced and spat into the grass. "Is this what ferraleaf tastes like, then?"

"Indera overdid it," Mirei muttered, and headed back toward the camp.

Lehant was there, ducking her head into the spring in order to clear it. The water streamed over the girl's bald head; she blinked her eyes clear and said, "Now what?"

Mirei knew before she tried that it wouldn't work, but she had to try anyway. Maybe it would work for her, with her different flavor of magic.

She sang the spell that would locate a human being.

The result was not like trying to find someone hidden behind a blocking spell. Instead of the painful silence, she suffered a wash of dizziness that dumped her on her ass.

She should have given the girls warning. They had no way of knowing what spell she was casting. By the looks on their faces, they had half-expected that she was going to rain fire down on their heads for letting Indera slip off. Her fall clearly hadn't helped their confusion.

"Damn it to Void," Mirei said, not even able to put any real force behind it. She had known the spell would fail. That, then, must be what it felt like to try and find a person who was in two places at once. Sharyo was hopefully at Starfall, and Indera was Goddess knew where.

"Are you okay?" Amas asked, not approaching her.

Depending on what you mean by "okay." "Yes," Mirei said, tucking her legs underneath her. *Crone on a crutch. So what now?*

After she had sat there for a moment, pondering that question and coming up with nothing useful, Amas spoke again. "Can't you just get her back with magic?"

"No," Mirei said shortly, and left it at that. *Better not to tell them they're untrackable by spell. Don't want to give them any ideas.*

Another few moments of silence, and then Amas's voice. "Shouldn't you be following her? Before she gets too far away?"

"I have no idea which bloody direction she's gone in, and I have you two to worry about," Mirei growled. "Need to figure out what to do with you, before I go after her."

"What to *do* with us?" This time it was Lehant, rising from her crouch beside the spring and coming a step toward her.

"Remember me saying your lives were in danger? I've lost two of you already, at least in the short term. I'm going to get you two safely stowed with somebody before I go haring off after Indera." She closed her eyes and tried to recall where the nearest group of Cousins was likely to be. No, not Cousins; she needed at least *some* witches to protect these two. And she couldn't just recruit the nearest Water Hand. This was going to be a nightmare. Every minute she spent on this, Indera was getting more thoroughly lost. Or being found by the wrong people.

Amas's voice broke through her thoughts, *again*. "I can help you find her."

"Will you stop distracting me?" Mirei demanded, rising to her feet in one smooth motion. Good; her sense of balance was coming back.

The trainee stood her ground against the anger. "I can help. I know Indera better than you do. If you can't get her back with magic, then you'll need to know where she's likely to have gone. And besides, she trusts me, kind of." The girl grimaced. "Okay, not really—but more than she trusts you, after what you said last night. I might be able to convince her to come with you."

"And I'm not letting you hand me off to some witch," Lehant put in, looking defiant.

Mirei's frustration boiled over. "In case you forgot last night's lesson, *I'm* a witch. And you'll damn well go where I *say* you will, because I'll hit you over the head or gag you with a spell or do whatever I bloody *have* to in order to keep your miserable, ungrateful skins in one piece."

"We're not ungrateful!" Amas shouted back at her, and for the first time, Mirei saw the girl's composure snap. "It's just that it's a little *hard* to deal with what you've told us—it's come out of nowhere, can't you understand that? And you're the only person we *know,* now. We can't go back to our schools and we can't go back to our parents and you want to pass us off to a bunch of women we've never met before, and then they're going to put us back together with some girls we don't know and we're not going to be like this anymore. We won't be ourselves. You've been through it, you're the only one, and so we want to stay with you, *all right?"*

The summer silence that followed her words, a quiet breeze and the buzz of cicadas, seemed incongruous, even silly.

Mirei stared at the two girls. Amas, skin flushed and hands clenched into useless, impotent fists. Lehant's gaze alternating between them both, its nervous flicker betraying that she was on the edge of snapping, too.

I don't know what to do with them.

She turned her back on them, walked a few steps to an elm and leaned against it, arms propped on the cracked gray bark. The remaining horses were not far away; they sidled a little, made uneasy by the shouting. Horses she could deal with. Witches she could deal with. Eleven-year-old girls? She was twenty-five, and when she was their age she'd spent the last six years of her life in a temple, learning to Dance for the Goddess.

"I don't know how to take care of you," she said, words muffled by her arms. She hadn't meant to say it, but out it came. "You're eleven. I don't know what to do with you."

Silence greeted this statement, until she had to straighten up and turn around to look at them.

Lehant looked startled. From the girl's expression, Mirei could only think that she'd managed to prove to her that, yes, even Silverfires were human. Crone only knew what kinds of stories Thornblood trainees were fed about them. Probably similar to the ones Silverfire trainees got about Thornbloods.

Amas had gone white, and her lips were pressed together. Her eyes were large in her face, light blue and lost; Mirei couldn't break away from her gaze.

The three of them stared at each other, and Mirei's gelding whickered and stamped one hoof.

Then Amas pulled herself up, squaring her thin shoulders in abrupt determination. "We're not children. We're Hunter trainees."

She said this as if it was supposed to solve all of the problems. Mirei couldn't see how. "And?"

"So don't think you have to treat us like children. Think—think like you're running a Hunter school. Your own school. With two trainees. And it's a different kind of school, because instead of having a compound, you're teaching us on the road. Like apprentices. We'll learn the trade by working with you."

"Being a Hunter isn't a *trade*," Mirei said; it was a silly objection, but it was easier to put into words than her other ones.

"Still," Amas insisted. "A two-trainee Hunter school— three, once we get Indera back—and you're the Grandmaster. And you'll teach us tracking, while we chase Indera, and how to find someone who's gone missing. That's work Hunters do. Jaguar told you to teach us."

He'd told her to teach them, not to have some kind of delusion about setting up her own school. The last time anybody had tried to create a new school had been over a hundred years ago, and Snowspears were still considered second-rate alternatives to Wildmoons, the school they had splintered off from.

Snowspears weren't doppelgangers, though.

Neither would these girls be, in the long run—but they would for a while.

Mirei wrenched her thoughts back from the road they were headed down. She wasn't *actually* setting up a school. It was just a way for her to deal with her growing—well, currently shrinking—pack of girls. A way for them all to relate to each other. They'd go back to their schools eventually, assuming Starfall let them go.

Don't follow that thought too far.

Then she remembered what training had been like, the way she'd gone through it. Mirei wasn't a teacher; the only way she knew how to teach was the way she herself had been taught. It had been brutal. "I'd be too hard on you," she said.

Lehant gave a short bark of laughter. "You've never been at Thornblood."

"*Be* hard," Amas said. "That's fine. You told us we're born for this. The teaching they give us at Silverfire—it isn't enough of a challenge anyway, because our year-mates would get flattened. You don't have to worry about normal people, though. Just us. We can take hard."

It was only true on some counts; training was hard in a lot of ways, not all of which were ways doppelgangers were gifted. But she was right that they could learn much more quickly than others could.

And they weren't starting late, like she had.

The more time she spent debating Amas's suggestion, the farther away Indera was getting.

"We do this," Mirei said, "and there's no more questioning. Understand? I tell you to do something, you do it, no arguing. Whether it's Hunter stuff or witch stuff. Most Hunter schools may have problems with witches, but for however long it lasts, *this* school is different. You're going to have to deal with it eventually; better start now. Got it?"

Both of them nodded.

"Fine," Mirei said. "Saddle the horses. You two ride double. We leave in five minutes."

THEY RODE NORTH, because in Amas's opinion, Indera would have gone back to Angrim.

"Why Angrim?" Mirei asked her as they led the horses toward the road.

"Because it's the only landmark she knows around here. And Silverfire is north."

"How sure are you?"

Amas thought it over. "Mostly."

She had to accept "mostly," because she had no better lead to follow. And, as Amas pointed out awhile later, Angrim was a large city, the capital of Abern; it offered more opportunity for Indera to lose herself in the crowds.

It wouldn't have done her any good against Mirei's spells if she hadn't been a doppelganger, and Indera didn't know that protected her—but she also didn't know much about how magic worked in general. Silverfire would have taught them eventually, because they needed to know how to deal with it, but that came much later.

Mirei gave them a lesson on it as they rode. Whenever they were walking or trotting the horses, she kept the gelding close to the trainees riding double, and told them how magic worked. Not just the side of it Hunters usually heard; she knew the witch side, and could tell them *why* things worked the way they did. With witches after them, they needed to know as much as possible. She didn't stint the practical aspects, though. Against a witch, their best defense would be to hit the woman in the throat.

They arrived in Angrim just before sunset, but the trio that rode through the gates was not a Hunter with two trainees. It was an aging mercenary with his two teenaged sons.

Mirei had cast it when they stopped for a breather during the afternoon; illusions were far too finicky and slow to be cast from the back of a moving horse. She had to define in close detail the appearances she wanted, constructing the images in the language of magic, and work through foci to channel the power. The trainees, to their credit, shut their mouths and accepted the spell. It seemed a good way to start breaking them of being nervous around magic, and anyone looking for them would not be looking for men.

"They haven't taught you about the agents yet, right?" she asked Amas quietly as they passed under the arch of

Angrim's southern gate and into the city's narrow, crowded streets.

Amas, disguised as a thickset fifteen-year-old with shaggy brown hair, shook her head. "We know they exist, because people have said, but we don't know who they are or how to find them."

Of course not. That information was held back until the last two years, when the trainees who were going to fail out had done so. Hunters did not want information about their agents leaking out into the rest of the world.

That would be one of the disadvantages to trying to set up a new school, Mirei thought, turning her horse down a cross street and moving to the side to avoid a wagon of beer kegs. *No network of informants in place.* Some agents were ordinary people paid to pass along information; others were Hunters too old or injured to actively continue their line of work. The latter would take time to build up, and the former, well, it was hard to find trustworthy people.

I could make use of witches, though.

"Then she won't go to them," Mirei said out loud, avoiding Indera's name. Too many listening ears. "But we can find out if any of them have seen her."

There were a variety of convoluted protocols for contacting an Angrim agent, because of the number of spies; Mirei had to choose one where the fact that she looked like a complete stranger would not be observed. The agent she'd chosen was savvy enough not to come if the one contacting her was described as unfamiliar.

Mirei waited for her that night in the cellar of the Horsehead, a raucous alehouse in the western quarter, while the two doppelgangers sat upstairs, losing miserably at dice.

A shadow appeared in the light from above, and a short figure moved into the cellar.

"Please hear me out, Wisp."

The knife-faced woman instantly went on guard. A hint of provocation, and she would attack or vanish up the stairs. Mirei was careful not to give her cause for either. She came forward slowly from her hiding spot among the cider kegs, pausing between each step, with her gnarled mercenary's hands held out wide. No way was she dropping the illusion, not without an opportunity to rebuild it later.

Wisp stared at her false face in the dim light and scowled. "You're none of ours."

"Actually, I am," Mirei said, halting where she was. "Not too long ago, you told me that just because you were once young and stupid didn't mean I had to follow in your footsteps. And I said that you had become old and wise." She came forward two more slow, careful strides. "It's an illusion. I'm Mirage."

Wisp's eyes narrowed and took in the entirety of Mirei's appearance, from her scuffed leather boots to what was left of her graying hair. Survey done, she said, "No disguise is that good."

"It is if it's magic."

Her words took the old Hunter visibly aback. "Who put that on you?"

"A witch," Mirei said dryly. "It *is* me, Wisp."

"What was the last thing you contacted me for?" the woman asked, still suspicious.

Mirei opened her mouth to say "refuge," and caught herself just in time. There had been another contact after that one, when she had gotten Wisp to send a bird to Silverfire, with a message for Eclipse.

The reminder of her missing year-mate sent a pang through her heart. In all her Angrim trouble, she hadn't thought about him for some time.

Concentrate on the moment, she reminded herself, seeing Wisp's suspicion grow with every passing second. "I asked you to send a message for me," she said. "To Silverfire. And that time I obeyed the protocols, because I knew you'd kill me if I bypassed them again, the way I did when I asked for refuge."

Wisp relaxed at last, as much as she ever did. Retired she might be, but the old Hunter had not gone soft. "Great."

Mirei had just enough time to wince before Wisp launched into her diatribe.

"What in the *Void* has been going on with you? You show up in town, send a bird to Silverfire, get jumped by a pack of Thornbloods, then leave town without so much as a word of explanation. Week or so later, you're back here again, demanding refuge for you and some other woman you won't name for me or even show me her face. Oh, and you drop the little tidbit that the Primes are on your tail, all five of them. Then you vanish *again,* this time out of a bloody *cloister,* and you don't even take your sword with you, you're gone for a couple more weeks, and next thing I hear you're dashing around the north end of town and some witch shows up dead. Now you're at my door again. With Eclipse's sword on your hip, when nobody's seen hide nor hair of him in weeks." Wisp glared at her. "Talk."

Mirei tried for a light tone. "Reminds me. Could I get my sword back? I hope you rescued it from the temple."

A knife sprouted from the keg behind her head. A thin stream of cider began to leak out and drip to the floor.

So much for humor. "Wisp, ask Jaguar for information. He knows what's going on, and he can decide how much is safe to spread. I didn't contact you because I wanted to see your pretty face again, or because I wanted to be your target for knife practice; I did it because one of ours is in trouble, and I may not have much time to get her out of it."

" 'Her.' So not Eclipse."

"I don't know where he is," Mirei said, not bothering to hide how much that upset her. "And I haven't had a chance to search because I've been riding herd on eleven-year-olds. I have two Silverfire trainees—well, I had two; now I've got one. The other one came back here, to An-grim, we think. I need to catch her before anybody else does. The Primes aren't trying to kill me anymore, but some other witches are, and they're after Indera, too."

Wisp took this in, then opened her mouth again. "Why—"

"Ask Jaguar," Mirei said, before she could even get the question out. "I'm serious. Wisp, that dead witch was one of the ones I'm running from, and she may have friends in town who are looking for Indera right now." She hesitated, debating whether or not to add the rest. *Ah, Void, go for it. She may already know.* "And they have another one. Not ours. A Windblade named Naspeth."

She could practically see the pieces click into place in Wisp's head. "These are the special ones. Aren't they. The ones who are like you."

"Ask Jaguar," Mirei said for the third time. Wisp would keep her here all night with questions, otherwise; collecting information was the woman's job. That, and lending assistance to Silverfires who needed help.

The sound of grinding teeth was nearly audible, but

Wisp was good at her job, and that meant swallowing her curiosity when bigger issues were at hand. "Tell me the details."

"Eleven years old. Red-brown hair. Was wearing Askavyan clothes as a disguise, but she may have tried to change those for something else. Riding, unless she ditched the horse. Would have been coming from the south. We're not certain she came here at all, though."

Wisp nodded. "It's enough to go on. We'll start looking."

BUT THE NEXT MORNING, Wisp delivered the news that there had been no sign of Indera.

There were any number of possible explanations. Angrim was a big city. Nobody had been looking for her at the time; she might have slipped through the gates unnoticed, and gone to ground well enough that they just couldn't find her yet. She might have ridden slowly, stopped along the road, so that even though she had a head start they had beaten her here—after all, she had saddle sores.

She might not have come to Angrim at all.

Amas still said she probably had. "Her parents lived in a town, or maybe it's a small city—she'd be more comfortable here than I am. She knows she can hold her own in a fight, and she doesn't have much to steal. She'd be on the streets. Not in an inn."

Plenty of street urchins in Angrim; easy to vanish among them. But still—"With a horse?"

Wisp went back out with a better description of Indera's bay mare. And there, at last, they struck gold: It was in a stable on the western side of town, not far from where Mirei and the others were staying. Not being boarded, though; Indera had sold the animal, and for a pathetically low price. *Well,* Mirei reflected, *horse-trading and haggling weren't skills I'd gotten around to teaching yet.* But it meant that Indera had coin enough to keep herself fed, at least for a while.

"She won't be in the west, though," Amas said, and Mirei agreed. Indera was smart enough to get away from that clue. But where would she have gone?

Mirei created a map on the floor of their room at the inn, using odds and ends from her saddlebag to demarcate the different areas of Angrim. The main temple district, the various markets, the residential quarters; she had to explain to Amas that yes, they were all called "quarters," even though Angrim's growth over the centuries meant there were far more than four of them. Lehant knew surprisingly little of the city for someone who had been living just to the north of it—Mirei supposed that Thornbloods, at least new ones, must not be let out often—but she was the one to make the next suggestion.

"There," she said, pointing at an area Mirei had identified as the Knot, which was currently being represented by a donated bootlace. "Easiest to get lost in."

She was right about that much; the Knot was a warren of streets where the overhanging structures had made good on their threat to merge together. The alleys were tunnels, and the buildings were roads. "But Indera doesn't know the city," Mirei said. "And that's *far* from where she sold the horse."

"She might hear about it, though," Amas said. "And I know she decided to run away from you, but that doesn't mean she's forgotten what you said about the witches who want to kill her. I think she'd be looking to hide from *everybody.*"

Mirei sighed and sat back on her heels. "Couldn't you tell me she would absolutely have picked, say, the temple district, where we won't have to spend a year combing the place for her trail?"

"You could smoke 'em out like rats," Lehant suggested. She was proving to be rather disturbingly bloody-minded. Mirei tried to convince herself not to chalk it up to the Thornblood influence, and failed. Lehant wasn't the only one with prejudices to get over.

"Don't tempt me," Mirei said, and remembered Wisp once warning her not to burn Angrim down.

She reached for the lace and began to thread it back through her boot. "Okay. In the absence of any better clues, we'll try the Knot. Goddess help us all."

"We?" Lehant said, looking up alertly. "You're going to let us help?"

"You two know what Indera looks like, which is more than I can say for the other people helping us search. And under an illusion, you should be pretty safe." Mirei cast a glance around, and scowled at the room; the walls were flimsy and thin. "But first I have to find a place where I can sing in privacy."

FEW PEOPLE WOULD NOTICE the addition of three new street rats to the Knot's population.

Some of the more charitably-inclined sects occasionally sent people into the warren to bring food or medicine or their flavor of faith to the children and vagrants there. Occasionally the Lady's town guards went in, to chase down someone who had gone to ground. And if you were too poor to pay anyone with training, there was muscle for hire in the maze of its streets. But few people paid attention beyond that.

The street rats paid attention.

Mirei found that out the hard way before she'd gone more than a street in.

She sent Amas and Lehant off on their own, with strict orders not to split up, and to scream their heads off if anything went wrong. Mostly she wasn't afraid for them, though she didn't say so. Even with the little training they'd gotten, they were more than a match even for children larger than them, and if they died—well, they would come back. She'd prefer them not to find that out the hard way, but it meant they had a margin of safety. The only *real* threat would come from witches, who would be unlikely to spot them. And Mirei could take care of herself just fine.

There were other kinds of trouble, though.

Six of them ringed her as she turned her first corner, where a fortune-teller's five-eyed sign leaned up against a wall. Mirei heard them moving into place, but didn't react until they showed themselves. There was more to disguise than just the surface.

"You ain't one of ours," the leader of this little pack said challengingly, crossing his arms over his chest. Mirei guessed him for thirteen or fourteen, to her own apparent ten.

She stuck her chin out and looked like she was trying to look unconcerned. "So? 'S a street. I can walk down a street."

"Not if your leg's broke, you cain't," one of the others put in. But he was scrawny, his voice shrill; he was here to follow the other's lead. Mirei kept her attention on the important one.

"*My* street," the leader said. "I say who gets to walk down it."

"Oh yeah?" Mirei said scornfully. "Ain't what I heard."

Standard posturing turned into indignation. "What do you mean?"

"I heard some girl came through here, some new girl, not from the Knot, an' she's been going anywhere she likes, an' beating up people who try to stop her." If what Amas said about Indera's temper and arrogance was right, then she probably was doing exactly that.

"Not *here*, she ain't," the leader insisted, and there wasn't the insecure edge that would hint at a lie. "I'd pound her into mush, any girl like that came here. She'd cry an' run home. Girls always cry."

As Mirei's illusion was that of a boy, she didn't bother to argue. But she was done here; none of these had seen or heard anything about Indera. Time to move on. Ideally without getting into a fight.

"Look," she said, dropping her tone confidentially and coming a couple of steps closer to the boy. "I ain't gonna stay. I just wanna find that girl. She beat up my little brother real bad the other day, an' her father told her she was gonna get a hiding, so she run off here. I wanna get her for that. Lemme on through, an' I'll get her out of here."

It came dangerously close to insulting the boy's strength. "You think we cain't get rid of her ourselves?"

Mirei responded with her own indignation. "It weren't *your* brother she beat up. I got a *claim* on her. Ain't gonna let her walk away from that."

Revenge and the restoration of pride were motives

these children could understand. The leader couldn't just back down, though; he had to make it into a favor, generosity on the part of the big man. "You just walk on through," he said, stretching to loom over Mirei. "You don't stop. You don't stop until you get to the Cripples' Corner, understand? I don't want you on my streets. But I'll let you through them."

Mirei assumed the Cripples' Corner would be easy enough to identify. "Thanks. I'll find her before long."

And that much, she hoped, was true.

She spread the same story in other places, knowing Amas and Lehant were peddling their own version from the other side of the Knot. At least they had started out at opposite sides; in the murky tangle of alleys, tunnels, bridges, and rooms that made up the place, it was impossible to keep a sense of direction for long. Mirei just hoped they'd all be able to find their way out at the end of the day. She should have made some way for them to contact each other. But putting spells into objects was even more finicky than illusion work, and not something she had ever tried before.

"I don't know where she is," the ninth or tenth kid she spoke to said. This one was a real piece of work, filthy, pox-scarred, and missing half her teeth. "But I can help you look. I can guide you through the streets."

Help couldn't hurt; Mirei had already gone in circles twice, thanks to the tortuous layout of the Knot. Still, she had to keep up her act. She gave the girl a suspicious look. "What do you want for the help?"

The girl thought it over for a moment. "If you give me a wheel, I'll do it."

"You think I got a *silver*?" Mirei said incredulously.

The girl looked defensive. "You might. But I'll help you for ten coppers."

"Two," Mirei returned. "You ain't big enough to be worth ten."

"Five."

Warrior's teeth, but she's bad at bargaining. "Three."

"Very well," the girl said, and led her up a rickety staircase.

They explored an upper level for a while, but ran afoul of a pregnant woman who threw a kettle at them. Then it was back down to the street—at least Mirei thought it was the street. Up, down, through buildings, out doors, with only occasional lances of sunlight to show that the sky was still there.

Mirei's "guide" was not much use. She didn't seem to have much idea where she was going, and Mirei still had to do all the talking, questioning people for hints of Indera. And then they squeezed through a gap between two buildings and found themselves back at an intersection they'd passed through not long before.

The girl squirmed when glared at. "If I wanna go in circles, I don't need you to help," Mirei said.

"I'm sorry," the girl muttered, and chose a new direction.

"You're dumber than a cowpat," Mirei said, following her, and wondered at the ineptitude. Why offer to be a guide, if she didn't know her way around?

And then other oddities began to click into place.

The way the girl looked so much dirtier, so much less healthy, than the other street rats Mirei had seen.

The way her speech didn't match her appearance—too polished, her grammar too good.

The way she seemed to be eavesdropping when Mirei questioned people.

A voice swam up out of her memory, from the Miryo part of her mind. The voice of Edame, the Fire Hand adviser to the Lord and Lady of Haira, when she dropped her illusion and revealed who she was.

"A tip, oh green one: If someone seems odd, check them for any kind of magic. Sometimes it'll be a fellow witch in disguise. Sometimes it'll be someone spelled by a witch, for any one of a number of purposes. Sometimes it'll just be somebody odd. But it's always good to know."

But how to do it without the girl noticing? A few streets on, the problem solved itself. A clump of children were playing a game with stones and singing a song to go with it, some vulgar rhyme about dead rats. One of them was on pitch enough to call up a resonance from nearby spells.

Like the one on the "girl" who was her guide.

Mirei's steps stuttered for a moment before recovering; she didn't think the girl noticed. Walking on as if nothing were wrong, she resisted the urge to swear. *A witch, or someone spelled by a witch? Either way, it's somebody who never learned that there's more to disguise than just the surface. Fortunately for me.*

She was tempted to just take a rock to the back of the girl's head. Witch or not, that would remove her from the situation. But then Mirei would be stuck with an unconscious body, and no Indera. Not ideal.

She decided to wait.

They'd moved into an area where there was even less light than usual; what there was filtered down through the structures above and didn't give Mirei any help in judging the time. Amas and Lehant were under orders to leave the Knot at dusk and go to a nearby safe house Wisp had set up for them, but Mirei was considering staying. There might be things to learn in the Knot at night. Like, for example, how anyone saw where they were going once the sun went down in a place where lighting even a candle posed a serious risk of torching the entire mess.

Then she heard shouting up ahead, in the high-pitched voices of children, and hoped her search might end before it came to that. Trouble could be a sign of Indera.

When she and her false guide came to the source of the sound, sure enough, there was a figure backed up against a pile of splintered wood left behind by a collapsing wall. The floor of two conjoined buildings above their heads, barely visible in the murk, slanted dangerously, as if the whole thing might be in danger of caving in. Several street rats had formed an arc facing their target, and some of them had crude weapons in hand—but the figure they had trapped was a scrawny boy, not Indera.

A scrawny boy Mirei recognized quite well, because she had carefully detailed what he should look like earlier that day.

She cast a swift glance around, but there was no sign of the disguised Lehant. *Void it—I* told *them not to split up!* Mirei wondered whether she'd prefer for Lehant to be lying dead or unconscious somewhere instead of wandering on her own. It depended on how badly this turned out.

Amas, in her boy's guise, was shouting at the pack facing her. "I didn't cheat! Like I'd *need* to cheat at your stupid game—a blind donkey could've beaten you!"

Mirei had just enough time to wonder where the quiet, thoughtful Amas had gone, and why the girl had decided to imitate Indera at such a bad time, before the kids charged her.

She only just barely held herself back from jumping into the fray. There was no reason for the boy she appeared to be to get involved; he didn't know these people. And she'd been avoiding scuffles all this time because she knew she couldn't fake a real ten-year-old's behavior in a fight. Her reflexes, though dulled, were far too highly trained. So she held herself back, and tried to think of a way to defuse this situation and find Lehant again.

While she thought, Amas moved.

She'd had less than a year's training at Silverfire. She knew only a limited set of moves. But she was a doppelganger, and it showed.

Amas dodged the first blow so fast it was almost comical. The lead boy, makeshift club in hand, stumbled past her and into the pile of broken planks. The second was there just a heartbeat behind him, with a jagged piece of metal he wielded like a knife; Amas slid to the outside of his strike and elbowed him hard in the kidneys.

Next to her, Mirei heard the girl who was not a girl inhale sharply at the sight.

Maybe the stranger had been about to sing. Maybe not. Mirei didn't get the chance to find out, because everybody, even the beggar children now dog-piling Amas, stopped what they were doing at the sound of a yell.

Indera launched herself out of a crumbling window and onto the hard-packed dirt of the area. She rolled with the landing, her form impeccable, and came to her feet with a feral grin on her face. "Stop right there!" she announced grandly. "I'm not going to let you beat him up!"

"Indera, you stupid little *bitch*," Mirei groaned, and then chaos broke loose again.

She ignored the brawl. It wasn't the problem. The problem was standing next to her, in the form of the girl who had just heard her say that, who spun at the sound. The element of surprise was gone; there would be no braining this girl with a rock while she looked the other way.

Mirei didn't punch her in the throat. Too much risk of collapsing the windpipe, and she wanted this one alive. But there were other ways to disrupt spells—if indeed this was a witch—and so she started by tackling the girl to the ground.

Or tried to. Mirei had forgotten that an illusion did nothing to change anyone's weight, and slammed into the bulk of a fully-grown adult. Instead of falling, they staggered backward into the nearest wall, which creaked alarmingly at the impact. Mirei grunted and went for a choking grip; her hands locked down, but the girl began to claw at her wrists, raising bloody gouges. Still she hung on, gritting her teeth at the pain and dodging the occasional swipe at her eyes, and tried not to wonder how the brawl behind her was going.

The girl's face contorted as she gasped for air, then went slack. Mirei held on, counting—and then let go in shock as the body beneath her hands transformed into a stout, red-haired woman.

Unconscious, she realized as the witch slumped bonelessly to the ground. *Well, at least I don't have to wonder how long to hold on for.*

Then she turned around to the rest of the fight.

Indera had squandered the element of surprise—bad tactics, and a corner of Mirei's mind made a note to chide her for that. But she'd obtained a cast-off horseshoe somewhere and was using it as a weapon, to devastatingly good effect; when the boy with the makeshift knife lunged at her with it, she hooked the blade out of the way, then smacked him over the head with the iron.

She'd also done Amas the service of breaking the focus on her. The dog pile had split up, some of them going for Indera, some of them staying with their original target, and the result was that there weren't enough on either doppelganger to pose an effective threat. But there was still chaos and struggling, howls of pain and muffled curses.

And as they brawled back and forth in the claustrophobic little area, bodies and makeshift weapons thudding into walls, the structures creaked and swayed alarmingly.

Mirei shot a swift glance upward, but she was no architect; she couldn't guess how likely the building was to collapse on them all. She just knew she didn't want to risk it. The girls would survive it, or at least come back, but she wouldn't.

So she gave up on the hope of maintaining her disguise in front of Indera. Whether or not the girl had pegged Amas for who she really was, there was no way she wouldn't notice this.

Mirei waded into the fight. She went for the ones facing Amas first; as long as Indera was busy, she wouldn't be running away. What should have been the work of mere moments for her took longer than expected—the slowing of her reflexes was nothing next to the oddity of a smaller body with the weight of an adult—but these were beggar children, and she was a Hunter. Amas was able to break away almost immediately, and then Mirei finished them off.

She turned in time to see Amas dive through Indera's fight and club the other girl over the head.

When the last of the street rats was down for the count or fled, she stared at the scrawny boy the trainee appeared to be. "What in the Void was *that* for?"

Amas shrugged. "It's easier than arguing with her, isn't it?"

It was, but it wouldn't make Indera feel too kindly toward her year-mate. Then again, Mirei was increasingly less concerned with how Indera felt. She could understand that the girl had some issues with her situation, but the problems she had led them into as a result . . .

One of which was lying on the ground not far away, her illusion fallen away with her consciousness. Mirei was getting heartily sick of smuggling comatose people through the most spy-ridden city in the world.

Which made her remember her concern of a short while before. "Where's Lehant?"

Amas at least had the grace to look guilty as she shrugged this time. "I don't know."

Mirei ground her teeth, then made herself say levelly, "Where did you lose her?"

"I didn't *lose* her," Amas said. "We just decided to split up."

"After I told you not to."

"It was faster that way. And I lured Indera out of hiding, didn't I?"

"Getting one back won't do us a damn bit of good if we've lost another in the meantime." Mirei stabbed a finger at the witch on the ground. "She was trying to find Indera. There may have been others. Lehant may be a prisoner now, thanks to your desire for efficiency."

Amas at least had the sense not to have an answer to that. She looked at her bare feet and kept silent.

The light was virtually gone; it had to be nearly dark out. Mirei swallowed and forced herself to handle the immediate, manageable problems first. "We're going back to the safe house. Bring Indera." She herself would carry the unconscious witch, and the Mother's mercy on anybody who got in her way now.

LEHANT WAS WAITING for them when they reached the safe house.

Mirei knew she was reaching the end of her rope when she realized she was angry at the trainee for being there, quietly, when everyone else had been in so much trouble. It was dark out by now; according to the instructions she'd given the girls, Lehant was right where she should be. *Be angry about them splitting up,* she told herself, *but happy that you're not having to break her out of witch custody, like you feared.*

When she trusted herself to be calm, she sang a cancellation to the illusion and said, "Care to tell me why you decided to ignore half of what I told you?"

Lehant, unlike Amas, decided to have an answer. "Because it didn't make sense."

"It *did* make sense," Mirei said, and unrolled the blanket she'd wrapped the witch in. The woman was stirring at last, but with her hands bound, her eyes covered, and her mouth securely gagged, there was only so much trouble she could cause. Mirei was willing to leave her be for the moment.

Lehant's eyes widened. "Where did you get her?"

"In the Knot," Mirei said. "Chasing Indera."

"We were disguised. She wouldn't have known us."

"Unless you fought somebody, like Amas here, and showed yourself to be a doppelganger. I actually found myself *hoping* you'd run back to Thornblood—since the other likely alternative was that you'd been picked up by a witch."

The words didn't have the effect she'd intended. The shaven-headed trainee flinched and turned away, but the brief flash of expression Mirei caught was not one of guilt.

Concern distracted her from her irritation. "What is it?"

"Nothing," Lehant said, but the flatness of her tone belied it.

"Share this 'nothing' with me."

The thin shoulders shrugged. "Just—you don't have to worry about me going back to Thornblood."

It was meant to be reassuring, no doubt, but it wasn't. "Why?"

She deliberately let the painful silence that followed grow. And sure enough, after a while, it forced Lehant into speech again.

"You were right about Ice," she mumbled. "I wanted to believe you weren't, because you're a Silverfire, but I knew you were right. And she's not the only one."

Mirei had a sudden, vivid memory of her own early time as a Hunter trainee. She followed the intuitive leap of Lehant's last statement. "You're not accepted there."

Lehant still hadn't turned around to face her. "Let's just say Ice isn't the only one who would have taken that kind of offer."

What could she say to that? Everything that leapt to her

lips was a standard-issue slander of Thornbloods, and this was not the moment for such a thing.

Then she heard what was behind Lehant's words.

"You don't *have* to go back," she said gently. "When this is done, I'm going to make sure you all *can* go back, if you want to. But you don't have to."

Lehant faced her again at last, and her eyes glinted with unshed tears. "What else should I do? Live with a bunch of witches?"

The answer was there, and getting more comfortable all the time.

"Be a part of my new Hunter school," Mirei said.

Chapter Ten

In a room without windows, there were only so many ways to count time, and none of them were reliable.

If food came twice a day, then it had been thirteen days. If the witch who sang a spell over him—the same spell every time, but he didn't know what it did—if she came once a day, then it had been seventeen days. But Eclipse suspected they were trying to throw off his count. He would have, in their place. The golden stubble on his jaw might be a more accurate measurement.

He retraced his capture in his mind, for the thousandth time; what else was there for him to do? There were only so many times he could analyze his situation and conclude that he had, at present, not a snowflake's chance in a bonfire of escaping. They knew how to keep a Hunter imprisoned.

Mirei had arrived in his room, appearing out of nowhere after her miracle: that was at night. The next morning, he'd left before dawn to continue his journey to Silverfire.

They'd ambushed him about an hour after Mid.

And they hadn't taken any chances. No witches, it was true—for the second time, too. There hadn't been any witches there when they took Miryo, either. But Cousins enough to swamp him under, certainly. Cousins enough

for him *and* Mirage, had she been there. They were suffi-
ciently careless to say that in his hearing. He wasn't the
real target; they'd come for Mirage.

But they'd kept him anyway.

They hadn't known about Mirei, at first. They did now.
Not that anyone referred to her by name, but there came a
point when nobody was talking about Miryo or Mirage
anymore, just "the abomination." Or sometimes just *"her."*
He could piece it together well enough.

No witches in the ambush, but witches soon after; he
didn't know why they'd been afraid of bringing witches
near Mirage, but it seemed obvious that she was the one
they'd been avoiding. He was only important to them because of his friendship with her.

He dragged his mind back to the count. The day after
Mirei left him, he'd been taken prisoner. They'd kept him
in some unrecognizable village that night, and that was
when he'd made his first attempt to escape. The next day
they'd ridden—that was day two—although it was inac-
curate to say *he'd* ridden, unless being tied hand and foot
across the back of his horse with a sack over his head
counted as "riding." His attempt to break free then had only
resulted in his near-death from trampling. Between that
and the bruises he'd taken simply from being tied up, he
wasn't in shape to try much of anything that second night.

On day three they drugged him, so he couldn't be sure
of time, but since he only remembered one round of drugs,
he was pretty sure it wasn't more than a day. Then arrival
here—wherever "here" was. And since then, somewhere
between ten and fourteen days had passed. Maybe.

He wondered where Mirei was.

He didn't think she was dead. If she had been, then

there would be no reason to keep him; his only value was as a hostage against her. They would kill him or let him go, and be done with this mess. So she was alive—but he had to assume her trip to Starfall hadn't gone well.

He never should have let her go. She'd made a persuasive argument at the time, pointing out that if she could convince the women in charge, then she could bypass a lot of other trouble. And with that look in her eyes, that crazy, peaceful faith, he couldn't bring himself to argue with her.

But now she was in trouble, and he couldn't do a damned thing to help her.

Eclipse realized he was twisting his hands within his manacles again, trying to slip free. He kept on doing it, even though he'd proved days ago that it was a waste of his time. They'd locked him up too well; even the slickness provided by scraping his wrists until they bled hadn't let him slide his hands out. And even if it had, then he was still in a windowless room, behind a locked door too thick for him to break down, with a grating they looked through every time before they came in. If he didn't show them his hands, still safely in their irons, then they didn't open the door. He'd missed a few meals that way, which was why he wasn't too sure of his count. And the witch who sang the spell, whatever it was, never came in at all. She just watched him through the grating, and left when she was done.

They weren't going to let him go any time soon.

When the two Cousins came in to bring his food—one with the food, the other to watch and make sure he didn't try to attack her—he said, "Tell whoever's in charge that I want to make a deal."

* * *

A WITCH CAME before long. Not the one who sang at him through the door, which made her the fourth witch he'd seen since coming here. Slight curl to her hair, narrow gray eyes. No way to tell if that was her real face. They weren't, always.

She eyed him from the safe distance of the other end of the room, with two armed Cousins at her sides. He was almost flattered by the precautions they took in dealing with him. "They say you have some deal to offer."

Eclipse nodded. He was standing next to the pallet on the floor that served as his bed; they were careful not to put any furniture in the room that he might conceivably use to escape. There was just the pallet, and the latrine hole, and him standing between the two, looking as nonthreatening as he could. "I can guess what this is about. You're after Mirei. You're holding me because you think I'll be useful against her. Maybe lure her into a trap, with me as bait."

He paused, wondering if she'd respond and give him any other crumbs of information he could use in this negotiation, but the witch held her silence.

So he forged ahead. "You can't find her, is my guess, or you can't get at her wherever she is. Well, fair enough; that kind of work is hardly your usual job.

"But it's very much *my* job."

The witch's lips thinned into a tight line. "So you're saying—"

"I'm offering to Hunt Mirei," Eclipse said levelly.

The Cousins exchanged brief glances, behind the witch's back, where she could not see.

"It's what I'm *trained* to do," Eclipse said. "I'm not

just a Hunter; I'm a Silverfire. I'm sure you know that.
I'm not a bodyguard specialist, or a spy—"

"Or an assassin," the witch said, unencouragingly.

Eclipse was not fazed by her response. "But I can do
all of those things. I can find Mirei, wherever she is; I
know the resources she's likely to call on. I know how she
works—Mirage and I were *year-mates*. And she'll let me
close to her. We've worked together before."

"Exactly," the witch said, biting the word off. "You are
fellow Silverfires. Year-mates. *Friends*. You will not betray her. This is a poorly thought-out ploy to make us release you, and then you will run back to her side."

He shook his head. "You're leaving one thing out of
your calculations."

"Oh?"

"She's not Mirage." Eclipse smiled, bitterly. "She's not
the woman I knew in training, the sister I've fought beside.
She's someone else. And it's her fault I've been stuck in
this hole all this time." He lifted his manacled hands, with
the blood still crusted on them. "No offense to you, but
she's a witch now. Hunters don't take kindly to *your* kind
trying to pass as one of us. Who knows what secrets of
ours she's already betrayed? The Grandmaster of Silverfire may even have given orders for her to be eliminated."

The witch studied him for a long moment, one slender
finger tapping against the side of her leg. Then she shook
her head abruptly. "No. Your loyalty goes deeper than that,
I think. It was a clever attempt, Hunter—but not good
enough."

She snapped her fingers at the Cousins, and the three of
them left him alone in his cell.

* * *

TWO DAYS LATER—four meals, two spells; he was pretty sure of his count—the witch returned.

"Commissions," she said crisply, after a minute or so of studying him, while the Cousins stood ready to kill him if he somehow managed to slip his bonds after weeks of failure. "How do they work?"

His heart beat faster. She would only be asking if she were considering his offer. "They're more formal than hires. Pay better, too. Record is made of them, unless they're for work you wouldn't want known publicly. Whether there's a record or not, all the parties involved swear a sacred oath on them—the Hunter to complete the task, the employer to deliver the reward and to provide any help they've promised."

"An oath," the witch repeated. "The blood-oath?"

The ambush had not been kind to his clothing; anyone looking for it might have been able to spot the scar on his right wrist. It was the only visible relic—and, he guessed, the only record—of his one previous commission, when he and Mirage had been hired to find out who assassinated Tari-nakana.

"No, Katsu," Eclipse said. "Not for normal commissions. Blood-oaths are rare."

"But they cannot be broken."

He chose his words carefully. "Breaking them, or failing the task, means the Hunter dies. But no one would break even an ordinary oath—"

"No one except a desperate man," the witch said, watching him closely. "No one except a man who, perhaps, believes the Goddess will forgive him his transgression, if it means saving a friend."

Eclipse snarled at the word. "I told you. She's not Mirage. She's not a Silverfire. She's one of yours, and I'll gladly kill her if it means getting out of this hole. If I wanted to die instead of being in here, I could arrange that, trust me."

"And so you expect me to believe that you will not break your word."

He met her eyes coldly. "You have a low opinion of my honor, Katsu."

"I have a practical opinion of it, and all the honorifics in the world will not blind me to who and what you are." The witch snapped her fingers to the Cousins again and left. Eclipse sagged against the wall, teeth gritted in frustration.

THIS TIME, she waited only one day before returning.

"This is our offer," she said without preamble. Eclipse had been sitting on his pallet, fed up with the dance of courtesy, but he looked up sharply at her words. "We will free you—if you swear to Hunt and kill the abomination known as Mirei."

Eclipse rose swiftly to his feet. "I will—"

"Swear," the witch interrupted him, "with a blood-oath."

He stood very still, praying that he could keep his true thoughts hidden from her eyes.

"Katsu," he said when he could speak safely, "do you know what the blood-oath means on your end?"

"Yes," she said, indifferent. "Money for you—we will pay, easily. Glory, if you wish to claim it; we will not stop you. In fact, you will publicly have the gratitude of Starfall, for the elimination of this threat."

"And three boons."

Even that did not surprise her; she must have done research during that day of waiting. "Of course. Any three things you wish to ask of us, we will grant, if it is within our power."

If I asked you all to drown yourselves, would you do it?

He put his hands behind his back, approximating a Hunter's formal stance, hiding the rigid fists his hands had become. "Out of professional curiosity," Eclipse said, "what happens if I refuse?"

The witch shrugged, but her casual manner carried just the right amount of menace. "The abomination has not come for you yet. She tried to find you with magic and encountered our blocking spell, but after that she seems to have given up the search. There are ways for her to find you without magic. But as she seems not to be interested in following them, your usefulness is at an end."

Meaning that this "offer" was no such thing. He would accept, or he would die here, and never get a chance to accomplish anything.

The knowledge that Mirei hadn't kept searching for him hurt, though he couldn't let it show. *Come on, idiot, she said that in* order *to hurt you. It probably isn't even true.* He prayed it wasn't true. He'd spent the last several days telling himself Mirei meant nothing to him, so he could lie and be believed—but what if he meant nothing to her?

Then he was dead either way, because as slim as his hopes of saving himself were, they depended entirely on her.

The witch was still watching him; he couldn't delay any longer. "So she gave up," Eclipse said, and pasted a cynical grin onto his face. "Told you she wasn't Mirage.

My year-mate would never quit on me that easy." He rubbed at his wrists, scraping off some of the dried blood. "My services won't come cheap, Katsu."

"You believe you're in a position to negotiate?"

"Can anybody else offer you the advantages I can? But this will be risky for me. She's got all the training I have, plus magic. I'm going to need resources to go after her. I'm going to need money."

"You'll get it," the witch said, and nodded at the Cousins to unchain him.

FOR THE FIRST TIME in sixteen to twenty-one days, he left the cell they'd placed him in.

They'd even given him water to wash in—though nothing to shave with. Eclipse scrubbed himself as clean as he could, then followed his guard of Cousins and witch through the halls. They still had shackles on him, as if he might run away, but it was more freedom than he'd had in weeks.

He hadn't seen much of the building when they brought him in, because at the time the only light had come from torches. Now the place was no longer deserted; tallow candles stood dripping in sconces on the walls, and he could hear murmurs behind some of the doors he passed.

Has the feel of a headquarters, he thought. *I wonder where we are?*

The walls and floor were dressed stone, and utilitarian. Didn't feel like a house. A small fort, maybe. He had to be within three or four days' ride of Sethick, where he'd spent the night before the ambush, but that didn't help; Palend, the previous Lord of Abern and father of its current Lady, had inherited from his predecessors an ongoing squabble with Eriot and Miest that peppered Abern's northwestern border with small forts. They were mostly abandoned now, since Palend had made peace with his neighbors. This could be any one of them.

His escort brought him into a room where a number of other women were waiting—and, he saw to his surprise, several men. The light in there was dim, but he memorized what details he could of their appearances. Two short, one tall, and all thickset; two wore the embroidered vests of Kalistyi. What were they doing here?

Another, older witch stood in the center of the room, in front of a table with tools he recognized all too well. She had a pinched, ugly look on her face, as if his very presence in the room offended her.

The escort brought him to the center of the room, and then moved back.

In the moment before anyone spoke, Eclipse sent up a silent prayer, more fervent than any he'd ever framed.

Warrior, Huntress, Lady of Blades. You can kill me later if you want, but if I can beg any mercy from you—don't kill me now. Let me swear this oath, with lies in my heart; let me convince them I mean to kill Mirei. Let me swear, and get out of here, and tell her everything I can, before you exact your retribution for my falseness.

It was all he dared ask for. If there was any way out of a blood-oath, he would have to find it later. And hope in the meantime that there *was* one.

On the table before him were a knife, a silver bowl, and a faceted, clear crystal. Two blood-oathed commissions in less than a year; it had to be a record. Assuming he lived through the swearing. A spell enforced the task of the oath; he had no idea how soon it would kill him for failure. He just knew two things: He wasn't going to die in a cell, and he wasn't going to kill Mirei.

The older witch was apparently the one who would conduct this ritual. Her eyes were almost colorless in the dim light, and the look she gave him was a snarl. "You know the wording of the oath?"

All Hunters learned it. Eclipse nodded.

"We will be changing it," she said.

The bottom dropped out of his stomach. "What?" he blurted, unable to hide his shock.

"As it stands, the oath is insufficient for these circumstances. We have an addition to make to it."

He swallowed the curse words he wanted to spit and instead said, as levelly as he could, "The oath is traditional, and sacred."

Her mouth thinned unpleasantly. "And we are adding to it. You swear what we tell you to, or you die here and now. If you will not Hunt her, we have no use for you."

A good dozen people in the room, several of them witches, and his hands chained in front of him. *I will not die until I have to.* "What's your addition?"

"In addition to binding you to Hunt the abomination, we will require two more things. First, that you tell no one what your task is. Second, that you divulge nothing of what you have seen here—who we are, and where this place is."

Which brought his plans to a crashing halt. If he couldn't say anything, how much good would getting out of here do?

It's better than dying here. You don't have a choice. Swear it, and look for loopholes later.

"What you ask is already a requirement of my honor as

a Hunter," Eclipse said coldly, looking as affronted as he could that she would dare to impugn that honor. "But I will swear it."

The witch wasted no further time. The woman who had cast the spell the first time had made something faintly artistic out of the ritual; this one did not. She took his shackled arm in a clawlike hand, shoved his sleeve up, and slashed the knife across his wrist.

She did it fast enough that he hoped no one noticed the scar right next to it.

His blood fell into the silver bowl, or at least most of it did; he was leaking more energetically than he wanted to. The witch's mouth thinned again in distaste as droplets spattered the table and even her sleeve. *It's your own damn fault for cutting so deep,* Eclipse thought, teeth gritted against the pain. *Now finish the spell before I bleed to death.*

She obliged him on that count, at least. The crystal was in her left hand, humming audibly in the quiet room; she held it above his bleeding wrist and the bowl. "You are charged with the task of Hunting and killing the abomination known as Mirei. Until your Hunt is ended, you will not tell what task you have sworn to, nor what happened to you following your departure from Sethick, nor who and what you have seen since coming here. Should you fail, or break the terms of this oath, you will die. Should you succeed, we who have hired you bind ourselves to grant three boons to you, whenever you might require them. Do you accept?"

Warrior. Do not kill me for these words.

"I swear," Eclipse said, his voice hoarse with tension, "on my oath and my name as a Hunter, that I will devote my utmost efforts to the task, or accept the retribution of the Divine Warrior who holds my oath."

The witch sang the spell itself then, crisp, quick notes that Eclipse had to fight not to flinch back from. The blood rushed upward, past and across his wrist, in utter defiance of gravity, and flowed into the crystal. The witch pocketed the ruby and took his wrist once more in her cold fingers, covering the wound, getting more of his blood on herself.

"Your oath is accepted. You are free to Hunt."

THE TWO SCARS DIDN'T MATCH.

Eclipse took a small amount of solace in the fact that he still had enough of a sense of humor to think such thoughts. The old scar was greenish-brown; if the tales older Hunters told were true, that meant an Earth witch had cast the blood-oath spell. He'd never found out for sure. The new one, though, was silvery-white. Air, he assumed. They looked odd, side by side.

At least only one of them still had the power to kill him. The old commission was fulfilled.

He dragged his eyes away from the scar and looked to the road ahead. The witches had knocked him out and dumped him on the road, so he had no idea where he'd been, but now he was almost to Silverfire. It was the best start he could think of. Mirei had taken with her the enchanted paper that allowed them to communicate with the rebel witches who had given them that old commission; he had no way to contact them now, except to look in the places where he'd met them before, and if they had the brains the Goddess gave mice they wouldn't be there. So he had to start with Jaguar.

One of whose people he was sworn to kill. And Eclipse couldn't tell him that. Or where he had been.

The Silverfire wall appeared on the horizon all too quickly.

The guard was familiar to him: Sickle, the oldest Silverfire still living, whom some said could have been Grandmaster if he had wanted to spend his silver years with the daily headaches the position carried. He'd been clever enough to pass the job off to Jaguar.

Sickle might be old, but his eyes were still sharp. He shouted to Eclipse before the rider even reached the wall. "Go straight in. They've been looking for you."

Eclipse swore yet again and put his gelding to a gallop.

The wall stood a goodly distance from the school itself; he covered that distance in record time. Briar emerged from the stables to see who was arriving in such a hurry, and opened his mouth as Eclipse reined to a halt. "I know," Eclipse said, and threw the reins to Briar as he slid from his saddle. "I'm already going."

The ground-floor room of the building that served as Silverfire's administrative heart was dim, after the brightness of the day. The voice seemed to emerge out of nowhere, before Eclipse's eyes could adjust. "Where in the Void have *you* been?"

"Where's Jaguar?" Eclipse asked. "They said you've been looking for me."

"We have," Slip said acidly. "So nice of you to drop in. The stubble looks lovely. Jaguar's in the main salle, evaluating the twenties."

Back out into the sunlight, now just as blinding as the darkness inside had been. But Eclipse's feet knew the way; he crossed the compound and went into a low building with many oilskin windows to let in the light.

Inside, there was a large, open room with benches and practice equipment lining the walls. Some of the benches were occupied by lean people in dusty uniforms who looked, to Eclipse's jaded eye, like fresh-faced young idiots. The oldest class of trainees at Silverfire—those few who had made it through the ten years of grueling work— they no doubt thought they were ready to take on the world. But Eclipse had been on the road for five years, and neck-deep in witch business since before Midsummer; to him, they looked like green fools.

The pair of men at the far wall were a different story. Both far older than he was, they were watching two of the trainees chase each other around the inside of the salle, blades flashing in the light. Their eyes flicked up at Eclipse's entrance, though, and the older of the two straightened at the sight.

"Continue," Jaguar said to Granite, the advanced weapons master, and beckoned sharply for Eclipse to come to him. Eclipse dropped his salute, crossed the room in the fighters' wake, and followed the Grandmaster through a small door at the back.

The room was an office shared by the Silverfire combat masters; the walls were decorated with charts showing which classes were doing what work at what hours under which instructor, and the shelves held stacks of sheets with observations about each trainee's progress. It was a time-honored tradition among the trainees to try to break into this room and look at their own records. Eclipse himself had not succeeded at the task until he was eighteen. Now, it seemed insignificant.

"Sir," Eclipse said, before Jaguar could get started, "I have a question I need to ask you."

The Grandmaster gave him a narrow, measuring look. "All right."

Eclipse rolled up his right sleeve and displayed the two mismatched scars. "If you violate a blood-oath, how exactly does it kill you?"

Jaguar had gone still at the sight. He knew about the first commission; in fact, he had chosen Eclipse to carry it out, no doubt knowing that Eclipse would choose Mirage as his partner for it. To show up with a second scar so soon, though . . .

"If you break your oath," Jaguar said, his voice low even though they were alone in the room and the door was shut, "then the scar begins to bleed. And no bandage or spell will stop it."

I wonder how long it will take me to bleed to death through one wrist, Eclipse thought with detached curiosity. *If it starts, I'm going to tell Void-damned everything I can before I die. Because at that point, it won't matter.*

"How—" Jaguar began. Eclipse stopped him with an upraised hand, fully aware of how badly he was violating protocol and the respect due to the Grandmaster.

"Sir, unless you want to run the risk of me bleeding to death right here in this office, please let me explain what I can, and forgive me for what I *can't* tell you."

That silenced the older man. He knew the standard wording of the blood-oath as well as anyone, and this had nothing to do with it. Which meant, without Eclipse saying it outright, that he'd sworn a modified version of the oath. And probably not by choice.

Now, the coldly rational part of his mind said, *I find out how far I can go without dying. Carefully. And depend on Jaguar's ability to listen to how I say things, and hear what isn't said, and put the pieces together.*

And hope the Goddess doesn't blast me for giving things away semi-on–purpose. They told me I couldn't say stuff. Not that I couldn't betray it by other means.

The intent had been obvious. The wording hadn't. Hopefully the loophole would be enough.

Eclipse took a deep breath. "Sir. The first commission is finished, you'll be glad to know. I haven't seen my employers in a while, so I haven't been able to collect the rest of my fee, or ask for the boons I'm due." *Taking this damn thing off me will be boon number one.*

Jaguar nodded, processing this information, hopefully picking out the hint that the original set of witches were *not* the ones who had placed this second oath on him.

So far, so good. "Unfortunately," Eclipse went on, "I can't tell you where I've been." True in two senses; even without the oath, he still didn't know specifics. "But I have other information I'm supposed to give you, which Mirage asked me to bring here."

"I know," the Grandmaster said. "It's how we knew to be missing you. She showed up here not long ago."

The bottom dropped out of Eclipse's stomach, sickeningly. "She's *here*? Mi—Mirage?" He'd almost said Mirei.

Unblinking, Jaguar took in his reaction. And the stutter. "I know what she sent you to tell me, and more besides," he said. "I know how she's changed. She came here to take the two trainees—the doppelgangers—to Starfall."

His words took Eclipse completely by surprise. "To *Starfall*?"

"She said it was the only place where they would be safe."

The world inverted around Eclipse, leaving him with no clue which way was up. How long had he been gone, and what in the *Void* had happened while he was? "Last time I spoke to her, Starfall *was* the danger."

"Not anymore," Jaguar said. "Not exactly. She said there were problems among the witches. The Air Prime still wants to kill these girls. And she knows where they are—or rather, where they have been—so those who want to keep them alive are taking them to Starfall." His aged faced shifted into hard, bitter lines. "They were not safe here."

"But the other Primes are on her side now?" Eclipse asked, trying to wrap his mind around the sudden change. "Where *is* Mirei?"

He would have taken the question back if he could have. As long as he didn't know that, he was one step further away from having to kill her or die. And that impulse, his dread of the answer, must have shown on his face, because Jaguar went instantly wary.

"We don't—" the Grandmaster began, then checked himself. "Mirei?"

Did I just make two mistakes at once? "I thought you said you knew how she's changed."

"I do," Jaguar said. "But 'Mirei'?"

"It's who she is, now. The Goddess gave her a new name."

"The Goddess," Jaguar repeated, his tone flat.

"When she became whole again. When Miryo and Mirage became a single person."

The Grandmaster's eyes had narrowed again, taking this

in. Eclipse glanced down and saw that the man's hands had gone tense, where they hung at his sides. "I thought," Jaguar said, "that it was a spell."

"It was." How had Eclipse gotten saddled with trying to explain this? Nearly everything he knew about the theory behind magic, he'd learned from eavesdropping on Miryo's explanations to Mirage. That hardly qualified him for this. "Magic is religious, apparently. New spells get invented through divine inspiration; particularly devoted witches learn how to do new things. Or something like that. Miryo and Mirage were praying, and then poof, they were one person again. And she told me the Goddess had given her a new name, like she did for the first witch."

Jaguar shook his head, with an expression more unguarded than any Eclipse had seen on him before. "So she really isn't the woman we knew."

Eclipse shrugged awkwardly. "Kind of. She half is and half isn't."

"I know." The Grandmaster sighed and sank down to lean against the edge of the desk. "I knew. She told me that. But hearing a different name . . . makes it harder."

Time for another gamble, Eclipse thought, and hoped for luck. "I said something like that not too long ago myself, about her not being my year-mate anymore. I didn't really mean it, but sometimes people take you seriously anyway."

And that visibly snapped Jaguar's attention back to the clue of a moment before, forgotten in the confusion over Mirei's name. "You wanted to know where she is."

"Might be useful, if I had some reason to find her," Eclipse said, not even trying to pretend his attitude matched the casual words.

"I imagine she might like to see you," Jaguar said, watching him closely.

"At first, sure. Might not be real happy with me for long, though."

Jaguar nodded, slowly, gaze still intent. "Well, as I started to say a moment ago, we don't know *where* she is. We even got a message from Starfall, asking what's happened to her. I don't think anyone can find her."

Relief washed over Eclipse, taking away a tiny fraction of his tension. *Looks like the Goddess is on my side, at least a little.* "I might have to go looking for her, then. I wonder how long that'll take."

It was enough. Jaguar gave a quick, sharp nod, and Eclipse knew to shut his mouth before he could say the wrong thing and bleed to death. The message had been conveyed, without ever being said outright. The Grandmaster knew what job he had sworn to.

Now, Eclipse thought, *let's find the bitches who did this to me.*

Chapter Eleven

❦━━◆━━◆━━❦

THE CONVOY THAT TRAVELED south to Starfall was not a subtle one.

Witches, Cousins, eleven-year-old girls, and one prisoner tied up in the back of a wagon under constant guard; there were over twenty women in the group, all told. Satomi was taking no more chances. Well, almost none; she had ordered Mirei back to Starfall, told her to translocate and let the others catch up later.

Mirei had refused.

She owed it to the girls to stay. To Amas and Lehant, anyway; Indera wasn't speaking to her. Mirei had promised Jaguar to train them, and had semi-promised the same thing to them directly. She was the Grandmaster of this minuscule school, and the closest thing they had to a friend in this group of strangers. She couldn't abandon them.

Satomi had disagreed. Mirei had ignored her. She was not looking forward to the confrontation she expected when she arrived with them in Starfall.

But for now, she rode south, and trained the girls as they went. Indera sulked at first, refusing to participate, but in the end her love of her body's strength won out; she was silent as she trained, but driven. As if she was going to enjoy every minute of this while she could.

As if, perhaps, she was hoping she could get strong enough to escape for real. But Mirei would worry about that later.

They were more than halfway to the domain's border when Amas finally worked up the nerve to ask Mirei the question that had clearly been on her mind for some time. "What's it like?" the doppelganger asked, her voice quiet, barely audible over the irregular rhythm of hooves along the hard-packed dirt of the road. "Meeting . . . the other one?"

Even though it was Amas, the ever-level, Mirei could hear the unease behind the words. For the first time, she considered that in some ways it had truly been easier for the Mirage half of herself, not knowing that the meeting was going to happen.

"Odd," she said after some consideration. Lehant, riding to her left, edged her own horse closer to hear. The girl's hair was growing out into a coppery stubble; she looked very different without the smooth scalp. "I won't pretend it's anything less than odd. But it isn't *bad*."

"You don't sound very sure," Lehant said.

Mirei shook her head. "You've got to understand the situation I was in. The witch-half of me, Miryo, was trying to convince herself to kill the doppelganger-half of me. Mirage, on the other hand, had no idea Miryo even existed. So from the one perspective, it was all shock and confusion and the very real possibility that I was going to die, while from the other, it was fear and revulsion and the very real possibility that I was going to kill someone. Not a very good way to begin."

She paused, looking without seeing at a spot between her horse's ears. She was back on Mist, the gray mare she'd left in Angrim when she rejoined, and the saddle felt like an old friend. "Yet for all of that . . . I was meeting myself. That's the only way to describe it."

The dull thudding of hooves on hardpack filled the silence before Amas said, "But you didn't *know* her. The witch."

"Or the doppelganger," Mirei reminded her. "I know you look at me and see Mirage, but I'm both. Neither half of me knew the other. But it didn't matter, and that's the point. That's what made it so strange. There was familiarity, even though I'd never seen myself before. Seen the other half of me, that is."

Lehant jerked her chin over her shoulder at where Indera rode among a guard of very beefy and well-armed Cousins. "You think that'll convince *her*?"

Mirei hoped meeting Sharyo would soothe Indera's fears, but it might not be that easy. "I pray so," she said. "For her sake."

More silence, more riding; Lehant seemed about to move off when Amas asked one last question.

"What are their names?"

Mirei closed her eyes and ran through the list in her mind, pairing girls up. Urishin was Naspeth's doppelganger; there would be no meeting between them, yet. The witch Mirei had captured was tied up in the wagon that trundled along in their wake, heavily guarded; whether she knew anything of use would have to wait for others to discover. There were no other leads on the missing girls as yet.

"Yours is Hoseki," Mirei said. "Lehant's is Owairi. You'll meet them soon enough." *And Indera will meet hers sooner than she wants to.*

* * *

THEY DID NOT STOP for the night in Samalan. Everyone who had been recruited for the escort plainly felt they would only be safe once they crossed the border into Starfall, or better yet, once they reached the settlement. With a witch tied up in a wagon behind them and three walking targets in their midst, Mirei couldn't argue it. And by then the trainees were tough enough to stick out the extra hours in the saddle.

The town, lying on the border between Starfall and Currel, was familiar to Mirei; she had passed through it more than once. She described it to the girls as they rode by its western edge, giving them details on the witches who lived there, the inn she had stayed at, the effort it took to make sure the townspeople didn't gouge travelers with their prices.

Nothing terribly exciting on its own, but the trainees' interest in her words was clear enough that she kept talking as they rode on. It was easy to forget that none of them had journeyed much from home; these southern mountains were exotic and new to them. If they were to be expected to stay here for long, of course they would want to know what the place was like.

So Mirei told them about the domain of Starfall, which had been her home for fifteen years. With fond detail, she described the orchards on these slopes, the farms on the coastal plateaus, worked mainly by Cousins, with assistance from Earth witches who kept the weather in balance. The main settlement lay in the mountains proper, and she told them what to expect when they came there. She sang the sentry spells into quiet, and explained about their presence; she mentioned that there would be guards when they reached the Starfall settlement, but did not bring up the patrols in the area. If Indera was hoping to escape again, no sense giving her extra information.

They arrived in the settlement after dusk, when hardly anything could be seen of the place but the dark bulks of the various buildings and the lofty, glowing windows of Star Hall. No reconstruction had yet been done on the shattered crossing; jagged edges of stone still outlined themselves against the stars. That was a story she still hadn't told them.

It would have to wait. Mirei hadn't even dismounted yet in the front courtyard when a Cousin was at her stirrup. "The Void Prime commands your presence."

"I'll bet she does," Mirei murmured under her breath, too quiet for the woman to hear, then raised her voice to the rest of the group. "They have rooms for you. I'll come find you tonight if I get a chance. If not, then be out here at dawn."

"Dawn?" Lehant said, clearly startled.

Mirei grinned. "Training doesn't stop just because we're here. Meet me in this courtyard. Now that you're not riding every day, I can *really* start to work with you."

Assuming Satomi leaves me alive, she added inwardly, and followed the Cousin.

THE VOID PRIME'S ANGER had cooled to solid ice during the long days of Mirei's ride south with the doppelgangers. She regarded Mirei now over the expanse of her desk with hard, unforgiving eyes, and Mirei reflected with only a weak shadow of humor that this was probably not one of the times she could take liberties and sit down.

"Your behavior," Satomi said, enunciating each word as if it were a weapon, "is unacceptable."

Mirei chose her own words carefully. "With all due respect, Aken, the doppelgangers are very nervous. I didn't feel I could in good conscience leave them alone on the journey down here."

"That's not the *point*!" Satomi shot back, and one hand slapped the surface of her desk. Mirei jumped at the sound. "The *point* is that I did not hear from you for *days*. A message after you left Silverfire: you had the two, and your friend was missing. Then *nothing*. Nine days without a single *word* from you."

"Aken, when I sent that first message I told you I would write once I had something new to report. There was nothing to say, on the ride to Angrim, and then once I got there I was so busy—"

"So busy that in all those days, you couldn't find a spare moment to notify us of your progress?"

"It took us a long time to reach Angrim," Mirei said, feeling defensive. "Longer than I expected. And I didn't want to use magic in front of the girls—"

It was a mistake, but she realized that too late. Satomi's expression grew poisonous. "You *what*?"

Now how in the Void do I explain this without making her even more angry? "Amas and Indera knew of me as Mirage," she said, trying to keep her tone placatory. "The easiest way to get their cooperation was to keep that image up. I wanted to tell all the doppelgangers at once, too; it's a complicated thing to explain, and I didn't want to have to do it over and over again. So I let them think I was still Mirage. And when they learned the truth—well, Indera ran off. I had to find her before she got too far away."

Satomi stood, but did not move out from behind her desk. She placed both hands on the polished wood and leaned forward to glare at Mirei. The woman was truly furious; Mirei had never seen her in this state.

"You are *not* Mirage," the Void Prime spat. "You are *not* a Hunter, a free blade wandering where you please, without answering to anyone else. You are a part of something much larger, now, and it is *unacceptable* for you to assume that you may put off informing others of your actions. While you were riding around Abern, a newborn doppelganger died. While you were concerned for the tender sensibilities of those few girls, a second Prime left Starfall, and took a great many witches with her. We are splintering apart, and you seem to think that you are still an independent agent. *You are not.* We must act together—all of us who hope to change our traditions—if we are to have any hope of surviving this strife."

By the end of it, Mirei couldn't meet her gaze. She looked down at her own hands, fingers twisted around each other. Mirage's hands, with their calluses, hard knuckles, tendons standing out against the skin.

But she was not Mirage. And she *had* forgotten that. There were moments when she could have written to Satomi, given updates on her progress, and she hadn't.

That was a mistake.

Satomi was halfway right. The Void Prime was too quick to forget her Hunter loyalties, and that was an error—but these past days, it was true, Mirei had been too quick to forget her loyalties to Starfall.

How in the Goddess's many names am I supposed to balance the two out?

She didn't know. But she could—she *must*—begin by apologizing to Satomi. "You're right," Mirei said, still not looking up. "And I'm sorry. I'm used to assuming that I'm the only one I can rely on in a crisis. The work I was doing—it was Mirage's kind of work. It made me forget what other resources I have. And what responsibilities."

A long silence followed that, during which she could not quite work up the nerve to meet the Void Prime's eyes. She had seen Jaguar like this a handful of times. She hadn't realized Satomi was capable of the same withering fury.

"You are right about the responsibilities," Satomi said at last. Her voice was quieter, but still unforgiving. "And I'm afraid you will find them heavy indeed. I must have your promise that you will not forget them again."

"I promise," Mirei murmured, not allowing herself to hesitate.

"Good." There was a scrape of a chair across the tiled floor as Satomi sat again. "Then sit down, and let me tell you what you have missed."

Arinei's departure Mirei had heard about, but Satomi filled her in on the details. They made Mirei cringe. One dissident Prime had been enough of an issue, but two was far worse, especially with Arinei's political influence.

"Now that you're back," Satomi said when she was done, "we have work for you. There is a very valid concern among many of the witches that we don't know enough of how your magic works, and what repercussions it may have. You'll be working with a group we've put together, who will put you through various tests."

Not a problem in and of itself, but Mirei had been contemplating other plans. "Aken, we're still missing Naspeth—"

"And others as well." The Void Prime cut her off coolly, before she could even make her argument. "We'll be following up on that, and questioning the witch you brought to us. But other women will work on that matter. No one else has your magic; therefore you are needed here."

"I made a promise to the Grandmaster of Windblade," Mirei said in a low voice. "I feel personally responsible for getting her back."

Satomi's mouth thinned, perhaps at the allusion to her Hunter loyalties. "She *will* be retrieved. But at the moment, that is not your concern."

Mirei should have left it at that, but there was one more issue she couldn't brush off. "And what about Eclipse? Am I forbidden to search for him, too?"

The Void Prime's reaction startled her. Satomi closed her eyes, looking pained, and did not answer.

"What is it?" Mirei said, her stomach twisting into a knot.

Satomi rose again and went to the window. Mirei was beginning to recognize that as a mark of uneasiness, an action the woman took to calm herself when distressed. Seeing her do it now was not reassuring.

"Your year-mate has been found," the Void Prime said.

Mirei gathered her emotions under tight control. "Is he dead?"

"No."

Relief washed over her like cool rain. "Then what's the problem?" Because clearly there *was* one.

Satomi placed her hands on the edges of the window, her slender fingers pale against the stone. "He has not been able to tell anyone the details of his absence, but we can fill them in. Before your rejoining, when we had Miryo in captivity, we made plans to capture Mirage, as well. We could not search for you directly then—not with a spell— but we had gained enough information on Eclipse to find *him.* Assuming you would be with him, we sent a very large detachment of Cousins to capture you."

But Mirage had left Eclipse, sending him to Silverfire with information for Jaguar, while she herself went after Miryo. A stupid plan that had also, apparently, been very well-timed.

Then anger boiled up inside her as she mapped out the timing in her head. "And you didn't bother to call them *off?*"

"I did," Satomi snapped, and turned to face her. "I am neither a fool nor a tyrant." The annoyance drained out of her with visible speed. "But Shimi was the one responsible for coordinating that group."

It wasn't hard to fill in. "She never told them to stop."

"Apparently not." Satomi looked tired. "They captured him, and kept him prisoner, and she did not tell us."

Mirei took a deep breath, forcing her anger down. If Shimi had still been there at Starfall . . . but she wasn't, and so there was no one to vent her fury on. "You said he's been found," she said once she was calmer. "Where?"

"He reappeared at Silverfire," Satomi replied. "Your Grandmaster sent us a message. And I am told he is not physically harmed."

Mirei's eyes shot to her. "Not *physically.*"

Satomi put her hands on the windowsill behind her, as if she were too weary to stand without support. "Your Grandmaster has been forced to piece this together from what Eclipse has *not* said, as it seems he's been placed under some magical compulsion not to speak. But it appears he did not escape; he was released. And there was a condition of that release."

Her mouth was dry with fear. "Which is?"

"We believe he has sworn a blood-oath to kill you."

The chair skidded on the tiles and fell over backward as Mirei shot to her feet. "That's not possible."

"Mirei—"

"He's my *year-mate*. He's a *friend*." The words would hardly come out; her jaw was stiff with shock and disbelief. "He isn't— He would never—"

"He wasn't given a *choice*," Satomi said, over her continued stuttering protests. "He can't tell the details, but we are sure of that much."

"So what, he was *forced* to swear the oath?" Mirei realized she was shouting, and realized she didn't care. "How can the Warrior accept it, if the person doesn't mean the Void-damned words they're *saying*—"

Satomi came forward with quick strides and tried to take her by the shoulders; Mirei slapped her hands away. The Void Prime's face hardened. "Control yourself," she snapped. "You will not help him by attacking me."

Mirei wrenched herself back a few steps, out of the range where she would be tempted to use her fists on the other woman.

"The blood-oath is a spell," Satomi said grimly. "As we have been painfully reminded of late, though spells are created by acts of faith, they continue to function even if that faith is misguided. Even if it is gone. How many of the women here truly feel personal devotion to the Goddess, the way Misetsu did? We began that way, but we have not continued in that path. If you know the words, know the pitches, have the power to fuel them, then the spell works. Eclipse, as far as I'm aware, has not cared to test whether the oath truly binds him, and that is wise of him. I'm sure it's effective. The spell holds you to the words you have spoken—not what is in your heart."

"That's a *shitty* system," Mirei muttered, and knew the protest was childish even as she said it.

Satomi, kindly, did not point that out. "He's safe for now. Be grateful for that. But you must not go anywhere near him."

Mirei wanted to rebel against the order, but it wasn't for her own good; it was for Eclipse's. The farther he stayed away from her, the less risk that the spell would consider his oath broken. She wouldn't risk his life by pushing that. "I understand," she said, and meant it, even though the words came out through clenched teeth. "I'll just have to work at a distance."

"I beg your pardon?"

She bent and righted the chair she'd knocked over, but did not sit again. "Is there any way to undo a blood-oath?"

A painful pause, and then Satomi's quiet answer. "No."

Mirei smiled, with no humor in it. "Just like there's no way to cancel a spell outright. Or to translocate a living creature. Unless, of course, you're me. Void magic has proved its ability to do things we thought were impossible. It'll just have to do so again."

She didn't voice the doubts already growing in her mind. The things she had done so far, she had learned through divine inspiration, because the Goddess was with her. They didn't happen on demand. To consciously reach for a specific effect—

She would just have to do it. Because otherwise, Eclipse was dead.

"May the Goddess aid you in your search," Satomi said, and there was a quiet faith in her voice that steadied Mirei's nerves. To save the life of a friend: It wasn't a selfish goal. Surely the Goddess would look with favor on it.

Even if he swore an oath falsely?

She couldn't let herself think about that.

"Sit down," Satomi said, and Mirei did.

Her mind was already shunting the fear aside, focusing on the problem of how to undo the oath—could she cancel it? But each kind of spell canceled differently, and she was having a hard time learning how to do new ones. The blood-oath was especially complicated. But if she studied how it was constructed—she knew the general theory, of course, but it wasn't something they taught witch-students about in exhaustive detail, as it was so rarely used—she might be able to work it out logically. . . .

"There's one other thing I must tell you about," Satomi said, breaking her reverie.

Mirei looked up. "Oh?"

Satomi's expression was startlingly somber. "Has anyone spoken to you about Eikyo?"

"No," Mirei said slowly, wondering what the woman meant by it. Their caravan had only just reached Starfall; she'd had no chance to speak to anyone else since arriving, let alone find Eikyo.

Then she remembered how much time had passed—and what was supposed to have happened.

Mirei opened her mouth to say something more, but the words died as she looked into Satomi's eyes.

"I'm sorry," the Void Prime said softly.

Mirei sat, numb.

"The Keys passed her in the initial questioning," Satomi went on, her voice too gentle for the terrible words. "If that is any small comfort. But when it came to the test itself—I'm sorry. Eikyo has become a Cousin."

Hands shaking, breath almost stopped, Mirei sat frozen in her chair. Not dead. A Cousin.

Eikyo had feared that as much as death. Maybe more. She might as *well* be dead.

"Where—where is she?" Mirei heard herself ask, as if from a great distance.

"You know I can't tell you that," Satomi said; under the compassion, there was an uneasy edge. "She must begin a new life, away from those who knew her. That is kindest."

Mirei opened her mouth again, found she had nothing to say. The shaking had grown worse. Fear welled up from where she'd shoved it out of the way. Eikyo gone, Eclipse gone—the dearest friends of her two halves, each of them taken away, maybe forever. A Cousin, her memory wiped clean. And a blood-oath, that would drive him to kill her— but he would never do that. Which meant he would die.

Hot wetness splashed her hands: she was crying. Realizing that broke through the last of her self-control, and she buried her face in her trembling hands, too hurt to care that she was breaking down in front of the Void Prime. Satomi was on her side, but she was not a friend. *They* were friends. Had been. Both of them, gone at the same time. Blows she hadn't seen coming, and the pain was too much to take.

Distantly she felt a touch on her shoulder, heard a voice speaking words that came and went without meaning. She wanted to leave, but couldn't get up.

A change in Satomi's voice. The woman was singing. Mirei sensed the power move, but couldn't be bothered to figure out what it was. She didn't really care.

"Mirei," Satomi said again, and this time the insistence of her tone broke through. "Listen to me. *Listen.* What I said to you was a lie."

It startled her enough that her breath snagged in her throat; she let it out again to speak. "What?"

"Eikyo is fine," the Void Prime said, and Mirei, lifting her chin, saw that the woman was pale but sincere. "She isn't a Cousin."

Wonderful words, but they made no sense at all. "I don't understand."

Satomi sighed and crouched in front of Mirei, dignity and rank momentarily laid aside. "The Keys questioned her, and then we took her into Star Hall, and as far as anyone remembers—other than she and I—she failed, and became a Cousin. But it isn't true."

The meaning of that sank in slowly. "Why?" Mirei rasped.

"Because I needed someone to spy on the Cousins for me. And she had offered to help." Satomi ran one hand over her face. If she had looked tired before, now she seemed weary beyond death. "They're a part of this world of ours, here in Starfall, and out in the domains; I wanted to know more about them. Since they won't answer questions, this seemed the only way. But Arinei knows. She doesn't remember, but she knows; she left a note for herself, because she was afraid I was going to do . . . well, exactly what I did. I think it's part of why she left."

Mirei didn't give half a damn about Arinei at the moment; she was drowning in relief. "Where is she?"

"Insebrar," Satomi said. "Or rather, she's on her way there. I want her to try and find out how Mirage survived. Whatever she learns out there, she'll send back to me, in code."

Had Satomi asked her, Mirei would have said that Eikyo was not at all suited for the life of a spy. The Void

Prime should have waited for a more suitable candidate; nobody at Starfall was formally trained in espionage, but at least there were some better liars. Mirei was too drained to try and argue the point, though, and it wouldn't help anyway. Eikyo had been sent. If she gave herself away, they'd deal with it.

Satomi glanced at the walls of her office. "I don't dare keep the spell up much longer, so let me say this quickly."

Spell? Mirei recalled Satomi singing a moment before. *Something to block eavesdropping.*

"Let *no one* know about Eikyo," the Prime said. "Everyone thinks she failed the test—even the other Primes. I even intended for you to believe it, but you . . . I had to tell you the truth. Still, though, you must keep the fiction up. If for no other reason than that I'm not at all certain how the Cousins would react, if they knew."

Mirei would no more endanger Eikyo's safety than she would Eclipse's. "I understand."

"Good." Satomi sang again, more briefly, and around her Mirei felt the spell subside.

The Void Prime returned to her desk and sat down. "Now," she said, her tone more businesslike. "We have tasks for you here. See Hyoka after you leave me; she will give you the details of the tests she wants to conduct."

"How long will those take?" Mirei asked.

Satomi favored her with a cool look, devoid of any sign of the compassion she had shown moments before. "As long as they have to."

Mirei told herself to accept that and not argue. *She's right: It* is *important.* And it would give her time to research some more immediately pressing questions.

Like how to keep Eclipse from dying.

PART TWO

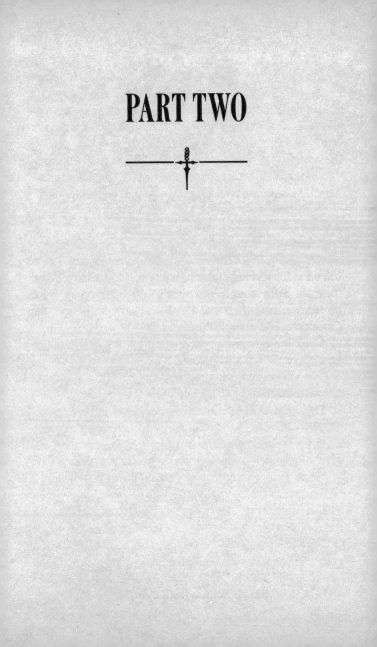

Chapter Twelve

⸎⸎⸎━━┼━━━━┼━━⸎⸎⸎

Edame waited until the heavy, carved door had swung shut and they were alone in the room before she turned to Mirei and raised one eyebrow wryly. "Well," she said, "that could have gone better. But it also could have gone worse."

Mirei dropped bonelessly back into the plush embrace of her chair. "I know."

The Fire Hand shrugged philosophically. She wasn't much older than Mirei—surprisingly young to be a domain-level adviser—but her experience here in Haira, working with Lord Iseman and Lady Terica, meant that meetings like the one just concluded were old, familiar territory for her. "Don't be too discouraged," she said, her face re-assuming much of the cocky cast it usually wore. "The ministers may be giving you squint-eyed looks, but you have Iseman and Terica on your side, and that's what counts. They can work on the ministers for you. Or just step on them, if it comes to that."

Rubbing her eyes in weary silence, Mirei tried to take encouragement from the words. She *did* have the Lord and Lady of Haira on her side, and that was no small thing. A deft bit of diplomacy—mostly Edame's work and Satomi's, but Mirei had done her part, too—had turned some of their most inflexible opponents into their strongest allies.

The married couple who ruled this domain were staunch Avannans, followers of a sect that was strong in Haira. Avannans honored a form of ceremonial Dance as the highest form of worship. The body in motion was the domain of the Warrior. Therefore, Avannans revered the Warrior particularly. A neat little chain that had, in the past, made them not particularly friendly—though not actively hostile—to witches, for the Warrior was by far the most neglected Aspect among Starfall's people.

Edame had used that very dislike to get her Lord and Lady on Satomi's side. Or rather, on Mirei's.

Mirei was not only a former Temple Dancer herself; she was a correction of the very imbalance that had set Avannans against witches. Once that was made clear, Iseman and Terica had seen it almost as a divine duty to help the witches make this change. In other words, to oppose the dissidents under Shimi and Arinei.

Mirei would have taken more comfort from that knowledge if she weren't so tired. Haira was not the only place Satomi had been sending her over the last few months, since she brought the doppelgangers to Starfall. In fact, she'd ricocheted all over the land, going to every domain but Kalistyi. She was both the strongest advocate they had for the new way, and the only one who could get herself to wherever she needed to be without losing weeks in travel. Not all the places she went, though, were success stories like Haira.

This domain was on their side. So was Eriot, the other major center of Avannan worship. Kalistyi, on the other hand, was solidly with Shimi's people. The rest were a patchwork of political battlegrounds, and Mirei was not cut out for politics.

She must have said that last out loud, because Edame laughed and said, "No offense, but I agree. Not this kind of politics, anyway. But you'll have to learn to do *some* of this, if you're going to survive in the Void Ray."

That startled Mirei into dropping her hands and staring up at the Fire Hand. "I *what*?" Sometimes it was hard to follow Edame's mercurial shifts, but this one had truly come out of nowhere. "I'm not going to be in the Void Ray. I'm planning on choosing Air." She hadn't even thought about that for a while. The troubles among the witches had driven such traditions straight out of her head.

Edame pursed her lips in a way that meant she was trying not to grin and said, "Sure."

"I mean it," Mirei said, sitting upright.

"Oh, I don't doubt you mean it. That's not where you're going, though." Edame looked at her, then made an exasperated noise. "Oh, come *on*, Mirei. Either you're ignoring it on purpose, or this blinking about that you do confuses the brain worse than I thought; there's no way you're dumb enough to miss it otherwise. You're being groomed, my dear."

"For what? Void Prime?" Mirei said it sarcastically, and got raised eyebrows in return. "You've got to be *kidding*."

"Who else is like you are? Sure, there'll be more eventually, but right now, we've got precisely one of you."

"So?" Mirei raked her hair out of her face in irritation. It was getting longer; she needed to decide whether to cut it Hunter-style again, or let it grow out. *What are you doing, dodging her point?* "The Rays don't have to do with magic—come on, you know that! They're about who you work with and what problems you solve. And the Keys and the Primes are administrative jobs, organizational ones.

Being able to use Void magic doesn't give me a damn bit of qualification for that."

Edame nodded, infuriatingly smug. "Which is why they're grooming you. So that you'll *get* qualified." Smugness faded to exasperation. "Do you really think they're going to let the first witch of your kind live out her life as some random Air Hand? They're going to keep you at Starfall—when they're not sending you on training runs—make you a Void Key the first chance they get, and then stick you in Satomi's place when she croaks."

Mirei remembered to close her mouth so she wouldn't sit there gaping like a landed fish. *That's not what I want to do with my life,* she thought, and then *So? What you wanted was never going to carry much weight. Not since you decided to be all clever and find a new way of doing things.*

"Uh-huh," Edame said, as if she could read Mirei's thoughts. "Come on, let's get out of here."

They left the chamber where they'd met with the council of ministers, and went through the halls of Haira Keep back to the guest quarters where Mirei was being housed. They kept them in readiness for her, these days; she was in and out often enough to merit it.

Their path took them through a small hall Mirei remembered very well. The chairs and curtain that had been there were gone, leaving the room empty, but she recognized the lurid sunset mural on one wall and the galleries that overlooked from above. Temple Dancers had performed here, once, dancing the Aspects of the Goddess for the Avannan devout of Haira.

Edame, seeing that Mirei had lagged behind, paused. After a moment, she asked, "How strange *is* it?"

It was the first time the Fire Hand had ever asked about Mirei's experiences. For all her garrulous chatter, it was the one topic she had conspicuously avoided.

Mirei shook her head, still looking around, remembering the various Dances and the responses they'd called up from her unstable magic. "Not as strange as it was. If I stop and think about it, I know that some of my memories are Miryo's, and some are Mirage's. But these days, if I don't stop, then they're my memories. That's all. I just have more of them than most people do."

"It makes me wonder," Edame said softly, then stopped.

Wonder what her doppelganger would have been like. Wonder what it would feel like, had she become what Mirei was now. It was a sentiment Mirei had heard from dozens of witches, all aware of what they had lost. She had no answers for them, or for Edame, either, and after an awkward moment of silence, they continued on out of the hall.

"So you're leaving again?" Edame asked, as Mirei folded a shirt and tucked it into her pack.

"Again," Mirei said, trying not to make it a groan.

"Where to?"

"Back to Starfall. Satomi's promised me I can take a break." Not very willingly, but the Void Prime had promised. Mirei had nearly resorted to admitting how much of a toll translocation exacted from her. The spell was an exhausting one, but its usefulness was such that Satomi was constantly sending her to one domain after another, back to Starfall, back out again, like a hawk being trained to fly from the wrist.

Edame nodded. "Tell her there's a new delegation

arriving from Teria soon, and that we'll go to work on them. Could be I can wheedle some support out of them."

That was a political task Satomi *hadn't* assigned to Mirei, so she gratefully left it to Edame. She slung the pack over her shoulders, tied it in place, and went into the sitting room. The furniture that had once occupied it was mostly gone; she had less need of furniture than of space. With Edame watching—the Fire Hand had seen it often enough that it no longer startled her, though she watched every time—Mirei used her voice and body to weave the spell that would take her back to Starfall.

She landed hard, it seemed, or perhaps it was just the vertigo that overtook her as she arrived. Her ears rang and her vision momentarily grayed out; she took two lurching steps before catching herself and waiting for it to clear.

She felt a hand under her elbow. When she could see again, the hand proved to be Rigai's. The Void witch was a tiny thing, a full head shorter than Mirei and slender enough to break in a good wind, but she looked prepared to catch Mirei should she fall. Or at least prepared to try. "Are you all right?"

"Headache," Mirei said through her teeth. Rigai led her across the room that had been set aside as her translocation target, seated her in one of the few remaining chairs, and pulled a feather out of one sleeve. Seeing it, Mirei said, "Were you waiting for me?"

"Hyoka said you were due back this afternoon." Rigai sang quietly, brushing the feather across Mirei's forehead. The sensation of power weaving into a lacework made Mirei wince, but then its effect settled in, and the pain receded. "I thought you might need help," the witch said when she was done, tucking the focus away once more.

Mirei didn't want to think about the predictability of that need. "Thanks. I promised to work with the girls today. And no doubt I've got paperwork waiting for me, too." Would they really try to make her a Void Key? She hadn't even been inducted into the Ray yet.

"Before you go," Rigai said as Mirei made to rise, "I'd like a moment of your time. I believe I may have found something that could help you."

Moments of Mirei's time were a vanishing commodity these days, but Rigai's words nailed her back into her chair. One of Mirei's first actions after returning to Starfall with the doppelgangers had been to call in one of the three boons she and Eclipse were owed from their commission. She'd asked for help in finding ways to break a blood-oath, and Rigai had been taking care of archival research for them.

Had been. "I thought you weren't working on that anymore," Mirei said.

"I wasn't," Rigai admitted. The archival approach had proved fruitless, so they'd given it up. "But I came across something while researching a subject Satomi-aken assigned to me."

Knowing Satomi, that could be anything. Mirei tried not to feel too hopeful; there had been dead ends before. Still . . . "What is it?"

Rigai sat down in a chair opposite her and folded her hands neatly in her lap. "The Prime asked me to look into the history of the Nalochkan sect. She hopes that knowing more about them will help us against Shimi and Lady Chaha."

The woman's mind worked at odd angles, but this seemed odder than most—what could it have to do with the oath? Mirei was willing to clutch at any strand of hope she was offered, though; they were few enough already, and the danger to Eclipse grew with every day. She bit her tongue and waited for Rigai to explain.

The witch seemed more hesitant to do so than usual. "The first thing you must remember is that the text I found this in is *very* old. It's a copy of an earlier manuscript from the opening days of the Three Kingdoms period, from Tserenar, and the practices it references are even older than that. They may well predate Misetsu's miracle."

As Starfall's view of history tended to begin with Misetsu, disregarding practically everything before her, that was especially startling. *And how can this help with the blood-oath, if it's before magic?*

"The warlords of eastern Tserenar had a practice at the time," Rigai went on, warming to her subject. Like most of Hyoka's theory witches, she could talk endlessly about her pet research. "If one of them fell ill and seemed in danger of dying, then his priests would attempt to appease the Warrior, so she would not take his life."

Now that sounds more promising. The Warrior is the one who judges a blood-oath. "Did it work?" Mirei asked, mostly succeeding at keeping her voice level. Everything else had led to a dead end so far. Breaking the crystal used in the ritual would do nothing. No healing could save him once his judgment came. She had no way of canceling or counteracting the spell, and even if it was possible for the original caster to release him from it, she didn't know who that had been.

"The stories say it did, but we must take them with more than a few grains of salt, I'm afraid. The common folk today claim efficacy for various charms and wards, but many witches have studied them, and have found no proof that they function. There's a theory that such practices may have held more power before the advent of true magic, but we have no way of proving that."

Mirei forced a smile. "I'll try anything. What did they do?"

Rigai hesitated again, and the reason was soon clear. "They offered the Warrior a different life in place of the one they feared to lose."

"Another life?" Mirei looked at the witch's expression, and felt her budding euphoria drain away. "You don't mean—"

"Human sacrifice."

Mirei stared at her. "You're joking."

"Not at all. The Nalochkans arose as a sect because they abhorred this practice. Over time, that attitude grew into an abhorrence for the Warrior, who supposedly accepted such gruesome trades. From there, it was a short step to demonize that Aspect, and name her an entity entirely separate from the other four faces of the Goddess. There was an offshoot sect, the Velejkans, who denied the existence of the Warrior entirely, claiming she was a false and powerless idol, but they died out during—" Rigai saw Mirei's face, and broke off. "At any rate, this is how I came to uncover the reference."

"Are you suggesting," Mirei said, "that I kill someone else to save Eclipse?" She ignored the vision of Ice dancing in the back of her mind, and the vision of Shimi.

Rigai at least had the decency to look startled. She probably *had* considered it, but only in the distant, theoretical way the witches of the Head tended to. The idea that Mirei might *do* it had likely never crossed her mind.

"I just thought it might be of use," Rigai said. "A new angle for you to follow. Undoing the oath isn't really your goal; saving this man's life is. Without, of course, losing your own. If you can find a way to do that, then the rest is irrelevant."

From a practical standpoint, she was right. And Mirei was not about to stomp on the one lead she'd been offered in weeks. "Thank you," she said. "I'll think about it."

"How is he doing?" Rigai asked, hesitant once more.

Mirei shrugged and looked away, gazing across the mostly empty room. It wasn't hard to visualize him there, his face drawn and shoulders sagging with weariness. Jaguar said he wasn't sleeping well. "I don't exactly know. We're not communicating directly; it isn't safe."

"No, of course not," Rigai said. The silence that followed hung leaden in the air. Mirei hated not being able to talk with him. Their partnership on the commission had reminded her how well they worked together, and he'd been her main support during the long days when she fought not to kill herself. She missed him fiercely, and the knowledge that she might be responsible, however indirectly, for his death . . . that burned like poison.

Rigai said, "I'm sure you'll find an answer soon."

She wasn't at all sure, and they both knew it, but Mirei appreciated the words nonetheless. Lies of that sort were the only comfort she had these days.

TWO COUSINS FOLLOWED HER as she went through the corridors. Their presence drove Mirei up the wall, and she was grateful that Iseman and Terica had refused to allow her a permanent escort in Haira; otherwise, Satomi would have given her a pair of babysitters there, too. Mirei wasn't sure what the point of their presence was, other than to make her feel like an idiot. If someone attacked her, she had more ways of defending herself than the Cousins did. But while she was at Starfall, Satomi refused to let her go unattended.

At least they stayed outside her quarters, taking up sentry positions on either side of the door. And there was one perk to Satomi's concern for security: Mirei had been given the rooms vacated when Shimi fled from Starfall. Keys and Primes always lived under at least a minor guard, just in case, and the rooms were much more defensible than the usual quarters allotted to new witches.

Mirei tossed her pack on a chair. She still wasn't used to having a Cousin serving as her personal maid, but at least there she could see the point of having one. There were other things demanding her time and attention, things that a Cousin could not take care of.

Like Satomi's little spying program.

The latest message from Eikyo was discreetly buried in a stack of unrelated papers. Satomi had assigned Mirei to work with her friend, but there wasn't much "with" to it; Eikyo sent messages, Mirei translated them out of code, and Satomi presumably did something with the information. Mirei couldn't risk translocating messages directly to Eikyo, and anything sent with the usual packets to the Cousins had no guarantee of getting to her friend. In all likelihood, Eikyo didn't even know that Mirei was the one reading her messages.

Bit by bit, the information had dribbled in. Some of it wasn't of much use. They complained about their work, but no more, it sounded like, than normal people would. Some of them were mildly resentful of witches, but some weren't, just as people felt about their Lords. Nothing in particular there.

But of late Eikyo had begun to uncover things that looked much more important. The Cousins had a distinct hierarchy among themselves, it seemed, that did not necessarily follow the tasks the witches gave them. They were *very* aware of those among them who were failed witch-students—not just "Kyou," but women far older than her, too—and though those women weren't necessarily at the top of the hierarchy, they received a certain odd respect.

It was maddening, trying to tease meaning out of the terse messages Eikyo could transmit; Mirei wasn't sure what to make of everything her friend said. The Cousins *had* arranged for the survival of doppelgangers in the past—but why? For that, she had only one cryptic reference to "hope." Hope for what?

She scanned the newest note quickly, picking the code out of its surrounding, unrelated text with the ease of practice. Perhaps she would get that answer this time.

They suspect me.

The words lay there, buried in their protective camouflage. It was the only complete sentence Eikyo had ever sent, and it chilled Mirei to the bone. If Eikyo meant that her charade was in danger of being uncovered . . .

Then what? Mirei had no clue what the Cousins would be likely to do. Stop working for the witches? The thought was unfathomable, but she couldn't rule it out. *Satomi should never have done this. Eikyo's no good as a spy, and if they know Satomi set her to watch them—*

She grabbed a scrap of clean paper and scrawled a quick note for Satomi. Perhaps now she could persuade the Void Prime to recall her friend. That might look diplomatically awful—how in the Goddess's many names had Satomi ever planned to bring this to an end?—but there might not be a better choice. Note completed, she sang it to Ruriko's desk. The one time she'd sent a message to Satomi directly, the Prime had verbally flayed her alive. Ruriko was there for a reason.

By then she was running late. Mirei stripped off the embroidered long coat she'd put on for her politicking in Haira, changing instead into something she found far more comfortable: loose pants, sash, and a jacket, all modeled on the outfits worn by the training-masters at Silverfire.

Her escort of Cousins followed her downstairs as she left her quarters and went outside to a small, level clearing just east of the main part of the settlement. The buildings there were storehouses, one of which had been given over to Mirei's use, but today her charges were waiting for her on the pounded dirt outside, breath steaming in the autumn air.

There were six of them. Only Amas, Indera, and Lehant were technically old enough for Hunter training, which began at ten, but Mirei had decided to bend that; she had been put into physical training as a Temple Dancer at five, and saw no reason why she couldn't do the same here. So there were three additional girls in the group: Falya, Ometrice, and Ranell, ranging in age from nine down to six. Together, they made up the tiny ranks of her so-called Hunter school.

The work she was putting them through was a mix of Hunter and Dancer that would have given any proper teacher from either tradition a fit. Even some of her students complained—mostly Indera, but occasionally Lehant. They thought of themselves as Hunters, and didn't see

why they should learn things that weren't about combat.
To Mirei, though, it was all of a piece. The faith drummed
into her as a Dancer had gotten her through the trials of
Hunter training; she had come to view the movements of
fighting as their own kind of Dance. And that faith, ex-
pressed through her body and voice, had saved her life
and made her whole again. More than anything, she
needed these girls to understand that.

She reached the clearing just as the bell on the main
building, hidden now behind trees, began tolling High.
The air today had a real bite, hinting at winter to come,
but by now they all, even little Ranell, knew better than to
complain.

The first part of their work needed no discussion.
While the Cousins stood sentinel nearby, Mirei led the six
doppelgangers through their usual warm-up. When she
was away, Ashin oversaw their practices; the Air Key
couldn't teach them the way Mirei could, but she could at
least make sure they worked out. It was better than having
them sit around and do nothing. The girls had morning
exercises with those Cousins who were being taught to
fight, training themselves for strength and flexibility, and
then afternoon drills with Ashin. And every day Mirei was
at Starfall, she set aside time to work with them.

Warm-up completed, she divided the girls into groups.
The younger trainees practiced basic tumbling, rolling
back and forth in the dirt, while the ones who had been at
Hunter schools worked on kick forms.

It plainly drove Indera up the wall that Mirei was not
having them spar. The decision was a deliberate one:
They were all far too focused on the idea of combat and
the potential for exerting force against others. That was a

part of the Warrior's nature, of course, and they would come to it eventually, but before that, Mirei needed them to understand their own bodies.

The question of why movement was a Void focus had much occupied Hyoka's theory witches when Mirei first returned to Starfall. Answering that had been Rigai's big contribution to the group. The Void was traditionally seen as the opposition of the world, the antithesis of concrete existence. Rigai had speculated that, while that was true, the Void was also emptiness *in* the world: that was to say, the space between objects. And movement defined space by bridging it and passing through it. Tajio, her main rival, still argued that the space was filled with Air, and therefore wasn't empty, but most of the other theorists seemed to think Rigai was on to something.

More importantly, *Mirei* thought she was on to something. Which meant that her young protégées needed to understand movement, and how to express it with their bodies. There was a relationship between the flow of a spell's music and the flow of a body in motion; Mirei was working on her own in what few spare moments she had to try and integrate the two as closely as possible. If the trainees could learn that now, rather than working it out the hard way when they came of age, so much the better.

Hence the forms. The same limited set of kicks, the same punches, the same grapples and pins against an imagined opponent, executed at a whole range of speeds, with Mirei singing as they moved. Not spells; she just wanted them to get used to relating movement to music. She'd tried to have *them* sing, but it had been exactly as painful as she expected.

There was another way around that, though, and they shifted to it as the bell rang the third hour of High.

Ashin arrived with seven more girls in tow. Mirei was finally used to the sight of them, but at first it had been so very strange, seeing them all lined up. Amas with her red-gold hair grown long, no remaining dyed ends—but it wasn't Amas, it was Hoseki. Sharyo, showing what Indera would look like if her face weren't so permanently bitter these days. Owairi, who had cut her copper hair short even as Lehant's grew out, so that only Lehant's harder build made them distinguishable from each other. The witch-doubles of the three younger girls. And thin-faced Urishin, the only one who stood alone, the other half of the missing Naspeth.

This was the point at which the Hunter aspect of training went more or less out the window, and Mirei started inventing wholesale.

There were some Temple Dances that were choreo-graphed for pairs—not just for two people, but for two people moving together. Most of them, unsurprisingly, were somehow related to the Bride. Mirei was drawing on memories of her years in the Temple and some of the more dancelike Hunter forms, and creating paired exer-cises for the girls to perform together.

So far as she knew, there was only one spell in the world designed to be performed in that manner, by two people, one singing, one dancing. It was the spell that brought those two back together into one body. Each of these girls would have to perform it some day, and the thought that she should teach it to them had led Mirei to invent this practice.

Ashin came over to stand at her side as the witch-students began to stretch—an activity they had taken to far less naturally than their doubles, but they had learned. "How are things going?" Mirei asked her, eyes on the now-sizeable herd of girls scattered around the clearing. Her headache hadn't quite gone, even with Rigai's help.

The Air Key sighed. "About as usual. They told Ukotto to pack her bags yesterday; they're sending her to Razi. Which means the students need a new teacher for political history."

"Razi? Why, what's happening?"

Ashin shrugged. "Nothing special, I think; just that Ukotto was once very friendly with the domain chronicler there. Had two children by him, in fact. That was years ago, but Satomi is hoping she'll be of use."

Once again, the demands of the political war against the dissidents had created a gap in the teaching staff at Starfall. Mirei remembered the orderly, well-regulated progression of her own childhood education, and wondered just what impact this chaos was going to have on the current students. She did not envy them, when the time came for them to face the fifteen Keys and prove their knowledge.

Assuming everything's still running that way by the time they make it that far.

Another witch-student had been tested since Eikyo's supposed failure; much to everyone's relief, she had passed without incident. Otherwise, the faction insisting that they suspend all testing until the full complement of Primes was restored might have grown to the point where they won their case.

But that was Satomi's problem, not Mirei's. "Do you think this is doing any good?" she asked Ashin, nodding at the girls.

The witch didn't answer immediately, which Mirei appreciated. Ashin's honesty would do her more good than the platitudes so many people gave her. "Yes, though the degree depends on what kind of good you're talking about," Ashin said.

"Oh?" Mirei glanced at her, curious.

"As a morale-booster, it's fine," the Air Key said. "Plenty of witches here look at these sessions and say, you see? She's building our new way of life."

"Don't tell them I'm making this up as I go along."

Ashin grinned. "Of course not. You're also encouraging the girls, giving them a structure to hold on to. It's a strange education, by our usual standards, but they can tell themselves it's preparing them for their future. It's a comfort."

For most of them, anyway. Mirei found herself looking to where Sharyo was stretching. Indera was several paces away, repeating the kick forms while she waited for practice to resume. Her technique was sloppier now; the energy behind it suggested she was vividly imagining herself in a real fight.

But she wasn't in a mood to deal with Indera's resentment today, and she no longer wanted to hear Ashin's assessment of how little *real* good these exercises were doing. Mirei stepped forward and clapped her hands sharply to get the girls' attention.

"Right," she said. "Same dance as yesterday. Owairi, Lehant, you're up first."

They started out facing each other, hands raised and laid palm-to-palm. Owairi waited for Lehant's nod, and then she began to sing.

The tune was a simple one, a farming song from Teria,

where Owairi had been raised. The melody was plaintive, and the two girls mirrored it with smooth, flowing motions, always keeping at least one hand in contact with each other. Movement with music was part of the point; two bodies moving as one was another part. She was starting them off with choreographed steps, but hoped that soon they'd learn to improvise, to anticipate each others' actions.

They passed into a complex move, and Lehant lost her balance.

Owairi stopped when her double stumbled. After, or at the exact same instant as? Mirei couldn't be sure. If the two happened at the same moment, that could be a good sign. Perhaps they were feeling the connection between them.

"Here," she said, coming forward. "You pressed too hard on her hand, Lehant—leaned too much weight into her. The point of this one is that you should be touching, but without pressure. Keep your own balance, and let her keep hers." She glanced at the watching audience. "Why was she off balance?"

Indera answered; as much as she might dislike this entire situation, she never passed up a chance to show the shortcomings of the girl she still thought of as a Thornblood. "It started before that, when she did the turn."

"Right, but incomplete," Mirei said. "Anyone else?"

This time it was Urishin, surprisingly, who answered. "She turned too fast, and had too much momentum."

Another sign of hope? The doppelgangers were usually the ones to understand the mechanics of movement, not the witches. "Exactly. Watch, Lehant. Imagine a partner next to me; I'm touching her, but not leaning on her. I extend, and then I turn—"

And as she spun, the world spun with her, and she fell on her ass in the dirt.

Indera's bray of laughter was excessively loud; everyone else gasped. Mirei sat where she was, eyes wide, disoriented, and tried to figure out what had happened.

Ashin appeared at her side. "Are you all right?"

"I thought so," Mirei said, momentarily indiscreet. "Maybe not. What in the Void happened?"

"You *fell*," Indera said with satisfaction. "Even the *Thornblood* only stumbled."

"Let's get you into the shade," Ashin said, as if the weak autumn sun were to blame, and helped her to her feet. Mirei's knees felt like wet paper; the Key had to support her over to a tree root she could sit on. "Have you eaten?" the woman asked, taking her pulse as if she could tell something from that. Ashin could cast simple healing spells, but that didn't make her a healer.

Mirei's stomach churned in response. "Yes. In Haira."

"And how long ago was that? You're pushing yourself too hard, Mirei."

But I'm not, Mirei thought, both irritated and confused. *I've done much worse than this before. Not that past stupidity should excuse present—but this isn't a fraction of what I did to myself when I first arrived at Silverfire.*

Granted, she no longer had one of the advantages she'd possessed then. As a young Temple Dancer, she'd learned to retreat inward, to a quiet place within that she could draw strength from; she'd reached for it since rejoining and had found nothing. She suspected it was her connection to Miryo she'd drawn from, and was half entertaining ideas for how to test that theory. Now that she was whole, though, that source was gone.

Still, she wasn't doing a fraction of the physical work she'd done then. And tiredness wasn't excuse enough.

"I'm fine," she said, shaking Ashin's hand off. "You know how sickeningly rich Hairan food is. Something just didn't agree with me."

It sounded lame even as she said it. Ashin gave her a skeptical look. "Am I going to have to talk to Nenikune?"

Mirei had already been through a blizzard of examinations at the hands of the witch who ran Starfall's infirmary, back when she first showed up and the woman was determined to study the miracle of two bodies made one. She didn't relish the thought of revisiting the place. "Misetsu and Menukyo, no. I'll be fine."

Urishin came trotting up with a cup of water; Mirei accepted it and took a sip, wondering what could be causing this. Dehydration? She knew better than to fall victim to that, although the drink was still appreciated. She'd eaten recently enough, whatever Ashin might think. She was sleeping.

Mostly. She had nightmares about Eclipse on a regular basis. But she didn't want to bring that up, not to Ashin, not in front of the girls.

"Okay, practice is over," Ashin said, standing up from her crouch.

"What?" Mirei got to her feet, and was pleased to find her knees had solidified into bone and muscle again. "It isn't time."

Ashin looked at her with an uncompromising expression. "Yes, it is. You're going to rest. Owairi and Lehant are the oldest girls here, and they're barely twelve; they've got plenty of time to learn what they need to. Practice is over for today."

The Air Key could compete with a boulder in a stubbornness contest, and Mirei didn't have the energy to argue. "Very well," she said, and handed the cup back to Urishin. "Dismissed."

The girls made their bows to her, Ashin smiled in satisfaction, but Mirei did not rest when she went back inside. Instead, she turned her mind once more to the endless, fruitless question of how to save Eclipse.

Chapter Thirteen

ECLIPSE WOKE TO SEARING PAIN, and found his sheets stained with blood.

He was out of bed and halfway across the room before he knew it, one hand clamped over his wrist as though that would save him from the Warrior's retribution—and he found the scar smooth, closed, not bleeding.

His hands shook badly as he fumbled with flint and tinder, until he gave up and took his candle into the hallway to light it from a sconce there. Alone in the corridor, he turned his wrist up into the light and examined it.

There was blood on his skin; it hadn't just been a nightmare. And it was still wet. But the scar was quiet—no sign that it was the source. *Had to have been, though. I'm not cut anywhere.*

Back into his room, candle in one trembling fist. Stains on the bedsheets, yes, but small ones. It hadn't been much blood.

But it was a warning.

"THEY KNEW this might happen," Jaguar said, tapping one finger on a paper that lay on the desk before him.

Anger was much easier to deal with than the heart-stopping terror that had woken him up. "Nice of them to *tell* me."

"They didn't want to worry you unnecessarily."

"This is my Void-damned *life* on the line. I'm *already* worried."

"Apparently the Warrior gives warnings when an oath is in danger of being broken. I'd heard of it, but didn't realize it would take this form." Jaguar sighed. There was no sign in his immaculate appearance that he'd been woken abruptly in the small hours of the morning; his weariness was not physical. "They recommend taking certain steps to prevent the situation from growing worse."

But it will *grow worse,* Eclipse thought. *It's unavoidable. Unless Mirei finds me some way out of this.* He prayed for that, but with each passing day his hope grew frailer.

Jaguar was looking at him as if he could hear the tenor of Eclipse's thoughts. Shoving his dread down for the thousandth time, Eclipse said, "Tell me."

"Make plans," the Grandmaster said. "Gather information. It's legitimate that you would have to plan this assassination carefully; she's as highly trained as you are in combat, and has magic to defend herself with. Moreover, she's very well-guarded. Caution is warranted, and caution takes time. They advise you to be as methodical as you can." The Grandmaster smiled briefly. "And they inform you that under no circumstances will they tell you the first thing about Starfall's defenses."

"I'm shocked," Eclipse said ironically. The only way they could be more helpful would be to feed him misinformation that he'd have to spend time sorting through. But even without that, he could spin it out.

That tiny flash of humor evaporated in no time, though. He didn't want to do this. Mirage had been his dearest friend in the world, and he'd grown fond of Miryo in their travels. He didn't want to spend his days planning how to kill the woman they'd become.

Was it his imagination, or did he feel a twinge in his wrist?

"This may take time away from your other work," Jaguar said, dragging his mind away from his fear.

Other work. "Who needs sleep, sir?" Eclipse asked, taking refuge in irony once more. "You'd be amazed how much I can get done. Speaking of which, is there anything new?"

The Grandmaster gave him an unreadable look. Was it the flickering light of the candles, or did he see sympathy and concern? Probably just Eclipse's tiredness talking. Jaguar took care of his own, but nobody would ever accuse him of being soft-hearted. "In the morning," Jaguar said. "You can't afford to make mistakes out of weariness."

True enough, given the game he was playing. But Eclipse doubted he would get any sleep. "Very well, sir."

SATOMI TOOK A SEAT before the mirror in her private quarters, arranged her skirt, and waited.

She was in place early, because not every bell tower kept precisely the same time, and she did not want to be late. It was worth enduring the tension of waiting to be sure she didn't miss this opportunity.

Not long after the Starfall bells chimed Dark, her mirror began to hum quietly.

She sang the answering phrase, her voice clear and steady, and an image of Kekkai formed across the glass.

Satomi had not been at all sure the dissident Fire Key would hold up her end of the arrangement. And to tell the truth, Kekkai's pointed jaw was set in a manner that did not bode well for the conversation—but at least she was there. And she spoke. "Satomi."

No honorific; also not the best of signs. But Satomi did not expect this to begin warmly. Or to end that way. "Kekkai. Thank you for agreeing to speak with me."

"I hope it won't turn out to be a mistake." The room the Key sat in was dim; one light, a lamp or a candle, sat past the edge of the image, but it illuminated little more than her face. Clearly she did not want anyone to know she was awake, nor what she was doing. Much like Satomi herself.

Kekkai hesitated briefly, then added, "Even with the differences among us, I think we should be communicating more. We will not solve anything with silence."

Was it Arinei who had slapped her down for making a suggestion along those lines, or Shimi? Clearly *someone* had bitten Kekkai's hand off for saying it. Probably Arinei; Hyoka had rewritten the suspension ritual to work with three Primes, and Satomi doubted the woman had taken her loss of authority well. Satomi put a smile on her face, not too warm, lest it be seen as insincere. "I agree, we *should* be communicating. That's why I contacted you."

"Before you ask, no, I will not tell you where we are."

Satomi hadn't even planned on asking. She'd sent women to infiltrate the dissidents in the hopes of finding out where in Kalistyi they had set themselves up; she hadn't heard back from a single one. With security like that, Kekkai was hardly likely to betray anything. "No, I wanted to speak to you personally."

"Why me? Why not one of the others?"

"Because I have information for you."

Kekkai's face closed off like a stone wall. "For *me*. Personally."

"It affects you more personally than others. I thought it best to tell you first, and then to consider, step by step, who else ought to know."

Kekkai was Key of the Fire Heart; she was no stranger to politically volatile secrets. Satomi could have wished for her to look more receptive, though. Finally Kekkai said, "What's to stop me from telling other people, once you've told me?"

"Nothing," Satomi said honestly. "Except your own conscience. Your own evaluation of whether our people would be best served by truth or by silence."

"*Our* people."

"Yes." Satomi met her gaze without blinking, hands folded quietly in her lap so she would not betray her nerves. "Contrary to the rumors that have been spread about me, I do still have a care for witches other than Mirei, witches without their doppelganger halves. I even have a care for those who disagree with me about this new way. They are still my people, as those who agree with me are yours. We cannot allow this to divide us."

Kekkai weighed this in silence, still clearly suspicious. Between the two of them, Arinei and Shimi had mounted quite a campaign to paint Satomi in a poor light, one she was fighting to counteract. But Kekkai had agreed to this conversation; she hadn't ignored Satomi's clandestine message, nor insisted on discussing the matter through intermediaries. She was here, in the darkest hours of the night, when virtually everyone was asleep—including the witches she had allied herself with. Surely that must count for something.

Satomi let her think the matter over, then spoke again. "My information for you is a confession. If you will hear it."

That got the Key's attention. She nodded, sharply, eyes slitted with curiosity and wariness.

"I will not preface this with explanations of our reasoning," Satomi said. "I can give you those later, if you would like them; they don't excuse what we did."

"We?"

"The Primes. All five of us, before this split."

Kekkai nodded again, even warier.

Satomi took a deep breath and said, "The death of Tari, your predecessor, was not an accident. She was assassinated, by a Wolfstar named Wraith. We hired him to do it."

Kekkai was not as much of an actress as Arinei; she was visibly startled, and appalled, and disbelieving. "How do I know that's true?"

Satomi smiled wryly. "You could try asking Arinei. Or Shimi. Arinei might deny it, for political reasons; Shimi would admit to it proudly. It's probably the last thing she and I agreed on. Though I have since changed my mind."

"You *murdered* her."

"Yes."

"And now, what, you claim to regret it?"

"With all my heart." Satomi was not above a little manipulation of her own; she deliberately allowed herself to show some of the pain she lived with, accumulated from all the wrong decisions she had made, beginning with Orezha's death.

A small muscle was jumping in Kekkai's jaw, just visible in the dim light. "Astound me," the Key said through her teeth. "Explain why in the *Void* you did this—and why she didn't get a trial."

"She didn't get a trial for the same reason that some cities will lock plague victims up to die, without allowing healers to visit them," Satomi said, choosing the brutal image deliberately. "To minimize the risk that infection will spread."

"What *infection*?"

"Tari is the reason we have so many young doppelgangers alive today," Satomi told her. "It goes back at least thirteen years. She saw Miryo's doppelganger alive, realized what she was, and did not report it. After that she began deliberately arranging for more doppelgangers to survive. Isolated incidents have happened before, apparently by chance, but never before on this scale. We concluded that Tari would not be persuaded to renounce her scheme; the scope of her work made that clear. If she had received a trial, she would have been able to speak in her own defense and might have swayed others to her cause. As it turned out, she had already done so—but we didn't know that at the time."

"You murdered her," Kekkai said in a harsh voice, "for supporting the very cause you now champion."

"Yes." There was no way she could even attempt to deny it. "As I said, I've since repented of the decision."

She'd presented the information; now she had to let Kekkai decide what to do with it. Satomi had known from the start that this was a gamble, as likely to alienate the woman further as to do any good.

In the quiet, where the only sound was the wind rustling outside her window, her fingernails dug into the palms of her hands.

"So," Kekkai said at last, flat and bitter. "You tell me this because you're hoping to sway me back over to your side. But you were as much a part of this as Arinei and Shimi. *You* made that decision, too."

"I don't deny it," Satomi said. "And I have no expectation that weeping tears of regret would make you feel more kindly toward me. But I ask you to consider this.

"Arinei and Shimi do *not* regret what they did. That is a moral matter, but it is also a political and legal one. Arinei accuses me of disregarding our ways and laws, but she argued the most strenuously of us all that we should deal with Tari quietly, without a trial. We had no rightful grounds for doing that—merely our conviction that it was best for Starfall. Which is to say, the same position she now attacks me for taking. I don't deny that I'm making changes; of course I am. But at least I am doing so in the open, where others may see, and where they may question me if they feel they must. Arinei and Shimi operate in secrecy, and show no inclination to change their habits."

There was, of course, a degree of hypocrisy in her words. Satomi wasn't playing with all her cards on the table; she had her share of secrets yet. But for the moment, what mattered was persuading Kekkai.

"Openness and honesty," Kekkai said in a biting tone, clearly not persuaded. "Which is why, of course, you're telling me about this in the tiny hours of the morning, when everyone else is asleep, instead of making an open proclamation to all of *our* people."

It was a good point. Satomi didn't have much of a defense against it. "I'd like to avoid further division. It could split us in so many ways: my followers against me, Arinei's against her, unranked witches of all stripes against the entirety of their leadership. Witches against Hunters—and both your group and mine have among them girls who represent, to their minds, the Hunters. When people become upset, it's not difficult for them to see the nearest targets as representatives of the ones they want revenge on. In this case, the man who murdered Tari."

Kekkai's mouth twisted unpleasantly at that, illustrating Satomi's point whether she meant to or not. "Where is he?"

"Dead. Mirei—no—*Mirage* killed him."

"And again I must take your word for it."

Satomi shrugged. "Gather information on him; you'll find out easily enough. Mirage and her partner Eclipse took on a blood-oath to Hunt Wraith, and carried it out this summer. Tari's friends hired them."

Kekkai's expression grew distant. "Wraith. Wait—I *have* heard that name. The ab—Mirei mentioned it, when she appeared in the ruling hall."

An incident Satomi kept meaning to thank Mirei for. The woman had nearly told the truth about Tari that night, but had sidestepped it in favor of addressing the real issue. Satomi did not want to consider what chaos might have resulted had everyone learned about the assassination at that moment.

The slip in Kekkai's speech just then hadn't escaped her. She'd started to say "the abomination," but had changed it to Mirei's name. Satomi took it as a faintly hopeful sign. The more Kekkai let go of the dissidents' rhetoric, the better.

But all Satomi said in response was, "Yes."

More silence; Kekkai's arched, plucked eyebrows had dived inward as she considered the revelations. Watching her, Satomi gauged this as good a time as any to end the conversation. The hooks were in place, she could hope for no more.

"I will not keep you any longer," she said, breaking Kekkai's reverie. "You have the information I promised you. You must decide what to do with it."

The Key's response was caustic. "Like telling the world."

Satomi's hands clenched again, but she answered with a fair semblance of calm. "If you truly think that's the best course of action. I can do nothing but ask you not to. I can't prevent you."

Technically, she *might* be able to. There were ways to harm someone with magic. They required the witch to see her target, but the mirror image might suffice. Satomi had learned long ago, though, not to let her more pragmatic thoughts show on her face.

"I'll think about it," Kekkai said at last. Her attitude seemed more uncertain than hostile; it was the best Satomi could hope for.

"May the Goddess guide your thoughts," Satomi said.

Kekkai didn't bother saying farewell. She sang again, and the mirror went blank.

"THERE IS NEWS FROM SILVERFIRE," Hyoka told her the next morning.

Satomi's schedule had become, more than ever, a rotating sequence of meetings. Rana and Koika every day, Hyoka every few days, Mirei every few days, a steady stream of the Keys of various Paths, both those confirmed in their office and the interim Keys who had been appointed to take over the duties, if not the spell-granted authority, of their sisters who had left Starfall in protest. She had always known that her fellow Primes did large amounts of work, but never until she had to take on half their duties herself had she appreciated how *much*.

It took a few moments for Hyoka's words to acquire meaning. Satomi had spent much of the previous day worrying over Eikyo's latest note, and then had stayed up to meet Kekkai. She'd only gotten a few hours' sleep, and as a result was feeling extremely slow. "Yes?"

"Eclipse suffered a warning flare from the oath-scar last night. We've already passed along to him our best advice, but we thought you should be informed."

One oathbound Hunter three domains away was the least of Satomi's concerns at the moment, but still, the news was worrisome. If the scar was bleeding, then his time was running out. And Mirei's hopes aside, there were only two possible outcomes to that.

"What advice did you give him?" she asked.

"To begin planning how he would go about Hunting Mirei, as if he were actually going to do so. It should keep him occupied for some time; she's hardly what you might call accessible."

Hyoka, clearly, thought this was an appropriate answer to the situation. As usual, she was thinking like a theorist. Satomi did not have that luxury. She did not like the idea of this man making any plans that could eventually lead to the death of the only complete witch in the world.

"Is he still at Silverfire?"

The Key nodded. "Until we tell him to leave."

"Don't," Satomi said sharply. "Do not give him *any* instruction to move without consulting me first."

Hyoka looked taken aback at her tone, but nodded again.

They moved on to other topics, then, to the various researches Hyoka's contingent were still carrying out, but Satomi only listened to it with half an ear. When the Key departed with her stack of notes, Satomi sat for a moment in silence, thinking, before she rang her desktop bell for Ruriko.

The secretary was there immediately. If anything, she was the second most overworked person in Starfall at present.

"Close the door," Satomi said.

Ruriko did, and at her Prime's nod came forward and took a seat.

Satomi considered her words for a moment, then set her jaw. "The situation with Eclipse is deteriorating. Mirei will not be able to save him. She's been trying for two months; if she hasn't succeeded by now, she won't."

"Does he know he's running out of time?" Ruriko asked.

"Yes. Which is why I called you in here." Satomi laced her fingers together and stared at them. "Mirei is confident that he won't hurt her. She cares for him a great deal, and is certain that he feels the same way—enough that he won't try to carry out the oath."

She paused there, and it stretched out long enough that Ruriko finally said, "You want to make sure he doesn't."

Satomi closed her eyes. "Yes."

Ruriko's pen scratched quietly across the paper. Satomi let her make the note; the woman had an impenetrably arcane method of documenting things, and Satomi had no fear that anyone else would be able to sort out what this one meant.

"We can't lose her," Satomi said, her voice hardly more

than a murmur. "This oath has made it so that one of them must die. He volunteered for that. But if it seems that he is going to lose his conviction—if he makes even the *slightest* move in Mirei's direction—then I want him out."

Out, her mind repeated mockingly. *You won't even say "dead."*

"I understand," Ruriko said. Her pen scratched again, and Satomi felt a tiny amount of relief that she could leave the specifics up to the secretary.

You can pretend your hands won't have more blood on them.

After a diplomatic pause, Ruriko said, "Is there anything else, Aken?"

Satomi opened her eyes and forced herself to sit up. There was another meeting very soon. "No, Ruriko. That will be all."

IN THE CONFERENCE with Rana and Koika later that day, she told them what she had done with Kekkai.

The Earth Prime stared at her in disbelief. "And you didn't tell us ahead of time."

"No." Satomi sighed and drank a substantial gulp of water. Her head was pounding, and she wanted very much to sleep.

"Mind saying *why*?"

"Why I told Kekkai, or why I didn't tell you?" Satomi waved away Koika's irate response before the woman could make it. "Both, of course. I told her because we *need* her back. Having three-quarters of the Fire leadership holed up in Kalistyi—having nothing but the Head Key left here—Onomita's hardly any use. She played support to the other two, and to Arinei. She doesn't take her own initiative, and we don't know how to make the best use of her. We're not getting Arinei back, so it was Kekkai or Mejiki, and of the two, Kekkai has shown the most indication of thinking that we should still at least be talking to one another."

"And her predecessor's the one we had *murdered*."

"I thought that might carry weight in our favor—not that we did it, but that we confessed it." Satomi drank more water. She might have to switch to a stimulant tea before the day was over; her energy was flagging and she still had plenty of work to do. "And it may have. It certainly didn't go as badly as I feared it might."

"I'm still waiting to hear why you didn't tell *us* you were taking that risk."

Because I'm still waiting to see which one of you will walk out next.

The thought jolted Satomi into temporary wakefulness. Was that it? Did she not even trust her two allies anymore?

Rana was sitting in her chair, eyes on the table, not participating in the argument. She was listening, Satomi was sure, but the elderly Water Prime was speaking up less and less often in these councils. Reconsidering her allegiances? And what of Koika, the most vocal Earth Prime Satomi had ever known, diving so eagerly into the situation when many of her predecessors had hardly paid attention to the human politics of Starfall at all?

She reached for her water cup, hand shaking, and knocked it to the floor.

Rana jumped at the sound of shattering ceramic; even Koika jerked. Satomi stared at the spilled water and for a moment couldn't even think what to do about it.

Then Koika muttered a quiet imprecation and pulled the sash from her dress to mop the table dry. That done, she dragged her chair closer and put one hand on Satomi's. "What's wrong?"

"I just need sleep," Satomi said. Had it been anyone else asking, even Ruriko, she would have put a facade over it, presented the same calm, level face she always did. But Koika was the one person here she truly trusted, apart from Mirei.

Dear Goddess—let her be safe to trust.

Koika therefore saw exactly how tired Satomi was. "Mother's tits," she swore. "Satomi, I've been telling you all along—you can't do everything yourself."

"We're shorthanded," Satomi reminded her. "Appallingly so. There are witches on our side, yes, but how many of them are qualified to teach the students? How many have the knowledge and skills necessary to handle our political affairs? I'm not the only person who's tired."

"I know," Koika said, with real bite in her voice. "Mirei collapsed yesterday. Only briefly," she hastened to add, as Satomi jerked in worry. "Just a bout of dizziness while she was trying to demonstrate some spinning something-or-other to her trainees. Ashin told me."

If there was one good side effect to this schism, Satomi reflected with sour humor, it was that more witches of separate Rays were talking to each other than ever before.

Koika was still talking. "The point is, neither of you is dispensable."

"I know," Satomi said in weary frustration. "That's why I'm pushing so hard."

"You're missing my point completely," Koika replied, shaking her head. "If you two fall apart, we're in trouble.

So you *need* to rest, and we'll just find ways around you while you're doing that. We'd rather cope without you in the short term than the long."

Satomi bent to pick up the shards of the cup and placed them back on the table. "You two are just as important, you know—you and Rana."

Koika smiled in triumph, as if Satomi had walked into a trap. "Yes. Which is why *we* are making sure to get enough sleep every night. Right, Rana?" She looked to the Water Prime for support.

"Mostly," Rana said in a soft voice. Her lined face looked older than ever.

Pulling Satomi to her feet, Koika said briskly, "We'll deal with Kekkai later. Tomorrow, say. For now, you're going to rest."

Satomi snatched her hands from the other woman's grasp before she could be led toward the door. "There are things I need to—"

"Oh, I'm sorry," Koika said blandly. "Did I give you the impression that you had a choice?"

She started singing then, and Satomi's tired mind took too long to sort through the notes and pitches and figure out what the spell was, and by the time she made it that far, Koika was done and she was asleep.

THE NEXT DAY, she was furious with Koika's autocratic decision, but the Earth Prime seemed unfazed. "You're not the only one who can make decisions without consulting other people," Koika said, and smiled cheerfully at Satomi's glare.

It had done some good, though; she had to admit that. The spell-induced sleep was the deepest she'd had in ages. Normally she woke up several times during the night, mind racing with the endless list of things she had to do. Her mind was sharper now, without even resorting to stimulant tea.

So when a sealed scroll landed on her desk, appearing out of midair a short distance above, her first reaction was irritation, rather than the slow-witted confusion she'd been wrestling with for days. Correspondence of this type was not supposed to come to her; it should go to the appropriate Key or Prime, and anything intended for her directly should go to Ruriko instead. That was what a secretary was *for.*

But now that it was here, calling Ruriko in would waste more time than it would save. Grimacing, Satomi picked up the scroll and cracked the seal.

After a moment of reading, eyes growing wider with every word, she reached for the bell and rang it as loudly as possible.

Ruriko appeared in the doorway. "Aken?"

"Bring the other Primes to the council room," Satomi said. "Immediately. Also Onomita and Mirei. And Ashin." She thought it over. Churicho and Bansu? No, best not to involve the interim Fire Keys. Best to involve as few people as possible. "Just those five. Tell them to come without delay."

The secretary nodded and vanished.

Alone in her office, Satomi reread the note, written in Kekkai's small, neat lettering.

> *Tungral, sunset, three days' time. Inn is the Bear's Claw. Send Mirei to get me out.*

Chapter Fourteen

❦

"IT'S A TRAP," Koika said flatly.

Mirei had just enough self-control not to crane her neck at the curled slip of paper Satomi had handed to the Earth Prime. *Trap?* she wondered, curiosity aroused.

Satomi took the paper back and showed it to Onomita. "Is this Kekkai's handwriting?"

The Head Key hardly needed to glance at it. "Yes."

"That doesn't mean it's not a trap," Koika insisted.

Mirei exchanged glances with Ashin. The Air Hand seemed as baffled as she was. Kekkai was on the enemy side, Mirei knew that much. But why was she sending Satomi messages? What kind of trap was she trying to set up? As the only unranked witch in a room full of Keys and Primes, she didn't quite have the nerve to ask.

Satomi did not leave them in the dark for long. Laying the curl of paper down on the table, she addressed everyone in the council room. "Some of you know that I've recently been in communication with Kekkai, attempting to convince her to come back to our side. According to this note, I've succeeded. She wants out of Kalistyi."

"And she wants us to send *you*, Mirei," Koika cut in, her voice heavy with mistrust.

"The parameters she's set require it," Satomi added. "She names a town in Kalistyi—Tungral, near the

Askavyan border—and an inn where she will presumably be waiting, three days from now. The only way to get there in time is by your magic, Mirei."

Hearing that, Mirei had to laugh. "Not a very good trap, then. Unless she crammed a very good description of Tungral onto that slip of paper. I'm not about to jump blind. Besides, there's no guarantee I could bring her back, not that way. I've never cast the spell on another person, or tried to take them with me. Hyoka's been nervous about trying."

Satomi gave her a sharp look. "Do you think you *could* do it?"

"Why ask?" Koika demanded. "We're not sending her."

"If Kekkai really wants to get out of there—" Onomita began hesitantly.

"If you believe *that,* you're a fool."

Satomi put up a hand to quell Koika. "I understand your suspicion; believe me, I share it. But if there's any way we can turn this to our advantage, then I want to find it.

"Consider the possibilities. If Kekkai truly does want to come back—perhaps she's had a falling out with Arinei; perhaps I convinced her on my own—then we cannot afford to miss this opportunity. Having her on our side would do us incalculable good." Satomi inclined her head toward the Fire Head Key. "No offense intended, Onomita."

The Key's round face bloomed with a fervent smile. "None taken. I'd love to have her back."

"So. If this is genuine, it's a stroke of great good fortune for us."

Koika instantly took up the countering side. "And if it's not?"

"If it's not," Satomi said, "then we may have a chance to capture her."

In the following silence, Mirei wondered if she was the only one who had known Satomi was going to suggest that.

The Void Prime continued on. "Kekkai has been with them for months. She will know things that could be useful to us. If this is genuine, we'll have her help willingly; if not, Mirei can knock her over the head and bring her back here, and we'll get the answers out of her by other means." The witch captured in Angrim had been of little use; she'd been acting as the agent of someone they already knew was on Shimi's side, but had been told no more than to search the city for a girl matching Indera's description. They needed someone else to question. Someone in a position to know things.

Koika was not so sanguine about the possibility. "Saying that Mirei will knock her over the head is fine and well, but she'll have a hard time of it if they've got a crowd of people waiting for her."

"She defeated *us,* didn't she?" Rana asked, a trace of bitterness audible in her voice. It was the first time she'd spoken since Satomi convened them in the council room.

Mirei snorted, forgetting to be polite. "Riding on the tail end of a miracle. I doubt I can arrange for that again."

"I understand your concerns, Koika, but this might still be worth the risk," Satomi said. "If we can find Mirei a good enough description to get there in the first place."

"Is there anyone else nearby?" Onomita asked. "Someone, or more than one person, who we could send in place of Mirei? I'd have to check my records, but I don't think I have anyone. The nearest woman in my Ray who I know to be on our side is Domeiyu, and she's all the way over in Buvailat."

"Would Kekkai go with anyone other than Mirei?" Ashin said dubiously.

Koika had clearly warmed to that idea, though. "We could put an illusion on them. Send a sketch of Mirei to whoever we use, have her cast an illusion, and then she can go to Tungral in Mirei's place."

"She'll check for that," Mirei said flatly. "As paranoid as she'll be? She'd know it was an illusion before your impostor got through the door."

Satomi was nodding. "Not to mention that I suspect she wants to leave instantaneously. No one else can do that, and maybe not even Mirei. Who can't get there, because she doesn't know the place." Sighing, the Void Prime seated herself at the table. "I'll have to try and get a message to her myself, telling her to change the plan."

But Ashin sat forward in her chair, looking suddenly eager. "We can still get Mirei there, though. All we need is for *someone* to describe the place to her. Surely there's a witch on our side who could provide that."

The words were hardly out of the Key's mouth before Mirei had an idea. "Or maybe someone other than a witch."

FALYA HAD MOSTLY gotten over being intimidated by Mirei; two months of daily practices had changed fear into the respect due to a training-master. But the nine-year-old Kalistyin doppelganger was clearly startled to have Mirei coming to *her* for information.

"You said you grew up in the north, right?" Mirei asked, trying not to overwhelm the girl with her drive to get the information. Some Hunter tasks she was good at; coaxing timid subjects into talking wasn't one of them. Intimidating, yes; coaxing, no. "Do you know Tungral?"

Her heart leaped when Falya nodded. "Da— I mean, that is—"

"You can call him 'Da,'" Mirei said gently as the girl looked uncertain. "He raised you. That makes him your father, even if you're not his seed."

Falya managed a small smile. "Da used to go there a couple of times every season. Not in the spring, during the melt; too muddy then. But in the summer and fall, or in the winter, when he could sledge. Took furs to market there."

"How about you? Did you ever go with your da?"

The girl shook her head, and Mirei's heart fell. "Not even *once*?"

"I never left Lyonakh," Falya said in a barely audible voice. "Not until Inei-mai brought me here."

Mirei sighed. Maybe Inei was still at Starfall, or could be contacted easily; she might have passed through Tungral on her way to Lyonakh. Although a description based on having passed through once was not something she wanted to trust herself to. *Come on, there* has *to be someone who knows that town. The others will find someone.*

Then a thought came to her. "Falya, where's Lyonakh?"

"In the mountains," the girl said.

"But where? When your father went to Tungral, which way did he go? And how far?"

She thought it over. "Northwest. He would be gone for

three days, when he went. One to go, one to market, and one to come back."

A day's journey. And that was with a wagon or sledge full of furs.

"Falya," Mirei said, keeping a death grip on the reins of her excitement, "tell me what Lyonakh looks like."

"THEY WON'T BE EXPECTING IT," Mirei said when they were all reassembled. "If it's a trap, they'll be looking for me to come into Tungral directly. To the inn itself. They won't look for me to be riding in from some mountain village."

"But they'll still see you coming," Koika said. "Unless you disguise yourself and, like you said, they'll be checking for that."

Mirei had recovered her manners, having received a pointed look from Satomi not long before. She smiled politely at the Earth Prime, even as she inwardly shook her head at the blindness. "I don't intend to use magic."

Ashin looked approving. "I've said it before—you'd do well in Air. *That's* adaptation."

"There's a good chance they'll make the same assumption you did, Koika-chashi," Mirei said, "which means they're less likely to spot a mundane disguise." *And that's diplomacy. You people forget to think about nonmagical answers.*

Satomi had been tapping her long fingers on the table during this discussion; now she stopped and spoke up. "It's a good plan. But if they have people waiting for you—"

"Then I sing myself out," Mirei said. "I can probably buy enough time for that."

"I'm not going to gamble you on 'probably.' You will only go if you can take someone else with you."

Mirei blinked. "Aken—I don't know if I can even do that."

"So you try. If you can't, then you would have to ride back from Kalistyi with Kekkai, and I won't risk that. Nor will I send you to Kalistyi alone."

Before she could protest, Mirei made the mistake of meeting Satomi's eyes. The look there reminded her: she was not an independent agent anymore. She had responsibilities.

"Yes, Aken," Mirei murmured reluctantly.

Koika looked marginally less worried now that Satomi had set her condition, but not much. "Who can we send with her, though?"

"Me," Ashin said.

Satomi shook her head. "Out of the question. You're a Key; we need you."

"With half my Path decamped to the other side? I'll do you more good out there. You need to send a witch; Cousins won't be enough. And not only am I an Air Hand and used to doing odd jobs, I'm also one of your more practiced subversives." Ashin smiled, with only the faintest trace of bitterness. "I spent quite a while planning what I would do if witches showed up to take me prisoner, or to—"

She cut it short as Satomi's eyes snapped to her. Mirei looked covertly at Onomita, but the Head Key appeared to be lost in speculation, and did not seem to have noticed.

"Name me someone better qualified," Ashin finished.

"You're too recognizable," Koika said.

Mirei raised an eyebrow at her. "Ordinary disguises

don't stop working just because they're put on a witch. Give me hair dye and some cosmetics, and I'll give you back a woman you've never seen before."

Satomi slapped one hand onto the table, not in anger, but to get them all back on track. "This is a moot point if Mirei can't do it. So first we test that."

"I'd recommend bringing Hyoka," Mirei said. "She'll cry for a year if she doesn't get to watch me do this."

THE VOID KEY'S FACE lit up when she heard. "I've been wanting to try! I wasn't sure that it was worth the potential risk, just to see if it worked. But if you have a good reason for doing it—"

They had not, of course, told her why they needed Mirei to translocate other people. Hyoka didn't care, so long as she got to take notes. "I hope the risk turns out to be exaggerated," Mirei said.

Hyoka nodded, beaming at Mirei and Ashin impartially. "Let me get my group together, then, and we can go to the translocation room—no *need* to do it there, of course; you could try it anywhere. But there we can observe you more easily. I'll have a Cousin brought."

Already in motion down the hallway, Mirei stopped dead in her tracks. "A Cousin?"

"To test your spell on."

Mirei almost swallowed her tongue. "I'm not going to experiment on some helpless Cousin."

Eyes wide in puzzlement, Hyoka said, "Why not? Who else are you going to experiment on?"

"Me," Ashin said, with the same confident blandness she had used before.

"But you're a *witch*," Hyoka said. "And a Key. What if it goes wrong?"

Ashin shrugged. "Then it goes wrong. I'm volunteering."

Mirei didn't much want to lose Ashin, but she hoped not to lose *anybody*. And no way in the Void did she want to conscript somebody who wasn't even a part of this. "If you can find another volunteer, I'll use her. But no Cousins. We can't even be sure it would work on one of them the same as it would work on a witch. And I need to know if I can move a witch."

Unsurprisingly, there were no other volunteers. Hyoka looked ill at the thought of using a Key as the first subject of this experiment, but Ashin was doing a good enough job of projecting an assured demeanor that the other theory witches gathered in the room were willing to let it happen. Satomi and her fellow Primes watched in silence. *And if you don't look too closely at them, you won't even notice how tense they are.*

Before Satomi had begun sending Mirei out on diplomatic missions, the translocation room had been where the theorists observed her casting the spell, so they could see how it worked. It was a long hall, and she'd blinked from one end of it to the other more times than she could count, performing obediently—if grudgingly—on command. Now they would repeat the process, but with a new twist.

"Do you want to send her alone, or try to take yourself and her both?" Rigai asked, since Hyoka was exhibiting less than the usual enthusiasm for this latest trick.

Mirei glanced at Ashin. The other woman shrugged. She was as far from a theorist as it was possible to get.

"Together, I think," Mirei said. "I'd rather pull her through with me than go flinging her around without a chaperone."

They stationed themselves at one end of the long room, and Mirei took Ashin's hands. "You sure you want to do this?" she asked in a low voice.

Ashin gave her a strangely blissful smile, and Mirei realized with a jolt of fear that she'd seen that look before. When she was Miryo and Mirage, and Ashin told them she was confident they'd find an answer to the problem of doppelgangers.

It was the look of faith that was perhaps a little *too* trusting.

Goddess, Mirei prayed, *Warrior, whose Void we're about to go dancing through*—please *let me not be about to kill her.*

Then she looked down at their hands. *Okay, first hurdle. How do I do the movements while holding on to her? I'm pretty sure I want to hold on.*

Maybe those bizarre exercises with the doppelgangers and witch-students would be good for something after all.

"Let's try it like the girls do in practice," Mirei said to the Key. "I need to move to cast this, and I don't want to lose contact with you, so give me your hands. I'll push or pull to show you where to go. Okay?"

Ashin nodded.

Mirei closed her eyes and centered herself, then began. She did it more slowly than normal; tempo wasn't a factor in spells. They could be rattled out in mere heartbeats when under attack, or stretched out into ritual choruses with long, sustained notes. What mattered was the flow, the relative durations of the notes, the way the parts compared to each other. She wanted to be sure she did this right, and so she sang slowly.

And moved slowly, guiding Ashin as she did, the two of them performing an odd, improvised dance at one end of the long room, with the power building around them, a blend of all five Elements, but most of it Void power that Ashin couldn't even feel—

The spell ended, and they were pulled into the Void.

IT WAS AS IF MIREI'S EARS had popped, as if she'd been deaf and then suddenly could hear again. One minute, the concluding note of her spell; the next, Ashin's screams.

The Key's hands pulled free of hers before she could stop them, but it was all right; they were back in the room, at the far end, and Ashin looked like she was in one piece, even if she had crumpled into a huddle on the floor, hands clutching her head.

But she kept screaming.

There was a generalized stampede in their direction, theory witches racing over to offer help or ask technical questions, depending on their bent. But Satomi must have begun moving to that end of the room before the spell was even done, because she was there before anyone else.

She took Ashin in her arms, a rare gesture, and began soothing her. "It's all right, it's all right—you've felt it before. It's all right. I wondered if this would happen."

The words penetrated the headache and dizziness that had overtaken Mirei with the conclusion of the spell. "If *what* would happen?"

From where she knelt on the floor, holding the slowly calming Ashin, Satomi looked up at Mirei. "Do you remember your test?"

Vividly; it had ended in the most excruciating pain she'd ever experienced, far surpassing even the times when she had died. "I don't see the connection."

"The trial of Void," Hyoka said, having arrived at their sides. Understanding was dawning in her eyes. "We all scream like this."

"Not *this* badly," Mirei said, still unsettled. Ashin had stopped screaming, but her breath was still coming in heaving gasps.

Satomi shook her head. "You weren't this bad. And neither was I. I should have known your doppelganger was alive, just from that—but I didn't make the connection."

Mirei finally saw what the more metaphysically inclined witches had already figured out. "Wholeness of self. That's what the Void trial tests. What you put us through isn't *actually* the Void—"

"But it mimics it," Satomi said. "I wondered if this would have a similar effect. Do you enjoy translocating?"

"Not exactly. But it's not *bad*."

"Since you are complete. It's harder on Ashin, it seems. As it would be for the rest of us."

The various observing witches suddenly looked less interested in this entire experiment, as if afraid they'd be asked to experience it firsthand.

Cousins might do better, *then*, Mirei thought. *Those who weren't born witches weren't ever split. I think I'm glad I tried it with Ashin. Better to find this out now then when we showed up in Kalistyi.*

Ashin had recovered enough to join the conversation. "This is worse than the test," she said raggedly, pulling back from Satomi to meet her gaze. Her eyes glittered from the depths of her high-boned face. "I remember it well enough. What you use there is an imitation of the Void. This is the real thing. It's worse."

Mirei began calculating whether or not to mention her Cousin theory. She wasn't sure she wanted them as backup—if she couldn't have more magic on her side, she'd rather not worry about other people at all—but if Satomi would only let her go if she had company, then it was worth suggesting Cousins.

But Ashin was rising to her feet, refusing all helping hands. She wasn't quite steady, but she made it. Satomi rose with her. "How bad?" the Void Prime asked.

Ashin didn't try to quantify the awfulness; she answered the question Satomi was really asking. "I'll go," she said. "I may need recovery time on the other side, but we're jumping to Lyonakh, not directly to Tungral. I can do it."

Mirei almost asked if she was sure, but if it had been her in Ashin's place, she would have been insulted by the question. So instead she looked at Satomi. "Aken, I'd like to leave as soon as possible."

ONLY THE THREE PRIMES were there to see them off.

Koika looked the two women over and finally nodded, looking impressed. "You told the truth about the disguises."

With the help of tea leaves, Ashin's hair had darkened to a brown that looked more appropriate to her dark eyes. Not that anyone could see much of it; it was braided tightly to her scalp and mostly covered by an embroidered kerchief Mirei had commandeered from an elderly witch who had spent most of her active years in Kalistyi. Carefully applied cosmetics downplayed Ashin's bone structure and gave her a sallow, pinched look.

Mirei's hair was also brown, but its length had posed a problem. There were no good wigs at Starfall—nothing she would trust to withstand even a minute's encounter with anyone—and short hair on a woman was rarely found outside of Hunters, mercenaries, and guards.

So she'd decided to be a man instead. She wasn't a very *large* man, but her tough build helped sell the image, and her breasts were small enough to bind flat easily. Men's clothing was in shorter supply in Starfall, but Mirei had decided they would be vagrants looking for work; some practical clothing from the Cousins, strategically frayed and rubbed with dirt, suited the image. And vagrants were expected to look patched and makeshift; the lack of properly Kalistyin styles wouldn't be noticeable.

Mirei didn't like having her weapons stuffed into a bundle of oddments and rags, inaccessible if she should happen to need them, but the disguise would keep them safer than her blades would. The main lack was horses. Not for the Ladyship of an entire domain would she attempt translocating *those* with them, not to mention that vagrants rich enough to ride would look odd.

"I don't think I need to give you specific instructions," Satomi said. "You know the situation as well as we do, and you know what we want to accomplish and avoid. As for how you'll carry it out, you'll have to decide that as it happens." She smiled at both of them, but especially at Mirei. "Fortunately, you're well-qualified for that kind of responsibility. So I'll merely remind you to be cautious, and promise that we will pray for your success."

"Thank you, Aken," the two chorused, and repeated

Chapter Fifteen

◄━━◆━━►

ONCE MIREI AND ASHIN WERE GONE, Satomi went to her office and tried to get work done. Her mind kept wandering, though, ricocheting endlessly between the problem of Eikyo and the question of what was happening in Kalistyi. Two days yet, before Mirei and Ashin were supposed to meet Kekkai. She had to be patient. What was she going to do about Eikyo and the Cousins if they'd discovered her ruse? Soon a message appeared on one of her many sheets of enchanted paper: Falya's description of Lyonakh was good, and Mirei and Ashin had arrived safely. Satomi exhaled a sigh of relief, and tried to make herself concentrate on other things.

The question she and Koika had debated privately was, why did Kekkai want to leave? And why so abruptly? Koika pointed to that as a sign that this *was* a trap; Satomi wasn't so sure. It might be that Kekkai had asked Arinei or Shimi about Tari's assassination, and that the response she had received had so appalled her that she felt the need to leave. Or that asking had led to a confrontation that made her fear that *her* life was in danger. It had to be something extreme; less than a day had passed between their secret conversation and the arrival of the note.

I should have tested whether Mirei could take multiple people with her, Satomi fretted, pacing her office. *Un-*

pleasant as the experience seems to be, she would be safer with a larger guard. Her one comfort was that, if it *was* a trap, Ashin knew full well that she had better sacrifice her own life to save Mirei's. The Key had seemed insulted that Satomi thought it even had to be said.

Ruriko knocked at the door, then came in. "Aken, Tajio would like to speak with you." Casting an ironic eye at the untouched stacks of paper on Satomi's desk, and then at the Prime, standing next to the window with her fingers twisted together, she added, "If you're not occupied with something else."

Sometimes Ruriko knew her too well. But Satomi welcomed the distraction from her worries. "Send her in."

Tajio entered and bowed. She was a fairly young witch who had come to the Void Head after Satomi left her position as Key to become Prime. Satomi recognized her, mostly by her hooked, prominent nose, but didn't know her well. *One of Hyoka's research group. But not here because of that, or Hyoka would have come.*

"Aken," the witch said, straightening from her bow. "I wanted to speak to you about the doppelgangers."

The word was an effective distraction. "Oh?" Satomi said, crossing the room and seating herself behind her desk.

"I was wondering who's overseeing their training, with Mirei and Ashin gone."

Satomi hadn't given it any thought. "They still have their lessons."

"I meant their physical training. I assume their morning work with the Cousins is continuing. But has anyone planned to take up their afternoon practices?"

"Not as far as I'm aware," Satomi said. "We don't have

anyone qualified. The training Mirei's been giving them is not like the Cousins'."

Tajio nodded. "Of course, Aken, we don't have anyone with Mirei's skills. But I thought someone might at least oversee the practices, the way Ashin does, and make sure the girls keep on with their work. That wouldn't take much expertise. From what I've heard, they're eager to practice; it shouldn't be hard to keep them at it. And I expect Mirei would prefer for them not to be left at loose ends while she's gone."

"She won't be gone more than a few days," Satomi said absently, reviewing in her mind the roster of witches who had taken up various teaching tasks, wondering who could be spared for those hours.

Tajio's voice broke into her thoughts. "If it's not presumptuous of me, Aken, I'd be willing to take on that task."

Satomi glanced up at her where she stood before the desk, hands clasped demurely behind her back. "I thought you were working with Hyoka."

"I am, but she can spare me."

It was an elegant solution. Satomi nodded. "Very well. Tell Hyoka, and ask Ruriko to give you the doppelgangers' schedule. Just make sure they do their usual practices; don't try to add or change anything."

"Of course not," Tajio said, and bowed again. "Thank you, Aken."

LATER THAT MORNING Satomi had her usual meeting with Nae, which of late had been more than usually tense.

The business they handled in these meetings was a routine that had remained essentially unchanged since Satomi took the office of Void Prime; for all she knew, it hadn't substantially changed in the last few centuries. Primes and Cousins might come and go, but the task of keeping people fed and clothed remained the same.

Today, she could hardly keep her mind on the matter, and when it was done, she spoke impulsively to the old Cousin.

"Nae," she said, "if I should ever . . . give offense . . ."

The Cousin waited impassively for her to finish, face no more expressive than a rock.

Satomi couldn't bring herself to admit her charade with Eikyo. Not directly. She tried another tack. "My hopes have always been for good relations between witches and Cousins," she said. "I hope I have done well. But if there is anything more I can do—some boon I can grant you, that would better your lives—then you have but to ask."

She said it on instinct, and for a moment she hoped that she might finally get some reaction from Nae.

But the old woman merely nodded, said "Thank you, Aken," and departed. Leaving Satomi wondering whether she had just made matters worse or better.

WITH ALL THE DEMANDS on Satomi's time, her day was scheduled from the moment she woke up until the moment she fell asleep, and no one got in to see her without going through Ruriko first. So she was startled to hear the door open and see, not her secretary, but Nenikune.

Nenikune, her normally rosy face white and sick, and marked with tears.

Satomi rose to her feet and moved swiftly around to the front of her desk. "What's wrong?"

The head of Starfall's healers sank into a chair without

asking permission. She was blinking rapidly, as if trying to stop fresh tears. "Anness—"

The two-year-old doppelganger had suffered a bout of sickness the previous night; Nenikune had brought her into the infirmary for care. "What happened?" Satomi whispered.

The healer looked up, devastation in her eyes. "She's dead."

Dead. But she was a doppelganger. She'd died before, when her mother tried to sacrifice her as was custom, and then had come back to life, because she shared a soul with Chanka. She would come back again.

"She wasn't sick," Nenikune whispered. "It was Chanka. They put her through the ritual. Two years old, and they opened her to power. It killed her—her and Anness both."

Satomi's own knees gave out; she barely reached a chair in time. Chanka was in Kalistyi. Captured by Shimi's people, along with several doppelgangers. They couldn't kill the doppelgangers while their witch-halves were safe at Starfall—but Chanka was not safe.

"She's two years old," Satomi whispered, unable to believe it.

Nenikune nodded, mute.

It was unforgivable. Whatever Shimi thought of the doppelgangers—this had to have been her idea—killing a *child,* someone that young and helpless . . .

A cold voice in the back of Satomi's mind murmured, *Can you use this against her?*

Satomi's stomach heaved in revulsion at the thought. To sit here, with two children dead, and think about using it for political gain . . . and yet she had to. It was one thing for Shimi to fight against the changes that had come to

Starfall. But if she was willing to go this far, then Satomi *had* to stop her, and sooner rather than later. Before she could find a way to kill the rest of the children, too.

And she knew, with icy clarity, that Kekkai had better have been honest in asking for help. Because if the Key was lying, and was captured anyway, then she would find no mercy here in Starfall.

CONSTANT TENSION HAD WORN AWAY at Eclipse; between a lack of appetite and a disinclination to train, he'd lost more than a little weight. If he really wanted to pretend that he was going to kill Mirei, he knew he should throw himself into practice, to build himself back up again. But there were other things occupying his time.

One of the rooms at Silverfire had been converted into an office for him. There was little in there other than a desk, a chair, and some shelves, but decorations weren't Eclipse's primary concern these days.

Information was.

Seating himself in the chair, as he had for days before, Eclipse reflected that he was getting a taste of the Grandmaster's life. Silverfire Hunters were independent, for the most part, operating off their own resources and ingenuity, but there were still times when the school helped them out. And though Silverfire's network of agents and informants paled next to, say, Cloudhawk's, they had people in every domain—and Jaguar had given him full access to them.

The most dangerous part had been the early stages. Eclipse could not tell anyone the details of where he had been, and who he had been with—but he could and did ask very carefully worded questions. Bit by bit, he had learned what he needed to know.

He knew now which fort he'd been held in, and where it stood along Abern's border. He knew that no obvious convoy of witches had left the area following his release— but there *had* been a suspiciously large group of non-witches, with no obvious reason for traveling together. Tracking them was made more difficult because they changed their disguise spells more than once, but their path led northeast, through the Bridewell Pass, and into Kalistyi.

Now he was trying to learn where they'd gone to ground.

That Lady Chaha had given her support to the dissidents was common knowledge. By the reports Eclipse was getting, she was doing more than just talking about it, too. She had given them soldiers and some manner of base; he thought it was in the mountains that formed the domain's western border, but nailing down specifics was difficult. The prevalence of the Nalochkan sect there meant that recruiting people to work for Hunters wasn't easy, and besides that, Chaha was doing her best to guard the security of the dissidents. So his spies were having to dodge domain guards while they went about their work.

There was other information he could gather, though, and he strongly suspected its usefulness was the main reason Starfall hadn't decided to play it safe and off him before he could be a threat.

Mirei would never stand for such a thing, he knew— but they didn't have to tell her. They could make it look like the oath had struck home. Then no more worries about his loyalties, no fear that he might try to save his own life by taking hers. The warning had to have made them nervous.

So give them a reason not to act on those nerves, he thought, and turned his attention to the newest reports.

The rumor that a Nalochkan monastery near Lavesye had all but emptied out seemed to be true, and more to the point, now he knew where they had gone. The write-up collated notices from other domains of Nalochkan monks proselytizing in the outlying villages and towns, preaching against the Warrior.

The witches might have heard about that one already, but Eclipse set it aside as information to be passed along, wondering as he did so how long it would be before one Hunter school or another took exception to the monks preaching against the Warrior. That track of thought made the next report catch his eye even more than it would have otherwise. It was a scrawled note from Slip, who occasionally passed Eclipse tidbits that Jaguar chose not to share.

Confirmation: Ice is dead, the note said. *Accepted story is Mirei killed her.*

Eclipse bit back an oath. There had been a rumor going around about Ice, but they had the story from Mirei and knew she'd left the Thornblood alive. If Ice was dead, then it was because somebody was trying to set Mirei up. The dissidents? They were the most likely candidates.

Next sheet. A trio of ships had sailed from a port on the western edge of White Bay. No reliable information regarding who'd been on board or where they were headed; the portmaster's logs had been suspiciously blank on the subject. Eclipse stared at the map nailed to one wall. The port was close to where he thought the dissidents were. If he could find out who the passengers were, then he could try and track where they'd come from.

Next sheet. Lady Chaha was drilling her troops, and had recruitment planned for the spring. Attached was an older paper that didn't look like a Silverfire report, a political and tactical analysis of where Chaha might strike, should she decide to make war on anyone. The mountains kept her domain largely hemmed in; her main options were to try and take the Bridewell Pass into Abern, or to go east, after the triangle of land between the rivers and mountains that was a long-disputed territory of Trine's. The analysis concluded that the eastern route was more likely, since there were gold mines in that area, and Kalistyi had been hurting for income since the silver mines in the north played out. Given the current alliance with the dissidents, though, Eclipse wondered if the Bridewell Pass weren't more likely. If they were planning a direct attack against Starfall, they'd have to get troops there somehow.

Next sheet, and this one made Eclipse's fingers go cold. Someone—no clear details on who—had visited the Wolfstar compound in Razi, and had bought up every unemployed Hunter in sight.

The fact that it was in his stack said that *somebody,* most likely Slip, thought it was related to Eclipse's own work against the dissidents in Kalistyi. Could it be? By all indications, both Chaha and Shimi were too rabidly Nalochkan to even dream of sullying their hands with Hunters. He knew that Shimi had been a part of hiring Wraith, but that was before her religious convictions had asserted themselves like this.

Who would even *want* that many Wolfstars? They

were assassins. People usually hired them singly, not in squadrons.

He tried to think of their potential targets. Hiring many assassins suggested there were many targets; otherwise it would be overkill, in a very literal sense of the word. Scattered targets, or a concentrated group?

Then a deeply unpleasant possibility occurred to him. *The Primes have hired a Wolfstar before, to kill one of their own. Shimi wouldn't be likely to use a Hunter again—but Satomi?*

It could be that the witches had successfully located the dissidents' base in Kalistyi, and hadn't told him. And they could be preparing to deal with the problem their own way.

Hunters against witches. The two groups had never come into open conflict; Eclipse tried to think through how it might work. Killing a witch could be done; Tarinakana's assassination had shown that. To kill a lot of them, though, you couldn't pick them off one by one; the others would become alerted far too quickly. A full-on attack, though, threw away the advantages the Wolfstars would have and put them right up against magic. They would have to find a way around that.

Poison? Wolfstars didn't use it as much as Stoneshadows, their bonded counterparts, but that didn't mean they didn't know how. They'd have to get in close, though, to make that work, and surely the dissidents had defenses just as much as Starfall did.

So they would need the help of witches. Which Satomi could provide for them.

He couldn't ask anyone if his speculations were right. All he could do was put the report in the stack of things he *wasn't* going to report to Starfall. It was a delicate game he played, convincing them he wasn't a threat to Mirei; exposing a plan to assassinate their own people wouldn't help him any.

In the meantime—just in case he was wrong—he went back to trying to find where the dissidents had gone to ground.

INDERA DIDN'T MIND the witch showing up to make them practice. She would have done it anyway. She wasn't like the others; she had drive. She *definitely* wasn't like the witch-girls, who grumbled every time they had to do something physical.

But it wasn't as satisfying with the witch there. However much Indera despised Mirei, who claimed to be Mirage but wasn't, at least that woman knew how to make them work. The witch just waved vaguely for them to do their "usual things," and left it at that. Even Ashin—Indera refused to think of the woman as her mother—had been better.

When practice was done with and the others were wandering off, Indera hung back. If she couldn't have a proper practice, she could at least have a longer one. Hone her body into a weapon, the way it was meant to be. She had to savor every moment while she could, before she lost it all.

The witch didn't leave, though. She waited, too, as the other girls went back to the main halls, and then spoke to Indera.

"I'm impressed by the skill you girls show."

"Thank you," Indera began without enthusiasm, and then realized she'd forgotten the witch's name and Ray.

"Tajio," the witch said with a faint smile. "Void Head."

"Tajio-ai," Indera finished.

"I'd never seen a doppelganger before, you know, and I haven't seen you girls much since you arrived. You truly are . . . interesting."

The woman was looking at her like she was some kind of new bug. Indera wished she would go away; the air was chilling her muscles rapidly. At this rate, she'd have to warm up all over again if she wanted to practice more.

Yet Tajio kept talking. "If you don't mind my saying so, though—"

I do, Indera thought furiously.

"You don't seem entirely happy." The Void witch gave her a sympathetic look. "Is there anything I might do to help?"

Indera threw her towel down and glared at the woman. "Not unless you can convince somebody to let me go back to Silverfire, where I could train for *real.*"

Tajio's eyes widened. "What do you mean, 'for real'?"

"I mean that if I were there, I'd be training every waking minute to be a Hunter. Not this slow, stupid—I'm not even going to get to *be* a Hunter. They could have at least left me there until it was time."

"As I understand it," Tajio said, coming closer, "you were in danger there."

Indera scowled. "Oh, yeah. Danger. Just because one stupid Windblade disappeared. And she's not even *dead.* If these other witches hate her so much, why haven't they killed her?"

Tajio smiled thinly. "Oh, I'm sure they'd like to. But they can't."

"*Can't?* What, you're telling me a bunch of big magical witches can't kill one girl? Or that some stupid Wind-blade is so amazing she defeats everybody they send against her? Or that they're afraid of what'll happen if they *do* kill her?" Indera snorted in contempt. "They're already in trouble with the Void Prime. I doubt they care what anybody would think if they killed some girl."

"No, of course not. What I meant is that they can't kill *Naspeth*. Not without Urishin."

That made no sense. "What?"

The Void witch's eyes widened again. "You mean—Haven't they told you?"

Now Indera was getting suspicious. "Told me what?"

"That you can't be killed."

It was like descending a staircase and thinking there would be one more step at the bottom. The ground thudded up unexpectedly beneath Indera. "I can't *what*?"

"You share one soul," Tajio said, and her tone took on the lecturing quality Indera was getting so very sick of here in Starfall. But this time the subject interested her, and so she paid attention. "Two bodies, one soul. If one body is killed, but the other survives, then the dead one will come back to life. They can't kill Naspeth without Urishin."

"You mean they need to, what, kill both at once?"

"Yes," Tajio said. "Or else to get one to kill the other. That's what they sent Miryo to do; did they tell you about that? If the witch and the doppelganger share a soul, then they are the only ones who can kill each other separately."

Indera was fascinated against her will. "What happens if they do?"

Tajio shrugged. "The witch has always killed the doppelganger, so far as I know. When she does, then her magic stabilizes; she comes home and takes up duties as usual. She has to do that; if she doesn't, then her magic will be out of control, and will kill them both." She caught herself, and smiled thinly again. "At least, that's how it used to be. But I've never heard of an instance of a doppelganger killing the witch." Her expression became distant as she considered it. "Well, I can only imagine that it would eliminate the magic, since the witch-half is the one power is channeled through. I expect the doppelganger would continue on as it has up until that point, just as the witch keeps her power when the doppelganger is dead."

Then the woman's eyes cleared, and she looked back to Indera, no longer lost in the airy land of speculation and theory. "But of course the entire point of this is to keep you both alive. And, eventually, to make you one person."

"Yeah," Indera said, losing her enthusiasm for the conversation. Her muscles had gone stone cold; there was no point in trying to practice more. She'd have to wait for tomorrow. "I should get back inside."

"Yes, of course," Tajio said, and gestured for the girl to precede her down the path. Indera picked up her towel and headed for the buildings, thinking about what the witch had said.

Chapter Sixteen

ASHIN HAD JAMMED a wad of cloth into her mouth before Mirei began the translocation spell, so when they came out of the Void she bit down hard on it and mostly muffled her screams. Mirei lurched off to one side the minute they reappeared, feeling none too well herself. *Damn. Pulling people through hits me harder than just moving myself.* She leaned against a rock and convinced herself not to vomit.

Falya had provided them with the perfect destination, she saw when she finally lifted her head. A stream wound its way down between the heavy granite knobs of the mountains, and plunged over a man-high precipice just to their left. In front of them, a gnarled cherry tree had taken root firmly enough that it formed a small, stubborn island in the middle of the stream, which flowed around it to either side before rejoining and continuing down into a meadow. This had been Falya's favorite place to come when she was shirking chores. It was sheltered, with a jutting ridge of stone between it and her family's cottage, and unless you went around the long way and came right up into the meadow, there was no way to see anyone here.

Ashin was regaining control of herself; her hyperventilation slowed, and she took the gag from her mouth. Righting herself from where she'd curled up on her side, she managed a shaky laugh. "When I first heard you could do that, I thought you could make yourself the most popular woman in Starfall, ferrying witches to wherever they needed to go. I'm sorry to tell you, but I don't think people will be lining up for this."

"It was brave of you to volunteer," Mirei said.

Ashin shrugged with a growing semblance of her usual composure. "We used you in our schemes. Saved your life, as it turned out, but still—we used you. We owe you a debt for that. And I owe you for Sharyo's life." Another shaky laugh. "And Indera's. Although I'm still not used to thinking of her as mine."

"Do you talk with her often?" Mirei asked, picking up the bundle Ashin had dropped.

"Indera? No. She doesn't like me very much."

"Nor does she like Sharyo. I thought getting the two of them to meet would put her fears to rest, but I don't think it has. Indera's too fond of being a doppelganger, with all the associated benefits."

Ashin shrugged again. "She'll have to get used to the idea of losing them. But she has years before that will happen, at least."

I hope time does the trick. Mirei pinched the nerve between her thumb and forefinger, trying to combat her headache, then gave it up as a lost cause. "Do you feel up for a little healing? I'd rather not be off my game while we're here."

The Hand Key gave her a sharp look. "You're not well?"

"I've been getting headaches lately." There was a bird's nest in a crook of the cherry tree; Mirei climbed up to it and found a feather Ashin could use as a focus. The lacework of power settled over her, and the headache and nausea faded. "Keep the feather," she said when the other witch was done. "With the distance we're going to be walking, we may need it again before we get to Tungral."

THE SUN WAS OUT when they began, but the sky soon grayed over and the air became quite chill. Mirei was glad they had thought to allow for how much colder it would be that far north and up in the mountains; otherwise they would have been a very miserable pair of vagrants.

Which they might yet become, if the weather decided to dump snow on them like it seemed to be considering. They made their way from Falya's family's cottage to Lyonakh itself, then skirted the village's edge. What the doppelganger had called "the big road" proved to be a rutted, stony track leading downslope from the village, which they found easily and began following.

"If I'm right about the distance, we could hurry and maybe reach it today," Mirei said, keeping her voice as low and her accent as Kalistyin as she could. No one was around, but the practice was useful. "Kekkai won't be looking for us until the day after tomorrow, though. I figure we keep our pace slow, camp out tonight, get to Tungral tomorrow. That leaves us the rest of that day to take a look at the town and figure out the situation."

"Sleeping in the cold," Ashin sighed. "What fun. Are we both going into the inn to meet Kekkai? I'd rather have a lookout, but on the other hand, if we have to get out of there quickly, we don't want to waste time trying to get to one another. Unless you think you could move me at a distance."

"Do you really want me trying that for the first time in the middle of an emergency?" Both of them shuddered.

"Can't say what the best approach will be until we're there. I'd like a lookout, too, but you're right about splitting up."

They passed other travelers on the road. By the look of the signposts, there were a lot of little villages scattered in pocket side valleys, their own paths leading off from the road. Traces of early snow lingered in sheltered areas, but the road itself was still clear; it looked like a number of villagers were making one last foot visit to or from Tungral before settling in to wait for the deep snows that would make sledging possible.

As they approached the first of these travelers, Ashin began humming a jaunty tune, fortunately choosing one that Mirei thought was Askavyan, and therefore not *too* foreign. Her timing might have been coincidence, but she stopped almost immediately after he was past, and then did it again when they came upon a slow-moving ox-drawn wagon on its way to town.

Once the wagon was well behind them, Mirei glanced sidelong at Ashin. "And I thought *I* was paranoid."

The answering grin was thin-lipped. "I wasn't exaggerating when I said I lived in fear of being killed. Even before Tari died, we were all on edge. I got in the habit of checking *everyone* for spells."

"So you're going to be humming nonstop the entire time we're in Tungral?"

"Maybe," Ashin said, and smiled with more feeling.

They stopped briefly around noon to eat from the meager supply in their bundle; then Mirei stood guard while Ashin hid behind a bush and quietly sang a healing spell over her feet. "I'm used to walking," the Key said when she returned, "but with actual *shoes* on." She gave her rag-wrapped foot a sour look.

The air grew colder as they walked on, and the threatened snow began to fall, thickly enough that there was soon a smooth layer carpeting the frozen ground. It muffled sound enough that the hoofbeats of the next travelers didn't catch their attention nearly as quickly. Ashin jerked in startlement and started belatedly humming as four riders came around a bend and began trotting uphill past them.

With four spells in such close proximity, the resonance was strong enough to vibrate in Mirei's bones.

It shouldn't have been a problem. Any on-pitch vocalization would alert any witch within hearing to nearby magic, but there were no spells on Mirei and Ashin; nothing pointed a guilty finger at *them*.

But in the stress of the moment, unaccustomed as she was to ordinary methods of disguise, Ashin forgot that, and responded as if she had been caught.

The Air witch began a song of force, probably intended to send the nearby slope of dirt and rock tumbling down on the riders. Before she was more than two notes into it, one of the riders, disguised as a heavyset man, spurred his horse directly at her. Ashin held her ground as long as she could, trying to finish the spell as two of the others began to sing, but she didn't make it; she had to dive out of the way to avoid a swipe of the man's sword. The power she'd summoned hung in the air, tense and incomplete.

Mirei didn't waste breath swearing. She couldn't sort out the spells the other two were building; they overlapped each other, muddling the words. Mirei went for something simple: a burst of light, shocking in the gray dimness of the snowfall.

The horses panicked and reared, interrupting both spells and sending those riders to the ground. Behind her, Mirei heard hoofbeats; the man had reined in and was headed her way. She dropped into a side roll, and he trampled past harmlessly.

Ashin was up and singing again. So was one of the other witches, a skinny woman who had disentangled herself from her horse. Mirei had fetched up against a boulder at the side of the road. She fumbled for a moment at the pack of their supplies, trying to get her blades out, but her fingers were cold and the knots weren't moving and she didn't have the time to waste. Mirei flung the pack at the rider and hit him in the back, knocking him askew in the saddle. Forget weapons. She'd use her voice.

Small explosions detonated underneath both Ashin and the skinny witch; they stumbled back from each other's spells. One of the other women was still on the ground. Her leg looked broken, but she was tough; with her face twisted in pain, she nevertheless began to sing. And this spell, Mirei realized, was aimed at *her.*

*Air and Water and Earth—going to choke me—won't be able to sing—*Everything had gone weirdly quiet and distant as adrenaline kicked in. *Heard this one before— Shimi, attacking me in Star Hall—canceled it then—but HOW—*

Syllables and pitches surfaced in her memory. Mirei rattled them out, as fast as she could, and felt the Void power cancel the building spell, cutting through the strands of energy and dissipating them.

Ashin and the skinny woman were still fighting. The

other two weren't singing—why not? Both looked like men; both had swords. *Cousins. Right. Worry about them later.* She focused on the woman with the broken leg. *Better if I don't kill her*—She began a spell to knock the other woman out.

Pain flared in her left shoulder. Mirei looked down and found a knife hilt protruding from her rags, a spreading stain around it. The unmounted Cousin had thrown it, and the one still on his horse was riding right at her.

Ripping the knife out, Mirei spun and took a running dive at the boulder, crashing to the snow-covered needles on the other side in a wash of screaming pain. *Damn me blind, should've worried about them*—She was temporarily hidden behind the boulder, and most of the things the enemy witches could do to attack her required them to *see* her. Mirei gasped in breaths of the freezing air and tried to think how to get out of this alive.

Cut down on their numbers.

Mirei lurched up to her knees and risked a quick glance over the boulder. No clear shot on either of the witches; their horses were still trampling around. The Cousin who had thrown the knife, though, was in the middle of climbing back into his saddle. Mirei returned the blade to him, and pinned the man's right hand to his thigh.

The other rider was an irritation she'd been avoiding long enough. He'd veered off from his course to intercept Mirei when she dived behind the rock; an explosion of power near Ashin had made his horse bolt down the path, back in the direction the attackers had come from. Now he was returning to the fray. Crouching so that she was hidden from the witches, but could still see the horse, Mirei gathered her strength and sang a spell of levitation.

The boulder at her side shuddered, rose, and hurtled through the air to smash into rider and horse alike.

Cover gone, she had to move. Ashin was holding her own against the skinny witch; the other Cousin had fallen from his saddle again and was trying to pull the knife free. Mirei turned to deal with the woman still lying on the ground with a broken leg—and felt a wash of sudden heat, blasting through the cold.

Ashin screamed.

The Air witch's clothes were on fire. She had sufficient presence of mind, fortunately, to drop to the ground and begin rolling through the deepening snow. Steam hissed into the air in thick clouds. Mirei didn't know how badly the Key was hurt, and she didn't have time to find out. The two enemy witches were turning their attention to her.

Mirei reached for the most obvious counterattack: fire of her own. But a bare three syllables into the spell, she knew something was dangerously wrong.

For one moment, she felt like Miryo again, able to call on power but not to control it. Then she realized the problem was outside her. Too many disrupted spells, cut off before completion; too much power drawn into the area without being resolved. The air rippled invisibly with it. As she drew in energy for her own spell, it roiled dangerously, like a drunken man juggling knives.

The other witches were briefly forgotten as she fought not to destroy *herself*. Seamlessly, not even letting herself question whether she could change midstream, Mirei wove her attacking spell into a canceling one, slicing through and dissipating the energy she'd called. It melted away, to her relief, and the immediate danger passed.

But she wasn't the only one who could set it off.

The witch with the broken leg was gasping in the snow, temporarily overcome by pain. The other one, though, was preparing more fire for Mirei.

Get out of sight! Mirei ran for the trees, just behind where the boulder had been, and felt a surge of heat, but nothing ignited. "Stop, you stupid bitch; we'll all be killed!" she bellowed as she ran, but doubted it would stop her.

It didn't. The witch began again, this time using force to rip at the trees Mirei had taken shelter in. *Can't she feel it? Like trying to sword fight on top of water*—Crouching out of sight, Mirei wondered desperately if she could try to cancel the unused power. *I could try*—

But failure could be even worse.

Fury and fear decided her. *It's them, or all of us.* And, snatching up a pair of rocks, Mirei threw herself back out into the open just as the trees shattered into wooden spears behind her.

The leap was part of the movement; the pitches were already pouring from her mouth. The rocks were foci, and more than that. Spinning in the snow, Mirei flung them at the two witches.

The power in the air followed the path she'd given it, and recoiled explosively upon the singer and her injured friend.

MIREI WASN'T SURE if she was temporarily deafened, or if it was just the muffling effect of the softly falling snow.

She clapped her numb hands, and heard only a distant smack. *Deafened. All right.*

The air was clear of summoned power. The landscape was a wreck. Several pine trees behind Mirei had been reduced to kindling. Debris from the slope on the other side of the path was strewn everywhere, half-buried in the snow. A boulder blocked part of the path downhill; the blood crusted on it was rapidly freezing. In its wake lay the shattered remains of a horse and a red-haired woman, no longer covered by an illusion.

Uphill, there was a patch of ground bare of snow. The falling flakes melted away on contact, from the heat.

Not much was left of the witches, the second Cousin, or their horses. The skinny witch had been singing Fire; that had been the catalyst and shaping force for the power that annihilated her.

Mirei stood alone in the quiet, shoulder throbbing— and then remembered Ashin.

She walked past the bloody pulp that had been a horse, stumbling with weariness, moving in the direction she had seen the Air witch roll. Ashin wasn't hard to find; her clothes made a blackened stain in the white of the snow.

The Key smiled weakly at her. "Next time, give a little warning."

Mirei's knees gave out. She sat down with a thump. "Mother's mercy. I thought you'd be dead."

"Thank the snow. But I'm feeling rather worse for the wear." Ashin struggled to a sitting position, wincing. Charred fragments of cloth fluttered loose, but it looked like the outer layers had been the ones to catch fire; she'd put it out before it burned all the way through to her skin. "For a moment there, I thought I'd go up with the rest of them. We nearly *all* went out in flames."

"I've never felt that before," Mirei whispered, still shaking. "Not on that scale."

"Doesn't happen often. Witches going at each other

with spells—not common. We discussed it, though, me and the others, before we guessed the Primes were hiring Hunters to kill us. If you can't back off and let it dissipate, aiming it's about the best you can do." Ashin touched the reddened skin of her face and hissed in pain.

Mirei tried to evaluate her condition, through the snow and char. "How badly are you hurt?"

"Nothing that'll stop me, once—" Ashin caught her breath sharply as she tried to get up. "Once I heal this. Couldn't you have left a horse or two alive, though?"

Glancing around at the wreckage, Mirei felt herself go suddenly cold, and not from the temperature. "Wait."

"I'm hardly going anywhere fast," the Key said with some asperity.

Mirei chopped one hand through the air, cutting her levity off. "These women. Two witches, two Cousins, all of them disguised, riding this way with a purpose. Why? What's up in these mountains that they'd be interested in?"

Ashin shrugged, winced, and switched to a verbal response. "Just passing through? On their way somewhere else?"

"But there *isn't* anywhere else. Villages up the slopes, then nothing. There's no pass. You can't get through to the other side." Mirei rose to her feet, scanning the remains of the bodies in the snow. Only one answer made sense, and it chilled her deeply. "They were looking for us."

After an ugly silence, Ashin said, "But who knew we were coming? Kekkai told us to come to Tungral, not Lyonakh. The only people—" Her breath caught again; then she scrambled upright, fear overriding the pain of her scorched skin. "The only people who knew we'd be on this road were Onomita and the Primes."

It was a sickening thought. A traitor that highly placed—how many plans had been leaked?

Then one blessed memory returned to Mirei, not exactly soothing, but at least less frightening than the alternative. "*No.* You said it in the room. Remember? When we were testing the spell. You said we were going from Lyonakh to Tungral. There were other witches present."

Ashin thought it over, swaying on her feet, then nodded slowly. "Yes. I did. But we don't have any proof it was one of them."

"They're more likely suspects," Mirei said. "It *isn't* Satomi, and I don't believe it's Koika, either. Rana—"

"Has been very quiet lately," Ashin said grimly. "Could be she's rethinking her allegiance. And then there's Onomita."

"Who didn't leave when Arinei and her fellow Keys did."

"Maybe they left her behind on purpose. As a plant."

Mirei pressed one hand to her shoulder against the pain there, mind racing over the possible permutations. "If it's one of the theory witches, then I don't *think* they know anything more. Just that we were going to Lyonakh for some reason, and from there to Tungral. Enough to point at a location where we could be found. And we're targets worth hitting."

"*You* are," Ashin said. "In that equation, I don't even matter."

"You matter to a zealot, and Shimi fits that description. But that's not the point. I'm thinking risk. If it was one of Hyoka's people, then they know where we're going, but not what we're doing there. If it's Rana or Onomita—"

"Then they know *exactly* what we're doing," Ashin finished for her, voice bleak. "They know the inn, the timing, who we're looking for. And they know to look for *her,* too."

"And to stop her from ever getting there."

"Unless it was a setup to begin with."

Mirei shook her head. "I don't think so. Why ambush us on the road, sloppily, if they could have a nice, well-planned ambush in Tungral?"

Ashin cocked her head to the side as a replacement for a shrug. "Fewer bystanders?"

"Could be." Mirei went hunting for their pack. Ashin took out the battered feather and placed a healing spell on her blistered skin. By the time Mirei found the bundle and returned to her, the damage had faded to a manageable level; the rest would have to heal over time, sped along by the energy Ashin had fed into it.

"So," Mirei said, when Ashin was done placing a spell on the knife wound in her shoulder. "If the traitor's one of Hyoka's people, we've put ourselves in mild danger by going to Tungral. If it's Onomita or a Prime, we're walking into a death trap. Do we press on, or go home?"

"You're asking *me?*" Ashin said.

Mirei smiled wryly. "You do outrank me, remember?"

"Right, and I care *so* much about that, in a situation like this." Ashin glanced around at the bodies as if they could provide some hint of what lay ahead. "Here's my opinion. We go on—as long as you make me one promise first."

"And what's that?"

"If it *is* a trap—or even if it isn't, but we run into serious trouble anyway—then you get out of there *immediately.* No hesitation. No waiting for me."

Mirei stared at her. "You mean leave you *there.*"

Ashin met her gaze without flinching. "Yes."

"I'm not leaving you to die."

A tight grin answered that. "Don't you have any confidence in me? The point is, I'm replaceable. You're not. Not for another ten or fifteen years. Satomi made me promise before I left that I would give up my own life to get you out alive. I would have done it even without her telling me. If we get in trouble, then you jump clear and don't wait to grab me. Make that promise, or we don't go anywhere."

The demand raised a mutinous feeling in Mirei. *I'm sick of being treated like I'm irreplaceable. And I'm doubly sick of abandoning friends to death.* Because Ashin *had* become a friend, though not as close as Eclipse.

"I've got my own tricks," Ashin said. "Don't assume that leaving me means I'm going to die. I've been at this game longer than you have. Not to mention that I knew when I started helping Tari that I was putting my life at risk. To see you succeed—to see you find the answer we'd all been looking for—and then to turn around and have my own *Prime* undermine that before it even gets started . . ." The Key shook her head; there was surprising heat in her dark eyes. "I'm still fighting for that cause. I never stopped. If there's danger, then I'll deal with it. But I don't need you to protect me."

She's a grown woman, Mirei thought, looking Ashin over. Scorched, exhausted, the witch still held herself with a determined air. *Not some child you need to look after.*

"All right," she said at last. "I promise."

There was nothing else for them there on the road, and they needed to get away from the disaster, fast. But more important than that, they needed to at least *try* to hide some of what had happened there.

"Let's deal with this," Mirei said, flicking a finger at the remains because nodding her head made her shoulder hurt. Cremation was one of three appropriate treatments for the dead, and the one witches preferred. The air was clear, so she could create fire without fear. "Then we move on and find a place to set up camp for the night. I have an idea that may keep us safer in Tungral, though."

"Oh?" Ashin said.

Mirei smiled mirthlessly. "It requires trusting Satomi. But if she's not on our side, we're dead anyway."

Chapter Seventeen

❧━━┼━━┼━━❧

PLEASE, ALLOW US to demonstrate our talents for you,"
Mirei said to the pockmarked man, who was giving her a
suspicious look.

Had she had an option, she wouldn't have chosen the
Bear's Claw as the place to carry out this charade. Packed
with benches under its low ceiling, the common room of
the inn was a place for raucous drinking, not other kinds
of entertainment. But Kekkai had chosen to meet here,
and she had to work around that. Fortunately, it happened
that Ashin knew quite a collection of vulgar drinking
songs.

Mirei's calculations had been simple. If the traitor was
Rana or Onomita—or, she supposed, Koika, though she
seriously doubted the Earth Prime would betray them—
then any ambushers would be looking for Kalistyin vagrants. Also, she and Ashin needed a more discreet way of
checking for illusions and other spells. Both problems
could be solved by changing their disguise.

Mirei told Satomi precisely where they were and
Satomi sent them extra supplies. Soon the Kalistyin vagrants became a much more flamboyant pair of Askavyan
entertainers. Neither Mirei nor Ashin had the blindest
clue how to play an instrument, unfortunately, but a drum
was simple enough. Ashin would be the singer, since

Mirei couldn't drop her voice low enough to fake a man's singing. Instead, she would beat out an accompaniment to the tunes the Key had picked up in her wanderings as an Air Hand.

After an extended scrutiny, the innkeeper nodded at last. Flexing her stiff shoulder—spells made the natural healing process go faster, but her knife wound was taking longer to mend than Ashin's skin—she tucked the drum under her arm and nodded to her companion.

With a four-beat intro, the Key began to sing in a rough, energetic voice that startled Mirei. It was completely unlike the mellifluous tones of a witch, while still being excellently on key. Ashin probably couldn't sing off-key if she tried, and it would defeat the purpose anyway. But the performance was everything Mirei could hope for.

The innkeeper seemed less impressed. When Ashin finished the song, he stared at them for a moment; for all Mirei could read from his expression, he could be considering the tune, preparing to throw them out, or doing the season's accounts in his head.

Finally he gave a curt nod. "You can try for tonight. Goes well enough, you can try tomorrow night. I like how you're doing a few days after *that,* could be we can make some deal for the winter. But no promises."

Ashin swept the man a florid bow. "You won't be disappointed, I promise you that. And having entertainers around can shorten the long, dreary nights of winter."

Unmoved by her poetic language, the innkeeper jerked a thumb at the staircase at the far end of the room. "Cupboard under there. Toss your things inside. Come sunset, you sit over *there*—" Another jerk of the thumb. "Play till the crowd leaves or I tell you to shut up. Any coin you get goes to me for food and space to sleep. Don't try to palm any of it; I'll know."

"Thank you," Mirei said, and went to stow their pack under the staircase.

Following her, Ashin murmured, "If worse comes to worst, we can *convince* him to let us stay another day."

By which she meant a spell. Mirei shook her head. "Not unless we absolutely have to. So you'd better sing well."

THEIR FIRST PERFORMANCE picked up no sign of magic anywhere in the vicinity, much to Mirei's relief. Ashin sang bawdy tunes, sacrificing tone quality in exchange for volume and not sounding like a witch, and if they didn't get much coin from the patrons, they got enough to satisfy the innkeeper and let them stay a second night, which was all the two witches wanted.

They had the daytime free, which let them scout out Tungral and get a sense of the place. The town sat just south of the border with Askavya, and had changed hands between the two domains more than once in its history. There was a narrow gap between the end of the mountains and the coast, and Tungral sat right on the road that ran through that gap. There were enough travelers through the area, even at this time of year, that their presence wasn't deeply suspicious. But with the failure of Kalistyi's northern silver mines, which Ashin briefed Mirei on as they wandered, Tungral's prosperity had suffered deeply. The townspeople had a grim look, and there were more than a few buildings that were shuttered or falling apart.

"Why here?" Ashin murmured to Mirei as they sat out

behind the Bear's Claw, cradling mugs of weak butter tea and waiting for sunset to come. "Why'd she insist on Tungral?"

Mirei also kept her voice low, in case someone were to wander by. If anyone was listening to them with magic, they were in trouble, but she had no reason to think they'd been pegged. Or that anyone was even here to peg them. "This isn't their stronghold; I'm sure of that much, after what we've seen today. But I think there have to be witches here."

"Have to? Why?"

"Because of the ones we met on the road. They had a day's warning, *maybe*, to get out there. They can't have been far away. And I doubt they were the only ones here."

Ashin nodded thoughtfully. "They wouldn't want to strip the town bare, I'd imagine. Not if they have some reason to keep witches stationed here. Unless, of course, they were just passing through, and were given orders to divert."

"Could be." Mirei brooded into her tea. "Just stay alert tonight. And be sure to sing on key."

"And *you* remember the promise you made. If there's trouble, and I'm not right there at your side—"

"I remember," Mirei said.

THE INNKEEPER WAS IN A FOUL MOOD, berating one of the serving maids for having forgotten to do some of the tasks he'd set her. The girl appeared to grow more and more flustered under his accusations, putting things in the wrong place and getting other details wrong. Mirei felt sorry for her, and very glad that this would be their last night in town.

She and Ashin were permitted a small meal before performing, a bowl apiece of rice noodles with spiced fish oil. Both swallowed it without complaint; as an Air witch, Mirei reflected, Ashin must have learned to live frugally, and to take what she could get. Much like an itinerant Hunter just out of training.

They both kept a close eye on the patrons coming in, wondering if any of them were under a spell of disguise. None of them looked around overtly, as if searching for someone they were supposed to meet, but Mirei hoped Kekkai was discreet enough not to be so obvious. Surely, after so much time playing politics, she had learned the valuable art of subtlety.

A decent crowd had gathered by the time they were done eating, and the innkeeper glared at them to get to work. Mirei dried off her hands and picked up the drum. She'd gained enough confidence with it the previous night to be bolder with her rhythms, so she gave Ashin a lengthier intro than usual, and then the witch began to sing.

She had to work to project her voice over the din of the crowd, but the answering resonance didn't depend on ears; it hit Mirei distinctly.

A quick glance to the side confirmed that, yes, Ashin had felt it, too.

When the song finished, she leaned close to the other witch, under the pretense of picking up her mug and taking a sip, and asked, "Could you pinpoint it?"

Ashin shook her head. "Too much interference from the noise of the crowd. Can't tell where it's coming from. Nor what it is."

"My money's on a disguise. Keep listening." Mirei straightened up hastily as a young trapper, bundled under what looked like half of his stock for sale, stepped up to where they sat. "Another song," he said in a hoarse voice, and dropped a coin down in Ashin's empty bowl. "Two songs. I like your voice."

Ashin flashed a flirtatious grin at him. "Two songs it is, and I hope my husband here won't be jealous." Mirei remembered she was supposed to be Ashin's husband and glowered.

Two songs later, they paused again. Ashin whispered, "It's moving."

"I know." Mirei had been looking around the room, trying to spot who might be the source of the resonance, but they were crammed off to one side and sitting to boot. Half the crowd was standing, wandering around, going to the bar for more mead, talking to friends, going for a game of darts against one wall and returning to their seats. She couldn't see clearly enough to pick the target out. "I only feel one, though. Must be Kekkai. We need to let her know it's us."

"How? Stand up and say so?"

"Not hardly." They'd been quiet too long. Mirei started on the drum again as the harried serving maid from before came by with a full tray.

The first words of Ashin's song called up a resonance so immediately that it felt like a kick in the teeth.

The Key managed to keep going, and in the noise, Mirei doubted anyone heard the slight stumble in her words. But Ashin's gaze snapped to meet Mirei's, and then back to the serving maid, who was beyond a doubt the source of the resonance.

Should've seen it sooner, Mirei thought with sudden clarity, understanding at last. *Forgetting tasks, doing things wrong—that* isn't *the maid. No wonder she's having such a hard time. Good cover, though.*

They finished out the song, because to do otherwise would look suspicious, but then Mirei put her drum down. "I'm going to approach her," she murmured to Ashin. "Let her know we're here, arrange to get her out. Keep singing without me." Rising from her seat, she scanned the crowd, found the serving maid, and began to work her way through the press of bodies.

She caught up to the disguised Kekkai just at the edge of the bar, not far from where the innkeeper was standing. Mirei sidled in close, to make it look less odd, gave the woman her best impression of a charming smile, and whispered in her ear, "Meet us out back after three more songs. We'll take you back to Starfall."

She got only that far before the innkeeper noticed her there. "Hey, back to your drum!" he snapped, glaring at her. "I'm not paying you to hit on my maids."

Mirei held up her hands in apology and faded back to her seat. "Three more songs, then we go out back," she said to Ashin, and picked her drum up again.

The songs seemed to take forever, even though Mirei knew by comparison to the previous night that Ashin was dropping verses out. When the three were finished at last, they stood up and headed for the inn's back exit, with a pause to swipe their pack from its place under the stairs.

"She's gonna throw up," Mirei shouted over the din at the innkeeper as they passed the bar, gesturing with her free hand to Ashin, who obligingly looked ill. She kept her pack low and out of sight. "We'll be back in a minute." Then they were past him and into the sweltering warmth of the kitchen, and it was too much hassle for him to pursue them. And as Mirei had no intention of returning, she didn't much care what he said when they came back.

Kekkai was waiting for them outside, shivering in the cold. "Let's go," she said fervently when she saw them. "I'm freezing. Where are the horses?"

"We didn't bring any," Ashin said, taking the pack from Mirei and slinging it onto her back. "Didn't work with our disguises."

The world snapped into focus around Mirei as she heard Ashin say that. *Horses?* she echoed in her mind, nerves suddenly harp-tight. *Why does she think we're riding out of here?*

Void it. If you're wrong, you can apologize later.

She slugged Kekkai with all her might and laid the woman out flat.

By the time the figure hit the ground, it wasn't the serving maid anymore, but neither was it the Key of the Fire Heart. It was a witch Mirei had never seen before.

"What in the *Void* do you think you're—" Ashin began, but then cut off abruptly as she saw the woman lying unconscious at their feet. "Damn me bloody," she whispered, staring. "We got the wrong woman."

"They're looking for her," Mirei said grimly. "We have to find her first."

She yanked the pack from Ashin's shoulders and ripped it open, digging her sword and knife out from where they were buried. Staring at the weapons, Ashin said, "What do you need those for? You have magic."

"They make me feel better," Mirei replied, and it was the truth. She was still as much Mirage as Miryo—and sometimes blades were quieter.

Ashin tied the pack closed again and slung it over her

shoulder. "I'll check the front. Maybe she didn't come in, maybe she's waiting outside." It was a thin possibility, but something to go on, at least. Mirei nodded, and looked down at the unconscious witch while Ashin strode off through the cold night. She was half-tempted to try and send her back to Starfall alone, and take her chances with the possibility that the woman might not arrive safely— but she didn't dare. If there were other witches around, then the surge of power for the spell would act like a beacon. It wasn't all Void energy, and they would be able to feel the rest of it.

Power. If Kekkai knows she's being hunted, she'll expect them to check for people under spells. Would she have the brains to go for a mundane disguise?

Before she could follow through on that thought, she heard a growing thunder of noise from the street.

Swiftly belting her weapons around her hips, Mirei slipped around the edge of the Bear's Claw to look out front.

An entire troop of mounted soldiers was pulling up in front of the inn. Mirei attempted a quick count of them in the bad light; she guessed at least twenty in the immediate spot, but saw more fanning out through Tungral's lanes, some on foot. By the torches the leaders carried, she could see the embroidered collars they wore over their armor.

A quartet of stars. The symbol of the Lady of Kalistyi.

And with the troop, there were witches.

"Fan out!" one of them barked, turning her horse so that she could watch the soldiers disperse. "Get around to the back of the inn. *Move!* If she gets away, it'll be *your* hides."

Mirei looked around desperately for Ashin, but the Key was nowhere in sight. Had probably taken cover when she heard this lot coming—but now what would she do?

That isn't going to matter in a minute. Not once they find the witch out back.

"Get them out here," the lead witch said, and more than ten soldiers trotted immediately through the front door of the Bear's Claw.

Blood and damnation—if I'm right, and Kekkai's in that lot . . .

Throwing caution to the winds, Mirei took her chance. As the crowd began to stumble out of the inn, milling and complaining and arguing with the soldiers, who responded with fists and kicks, she slipped herself into their midst.

She moved as quickly as she could without attracting attention and scanned the faces of the people in the crowd. The terrible light didn't help. *Not many women. Might be a man. Rule the tall ones out.* She was one of the few in the crowd who was armed, the only one she saw with a sword. Somebody would notice that before much longer. *If a man, then no beard, I doubt she could fake one—* No sign of Ashin. But she had to find Kekkai first. *So she'll look young . . .*

From somewhere among the snow-dusted houses of Tungral, but not at all far away, she felt power begin to move.

The other witches felt it, too. She saw them turn to each other, confer; a swift count by one of them seemed to show all present and accounted for. Whoever was casting a spell wasn't one of theirs.

Then a figure stepped out into the middle of the street and faced down the company of soldiers and witches that had come to take her captive. "Leave those people alone," Kekkai said in a clear, carrying voice. "I'm the one you're looking for."

At the sight of her—so clearly the target the soldiers were after—the noise of the drunken, confused crowd abated slightly. Just enough for Mirei to hear a despairing voice moan, "Oh, you stupid girl, *no!*"

Though her heart was screaming at her to go and help the witch who had just called the violence down on herself, Mirei wrenched her eyes away to find who had spoken.

The young trapper who had called for songs, beardless, not too tall, buried inside a wealth of furs that made his— her—build look larger than it was. Whose voice, absent the hoarseness, was the same as the woman who had just challenged the soldiers, and whose face, now that Mirei was looking for it, was Kekkai's.

The time for subtlety was gone. She lunged through the crowd and seized Kekkai by the wrist. The woman screamed and tried to pull away. Mirei snarled, "It's me, you blind bitch! Now we have to get to Ashin before she gets herself killed!"

"Ashin . . . ?" the Fire Key repeated, confused, but Mirei didn't have time for her confusion; soldiers had spurred their horses forward to ride the disguised Ashin down, and the witches were singing spells, and Mirei knew she had made a promise to Ashin but she couldn't just abandon the woman to die.

Power surged, and a roar of heaving earth filled the air. Over the startled yells of the crowd, Mirei could hear screams; the spell, she guessed, was Ashin's, ripping apart the ground beneath the horses' hooves. A cloud of

snow and dust clogged the air. Hauling hard on the
woman's wrist, Mirei dragged Kekkai out of the press,
drawing her sword as she went.

The scouting of Tungral paid off, as she ducked between houses and approached Ashin's position from the
side, avoiding the main avenue of attack. There were soldiers here, too, but Kekkai had recovered enough to sing
as she ran; the men were knocked to the sides, clearing
their path. But Mirei could feel power to her left, too,
from where the other witches were massed.

She broke through onto the street, Kekkai at her heels,
and found herself enveloped in a rising cloud of steam;
Ashin had conjured heat to melt the snow, hiding herself
for a moment longer from the sight of the other witches.
Mirei threw herself in the right general direction and saw
Ashin, a shadow in the mist, still looking like Kekkai.

No time to waste. The mist wouldn't last long. Ashin
saw her, grabbed hold, and Mirei began to cast the spell,
praying to the Goddess that she could take both of them at
once.

The power on the other side of the fog was building,
but she couldn't tell what it was, not through the weaving
strands of her own spell, shaped by voice and body and
desperate, frantic faith—

A flight of blades shot at them out of the mist, soldiers'
swords put in flight, and struck just as the spell snatched
them away.

Chapter Eighteen

MANY WITCHES MAINTAINED schedules that kept them up some distance into the night, because they favored the starlit darkness for working spells. Scholarly and administrative work, however, was mostly carried out during the day, so the archives were not at all crowded once the sun went down. But Satomi suspected that the corner of the archives she was perusing would have been deserted even at midday, for the contents were among the most tedious and uninteresting of those kept at Starfall. No one came here unless they had a specific reason.

Hers was a specific curiosity.

She ran one finger down the rows of identical, black-bound volumes, reading the characters marked on their spines. *Forty years ago would be my guess, but that's an estimate; I'll have to check for quite a span in either direction. This is going to be ever so much fun.*

Satomi found the book that contained records from exactly forty years previously; she would search outward from there. Opening it, she found herself eyeing pages with neatly ruled lines, and terse entries on the lines.

Oeba. Choukin. 23 Ara 62.3.244. Water Heart.
Shidau. Etsumari. 4 Gire 62.3.244. Earth Hand.
Hannen. Waki. 11 Paoli 62.3.244. Air Hand.

Tidy annals of witch-students tested, and where they had ended up. Name, mother's name, date of test, and then later some Void Head returned and added in the Ray and Path each woman had chosen. There were literally hundreds of records for her to search.

The one saving grace was that the entries she was looking for would be easy to spot.

She found one on the next page. *Urayomi. Yabure. 16 Riggio 63.3.744.* No Ray and Path. That omission was the silent record of a student who had failed.

"Died, or became a Cousin?" Satomi murmured to herself. No indication; she had known there wouldn't be. But it didn't matter for her search.

Looking for those blank spots, the search went quickly, if not fruitfully. Satomi went methodically in each direction, year by year, fanning outward from the forty-year mark. Every time she found a failed student, she checked the name.

Until at last she found an entry that caught her eye.
Omonae. Hinobi. 5 Paoli 58.3.244.

She stared at the words for several minutes before closing the book and returning it to the shelf. Not definitive proof. Other women had names like that. But it came from roughly the right time, and it could have been shortened to Nae.

Satomi was not certain why she'd gone to the trouble of checking. If Nae had been a witch-student, rather than a child of a Cousin, then she wouldn't remember anything of it. What difference did it make, if the woman in charge of the Cousins had been one of those who lost her memory in the test? What bearing could it have on the situation? She didn't know. But the question had crossed her mind, and once it had done so, she hadn't been able to shake it.

Omonae. Would any part of her remember that name, if she heard it again?

She left the test records and went to another section of the archives, equally deserted. This time her search went faster. Knowing the date she was looking for, she immediately located the relevant book and pulled it down.

> One is one and it doesn't continue. Then one sees one and one is more. More than one is a set, a group, a series. But there is only one. There are all the ones and none of them is more than one. East and west and north and south and from one domain to another it goes, hands carry the hope but there is no hope in their hands. More than one is death. More than one is war. War is one of five. You must see this before there can be more than one.

With a sigh, Satomi closed the book. Those were the words spoken by Omonae, the night she lost her memory, the night power broke her and made her a Cousin. Satomi could make no sense of them. She couldn't help but try to apply them to the current situation, but they could as easily be referencing the politics of Askavya, or nothing at all. And even if they *were* about the current time, she could not derive any advice from them. They were useless to her. Eikyo had hinted, tantalizingly, that the Cousins knew about the words, but with the young woman under suspicion, Satomi had little hope of learning more. Perhaps it was time to retrieve Eikyo, and pray there was some way of salvaging that situation.

Leaving the archives, Satomi went through the corridors with a brisk stride, nodding briefly to witches who sank into bows at her passing. *If nothing else, I accomplished one thing by going on that hunt: It distracted me from wondering what's happening in Kalistyi.*

The message from Mirei had shaken her deeply, with its suggestion that someone had betrayed news of their journey to Shimi and Arinei. Satomi was willing to trust— for the time being, anyway—that Rana and Onomita were loyal, but Hyoka's witches were another matter. Koika had taken charge of the search for the spy. Given a free rein, she would have used methods that would make a sledgehammer look subtle, but Satomi had talked her into more delicacy. If they could identify the traitor, they could use her to feed false information to the dissidents.

Depending on how the mission to Kalistyi went, though, delicacy might end up the least of her concerns.

Ruriko was out when she arrived at her office. Satomi passed through the secretary's room and into her own. There was another report from Hyoka waiting for her, detailing the various obstacles they'd run into; despite all efforts, it seemed there was no way to disrupt the communication papers without having physical access to them.

She turned up the lamps, sat down at her desk, and had just begun reading the report when she felt a twisting of power in the air.

It wasn't large; she didn't immediately go on alert. So she was completely unprepared when three figures appeared in the space before her desk.

Screams hammered the air.

Two of the three figures collapsed to the floor; the third, Mirei, stumbled and half fell against Satomi's desk, retching and trembling. Satomi shot to her feet. The screams continued. Mirei was filthy, ragged, bleeding. Beyond her, on the floor, Kekkai was curled into a tiny ball inside a giant mound of furs, shrieking, hands clamped to her head, and next to her—

Satomi began singing even as she flung herself around the end of her desk, reaching her hands out to the third woman on the floor. Her knees hit the tiles and skidded in blood. Power came to her call and went where she sent it, but it wasn't enough; healing was magic, but even magic had its limits. Wounds knit faster, under a spell, but some wounds were bad enough to kill even more quickly.

She felt the moment that Ashin died.

She kept singing for a span after that, reflexively, as if it would do any good now. Finally her voice trailed off, and in the silence that followed, she realized that Kekkai had stopped screaming, and Mirei was on the floor next to her, white and shaking with exhaustion.

Satomi's eyes met hers, and she saw the shock and horror in Mirei's face.

"Not fast enough," Mirei whispered, voice ragged and faint. "They couldn't see us, so they sent blades—if I'd been just a beat faster—"

What little color was left in her drained out suddenly, and Satomi caught her just as she collapsed.

NENIKUNE CAME OUT of the bedroom and closed the door quietly behind her, giving a quick glance to the phalanx of Cousins and witches that were standing guard in the outer room.

"Come with me," Satomi said.

They retired to a next-door chamber, and Satomi sang

into place a spell that would keep anyone from eavesdropping. When they were safe, she faced the healer, trying not to show the worry she felt.

"Tell me."

Nenikune was concise and clear, as always. Her businesslike tone belied her haggard face, still marked by the horror of Anness's death. "They both have a number of cuts. One, in Mirei's shoulder, looks older, and it's well on its way to being healed. We've put spells on the rest; they shouldn't pose a problem. Nothing too vital was struck."

Ashin had been the unlucky one. Two of the blades Mirei had referred to must have hit her squarely in the body.

"I've given Kekkai a sedative for the time being," Nenikune added. "It seemed the simplest answer."

Satomi appreciated the discretion. "What of Mirei?"

Now the healer looked less certain. "I've also given her a sedative, and something to abate the nausea and headache."

"But what *caused* them? Was she poisoned?"

"I don't think so." Nenikune hesitated. "With your permission, Aken, I'd like to question Hyoka-akara."

Satomi blinked in surprise. "Hyoka? Why?"

"I've heard that Mirei has been suffering headaches rather chronically of late."

"Overwork," Satomi said, grimacing. "She's been driving herself very hard." But there was still a hesitancy in the healer's expression. "Do you think it's more than that?"

Nenikune smoothed the front of her plain skirt, as if getting her clothing into order as a substitute for order in her thoughts. She was a relentlessly tidy woman; uncertainty and confusion were the bane of her existence. "This is purely unfounded speculation, Aken, which is why I'd like to talk to Hyoka-akara."

"Then give me unfounded speculation." *Crone knows we have little enough else to go on.*

The healer-witch nodded. "I fear that this may be a side effect of Mirei's . . . different magic."

After having ordered Nenikune to share her thoughts, Satomi couldn't justifiably fault her for having made such an appalling suggestion. She swallowed down her first several reactions and said, more or less evenly, "What do you mean?"

"I mean that the use of Void power—or something in that vein, at any rate—is taking a very hard toll on Mirei's body. One that's been growing the more she does it."

If that is true . . . Satomi jerked her head in a curt nod. "I'll send Hyoka to you tomorrow. Will that be soon enough?"

"Yes, Aken."

Leaving the room, Satomi sent a message to Koika. The loyalty of one witch, at least, they would establish before the night was out.

THEY USED UNSUBTLE METHODS, and when they were done, they were sure that Hyoka was not a traitor. And when she found out why they were asking, Hyoka forgave them their choice of approach.

She was dispatched to work with Nenikune, under strict orders not to share even the slightest whisper of the healer's concerns with anyone else. Koika had not yet turned her attentions to the rest of the group to flush out the spy, and until she did so they could take no chances. Mirei was still in the infirmary, under guard, recovering from her weakness.

In the meantime, Satomi and Koika had a meeting with Kekkai.

They brought her into the council room, put her in a chair, and sat facing her like a pair of judges. "Talk," Satomi said.

Kekkai was pale and still had bandages on the more severe cuts, but she spoke without reluctance. "I'm sorry, Aken, Chashi. I—I knew there might be danger to Mirei, if they found out I was leaving. I didn't expect anything on that scale."

No one had yet said a word to her about the traitor, and Satomi was going to keep it that way, at least for the time being. "Why did you decide to leave? And so abruptly?"

The captive looked down at the table. "It wasn't as abrupt as it seems. I . . . when I spoke to you a few nights ago, Aken, I'd already been questioning many things. The information you gave me was simply one more factor. And then the next day I met with Arinei-nayo and Shimi-kane, and I learned something they intend to do."

"Which was?" Koika prompted her when she paused. The Earth Prime had her hands tightly laced together on the table's surface, and the rigidity of her posture showed just how suspicious she still was of the Key.

Kekkai's eyes wavered for a moment, but then she lifted her pointed jaw and met Koika's gaze. The unease in her was clear. "They're planning to open the witch-child they captured to power. They intend for her to die, and to take her doppelganger with her."

"They've already done it," Satomi said flatly. "Chanka

and Anness are dead." She let that sink in, then leaned forward. "And your response to this hideous plan was to *leave*?"

The Key's hands were trembling. "I didn't know what else to do. I thought, if I warned you—"

"You could have done that immediately. You could have sent a message to me." And then perhaps they would have found some way to save the children.

Kekkai nodded. A tear slipped down her cheek. "I should have. But I was afraid— I tried to argue against it, and Shimi grew angry—I had to get out of there. I didn't know they would do it so soon. I'm sorry. I'm so sorry." Her head bent low over her clasped hands.

When the Key's quiet sobs abated, Satomi spoke again. "You will tell us everything you know about their plans."

Wiping at her cheeks, Kekkai said, "Yes, Aken."

"Start with Chaha," Satomi said. "Is Arinei funding her military ambitions?"

"Not exactly," Kekkai replied. Her voice steadied as she went on. "Chaha is paying for the drilling of her current soldiers out of her own pocket. But once this conflict is settled, Arinei has promised to fund more recruitment in the spring, and to help her press the claim on the disputed territory in Trine. With magic, if necessary."

Koika made a sound of disgust. Witches served rulers and common people all over the land; it was a shocking violation of Arinei's position as Fire Prime to directly support one Lady against a neighboring domain. She was selling Starfall out, putting it in the debt of an outsider. No wonder Kekkai looked upset.

"What else?" Koika demanded. She smiled at Kekkai, but it was a baring of teeth, not a gesture of warmth, as if the Earth Prime were one of the animals her Ray dealt with. "Keep talking, Kekkai—or we'll question just why getting you out of there was worth the death of a *loyal* Key."

The other witch's eyes flared at her unforgiving tone. "I wasn't finished, Chashi. The Kalistyin troops have been drilling because Arinei seems to think she'll find a way to use them against you."

"How?" Satomi asked. One of the great mercies of Shimi going to ground in Kalistyi was that it was one of the most inaccessible domains relative to Starfall. Quite a bit of land, plus a range of mountains, stood between the two, and the Lords of intervening domains would not be likely to let an outside army through. Not to mention that soldiers would be of limited use against witches.

And even if it came to witches fighting each other, spell against spell, Hyoka was trying to develop a ward that would protect Starfall against that.

"I don't know," Kekkai said. "You know as well as I do the unlikelihood of soldiers being useful. But a great many of them were sent off recently; the rest have been especially active to disguise the lack."

That wasn't good news. Could they be mounting operations against Trine already, despite the late season? Or might the tactical concerns about the Bridewell Pass to Abern be accurate?

They might have a chance to preempt any such actions, though, if they could get at the ones behind it. "Leave that for the moment. Tell us where they are in Kalistyi, and what kinds of defenses they have set up."

The already pale Key went even whiter, though Satomi would not have thought it possible. "I—I'm sorry, Aken."

Her expression turned desperate, pleading. "I can't tell you that."

Any charity that she'd built up with Koika vanished in an eyeblink. The Earth Prime glared at her. "You don't have a *choice*. Either you'll tell us, or—"

But she cut off short, the threat unfinished, because Kekkai had yanked up the sleeve of her dress and laid her forearm on the table, palm upward.

A silver-white scar shimmered on the inside of her wrist.

"A *blood-oath*?" Koika said disbelievingly. "But you're not a Hunter."

Lines had formed around the edges of Kekkai's eyes, her mouth; she looked ten years older, and still dead white. "It was Shimi's idea. She thought of it after sending some Hunter off on an oath to kill Mirei. She changed the spell. Used it on anybody who has access to their stronghold."

"Binding you not to say anything," Satomi said quietly. Like they had done to Eclipse. Perverting the original purpose of the spell, the contract between a Hunter and the Warrior to carry out a mission. Using it to seal people's lips, on pain of death.

Kekkai swallowed convulsively, as if trying not to cry. "Shimi wanted to make it so that we couldn't tell *anything* about what they're doing. Arinei talked her out of it. Said that it would cause more trouble than it's worth, that we needed to be able to say things or we'd be of no use at all. So they limited it. I can say most things. But I can't tell you where they are."

Staring at the scar, Koika growled, "Damn their souls to the *Void*."

The Key's gaze was jittering back and forth, from one Prime to the other to the scar on her wrist. It was easy to guess that she was afraid of what would happen to her now. Whether, as Koika had questioned, they would consider her presence here worth Ashin's death, now that she could not be as much use as they'd hoped.

Satomi had no real idea how Koika felt on that matter, but she knew her own opinion. This, undoubtedly, was part of what had started Kekkai questioning her decision to follow Arinei, and rightly so. The woman had risked her own life by leaving Kalistyi. And they had lost too many people to throw another one away.

She stood and came to where Kekkai sat, and raised the woman to her feet. "The guards will take you back to your room," she said. "We'll have food brought to you there. Koika and I will meet with you again later today to hear anything you're able to tell us about what Arinei and Shimi have done, and plan to do. We won't push you to say anything that would risk your life."

Relief flooded Kekkai's face; she sank into a deep bow, then seized Satomi's hand and kissed it. "Thank you, Aken. And you, Chashi. I swear before the Goddess's five faces—I'll tell you everything I can."

"I'M GOING TO GO QUESTION the rest of them," Koika said when they left the council room.

"Do you want help?" Satomi asked. The thought of forcing the traitor out into the open was attractive.

Koika shrugged. "Can you spare the time?"

"I—" Satomi began, but stopped as Hyoka came around the corner, nearly running.

The Key jerked to a halt by them and dropped into the very briefest of bows. "Aken. Chashi. Rigai is dead."

"*What?*" Satomi demanded. *Rigai—one of Hyoka's theorists—Misetsu and Menukyo, if the traitor has killed another one—*

"She took poison in her room," Hyoka said. The edges of her lips were white, as if she were hanging on to her composure by her fingernails. "There are burned papers in her fireplace. A few of them weren't entirely destroyed. She's been receiving messages from Kalistyi."

Koika grabbed her by the shoulders, fingers digging in. "Are you *certain?*"

Hyoka looked sick. "There's no doubt about them. Chashi, I'm sorry. I would never have suspected her. She—" The Key stopped and took a wavering breath, trying to steady herself. "She was *helping* Mirei. Researching the blood-oath for her. I can't believe—"

"Let me see this for myself," Satomi said, but she knew before she went that Hyoka would not have made that kind of error. The papers, when she saw them, were undoubtedly from the dissidents in Kalistyi.

Rigai's body had been covered with a blanket, but the smell was still sickening. Satomi clenched her jaw and looked at the shrouded shape on the bed.

I wanted to believe it wasn't one of mine, she realized. *I wanted Koika to do the search because I knew I couldn't be impartial. I wanted to believe it was someone from outside my Ray.*

But the divisions among the witches had not gone by Ray boundaries. More Air and Fire witches had left than Void, it was true, but there were some from every Ray on both sides. And by staying, and appearing to be loyal, Rigai had put herself in a position to betray them all.

"Get rid of the body," Satomi said in a low voice. Cousins moved forward to take the corpse from the bed. She left before they did, and went away to vent her rage in private.

ASHIN'S FUNERAL took place that night.

Satomi presided over it. Ashin's own Prime should have done so, but her Prime had been responsible for her death—a fact that no one would soon forget.

Witches gathered in Star Hall, arranging themselves in the branches for their Rays, with the witches of the Void circling the dais. Looking out over them, Satomi could see the splintering of her people, laid out before her. Some branches of the hall were emptier than others. Many faces were missing, that should have been there.

Rigai was one of the missing. She had not yet decided what to announce on that matter.

But now was not the time to think about that. This ritual was to honor Ashin's courage, and the sacrifice Rigai had forced her to make.

Satomi's eyes lingered briefly on two small figures. Most of the students were at the far back of each branch, choosing whichever of the four they preferred, but these two were up front, because Ashin had been their mother. Sharyo and Indera, with identical closed expressions, neither of them willing to show a reaction in front of everyone else.

Mirei was present, standing just behind the remaining Air Keys. Kekkai was not. No one would want to see her here tonight.

Satomi took a deep breath, then spoke into the crystalline silence of the hall.

"Before us lies the body of Ashin, daughter of Yukin. She was a woman of Starfall; she was a witch of the Ray of Air, and the Key of the Path of the Hand. In following the Element of Air, she served the people of the land, wherever she might lend aid. In leading the Path of the Hand, she carried out the tasks of her Ray.

"We honor her tonight."

"*Honor to the name of Ashin,*" the assembled women murmured, their voices whispering off the surrounding stone.

Facing the western arm of the hall, where the light cast its fiery glow on the figures below, Satomi bowed, then spread her hands wide in supplication. "Maiden, Youngest of Five, the beginnings of life: We beseech thee grant thy blessing to Ashin, whose journey through life began with thee."

"*We ask this, Maiden, of thee.*"

Next the south, all silver-white. Another bow, another prayer. "Bride, Second of Five, the joining of one life with another: We beseech thee grant thy blessing to Ashin, who loved others in her journey through life."

"*We ask this, Bride, of thee.*"

The east, with the soothing blues of Water. "Mother, Third of Five, the granting of new life: We beseech thee grant thy blessing to Ashin, who birthed a daughter on her journey through life." One daughter, or two? She had wrestled with the question for hours. The two shared a single soul, and in the end, that had decided her.

"*We ask this, Mother, of thee.*"

The north, the final arm of the hall, green and amber

with the colors of Earth. "Crone, Eldest of Five, the dwindling of life: We beseech thee grant thy blessing to Ashin, who sought your wisdom on her journey through life."

"We ask this, Crone, of thee."

Finally the part of the ceremony that had always seemed an afterthought, necessary for the sake of completeness, necessary because of the theology they could not simply ignore. Tonight it carried weight that it never had before.

Satomi tilted her head back and addressed her words to the space where the hall's crossing had once soared, the clear air that stood between her and the stars. "Warrior, Alone of Five, the ending of life: We beseech thee grant thy blessing to Ashin. Let her spirit not be lost to the emptiness forever. Guide her soul through the blackness of the Void, so that it may be born again on the other side, to begin her journey anew."

"We ask this, Warrior, of thee."

Turning to face the silk-draped platform that stood on the bier, Satomi stretched her hands out. "The spirit is gone. The flesh remains. With the Maiden's Fire, we shall burn away the Mother's water. When the Crone's Earth is all that persists, then let it be scattered to the Air of the Bride, in whose service Ashin dedicated her life. Her soul is with the Warrior now."

The spell was not a complex one. She sang it slowly, turning the practicality of pitches and vowels into a work of art, sustained by her voice with all the care she could give. The power swirled to her, gentle and obedient, and with the final note she released it into its home. The fabric ignited, and then the body beneath; fueled by magic, the fire did not take long. Satomi remained on the dais the entire time, refusing to retreat from the scorching heat.

When it died down, only a pile of ash remained.

Satomi sang again, with as much care as the first time. The wind arose from the southern arm of the hall, sweeping up toward the dais, swirling about in a loop to carry the ash upward, past the shattered ribs of the crossing and into the night sky. To where the eyes of the Goddess looked down on them all, and welcomed Ashin home.

Chapter Nineteen

⊸⊱━┼━┼━⊰⊹

MIREI LOOKED from Hyoka to Nenikune, then back again, trying and failing to read their expressions. "So this is killing me."

"Not *killing* you," Hyoka said hastily. Nenikune cast a look at her that suggested the healer disagreed.

"Hurting me, then."

Nenikune turned away from Hyoka and sighed. "Say that it's . . . putting a *strain* on you. On your body. One that is growing quite serious, and could, over time . . . cause you great harm."

"In other words, kill me."

"When you cast that spell," Hyoka said, retreating into her intellectual voice, "you're sending your body and spirit into the Void. The Void threatens dissolution; that is its *nature*. Every time you cross over into it, you're—that was a good word for it, Nenikune. You're putting a *strain* on your body, and its ability to hold together. Which is manifesting as headaches, nausea, faintness, and so on. I think the effect is worse when you bring others with you. They can't protect themselves against it, so you have to do it for them."

They were alone in the infirmary room, with the door closed; of course the two witches did not want anyone overhearing this conversation. Mirei's fingers drummed a rapid rhythm on her knees. It made her think of Ashin, singing in the Bear's Claw, and she stopped. "Do I recover from that damage?"

"We can't tell," Nenikune said tartly. "You haven't stopped for long enough."

"But we think you might." Again, Hyoka was quick to reassure her. "It does mean, however, that you should avoid casting the spells in anything like quick succession."

Mirei gave her an ironic look. "Which puts any further research sessions right out of the question." Not to mention that those sessions had helped put her in this state in the first place, sending her back and forth in the translocation room simply so the theorists could stare at her. If this damage was something she could heal, then she didn't mind—too much. If it was permanent, then she'd frittered away most of her potential in pointless experimentation.

She took a deep breath to quash that fear. "Is it just the translocation? Or is it all Void magic?"

An exchange of glances between the two witches. "We can't be sure," Hyoka said, reluctantly. "Since we're incapable of perceiving that energy ourselves, it's hard to guess what it might be doing to you. Or even what it *is*—to be honest, Mirei, I can't even wrap my mind around the notion of a power associated with something whose very essence is nonexistence. I can say with confidence, though, that if there's any negative effect from casting spells that use such power, it's a drop in the rainstorm compared to what moving through the Void does to you."

"Wonderful." Mirei leaned forward in her chair and propped her elbows on her knees. The floor beneath her shoes was warm, heated by spells that helped take away what sting the southern winter had. Her mind focused on that, irrelevantly. Magic built of Fire and Air, magic that did no harm to the women who cast it.

Did you expect your miracle to have no price?

Mirei straightened up, grateful for once that she had a schedule. If she couldn't translocate, then both research and diplomatic missions were ruled out, but she still had the doppelgangers to deal with. And Eclipse to worry about. It gave her something to concentrate on other than the possibility of her own degeneration. "Thank you for telling me. Does Satomi know yet?"

"We wanted to tell you first," Hyoka said. "But we'll be meeting with her later today."

"Don't bother," Mirei said. "I'll go talk to her myself."

SATOMI CURSED with a fluency Mirei didn't think she had.

"They say I may recover, if I hold off on translocating for a while," Mirei added, as a tiny balm for the bad news.

"We don't *have* a while," Satomi growled, rising to her feet and taking quick, restless strides to the window. "I was going to send you back out, this time to the Hunter schools."

The suggestion took Mirei aback. True enough, it was the one place where she might be competent as a diplomat. But why the schools?

"I thought they might become allies," Satomi explained when she asked, turning back from the window. "Much in the same way the Avannans have, by playing up the change in our attitudes toward the Warrior. Though I doubt that would persuade all of them. There is word from your friend Eclipse that the Thornbloods are saying you killed Ice."

Mirei blinked in surprise. "But I didn't. I was tempted, but I didn't."

"I know. Someone has, though, and is using that to set them against you."

It was surprisingly upsetting. After that struggle with herself, the debate over whether or not to kill a woman she detested on every count, now her decision had been made irrelevant. Ice was dead, and she was being blamed for it anyway. She wanted to say good riddance; the Thornblood had been an irritant to her since her first day out of Silverfire, and had sold fellow Hunters out at a moment's notice. Yet for all that, Mirei had to offer up a silent prayer to the Warrior, to guide Ice to rebirth. She might have damned the woman to the Void more than once, but she hadn't meant it literally.

"I suppose you can send messages," Satomi said, breaking the silence, but she didn't sound enthusiastic about the idea. "Instead of going in person."

To the schools. Mirei's mind came back to the problem at hand. "Maybe," she said, but doubtfully. How much attention would they pay to messages? Jaguar would, certainly, but Wall? Let alone the Grandmasters of more distant schools. The Cloudhawks had no more reason to listen to her than to a bird in the trees. What a pity *they* weren't the ones who owed her boons.

Which reminded her of the problem she still had not solved. "I want to call in our second boon," she said, looking up at Satomi.

Returning to her seat and picking up a brush to write with, the Void Prime said, "Oh?"

"I want to put someone under a blood-oath."

The brush clattered back onto the desk. Satomi stared at her. "To what end?"

"So I can study it. And figure out how to break it." Mirei waved one hand impatiently. "I won't swear them to anything important. Just something that will let me experiment."

"*Experiment?* With someone's *life*? It's out of the question."

Mirei's jaw clenched. She chose her words carefully as she said, "The terms of a blood-oath don't put limitations on the boons. But they *must* be granted."

"I honor that oath by choice," Satomi snapped. "It was sworn to Ashin and her friends, not me."

Something went cold inside Mirei's stomach, and caution went to the winds. "What a pity, then, that Ashin's dead."

An ugly silence fell between them. Mirei met Satomi's pale eyes, unblinking. She was running out of ideas for how to save Eclipse, but she *wasn't* going to give up. She cared about him too much to let him die. This was the only option she could see. She wouldn't abandon it.

At last Satomi said, her voice clipped, "How fortunate for you that we have a subject on hand for you to study."

The unexpectedness of that thawed her a little. "What? Who?"

Satomi smiled thinly. "Kekkai. All the witches close to Shimi and Arinei have had to swear modified oaths, built on the same spell. You can study Kekkai."

"*Modified* oaths," Mirei said. "How do I know that anything that works on her will work on him?"

"You'll just have to hope that it does," Satomi said.

* * *

AT THE SIGHT OF MIREI, Kekkai sank into a bow that was entirely unnecessary from a Key—even an imprisoned and treasonous one—to an unranked witch. From the depths of it, not rising, she said, "I didn't get a chance to thank you."

"Don't," Mirei said bluntly, settling into a chair. The room they were keeping Kekkai in was painfully bare, and chilly; it was as if someone were trying to minimize the risk of her breaking out with destructive Fire magic by limiting the amount of flame that could be used to heat the space. Pointless, of course. Or maybe they were just punishing her.

Kekkai straightened and sat as well. "You saved my life."

"At a cost I didn't want to pay. And don't assume you're in the clear yet." Mirei reached out. "Let me see your wrist."

The Key didn't bother to ask which one she meant. Pulling back her sleeve, she extended her arm for Mirei to examine.

The scar shone silver-white, smooth against the skin. "Air. Who cast it?"

"Shimi."

"A blood-oath? I didn't think she'd have anything to do with the Warrior."

"She doesn't." Kekkai reclaimed her arm when Mirei released it and tugged her sleeve down, as if ashamed to show the mark. "The Warrior was nowhere in it."

Mirei remembered the terms of the spell very well. "But the Warrior is the one who judges whether the oath is fulfilled."

"According to the traditional words, yes. Shimi changed it."

If the Warrior wasn't a part of the oath, then what could she possibly learn from Kekkai that would help with Eclipse? Fury surged in her gut. But it was all she was going to get from Satomi, and so she had to try. "What words did you use? Or can't you say that, either?"

"No, I can." Closing her eyes—whether to help her memory or to hide her emotions, Mirei couldn't say—Kekkai recounted it. "Shimi's part was, 'You are forbidden to betray, by speech or action, deliberate silence or inaction, the location and defenses of our stronghold that you now stand in. Should you violate this prohibition, you will die.' Then I said—we all said, every time she made someone swear this—'I swear, on my body and my reborn soul, that I will obey the prohibition, or suffer immediate death.'"

No asking whether she accepted. No promise of reward, because the oath wasn't a charge to do something; it was a ban *against* doing something. And because of that, the oath would never end.

No reference to the Goddess, anywhere in it. Just human pride and fear.

Into Mirei's thoughts came Kekkai's quiet voice. "She got the idea from her encounter with your friend."

Mirei's head shot up. "What?"

"The Hunter. The one who swore to kill you." Kekkai eyed her, now nervous. "Surely you've heard."

"I've heard." Mirei got up and went to the small fire on the hearth, reaching her hands out to the warmth. Her fingers were cold. For all that she was here for information that might save Eclipse, she didn't want to talk about him. Not to this woman.

"I believe she gave him the normal version of the oath, though," Kekkai said softly to her back.

It took a moment for Mirei to see the implication of the Key's words. She turned abruptly, hands still toward the fire. "Wait—*Shimi* cast the spell on Eclipse?"

The nervousness in Kekkai's eyes edged over into fear. Mirei wondered what her expression looked like, to get that response. "Yes," Kekkai said. "Even with the Warrior in it. Or so I'm told. I might be wrong."

Three quick steps across the floor, and Kekkai flinched back. "But it was *Shimi.*" The same bitch who had him taken prisoner and didn't release him when Satomi called the hunt off.

"She forced him into it," Kekkai said, her words rushing together. "They had him prisoner in Abern—he told them he wanted to do it, that you weren't his year-mate anymore, so he didn't care about you, but she made it be a blood-oath, and told him they'd kill him if he didn't swear. That he wasn't any use to them if he wouldn't. So the only way for him to live was to agree to kill you."

Mirei had known that an Air witch cast the spell. The color of Eclipse's scar had been reported to Starfall. But she hadn't known it was the Air Prime herself.

I'm going to make her pay.

Rigai's voice whispered through her memory, saying, *"Human sacrifice."*

A life offered to the Warrior, so that she would not take someone else's.

Who better to offer in exchange?

The thought repulsed Mirei even as she was attracted

to it. *Wouldn't it be poetic justice? She tried to set up Eclipse's death; I'll set up* hers *in his place.*

She was a Hunter, and she'd killed people before. But never in such cold blood.

What would Eclipse think of it?

But he didn't have to know. No one had to know.

I don't even know if it will work.

Will work, her thoughts had phrased it. Not *would* work.

I don't even know where she is.

Mirei dragged herself away from those thoughts with an effort, and looked back to Kekkai. The Key was staring at her, eyes wide. No doubt wondering what Mirei would do to her for having been the bearer of that particular bit of information.

I won't do anything to you, Mirei thought coldly.

"We're done for now," she said, and left without another word.

THE PRACTICE WITH THE GIRLS that afternoon was a quiet one. There had been so much bad news lately, starting with Chanka and Anness; Mirei had been nauseated to hear about their deaths. Now the business in Kalistyi. The girls didn't know where Mirei had gone, nor what exactly had happened there, but they knew that Ashin had gone with her, and that Ashin had come back dead. Indera and Sharyo were both stone-faced, and the others stayed gingerly away from them, as if not sure what to say.

Tajio had been watching over them in Mirei's absence; with Mirei's permission, she remained on hand to observe how the practices were normally conducted. Mirei wasn't particularly happy with having an audience, but she couldn't shake the memory of her conversation with Hyoka and Nenikune. She wouldn't be around forever, and someone else had to know what to do with these girls. Ashin, who had helped, was gone.

As they moved through their exercises, silence only broken by shouts as they punched and kicked, Mirei wondered privately if this was even a good idea. *If my magic is killing me—*

The thought left her feeling scared in a way she hadn't since the days before she rejoined. Back when she was doubting whether there *was* any alternative to killing her doppelganger. If the consequence of this rejoining was early death, then did she have any right to send these girls down the same path? Wouldn't it be better to lose Amas, than Amas and Hoseki both?

It all depended on what exactly was happening to her. And she didn't know the answer to that.

Practice ended; she waved everyone off, including her escort of Cousins. They didn't want to go, but she summoned up a glare that drove them into retreat. Alone at last, she exhaled slowly, breath blooming outward in a white fog. Standing in the wintry clearing, she relaxed her muscles, and began to move.

It wasn't a spell. There was no purpose to the power she drew. She simply moved, weaving her voice in counterpoint to the shifting of her body, and called up the power of the Void. Dangerous, perhaps—but she had to feel it. She had to touch it, and see if the healers were right.

She had to know if it was killing her.

The sensation was so different from other kinds of power. It was a paradox she didn't understand—how she could make use of something whose essence was nonbeing. But she felt it around her, flowing through her limbs as she moved, and knew it was there even as it was not.

And in that power, she felt no harm.

Work like this was not dangerous. She had no proof for Hyoka and Nenikune; they'd have to take her word for it. This was not where the damage lay. What was harming her was translocation, the journey through the Void, where the only thing that kept physical form together was the power of her will. That was what she had to avoid—no, not avoid. She couldn't afford that. She must use it in moderation, and accept that the cost would be paid in flesh and blood.

She drew her movements to a close and released the power she held. It did not hang in the air, as other Elements did; there was no need to cancel it. The minute she let go, it was gone, for it had never been there to begin with.

"A paradox," Mirei murmured into the cold air. But one that was a part of her now.

With her attention no longer bound up in movement, she realized there were eyes on her.

Turning around and scanning the thickets of gray, leafless underbrush, Mirei said, "You might as well come out."

Amas emerged from behind a tangle of branches, looking disgruntled. "I thought I'd gotten better at hiding than that."

Mirei was not in a mood to play teacher right now. "What do you want, Amas?"

"Well, it's not so much what *I* want, as what *we* want." Amas glanced back over her shoulder and called out, "We might as well ask her now."

Farther back, several more figures appeared. Lehant was

not much of a surprise; Owairi, Hoseki, and Urishin were. As they came up to join Amas, Mirei sighed. "Couldn't this wait until later?"

Urishin stepped forward. "I wanted to talk to you privately." Mirei gave a pointed look at the others; she flushed. "Privately as in, without witches and Cousins around. Without Tajio-ai, or A— Or any of those other people that are constantly watching over us."

"They're there for a reason," Mirei reminded her. "To keep you from getting snatched and killed."

"You're busy all the time, though. So when we saw you were alone . . ."

Mirei didn't want to waste more time arguing the point. "Fine. What did you want to ask me?"

The girl took a steadying breath. The others were still a little behind her; whatever this business was, they were supporting Urishin, but it was her affair. "Ashin-kasora told us a while ago that it's possible for a witch to tell where her doppelganger is."

"Not exactly. Just the general direction."

"But we can *find* them."

"That's how they were able to send witches out to kill their doppelgangers."

"Well," Urishin said, back very straight, hands clasped together, her whole posture proclaiming the nerves she was trying to hide, "do Shimi and Arinei have the missing doppelgangers with them? I mean, in the same place they're in?"

Mirei's eyes narrowed. "I don't know."

Urishin bit her lip. "If they do—if they've got Naspeth there—then I could find her."

The possibility had never even occurred to Mirei. Her

mouth fell slightly open as she considered it. All the fuss over Kekkai not being able to say, and they had the answer here all along—

And then I would know right where to find Shimi. And I could kill her.

Mirei shoved that thought aside. "You can sense her, right now? Even with the block still in place?" She'd never tried it herself, because she hadn't *known* to try until after her test. And it wasn't a blatant thing; she'd only sensed it when she specifically went looking for it. She hadn't even considered that it might have worked sooner.

But Urishin was shaking her head.

Mirei frowned at her. "Then what do you mean?"

The girl took another steadying breath. The others were watching her closely, eyes flicking occasionally to Mirei. "I mean that if the block were gone, then I could tell you where Naspeth is."

"But you're eleven."

"I know."

Mirei stared at her, then at the others. "Removing the block is the final part of your *test*."

"I know."

"But you— That isn't supposed to happen for another fourteen years."

"Just over thirteen. I'll be twelve soon."

"Thirteen, fourteen, it doesn't bloody *matter.* Urishin, you're not ready."

"Who says?" the girl asked quietly.

Mirei's head reeled. "Void it—you *know* what happened to Chanka and Anness. Shimi used exactly the kind of thing you're suggesting to *kill* those two. And that's what will happen to you."

"I'll know what's going on," Urishin said stubbornly. "Chanka was too young to understand. I'll be okay."

"It isn't just a matter of understanding. You've hardly begun your education. Everything you learned before coming here is just background. The spells, the detail— you're, what, finishing up your first study of Earth? You've done *one* of the five Elements. *You're not ready.*"

But Urishin wasn't fazed. In fact, her nervous posture was relaxing, settling into something more determined, more confident. "Misetsu didn't study for twenty-five years."

"Misetsu," Mirei said through her teeth, "was a holy woman, and a dedicated hermit."

Urishin nodded. "She was a woman of great faith."

"And you think *your* faith is going to replicate her miracle?"

Amas spoke up, startling her. "It doesn't have to. Misetsu got magic when no one had ever had it before. Urishin has the channel for power already in her. She just has to survive."

She couldn't believe they were saying this, when two of their number had so recently died. "What do you think the odds of that are?"

Yet Amas would not back down. "Look, we thought about this before we came to you. We've been talking this over with Urishin for ages. She knows the risks."

"I want to try," Urishin confirmed, thin face serene. "Even if it means I might die."

Mirei took one look at her expression and knew that now was *not* the time to try and persuade the girl that she was acting like a lunatic. She took refuge in something more concrete. "Look, I can't help you anyway. You need a *lot* of people for that ritual, and I don't even know how it works. And you're never going to convince Satomi to let you do this."

"But *you* might convince her," Amas said.

"Is *that* what you want?"

"We were hoping you'd try."

They faced her in a tight clump, the five of them. Owairi and Lehant, copper hair cut short, hardly distinguishable from one another in their practice clothes. Amas and Hoseki, standing side by side; more than anyone in the group, they had begun to work as a single unit, reading each other's movements and blending into one. Urishin, standing by herself in front, and it didn't look natural. There should be someone else next to her, someone with the same thin features. A Warrior half, a Void half: the other face of her soul.

In all the world, there were so few other girls like these. And Urishin was asking her to risk losing two of them.

"Just tell Satomi-aken," Urishin said softly. "Tell her I want to try."

That much, at least, Mirei could promise. Because Satomi needed to know about this lunacy. "I will."

Chapter Twenty

IT MIGHT EVEN WORK," Mirei said, shrugging.

"It doesn't stand a chance in the Void of working," Satomi snapped. "And you know it."

The young witch held up her hands. "I mean the part about finding Shimi. You said Kekkai told you she's keeping the doppelgangers close by."

Satomi ground her teeth. "That doesn't *matter*. The issue is Urishin, and the madness of this idea."

Mirei looked thoughtful, glancing into the autumn twilight outside Satomi's window. "I'm not so sure it's madness."

"She's an eleven-year-old *girl*—"

"Who trusts the Goddess." Mirei smiled sadly. "I recognize it when I see it. I probably had the same expression on my face, not long ago—both of my faces, if you want to put it that way. I saw it in Ashin a couple of times, too."

"Faith isn't enough."

"Isn't it?" Mirei's gaze came back to meet hers, and now it had sharpened. "Everything that makes us who we are has come to us through faith. Misetsu's gift, the spells we cast—what I am today. It all comes down to us having faith—opening ourselves to the Goddess and listening to what she has to say."

If Satomi had ever felt the sensation Mirei was describing, she didn't remember it. "She'll die, just like Chanka and Anness, and Naspeth will die with her. You don't know the numbers—how many students die, how many become Cousins. I do. And that's for women who have studied their entire lives. For an eleven-year-old girl? The odds are impossible."

"But this isn't about odds. It's about courage. Urishin has it. And as much as I know she might die—we all know that, very well—the more I think about it, the more I'm inclined to say, let her try."

Satomi pressed her fingers against her eyes. She felt a headache starting, spiking in from both temples. "There's no such thing as *trying*. There's no second chance. If this goes wrong, there's no trying again, no opportunity to make it right. That's what she doesn't understand. Or you, either."

Mirei received that in silence. Satomi began to hope that she'd convinced the young woman. The next words hit her from the side, out of nowhere, and knocked her completely out of the calm she'd achieved.

"Is this because of Orezha?"

Satomi's hands fell to her sides like stones. "She is none of your concern."

"With all due respect, Aken, I think you're letting your guilt cloud your judgment. Orezha died when she shouldn't have. Now you're clinging to these girls as if they'll make up for that mistake."

Satomi stood abruptly, hands clenching the edge of her desk until they hurt. "You may leave."

"I think you're afraid that if you let Urishin try, and she dies, then it'll be your fault again, you making the wrong decision. But the decision that matters this time isn't yours. It's *hers*. Young as she is. Children younger than she is are sent off to temples, never to leave again; they're forced into a life of pretended faith whether they want it or not. Is that better? Or is it better to make the choice for herself, and to try to help others in the process?" Mirei was unblinking, her face relaxed into a tranquillity Satomi found frightening. "Our job should be to help her as best as we can. Not to take her choice away."

"Get out," Satomi snarled.

Mirei stood at last. "If you can't trust me, or Urishin," she said quietly, "trust the Goddess. Pray, and see what you think of it then. But do it soon."

Then she was gone.

THE ONE PLACE in Starfall Indera had found where she could be private was on the roofs. She'd heard that students often climbed around on the roof of the hall where they lived, but other places were less frequented. There was a large storehouse where they kept jars of wine, with a tall pine growing right alongside it; Indera could climb that to the roof, and have some time to herself.

Alone. She hadn't realized how much she really was alone, until the night of the funeral. Until they spoke of Ashin's life, and said she only had one daughter.

Sharyo's the only one who's real to them. I'm a copy, and they'll get rid of me as soon as they can.

She sat glaring at the stars, pretending they were not blurring in her vision, and ignored the cold tracks that formed down her cheeks. She stayed until the air chilled her too much; then, reluctantly, she climbed back down to the ground. And there she found someone waiting for her.

"Are you all right?" Tajio asked.

Indera resisted the urge to scrub at her face. If any marks of her tears remained, that would only draw attention to them. "What do you care?" she asked rudely.

Instead of being offended, the witch smiled sadly. "I thought you might want to talk to someone, after your mother's funeral."

Indera turned away. "She wasn't my mother."

After a moment, she heard Tajio move, coming forward two steps, but not trying to touch her. "I understand. It's very brave of you, to face it like that. To be strong enough to stand on your own, at such a young age."

Startled, Indera turned to face her again. "You— Do you really mean it?"

Tajio nodded. "You're an impressive young woman. Strong and disciplined. I've seen how hard you work at your training. I can only imagine how well you would be doing if you were still at Silverfire."

The name lanced through her, awakening other pain. Indera turned away again, but this time a soft hand on her shoulder turned her back. "Tell me," Tajio said, full of compassion.

So Indera did. They walked through the woods, Indera hugging her arms around herself in a futile attempt to ward off the chill both inside and out, and she told the witch everything. How no one here really thought of her as a person. How they only cared about Sharyo. And then what she'd overheard—it was a lie, that she had years yet before she would be expected to turn into somebody else. They were going to do it *now*. With Urishin, anyway, and if that worked out then there would be no point in waiting, would there? They'd all have to do it, then, every last pair.

So Indera would stop existing, and in her place there

would be some witch. Sharyo, but with all the things *Indera* had worked for. All the Hunter training. All the things the witch-girl hadn't earned. And Indera would be gone forever.

"I'm going to *die,*" she said at last, miserably, and the tears began to run down her face again, against all her efforts to stop them.

"Hey, listen to me," Tajio said softly, and stopped and knelt. Indera turned to look at her, reluctant, sure she was going to hear another lecture on how it wouldn't be bad, she'd still be herself, just *more*. The same lecture everyone else gave her.

She was wrong.

"If you weren't here," Tajio said, "then they wouldn't do it. With the others, maybe, but not with Sharyo. It would be too risky, to open her to power when you're not around; she'd be in danger, then. Both of you would."

"But I can't get out of here," Indera said, struggling to keep her voice from going high and tight with tears. "I've looked. There's patrols, and I can't steal a horse."

Tajio hesitated, seeming to struggle with herself. "I could help you," she said finally. "Give you something to slip you past the guards. And once you're gone, they can't use magic to find you—you know about that, right? You'd have to fend for yourself after that—"

Hope had blossomed in Indera's heart at the offer. "Oh, I could do that," she said eagerly. "I did it in Angrim. When they were hunting for me. I could do it again."

The witch smiled. "Okay, then. Will you let me cast a spell on you? It'll keep the guards from noticing you go by."

Indera hadn't made any preparations—no food, no last-minute study of maps. "Does it have to be now?"

"Yes," Tajio said. "Before they have a chance to do anything with Urishin, or guess that you might run away. I'm sure you'll be fine," she added, correctly guessing Indera's fear. "You're smart, and very resourceful. You won't have any problems."

The confidence bolstered Indera's courage. Biting her lip in nervousness, she nodded.

"Give me a strand of your hair," Tajio said, straightening. "I need it for the spell." Indera plucked one out and handed it to her, then watched, fascinated. She'd seen witches cast spells in her months here—they did it all the time—but never anything like this.

Twining the strand around her finger, Tajio began to sing quietly, incomprehensible syllables weaving up and down in a weird melody that sounded nothing like music, yet had a beauty of its own. Indera listened to it, entranced, and for one brief, fleeting moment, wished that she could feel the currents the adult witches talked about, the strands of power that came together to form a spell.

But the desire was a stupid one, and she realized it quickly. She would never feel that power. She didn't *want* to feel it; to do so, she'd have to be a witch herself. And she wasn't a witch. She was a Hunter. *Her* life was out here, in the darkness of the night; *her* role was sneaking past guards, carrying out secret missions. Spying. Thievery.

Assassination.

To hunt, to fight—to kill.

After all, she was chosen by the Warrior. She *was* the Warrior—the fifth, independent part of the human soul, pure and uncorrupted by the softer, weaker parts. *That* was who she was, and Indera embraced it fiercely, understanding for the first time what it meant. Reveling in the power that it held.

And they wanted to take that from her.

They wanted to steal the strength she had, and give it to someone else. They wanted to condemn her to a life of mediocrity, doom her to being like every other person in the world. Take away her gifts. Make her slow and weak, like everyone else. The thought infuriated her and her anger rose up like fire, warming her body and mind, until her pulse beat in her ears, a swift, steady rhythm.

The answer was obvious. To escape that fate, she need only do what she had been made for.

She was, after all, the Warrior.

And she knew the Warrior's role.

THE SCREAMS BROKE THE QUIET of Starfall's night, starting a chaos of noise and terror, women running through the halls, people flocking to see what had happened, and no one would make way for anyone else, so that those in charge had to fight their way through, elbowing and cursing and finally using magic, forcing a passage that let them into the room where Indera, staring-eyed and trembling, was pressed against the wall, face whiter than bone, hands red with blood, staring down at the body that had been the other half of herself.

Satomi recognized that look. She had worn it, years before.

The room was a public sitting area, with several entrances. More and more witches were crowding in. Witches and Cousins and, slipping among them, smaller bodies squeezing through gaps, students. Children.

Including doppelgangers and their witch-halves.

Satomi reached out blindly, grabbed a fistful of fabric, dragged some witch toward her and snapped unseeing, *"Get them out of here."* Released, the witch began moving; Satomi paid only enough attention to be sure that she or someone else was taking care of the children, taking them away from the sight they should not see.

The crowd was growing ever larger, women in back demanding to know what had happened, rumors flying faster than thought and warping as they went. It would be a panic, soon. Satomi gathered the fraying strands of her wits and began to sing. Her voice couldn't be heard over the clamor, but it was enough for the Goddess; the power came, and with it Satomi forced everyone back, shoving them through the doorways, not caring who got bruised or stepped on, so long as they were *gone*.

Leaving her alone in the room with the doppelganger and no one else. Satomi swallowed the scream that would have demanded *Where in the Warrior-damned Void is Mirei?*

She couldn't wait for Mirei, who knew Indera, who could calm her down. Satomi had to do it herself.

She slammed a silencing spell down over the room, blocking out noise from outside, and with a last profligate expenditure of power flung the doors shut.

In the quiet that resulted, Indera's breathless, terrified whisper could be heard. "I—I—"

Satomi knelt by Sharyo's body and felt for a pulse. A formality; she knew the truth. Indera would not look like that if Sharyo were alive.

She tried to damp down her fury so it would not show in her expression, and knew that she had failed.

Indera pressed herself even farther into the corner she'd retreated to, as if she could meld with the stone by force of will. "I—I didn't—she—it just—T-t-t-tajio said—"

The name, the only marginally coherent thing out of Indera yet, brought Satomi to her feet. "What," she asked, low and dangerous, "did Tajio say?"

The banks broke; the river of Indera's terror and horror poured out in a flood of words. "I don't know she told me about the thing we can't die that's why they hadn't killed them and I thought about it I guess but I never would have except that all of a sudden I wanted to—they said Urishin was going to do it and then you'd make us all do it and I didn't want to, oh Goddess, Mother please, but I wouldn't have done it I *swear* except suddenly I knew, I'd be free if she were dead and I knew that's what I should do but I *shouldn't* have and oh Mother, I should have left I should have run away Tajio said she'd help but she started singing and I just—I just—"

And as the torrent came out, it cooled Satomi's anger, turning her skin and blood to ice and fear. She opened her mouth again, but this time she sang no spell; it was a held note, modulating to feel out the edges of the dissipating power that still lingered about Indera like a clinging, invasive net.

Mostly gone. They faded fast. But enough for her to be sure of what it was.

A spell of persuasion.

A spell, not to force—that couldn't be done—but to take the impulses already there, to fan the sparks into flame, to make that which had been thought of and imperfectly dismissed seem like the proper thing to do.

A spell to make Indera kill her other half.

* * *

WITH THE SILENCING SPELL around the room, Satomi could not hear what went on outside.

Others did, but Koika and a few others had tried to take control, to shepherd them away, and it took everyone a moment to realize the screams they heard were new ones, not Indera in her terror, but other girls.

MIREI DID NOT UNDERSTAND what authority she held in Starfall until that night. Unranked, neither Key or Prime, not even a member of a Ray yet, she found others responding to her as if she were in charge, offering her information—garbled, contradictory, but enough for her to follow. She didn't understand what had happened, but she knew it had to do with the doppelgangers, and enough people remembered which direction they'd been taken in that she could go in search.

She flew down the hallways with rapid strides, almost running—and then a sudden scream from a door she'd just passed jerked her to a halt.

The door, when she slammed into it, proved to be locked. She didn't waste time with subtlety. Mirei blasted the door open and threw herself through the smoking wreckage, and found herself facing horror.

Her eyes took in bodies, small ones, on the floor, and knew with sick dread who they were, but she could ignore that for the moment, because her concern was with the standing figure, the woman at the far wall, bloody knife in one hand, other hand flinging outward, as if hurling something at her.

Tajio's spell knocked Mirei back into the wall with bruising force, but she rebounded off the stone and charged straight at the woman. The room wasn't large. Tajio didn't have time to cast anything else. Mirei hit her shoulder first, felt ribs crack; they went down in a heap, the knife slicing them both, and Mirei snarled syllables, driving her fingers up at Tajio's ribcage to strike her diaphragm, and the movement and the words fused as one: force went where she directed it, into the body where her hand couldn't go, and crushed Tajio's heart in her chest.

The woman shuddered and lay still.

Mirei shoved ineffectively for a moment before she managed to right herself, and by then others were there; witches were screaming, chaos was spreading again, but two things occupied Mirei's attention.

First, three bloodstained bodies, small and unmoving. Falya and her witch-double Yimoe, and Chaiban at their sides.

And second, so that horror and relief warred for supremacy in Mirei's heart, six other witches and doppelgangers, not moving, but not dead; rigid with the spell that held them trapped, but alive.

Thank the Goddess.

THE INFORMATION HE'D BEEN WAITING FOR came at last, when he had given up on ever seeing it.

Garechnya.

Eclipse stared at the name for a moment, hardly believing. Then he pivoted and moved with two swift strides to the wall where the map hung, marked with notations that narrowed down, bit by bit, the area where the dissidents might be.

His finger slid over the paper, crossing roads and rivers,

up into the mountains of northwestern Kalistyi, to a small town with nothing to recommend it except solitude.

There, Eclipse thought, and then hissed in pain.

Blood flowered out of nowhere on his wrist, seeping from no visible wound in his scar. He clutched at it with one hand, whispering, "No, no, not now, not yet—" He lunged to the desk, fumbling for a brush—

Then it stopped.

Eclipse stood for a moment, panting, trying to slow his heart. Another warning. The third one, all told. Five, supposedly, was the magic number, but he wasn't about to gamble that he had one more warning before he died.

Which meant that he had finally come to the crossroads. He could no longer hope for Mirei to pull off another miracle and save him. All that remained was to choose how he would die.

He wanted to see her one last time, even if it meant bleeding out on the spot. It didn't seem fair, that he should have to die without being able to say good-bye. If he tried to go anywhere near her, though, the witches would kill him on the spot. They would not risk him changing his mind.

He could stay here at Silverfire, where the witches would leave him alone, and bleed to death one night soon—judged by the Warrior, and found guilty of failure.

Or he could choose a third road.

Eclipse picked up the brush once more. It had spattered ink all over the top sheet of paper: He pulled out a clean page and wrote a brief note in as steady and regular a hand as he could manage.

The instructions for Jaguar were clear, as were his reasons for them. Depending on how closely the witches were monitoring him, the charade might not do any good, but it was worth a try.

He wondered, one last time, whether the witches of Starfall already knew his information, and had sent all those Wolfstars to deal with the problem. They had to have been hired to kill *someone*.

One way or another, it didn't matter to him.

Eclipse folded the note, sealed it, and delivered it to Jaguar's office, sliding it under the door of the anteroom, where Slip would find it in the morning.

Then he went through the night to the stables, to saddle a horse.

Chapter Twenty-One

❖━━┼━━━┼━━❖

CHAIBAN, WHOSE DOPPELGANGER had been captured months ago, did not come back to life.

They pieced it together, painfully, while the surviving doppelgangers and their witches were placed under the most stringent guard they could arrange, with Indera held apart from the rest.

From Indera, questioned under a spell to keep her calm, they got the story of her encounter with Tajio. Other witches remembered seeing the woman shepherding the children away from the scene of Sharyo's death—and why shouldn't she? After all, she'd been taking care of them in Mirei's absence, and had showed such concern for their well-being. And Tajio must have informed her allies in Kalistyi of the situation. There was a crumpled note in the room where she'd taken them, telling her to kill Chaiban. The two halves of a pair didn't have to be killed at the *exact* same instant—just close enough.

The one saving grace was that Tajio had been trying to capitalize on an unexpected situation, and had not had time to plan. If there had been a silencing spell over the room she took the children to, Mirei would never have heard Chaiban scream. All the girls in there would have died. And maybe others, as well, if Tajio slipped away and managed to find the rest of them.

Mirei put another piece into the puzzle: Rigai's abrupt suicide, before Koika could question the witches to flush out the traitor.

Rigai's suicide, which now looked rather more like a murder.

It had distracted them all from the search. And why should Rigai have killed herself, anyway? Why not escape, or try to stay hidden? Satomi regretted now her decision to cremate Rigai quietly, and to hold no funeral. She would have to make amends for that somehow.

Koika, dragging herself away from self-castigation over not continuing to search, wanted to know why Tajio hadn't killed the children sooner. The traitor's merely partial success seemed to answer that: She'd been waiting for a chance to get all of them, or at least as many as possible. The situation with Urishin had provoked her into action.

Not long after that point came up, a message arrived from the rooms where the girls were being protected. It came from Urishin.

She didn't come out and say it, but Satomi and Mirei knew what she meant.

"I still want to do it."

"IF YOU KNEW WHERE THEY WERE," Mirei said, "what would you do?"

Koika glanced sideways at Satomi. The three of them were alone in the council room. Rana had retired to her rooms, her nerves shattered by the bloodshed. No one expected anything more out of her, after this. The elderly Water Prime was done.

As the silence from Satomi dragged on, Koika said

with a hint of her usual wryness, "I don't suppose you could transport an entire army to Kalistyi."

Mirei shook her head. "I won't even try."

Satomi roused enough to shake her head and speak. "Urishin would only be able to give us a direction. Not anything more specific. And we already know they're in Kalistyi."

Mirei took a deep breath. What Satomi would think of the suggestion she was about to make, she didn't know, but she would make it anyway. "I can get her closer. And if she pegs the direction from multiple angles, we can pin-point it on a map fairly well."

They were finally accustomed enough to her special-ized skills that they knew what she meant. Koika moved in startlement. "But I thought translocation was bad for you."

"It is," Mirei said, and tried to suggest by her tone that this was a minor concern. "But only in repeated doses. Urishin's never gone through it before, and it would only take a few jumps; I'm sure she'll be fine."

"But what about *you*?"

Mirei met the Earth Prime's eyes, unflinching. "I'll take my chances."

"No," Satomi said softly, and then repeated it louder. "No. It's all too risky."

Despite her best intentions, Mirei's temper snapped. "So what are you going to do? Sit around and wait for more of them to die?"

It produced an ugly silence. Koika seemed torn between agreement and shock at Mirei's lack of respect. Satomi just stared at her, pale green eyes flat and unreadable, but not happy.

Finally Mirei caved. "I'm sorry, Aken," she muttered,

and tried to sound like she meant it. "We may have a chance here. I don't want to miss it. But it'll be for nothing if there's no plan for what to do once we find them."

Koika exhaled, laying her hands flat on the table. "Shimi and Arinei are the largest problem. The Keys who have defected with them are a problem, too, but those two are the worst. Loyalty is what's keeping their followers with them, as much as fear and confusion and dissent with us. Cut that tie, and the group loses its organization; disorganized, we can bring them back in."

"Cut the tie," Mirei repeated quietly.

The Earth Prime looked at her, unblinking, for several heartbeats. "Could you do it?"

Had she still been Mirage, her answer would have been easy. But she'd known since she faced down the helpless Ice that she had changed.

"No," she said. "Not as an assassination."

Koika's jaw hardened. "You know what a threat they are. What damage they've already done to us. You want to leave that out there?"

"No," Mirei replied, this time with more strength. "No more than Miryo wanted to leave Mirage out there, with the danger she posed. But I don't want to just kill them off, either. They're a part of us, Chashi; we can't just cut them out because of a split between us. We have to bring them back in, somehow."

The Earth Prime shook her head, but before she could muster up a response, Satomi spoke. "She's right."

Mirei turned to look at her.

Satomi's face was weary but resolved. "They're our people, Koika. And some of their concerns are valid. I can't condone their methods—but neither can I send Mirei, like a shadow in the night, to kill them while they sleep."

Koika slapped one hand on the table. "So what—are we just supposed sit here? Mirei, I thought that's what you were arguing against just a minute ago!"

"It was," Mirei said. "It is. I'm not going to assassinate them. But I want to know where they are, because we can't do a Void-damned thing until we have that information. And that means Urishin."

In this room, insulated as it was from the outside, layered with permanent spells to prevent eavesdropping, there was no sound apart from the quiet breathing of the three women as they faced their dilemma. Mirei's heart beat in her ears, marking off the moments as Satomi considered it.

Finally the Void Prime spoke.

"Very well."

THE RITUAL REQUIRED five women to work, so they had to recruit help.

They did it privately, because no one wanted to admit to Starfall that they were taking such a risk. Which meant they could not use Star Hall; instead, they went outside. And besides, the original miracle of Misetsu's power had come in the wilds of these mountains, atop a rocky crag where the woman had prayed all night long. It seemed fitting to return there.

Mirei studied the necessary spells ferociously, committing the syllables and pitches to memory. Satomi had granted her the right to stand for Air, even though Naji outranked her. It was the closest she was ever likely to get to the Ray she had once thought would become hers. With her were Churicho, the interim Fire Heart Key, and Paere, the Water Heart Key. No one trusted Kekkai to be a part of this, and Rana refused to participate.

Together they studied, and together they prayed. None of them wanted to make the slightest mistake that might endanger Urishin.

Any more than she's endangering herself already.

But they couldn't wait long, because Tajio had certainly told *something* of the plan to Kalistyi, and no one could be certain how much. If they were going to do anything, it would have to be soon.

IN A BACK CORNER of her mind, where she could pretend that she hadn't been considering it, Satomi had thought through the question of testing Urishin.

The complexities of the ritual were not for decoration. They had been developed as a means of ensuring that the young women stood the highest possible chance of succeeding. In theory, one could simply remove the block that stood between them and power; there was no need for the rest of it. But if one instead worked them up to it gradually, then the shock was less, and the odds of success— of survival—were greater.

She would lessen the shock for Urishin as much as possible.

There was no testing by the Keys, no exhaustive questioning designed to make sure she had learned her lessons, for her education was incomplete. Leaving behind a careful facade of excuses for their absence, the witches took Urishin south of Starfall, up to a small, sheltered valley where they left her at sunset, tucking her under a blanket with a warming spell on it so that she would not grow cold in the mountain winds.

At midnight, they returned, and stood in the dead grass around the girl. The columns of Elemental light they ordinarily stood on were a part of Star Hall's power. Nor would they have the Hall's structure to assist them; each woman held a focus in her hands. What they did tonight was far too complex to manage without them.

Urishin shed the blanket and stood up, a slender figure in the darkness, and the witches began to sing.

"Who comes?"

"A sister," Churicho sang. Her voice, at least, betrayed no hint of doubt.

"Who comes?"

"A student." Mirei, confidence and faith written in every line of her body.

"Who comes?"

"A daughter." Paere, singing for Water.

"Who comes?"

"A candidate." Koika's hands were tight, her jaw set.

"Who comes?"

Satomi's turn, and her voice rang out clear and true on the weird intervals of her response. "One of ours, who is not one of us; one who would join us under the stars, who has not been tried."

And then the testing began, though Urishin didn't know it. Perversely, it began with Mirei, who had argued in favor of this entire attempt.

"Aken, I stand in protest."

The young witch chanted the line in a monotone; the entire ritual, from start to finish, had to be conducted in song, even this false disruption. False, unless Urishin failed it. A part of Satomi hoped she would.

Failure now was safe.

"This student is not fit for testing," Mirei chanted. "She must not be allowed to continue."

Eyes wide with shock and fear, Urishin blurted, "But—Mirei—you told me yourself that I could."

The girl, fortunately, maintained the careful monotone pitch; that much she had learned. Mirei gave her a cold look. "I have realized my error."

"The ritual's started, though," Urishin sang-spoke. "And the ritual's a spell. We're supposed to finish spells that we start, never quit partway through."

Good enough for the purpose; now it was Churicho's turn. "Sister, she outranks you. Do you challenge her word?"

Urishin flinched. The look of betrayal on her face hurt, but Satomi steeled herself against it; if the girl couldn't get through this, then they *had* to know. "I'm sorry, Churicho-nakana—but I don't want to give up. I *can* do this. I *know* I can. I've already started."

"What has been started can be ended."

"But I don't *want* it to be," Urishin whispered. Her chant was hardly audible, but there was strength behind it nonetheless.

Koika took that as her cue. "Your desires do not dictate our actions, candidate. They are not the most important thing here."

"I know that, Chashi," Urishin said, looking offended that Koika should even suggest it. "That's why I'm *doing* this. We have to help the others—Naspeth and the other three." Her face fell. "The other *two*. I'm doing this for them."

"Even if it's against our will."

Urishin managed a wavering smile. "I'm hoping you'll change your minds."

And now, from Paere, the final step, a question that never varied regardless of the debate that proceeded it.

"Why do you wish to continue?"

Turning to face the Water Key, Urishin swallowed nervously before responding. "Because I want to help."

"You may die."

Please, beloved Goddess, let her not die.

Urishin paled at the declaration, but her answer, though quiet, was calm, backed by a conviction that seemed far older than her years. "If I don't do this, then maybe the others will kill me anyway. I'd rather try."

And that was good enough.

"The Goddess smiles; the ritual continues. The sister, the student, the daughter, the candidate; she has been tried, and not found wanting." Satomi sang the phrases, and tried not to be afraid.

The others sang their response in melodious concert once more. "Let the testing continue. Will you begin?"

Urishin's eyes widened as she realized, just as countless young women had before her, that the objections were part of the test. She recovered from the shock admirably, and sang without error the response she had so recently memorized. "I stand ready for Earth. May the Goddess as Crone be at my side, and lend me determination."

The spell they placed her under locked her body into a rigid statue, frozen in the center of the valley. Koika took the lead on this one, though they all participated. And, as

Satomi had cautioned her, the Earth Prime built it up slowly, one careful degree at a time.

These Elemental tests were dangerous in their own right, because they were precursors to the full power that came at the end. They served the same purpose as the preceding debate, which students were not told about in advance; they tested the qualities of character needed to survive the onslaught of power. And they did so by feeding the student, in measured doses, strands of the energy she would soon be handling.

Some students died in these trials. It seemed unavoidable. But according to the chronicles, many fewer died this way, encountering each Element singly before channeling them all together, than if they took the power without preparation.

The Earth power Koika was feeding to Urishin grew, and grew, and grew—

And then the Prime ended the spell, and the girl staggered in the grass, gasping for air. Gasping, but alive; she had passed the first test.

Four to go—and then power itself.

"I have mastered Earth," Urishin sang. Her voice was steadier than Satomi would have expected, and it gave her hope. "Its strength is mine."

"The Crone smiles," Koika sang, and she very nearly smiled, too.

There could be no pausing. "Let the testing continue."

Urishin set her feet, full of the determination of Earth, not realizing that it was not what she would need next. "I stand ready for Water. May the Goddess as Mother be at my side, and lend me flexibility."

Again her body went rigid, this time with Paere leading the spell. As Satomi worked her own part, she wondered at the way they performed these tests. Building up the power until it reached a sufficient strength, or until the student died. Crushed by their failure to stand against Earth. Snapped by their failure to bend with Water. Maddened by their failure to stay calm in Air. Destroyed by their failure to burn with Fire.

Annihilated by the Void, because they were not whole enough in themselves.

Did it have to be that way?

It did for Urishin, tonight, because they had no other way.

Paere finished her spell. Urishin wavered on her feet, but had voice enough to sing. "I have mastered Water. Its flexibility is mine."

"The Mother smiles," Paere sang in response.

"Let the testing continue."

"I stand ready for Air. May the Goddess as Bride be at my side, and lend me clarity."

Mirei, the least experienced of their number, had to take this one. She took a deep breath and began.

What dictated that the ritual be this way? The tests served a purpose; could they serve it in a way that wouldn't risk death for the student?

If they fed power in smaller amounts, yes. But smaller amounts wouldn't be enough preparation. Done over time, though . . . a tiny amount of Earth one day, then more a few months later . . . the students could develop the necessary qualities gradually, like the soldier Cousins lifting progressively heavier weights to strengthen their muscles.

Then everyone would know how the testing worked, though.

Was that really the only argument against doing it that way? Secrecy?

"I have mastered Air. Its clarity is mine."

Satomi was disciplined enough not to show her startlement at Urishin's sudden voice. She should have noticed the spell ending. This distraction was not good.

But the girl was still alive.

Mirei didn't bother to aspire to the impassive mask traditional for this ritual. She grinned at Urishin and sang, "The Bride smiles."

"Let the testing continue."

Urishin was sweating, even in the chill air, but she forged ahead, as she knew she must. "I stand ready for Fire. May the Goddess as Maiden be at my side, and lend me courage."

As Churicho took up the test, Satomi realized that the test of Void worried her far less than it ever had before. They knew it from Mirei: witches whose doppelganger-halves were alive came through the test less traumatized than their sisters. It still wasn't pleasant for them, but it wasn't as bad. And Urishin was the first one who would go through it knowing her other half was alive.

But there was one more test after it, and that was the one she feared.

Perhaps the Goddess *was* with them, though—with Urishin. The test of Fire ended, and Urishin moved again. "I have mastered Fire," the girl sang, her voice hoarse but still strong. "Its courage is mine."

No one doubts your courage, child, to come this far of your own free will.

"The Maiden smiles," Churicho sang.

"Let the testing continue."

Satomi met the girl's eyes in the starlit darkness. "No one stands ready for the Void. The test begins. May the Goddess as Warrior have mercy on your soul."

Alone of the Elemental tests, this one was different. They could not feed witches Void power as they did the other types. Instead, they created an illusion, the closest they could come to approximating the nothingness of the Void.

Or they were supposed to.

Mirei's voice laced into the chorus, not where she was supposed to be, and her hands gestured toward Urishin, describing graceful arcs in the air. Halfway into the spell, Satomi did not dare stop to ask her what in the Goddess's many names she thought she was doing.

But the strangest part was that she could feel no power. *Of course I can't. Which is how I know what she's doing.*

Urishin stood with her eyes closed, suspended unknowing while they built the illusion that, once formed, would last for only an instant. And whatever Mirei was doing, presumably, wove around her. Testing her, in the way that only Mirei could, with her connection to the Void.

Satomi just had to hope the girl would pass whatever test she was being given. *If this change harms her, Mirei, you will live with the guilt of it forever.*

The illusion was finished; they unleashed it. And Urishin jerked convulsively, and screamed.

She screamed. It meant she was still alive. Which meant there was only one more threat facing her.

"You have glimpsed the Void, for an instant only, and it has marked you," Satomi sang. *Along with whatever it was that Mirei just did.* "The Warrior has tested you, and you have not been destroyed."

"Let our newest fly on the wings of power."

And together, praying silently that this would not be the end of her, the five women sang the phrases that removed the block placed just eleven short years before, opening Urishin to the Elemental powers of the world.

Chapter Twenty-Two

━━◆━━◆━━

IN THAT MOMENT, Satomi knew exactly what to pray for.

Receiving power for the first time was a painful experience, akin to spending twenty-five years in darkness and then staring straight into the sun. It jarred every woman who went through it.

Women whose doppelgangers were still alive suffered more. The power, as it flowed into them, tried to rebound into the doppelganger; finding no home in the nonmagical half, it then snapped back into the witch. The impact usually rendered both her and her doppelganger unconscious for a time.

This was what Satomi hoped for.

There were two alternatives to that hope.

Some women, despite all the preparation of the Elemental tests, failed when the power came. They didn't strike the right balance with it, and were annihilated by its force, screaming themselves to death in what seemed to be a doomed attempt to vent the energy.

This was what Satomi had remembered to dread.

What happened was the third possibility, which she, so afraid that Urishin would die before making it this far, had not even thought to fear.

Urishin gasped, face twisting in pain, and her head snapped back until she stared at the sky. Her entire thin frame shook like a leaf in the wind, and then, abruptly, it stilled.

And she began to speak.

"The answers," she said in a whispering voice that hardly sounded like her own, "are coming. From the forgotten overlooked lost they come. The path will move slip-side not straight not through, but *through,* with help. Two sides, one seen, one not, but the answers coming will open the eyes, and it may be in time, while the other eyes are gone, seeing the truth that lies elsewhere. New hope will help; the loss of fear. No more will be lost. No more save that which is always at risk. No more, in time; you will remember."

There were no words in Satomi's mind as she listened to the stream of ravings whisper from Urishin's mouth; no words that could begin to express the soul-sick horror she felt, seeing the girl standing there with her head thrown back and her mouth moving as if on its own, realizing what they had done.

They had made Urishin a Cousin.

Across the circle, she met Koika's eyes, and saw the same dead shock she felt herself. Koika knew. The others, new to this ritual, did not.

They had destroyed her forever.

The words ghosted to a halt. Satomi closed her eyes, too hurt to even weep, waiting for the sound of the small body hitting the grass, later to wake with her memory gone.

Instead, she heard a deep, shuddering gasp.

"Did it work?"

Satomi's eyes flew open.

Urishin was looking around the circle at the five of them, dazed, unsteady on her feet, but speaking. "Did it work? Am I a witch now?" Her eyes alighted on Mirei, standing for Air in the west. "Mirei, did it work?"

Then she collapsed.

WHILE URISHIN SLEPT, the five who had initiated her convened once more.

"She's a Cousin," Koika said, voice unsteady. "That's what *happens* to them. They receive power, they babble some words that would probably be important if we could figure out what in the Void they meant, and then they pass out."

"But she *remembered*," Mirei replied. There was no question of it in her mind. "She knew me, and she knew herself."

Koika shook her head, not as if she was disagreeing, but as if she hardly *dared* agree. "Will she still remember when she wakes up?"

Paere, silent up until this point, spoke up quietly. "She can still work magic." Heads swiveled to stare at her. "I checked," she added, looking around at them all. "The channel is still there. In Cousins, it's gone."

"Then what in the Void *was* that?" Koika demanded.

"More proof," Satomi murmured.

Now everyone was staring at the Void Prime. She had been sitting at the table with her hands sedately folded, hardly seeming to be present at all. Now she was alert, and there was a fragile joy in her expression, such that Mirei hardly dared breathe lest it shatter.

"Her mind survived an experience that has destroyed every other woman who's gone through it," Satomi said, her voice stronger now. "Because she is eleven? I doubt it. If there is an oddity here—something we've never seen happen before—then we must look to the characteristics that are peculiar to Urishin."

It wasn't hard to figure out. "Naspeth," Mirei said.

"Naspeth," Satomi repeated. "The other part of her self. If one half is killed, but the other survives, then the slain one recovers. As if the duality of their existence somehow protects that life, providing a refuge for it. The same must be true of the memories—the mind."

The joy faded into something closer to practicality. Satomi turned to Mirei. "But it could have been something else. What did you do to her, during the test of the Void?"

Mirei was hardly confident she could explain it, but this wasn't the time to tell the Void Prime "no." She scrambled for words. "I . . . something like the way the Elemental tests work, only not. In the same way that the Void itself is . . . not." The expressions aimed at her were unencouraging. *Blast it—this is like Hyoka and her friends all trying to study Void power when they're incapable of understanding what it is in the first place.* "The Void is non-essence, empty space, nothingness, and you make an illusion of that. But it wouldn't really prepare her to understand how she can use the *power* of that concept. I fed her Void power, so she could learn." Mirei couldn't suppress a smile. "She handled it pretty well."

"How did you know how to do that?" Churicho asked, confused. She and Paere were sitting together, slightly apart, as if in deference to the Primes—but Mirei was included in that deference.

Mirei shrugged. "I just knew." As all new forms of magic were just known. Perhaps her faith had slackened from the fervent, driven surrender that preceded her rejoining, but the Goddess still saw fit to give her that gift.

Satomi was more concerned with other matters. "Could that be responsible for Urishin?"

Again, Mirei shrugged. "I have no idea. But at the moment, it doesn't matter."

"What?" Koika asked.

Mirei smiled grimly at the Earth Prime. "Urishin passed out. I'm willing to bet Naspeth did, too. Shimi and Arinei know what we're up to. So if we're going to use her to find them, we'd better do it soon."

CHURICHO AND PAERE having been sent away, the remaining three bent over a map spread out on the council room table.

"Kalistyi," Mirei said, laying a finger on it, tucked into the northern bend in the coastline that formed White Bay. "We know they're in there. Specifics are what we're missing. So I figure Urishin and I go here—" She tapped the letters marking Olpri, a town in northern Haira. "Been through there a couple of times; I remember it well enough. And then we go here." Her finger moved to southern Liak. "Triangulate the two senses of direction that Urishin gets, and see where they meet up."

"It's distant, though," Koika said thoughtfully. "At that range—"

"She'll still feel Naspeth, trust me. It won't be precise, but it'll be more than we have now, and we can do it in just three jumps."

Nodding slowly, Satomi said, "And even if they find out what we've done . . . they're in trouble whether they relocate or not. If they stay put, we find them, and if they move, we'll hear about that, too."

A knock at the door interrupted them. Mirei, in deference to the Primes, went to open it.

Ruriko was outside. "Aken," she said. "Chashi. Mirei." She held out one of the many message sheets the witches used to communicate with distant places. "This just arrived from Silverfire."

A clatter of heels on the floor alerted Mirei before the two Primes appeared at her shoulders, bending to peer at the words on the sheet. Mirei recognized Jaguar's hand, even in the brief message it conveyed.

> *The dissidents are near Garechnya. With this information, Eclipse renders his final service. As the last of his boons, he requires that you not seek him out. He gives you his sworn word that he will not endanger Mirei's life.*

Her stomach lurched at the words. Flat and unemotional as they were, she read what lay behind them. *He's going to die. Warrior, there* has *to be a way to save him*—

"Garechnya," Koika whispered, and then swore. "We didn't need to risk Urishin."

Mirei didn't give a damn about that at the moment; her mind was entirely on her year-mate. She wasn't bound by the boon. She could search for him—

For what purpose? To kill him more quickly?

She became aware of noise. Shouting in the corridors, as witches called out to one another. The Primes and Ruriko were looking up, message forgotten, when a figure Mirei had not seen for months came into view at the other end of the hallway.

"If you'll pardon the interruption," Eikyo said, pink

with nervous excitement, "there are women who want to speak with you."

A SMALL CROWD OF RIDERS waited in the morning sunlight of the courtyard. Red-haired, every one; it took Mirei a moment to realize they were not witches.

They were Cousins.

Cousins as she'd never seen them before. The quiet, near-invisible servants of the witches were standing, reins in hand, facing Satomi and the rest of the growing crowd, and somehow they were more *there* than ever before. Drawing attention to themselves, rather than fading into the background as they usually did. She hadn't realized how good they were at fading until she saw them stop.

In front of them stood one woman who was not a visitor. Nae, her old face hard with determination, was waiting for the Primes to arrive.

Satomi stepped forward, every bit as imposing as the Cousins, and spoke. What she said, though, was not at all what Mirei expected.

"I hope," she said in a quiet voice that carried no farther than the newly arrived group, "that you have the answers I was recently promised."

THE COUNCIL ROOM was not suitable for a group of this size; they took over one of the teaching halls instead, rearranging the seats more appropriately. Or rather, Mirei and Eikyo rearranged the seats. Satomi and Koika, whether they realized it or not, were obviously expecting the Cousins to do that work, and the Cousins were just as obviously not going to do a bit of it. Mirei and Eikyo, so very junior to most of the other people there, took care of it, while the Primes fiddled with foci and cast spells warding the room to the Void and beyond against any eavesdropping or meddling.

Mirei whispered to her friend as they moved chairs. "What happened? Your last message—"

"Were you reading those?" Eikyo whispered back. She cast a sidelong glance at the women milling around, but no one was paying attention to them. "They knew all along. They just made me think they believed it. I've been talking to them for days—" But then the seats were arranged, and they had to shut up, waiting for the others to talk.

Songs completed, Satomi took possession of a chair, and opened her mouth to begin the meeting—but Nae beat her to it.

"We have decided to offer you our help," the old woman said, in a tone of voice no more meek than that which a Lady might have used.

"I see," the Void Prime said, seemingly unfazed. "First I must ask, though—what of Kyou?"

Mirei winced.

Nae's mouth pinched tighter. "*Eikyo,*" she said, "has been an ambassador on your behalf. Fortunately for you, she is more competent at diplomacy than spying."

Satomi went very tense.

"We knew right away that she wasn't really a Cousin," the woman continued. "As soon as she woke up. There is one thing the touched remember, even when they've forgotten everything else: They remember the words the Goddess passed through them. Eikyo had no words. By that, we knew she was an impostor."

Koika, seated next to the Void Prime, gave the Cousin a startled and confused look; then, comprehension dawning on her, she turned to stare at Satomi. And Mirei remembered that Satomi had lied to her.

Satomi glanced sideways at her, a quick flick of the eyes. "Later," she murmured, and Mirei heard the plea in her voice. *Don't ask about it right now. Don't show weakness, dissent, division, in front of them.*

Since she happened to agree that now was not the time for Satomi to explain her lie, Mirei threw herself into the conversational breach. "The 'touched'?" she repeated.

Another Cousin answered her. "Those who were raised to be witches," she said. "Who lost their memories in the test. They're touched by the Goddess."

"The words they say," Mirei said. "That's the touch? What causes it?"

Nae took over again, her voice tight with offended pride. "You needn't say that as if it were a curse."

Mirei felt obscurely as if she should address the woman with some honorific; the rest of the Cousins were clearly deferring to her. "I didn't—"

"It *isn't* a curse," Nae snapped, before Mirei could finish her half-formed apology. "It's a blessing we're too weak to handle."

As diplomatically as she could, Mirei said, "Please explain."

"Being touched is not a form of *failure*," Nae said. Her posture was ramrod-straight in her chair, and her hands were stiffly folded in her lap. Looking at her, Mirei thought, *She's nervous. This confrontation is not easy for her, after who knows how many years of invisibility.* "Failure is being destroyed by power. The ones who become witches control their power. The touched, though, find a different way to survive."

Satomi's quiet voice slipped in when Nae paused. "Do you remember it?"

Nae was a witch-student? Mirei thought, startled, as the old Cousin turned to the Prime.

"No," the woman said, and there was a wealth of sadness in the word—yet pride as well. "But from our words, and from the stories we preserve of who we once were—stories given back to us by those Cousins who knew us before the touch—we know what happened."

She looked at each of them in turn, eyes intense, and Mirei resisted the urge to prod her into going on.

"In the moment of crisis," Nae said at last, "when others control the power and live, or else succumb to it and die, we who are touched surrender ourselves into the Goddess's hands. We give ourselves to her, completely, because we are faced with something beyond our strength, and only through her merciful grace will we survive it. In that surrender, we open ourselves to her voice."

Remembering the perfect faith in Urishin's eyes, Mirei believed it. *She was relying on her faith to get her through. And it did—though not in the way we expected and hoped for.*

"The volumes in the archives," Satomi said. "Pages and pages of incomprehensible babbling, as written down by the witches who heard it from the—the touched. That's the Goddess speaking?" There was a faint, skeptical edge to her words.

"She requires us to work to understand her meaning," one of the other Cousins said sharply.

"Or else human minds are too dumb to translate her message," another suggested, more cheerfully. "It gets garbled along the way."

"Either way," Nae said, on the heels of the second one, "our words are divine messages. There *is* meaning in them."

Satomi made a conciliatory gesture. "I don't doubt you. But we've looked for that meaning. I read your words, Nae— Would you prefer to be called Omonae? But I couldn't get anything from them. I can't even be certain these are the 'answers' I recently heard of."

"You haven't tried hard enough." Nae's expression was harsher and less forgiving than stone.

"Nae," another Cousin said quietly. She had been at the forefront of the riders in the courtyard, and she locked gazes for a moment with the old leader of the Cousins. Surprisingly, Nae bowed her head and indicated the other woman should speak.

"I've been keeping an eye on Eikyo since she arrived among us," the newcomer said. "The fact that you sent her to spy on us is only partially counterbalanced by your intentions in doing so. You have Eikyo herself to thank for persuading us to come forward like this. She learned much about us, in such a short time." The look she bestowed on Eikyo carried a hint of pride.

Eikyo smiled back at her and then spoke, diffidently. "Aken, Chashi—may I introduce Rin, leader of the eastern Cousins." One by one, she named the others, while Mirei tried not to glare at Satomi for not having thought to ask sooner.

"It is an honor to meet you," Satomi said when they were done, and at least she sounded sincere.

Rin looked to Nae again, and having received a nod, she continued speaking. "As Nae told you, there *is* meaning in the words the Goddess gives to the touched—but, as you pointed out, it isn't very clear. This is what we've been debating among ourselves. We all agree that some of the words apply to this situation; what we don't agree on is which words, or what they mean. But on the whole, we're willing to support you, because we think that the changes Mirei has brought hold hope that the touched might not have to lose their memories when the Goddess's presence descends on them."

It was good to have reasons for real, heartfelt smiles, after the stress and grief of recent days. "More than a hope," Mirei said, grinning and not caring whether she was stepping on Satomi's toes. "We have to wait for her to wake up to be sure, but we're pretty positive Urishin still remembers herself."

"What?" Nae demanded, echoed by several others. "Urishin *what*?"

"We tested her last night," Satomi told them, with a fleeting glare at Mirei. "At her request. So that she could find Naspeth, and through that, we could find Shimi and Arinei. She was . . . touched, during her final trial. But she seemed to remember herself, before she passed out."

This sent an excited murmur through the gathered Cousins. Mirei heard "could be what Barani's words meant," "I told you—'only by keeping will you not lose,'" "isn't she one of *them*?" and then, in an ironic voice, "We argued for so long, they beat us to the answer."

Satomi waited for the noise to die down. "We would be grateful for your support," she said. "What did you have in mind to offer?"

Rin's smile was predatory. *Here we go,* Mirei thought.

"We know where the dissidents are," the Cousin said.

"So do we." Satomi showed no hint that they had learned it less than an hour before.

The setback didn't faze Rin. "We can describe it for you, well enough for Mirei to send herself there. Yes, we know how her magic works," she said when Koika shifted in surprise. "And though some of our people are truly on the side of the dissidents, we have our spies among them."

"How did they give you this information without violating the oath?" Mirei asked.

The answering smile was both pained and smug. "Shimi didn't immediately think of including Cousins in the oath. Once she did, she placed them under a stricter version than the witches, but by then, it was too late."

Invisibility had its uses, obviously. Mirei began calculating just what she could do in Garechnya, if she got herself there.

"But we can offer more than that," Rin went on. "Not just information, but aid. As I said, we have people among them, who can help you with whatever you have planned."

Possibilities began to flower in Mirei's mind. She couldn't take any large force with her, and alone she couldn't do much, but with help . . .

Satomi nodded, not taking her eyes from Rin and Nae. "In exchange for what?"

"In exchange for nothing," Nae said, but her cool tone belied the innocuous words. "Merely keep the promise you made to me."

Koika stared at Satomi again.

"A boon," Nae said. "To 'better our lives'—I believe that was the phrase you used."

Satomi's lips thinned. "I meant it when I said I wanted the best for witches and Cousins. The fact that you feel obliged to remind me of this boon means you intend to ask for something very large indeed."

A tiny incline of Nae's head and the faintest hint of a smile conceded the point to the Void Prime. Even with that warning, though, her response hit like a catapult shot. "Magic for our daughters."

Dead silence.

"I beg your *pardon*?" Koika said flatly.

"Magic. For our daughters. We have five candidates. Create the channel in them; educate them as witches. Let them be tested. Their mothers were witches, generations back. We see no reason why *they* cannot be, as well."

Koika was shaking her head before Nae had even finished. "But these candidates of yours—no doubt they're more than five days old."

"So?" Nae asked. "Five days is tradition, nothing more. Yes, they have souls already, but we know now that it's not a problem. They are all infants yet. They can be trained just like any other witch-child." She was smiling, but underneath it was determination honed over decades of quiet, unobtrusive service in a world that had once been hers. "We want that chance for them."

Mirei looked to Eikyo, and found her friend serene. Her eyes said that she supported this idea wholeheartedly. The thought was so alien, though—

More alien than what I did? Mirei was hardly one to throw stones at radical ideas. And as far as she knew, there was no reason other children could not become witches. Even children not of Cousins. The ability was not inborn; it was created. Misetsu's decision to create it only in her own daughters might have been her first step down the path of prideful error.

Satomi broke the silence. "On one condition."

This time everyone in the room stared at her. The reasons for staring varied between the witches and Cousins, though. "You offered the boon without conditions," Nae said.

Satomi disregarded that. "One of the five must be a boy."

Dead silence, again. Mirei was probably the only person who had seen that coming.

Koika said, "You can't be serious."

"I am," Satomi said, somehow both defiant and peaceful at once. "Can't you feel it, Koika? This is a time of change. Yes, our traditions are being overturned, but it's because they *need* to be. I know how we can reduce the risk of women dying in the testing. I realized it while we were testing Urishin. It will mean changing our entire way of conducting the trials—but should we cling to tradition, when lives are at stake? We know how to keep the Warrior part of our selves; we know how to save our memories. *'No more will be lost,'* Urishin said. And now this: a chance to increase our numbers. Why should it only be our own daughters who can become witches?" Satomi gave them all a smile that was almost creepy in its calmness. "We have a chance to change things for the better. I mean to take it."

Another silence reigned, until Nae broke it.

"Four girls, one boy," she said. "We will arrange it."

Chapter Twenty-Three

❦━◆━❦

IN THE QUIET, snowy darkness of Kalistyi's western mountains, two figures suddenly appeared.

Mirei fell to her knees, retching, shaking, trying not to make any noise. *Warrior's mercy—Warrior's complete lack of mercy—Goddess, please tell me I'll recover if I rest.*

She got over the nausea enough to see Urishin removing the gag from her own mouth. Mirei wasn't certain how the unrestored witch-half of a pair would react to being moved through the Void, so on the chance that she would suffer the effects an ordinary witch did, she'd gagged the girl. But Urishin looked fine—if suspiciously bright-eyed.

Instinct alerted Mirei. "Don't," she whispered, reaching one trembling hand out toward the girl. "Don't do it."

Urishin took a deep, ragged breath, and the gleam in her eyes faded.

Mirei could sympathize with what Urishin was feeling. Immediately after the test, the world looked different; she was aware of power everywhere, inherent in the world around her. Resisting the urge to reach out to it was not easy, especially when someone else cast spells.

That was why they were here tonight.

The Primes and the leaders of the Cousins were ensconced in the council room at Starfall, planning a full-blown action against the stronghold outside Garechnya.

Mirei wholeheartedly supported this, but one thing could not wait for their plans to be completed, and that was Naspeth.

Shimi and Arinei would know what had happened to her. If they were smart—and so far they had not obliged anyone by being stupid—they would move Naspeth somewhere else. It wouldn't keep their stronghold safe, not with the help from the Cousins, but they didn't know that, and it would mean all the information on this place's defenses would be useless in rescuing the doppelganger. And time was on the dissidents' side. All they had to do was keep the two apart for long enough, and Urishin's magic would kill them both.

She'd said all this to Satomi.

The Void Prime had told her to wait.

Mirei remembered very distinctly the fight she'd had with Satomi when she came back to Starfall from Angrim. She knew she had responsibilities. But she also knew that the time to go after Naspeth was *now,* right after Urishin's test, before the dissidents had time to make plans. A quick mission, in and out—exactly the kind of thing she'd been trained as a Hunter to do. She had the skills and the supplies to pull this off. The full-blown strike had to wait for preparation; the rescue of Naspeth could not afford to.

Urishin stood shivering in the snow while Mirei pulled herself together. *Only one more of these,* she reminded herself. *Jump back to Starfall, and you're done. For a while, anyway.*

With luck, they might even be able to get the rest of the doppelgangers—not just the one.

Mirei wondered what that would do to her. The strain

on her was stronger the more bodies she moved; the worst so far had been Ashin and Kekkai. Could she move four people besides herself? They were small people; maybe that would count for something.

I'll manage if it kills me.

She tried not to think about that.

To Urishin's credit, the girl didn't stand idly by while waiting. When Mirei finally pushed herself to her feet, brushing snow off the knees of the Hunter uniform she wore beneath her fur cloak, Urishin pointed off through the trees. "That way."

Mirei's original plan, before the message from Eclipse and the arrival of the Cousins, had been to use Urishin for broad triangulation. That had only been because she couldn't be more precise. With the description Rin had given her, she'd jumped much closer. They were far enough from the stronghold that their arrival wouldn't be noticed, but near enough to strike. And Urishin could guide her from here.

They moved off, snow muffling the sound of Urishin's footsteps. The girl wasn't bad; she'd been spending time with the doppelgangers at Starfall. At last they sighted lights, and Mirei paused.

"Wait here," she told Urishin, and continued on alone.

Garechnya itself lay somewhere nearby, but another, smaller town had sprung up in this sheltered valley to accommodate the exiles. Witches, Cousins, and soldiers lent by Lady Chaha, according to Rin and the reports from Eclipse. The guard on the area wasn't trivial, but she didn't have to penetrate it just yet; Rin had set up ways to contact the loyal Cousins among the dissidents. Mirei wondered whether the woman had suspected her intention of coming out here alone. Perhaps.

A broken pine stood just next to a large, flat-topped granite boulder. Mirei placed a spray of pine needles on the stone, then retreated.

With Urishin in tow once more, she found a clump of holly bushes thick enough to hide behind. Once concealed, Mirei turned to Urishin. "All right. Reach for her again."

Urishin closed her eyes for a long moment. Then she opened them and shook her head, looking unhappy. "That way." She pointed toward the settlement. "But I don't know where."

Mirei was afraid she was telling the truth. When Miryo had come to Angrim, she'd known Mirage was in the city, but nothing more. Directionality faded at close range. Mirage had pushed past that, once, but only after knowing Miryo for a while, and she'd done it by focusing on the things that made Miryo distinct from her. Urishin and Naspeth had never met.

But she couldn't accept that this time. "Close your eyes again," Mirei said. "Deep breath. Meditate like I taught you." She waited while Urishin obeyed. "Naspeth," she said softly, when the girl seemed ready. "Your other half. You are the Maiden, the Bride, the Mother, the Crone. She is the Warrior. You are Fire, Air, Water, Earth. She is the Void. Reach for her. Feel her. You two are connected. Follow that link. Which way does it lead?"

The winter silence stretched out. Mirei hardly dared breathe.

Then, as if of its own accord, Urishin's arm rose to point. This time it aimed, not at the main body of the settlement, but off to one side.

"Hold that," Mirei whispered, and waited.

It was a cold wait, but eventually a heavily bundled woman appeared, scouring the area for firewood, though it had largely been picked clean. From behind the holly bushes, Mirei mimicked the call of a cardinal.

The woman stopped. "Friends to Misetsu?"

"Misetsu made mistakes," Mirei said. The pass phrases the Cousins had chosen were . . . interesting.

The woman didn't approach them. "What do you need?"

"A diversion," Mirei said. "South end."

"How big?"

"Enough to draw guards away from where the children are kept."

The Cousin's face went tight. "Dangerous."

"Necessary," Mirei said. "We have to get the girls out if possible. Can you do it?"

The Cousin hesitated. At Mirei's side, Urishin was breathing slowly and evenly, maintaining the trance that pointed the way to her doppelganger.

"Yes," the Cousin said at last. "If this is the time."

"It is," Mirei told her softly. *It had better be.*

With a nod, the woman said, "Then wait here. You'll know when to move."

She vanished into the snow, leaving Mirei with Urishin.

THE DIVERSION, when it came, consisted of lighting a horse barn on fire.

It'll do, Mirei thought grimly, wishing that the Cousin had been a little more creative. Certainly some people would be involved in getting the horses out, and in making sure the fire didn't spread from the barn to the thatched roofs of the neighboring buildings. It wasn't very effective, though, and it looked too much *like* a diversion.

But if that was what she had to work with, she'd do it. Mirei took Urishin by the hands and led the girl out of the holly thicket.

They had just reached the outermost buildings, sitting on the slopes of the valley, when the rest of the diversion kicked in.

Mirei couldn't even quite be sure what was going on. All she could make out, at this distance and with only firelight to illuminate it, was that some kind of armed attack was underway on the far side of the valley. Some distance from the fire, but well away from the direction Mirei and Urishin were headed in.

Precisely calibrated to look like the fire was a diversion for *that*.

Mirei took back her unkind thoughts about the woman's creativity and began to move faster.

The town was beginning to swarm like a hornet's nest. Deep in her trance, Urishin continued to point when told, in a decidedly creepy way. Mirei took her direction, marked the buildings that were along its path, and then circled around the outer edge of the town. It kept them away from the people now swarming out of the buildings, and let her triangulate. Urishin seemed to be pointing at a one-story building that looked like some manner of barracks.

Let's hope the soldiers are busy outside.

Snatches of song were rising from the chaos at the other end; there was enough magic being flung around that Mirei could feel it even at this distance. She shot a quick, worried glance at Urishin, but the girl showed no sign of reaching for power. Still, Mirei moved faster. The sooner they got out of here, the better.

Urishin continued to point, unerringly—at least Mirei hoped unerringly—at the barracks building.

Hiding in the shadows of a storehouse's steeply canted roof, Mirei eyed her target. At a guess, the main door would take her into an antechamber where people could remove their snow-covered outer garments. Beyond it would be a mess hall. She'd seen the type before.

Urishin was pointing straight in. Not to the side. Probably at the mess hall, then.

I don't like this.

She especially didn't like the idea of taking Urishin in with her. But the alternative was leaving the girl here, or sending her back out into the woods alone, and both of those options were worse.

Mirei took a deep breath. *I'll just have to be ready. If there's trouble, I'll sing us out as fast as I can.*

"Come on," she whispered to Urishin, and together they ran across the intervening space.

Through the door, and yes, there was an antechamber, and then through that into the mess hall behind—

The girls were in there.

So were other people.

Clapping one hand over Urishin's eyes and closing her own, Mirei threw down a small ceramic container. It shattered on the floor, and the resulting flash of light bought them an instant of time, at least. Time enough for her to realize what she'd seen in there, and to make a decision.

But Urishin, without warning, began to sing.

Mirei flowed into motion. Blades out, she sliced into the two Cousins who had been waiting by the door;

blinded as they were, they both went down easily. But that wasn't Mirei's real aim. Weaving body and voice together, she built a spell, reaching frantically for power around the rippling chaos of Urishin's naive, untrained, uncontrolled attempt to help, *Oh please Goddess don't let her kill herself this has got to work PLEASE—*

With a wrenching effort that felt like it ripped her own body apart, Mirei slid through Urishin's spell, seized four bodies, and flung them through the Void.

Leaving herself behind.

THE AFTERMATH of Urishin's attempted magic rattled the walls, splintered tables into kindling, and sent everyone stumbling back.

Mirei collapsed to the floor, retching helplessly, hardly even alert enough to hope that she had just succeeded at getting the girls out of harm's way—even if she hadn't moved herself.

Got to get up got to get up she's here I have to get up—

She felt blows landing on her body, boots hitting her ribs, people attacking her who didn't realize she wasn't in any state to be a threat at the moment. Then a voice spoke sharply, cutting them off.

In the quiet, the voice spoke again, and she recognized it.

"You've achieved nothing. They're still going to die."

Footsteps on the wooden boards as Shimi came forward. But not too close. She wouldn't be stupid enough to do that. Mirei writhed on the floor, too weak to rise.

Void-damned trap *no guards outside she wanted me to come in and used them as bait—*

"Your unnatural magic won't save them. Starfall isn't safe. Arinei has seen to that."

What would have been a laugh turned into a gut-wrenching fit of coughing, which was probably just as well. *Good thing I accidentally sent them elsewhere, you bitch.*

Goddess, please tell me it worked.

And then, penetrating the fog of her disorientation— *Starfall isn't safe?*

Hands on her, taking away her weapons, wrenching her arms behind her back, yanking her more or less upright. Mirei's vision cleared to reveal Shimi standing before her.

The intervening time hadn't been kind to the former Air Prime. Lines scored her face, which had gone even thinner and harder than before. She looked exhausted. But her pale eyes burned with energy enough to keep her going, and hatred enough to kill Mirei where she knelt.

"You are a *monster*," Shimi hissed, literally spitting the words in Mirei's face. "A taint on the face of the Goddess's creation. An abomination in her eyes. You serve your twisted Warrior and cloak it in piety, you—"

Mirei gathered enough strength to cut her off. "Do you think you're going to *convert* me, Shimi? Save the theology lecture and just kill me already."

And when the former Prime's face contorted in rage, Mirei ripped herself free of the Cousin's grasp and threw herself forward.

She didn't have the blindest idea what she thought she would accomplish, other than knocking Shimi down. Not with other Cousins in the room. There would be no escape, no wending her way back through the chaos of the town to the cold woods outside, and she couldn't hope to jump by magic. She doubted she could manage even the simplest spell at the moment.

But if she could find a way to kill Shimi, then as the Warrior was her witness, she was going to do it.

They crashed to the floor, and as Mirei grappled with the woman, she heard shouts, thumps, a scream of pain. Not from Shimi. Mirei rammed with knees and elbows, twisting, scratching, yanking at the Prime's hair, anything to prevent a spell, and then another body fell on top of them, and she realized that something else was happening in the room.

She turned her head to look, and Shimi, by accident or design, slammed an elbow into her head.

Mirei's grip slackened, and the woman slipped free. But when the stars faded from her vision, she saw bodies on the floor—Cousins, fallen in bloody pools amongst splintered wood—and someone else.

Eclipse.

The Hunter stood, reddened blades in his hands, and he was staring at her in stark horror. Blood dripped from his right fist down to the floor—not dripped, poured. It grew stronger as she watched, as if some wound were opening up beneath the sleeve of his uniform.

Singing. Shimi was casting a spell. Pivoting where he stood, Eclipse threw his knife, and the tune died off in a vicious curse.

Mirei grabbed the edge of a nearby table and hauled herself to her feet, holding on desperately so she wouldn't collapse.

"Mirei," Eclipse said in a painful mimicry of a conversational tone. "Didn't expect to see you here."

"Eclipse," she whispered. Her eyes were on Shimi, who was pulling a knife from her thigh. *Bad aim,* she thought irrationally. *He needs to practice.*

He needs to not be bleeding.

"Just came to kill *her*," he went on, nodding at the witch. "Figured if I was going to die, I might as well try. What did I have to lose? Got some help along the way. Nice women, they were. Cousins." His voice was wandering, fading. With a shocking clatter, his sword slipped from his fingers and hit the floor. Mirei's heart lurched. Eclipse would never drop his sword.

He's dying.

Shimi opened her mouth to sing again.

Weaponless, Mirei flung herself forward once more, across the intervening space and at the woman who had, through her manipulations, killed the person dearest to her in the world.

The stiffened edge of her hand struck Shimi in the throat, crushing the woman's windpipe two syllables into the spell.

She knew, as she did it, that this was the moment to try. Offer Shimi's life up to the Warrior, in exchange for Eclipse. It might work. It was the only thing that could, now. She had no other way to save him.

But she wouldn't make that trade.

She struck to kill, but not in sacrifice. She killed Shimi because of all the damage the woman had wrought, the other lives wasted besides Eclipse's. Falya and Yimoe, Chaiban and Serri, little Chanka and Anness. Sharyo, dead at Indera's hand. Ashin. She killed Shimi because the woman had perverted so many of their ways, splintering Starfall, warping the blood-oath, murdering children for her cause. A trial would condemn her to death, but Mirei lacked the strength to take her back for one, and if she didn't kill Shimi then Shimi would kill her.

But she would not offer the woman's life to the Warrior, because it wasn't hers to give.

She killed Shimi, and knew she had lost Eclipse as well.

Three bodies hit the floor at once. Shimi convulsed, clawing at her throat, choking to death. Mirei rolled free of her, dizzy, and crawled across to where Eclipse had fallen.

He was white with blood loss. Mirei clamped her hand over the oath-scar on his wrist, but it did no good. Nothing would stop him bleeding; even if she could manage a healing spell, it wouldn't make a difference. She could not save him.

He managed a shaky smile. "It would've killed me anyway, even if you weren't here. Guess I'm glad you are. Get to say good-bye."

She stared down at him, seeing him with two gazes, two sets of memories overlapping. To Mirage he was so familiar, so loved, but too close to be seen as anything other than a brother. To Miryo, he was a newcomer in her life, but valued and trusted—a friend—because Mirage had always trusted him.

Both at once. Familiar and not. Too close and too far. In between them, in the blending of her memories, a middle ground. She would have explored it, given time, and she knew he would have, too.

But they weren't going to get a chance.

Mirei let go of his hand long enough to grab a piece of wood from one of the tables broken by Urishin's magic. There was plenty of blood available; she dipped her fingers in it and scrawled her message in a few short words.

Shimi dead. Dgs at Silverfire.
Starfall not safe.

Everything she knew. It wasn't enough; she didn't know what Shimi had meant. Were there more traitors in Starfall? What had Arinei done? Questions she didn't have answers to. She had to hope others could deal with them.

With what remained of her energy, Mirei sang the board to Satomi's desk.

She wasn't getting out of here anyway.

Mirei bent her head and kissed Eclipse gently. For the first time, and the last. She wished they'd had more time. But she would do what she could for him.

"You're not going to die," she said.

The prayer she sent up was resigned. *You probably won't take this. I doubt I could get out of here alive anyway, so it's not much of a trade. But damn it—he deserves to live, even if he did swear the oath falsely. He's dying for my sake.*

And I've done a lot for you. So I guess this isn't so much a request as a demand.

If you really do take trades—then take me.

"What—" Eclipse whispered, near-soundlessly, as she slipped one of his knives from his boot, and he tried to grab her hand. But he was too weak; he couldn't stop her.

Mirei placed the point of the knife under her chin, then shoved the blade upward.

Chapter Twenty-Four

THE DEBATE OVER what to do now that they knew where in Kalistyi to strike promised to go on for long enough that Satomi sent word down to the kitchens for food.

The council room was crowded with women: Satomi and Koika, plus an assortment of Keys and Cousins. Mirei, frustrated by the interminable disagreements, had left to take care of Urishin, though she promised to return later. Satomi dearly wished the young witch could take a force of people straight to Kalistyi; it would be the most effective solution. It just wasn't possible, though. Any attacking force would have to come by another route. The debate was mostly over what size that force should be: a small one, slipping in quickly to take out the leaders, or a large one, sent to subdue the entire area. That, and how they were going to get there.

"We could go in either through Liak or Abern," Kekkai said dubiously, tracing the various passes on the map. "But that requires getting cooperation from those domains."

"Plus everyone else we'd have to march through on the way there," Churicho pointed out.

Rin was shaking her head even before they were done. "Too slow. You'd be lucky to get there by spring. Arranging diplomatic permissions, then an overland march in winter, through the mountains—they'd be gone long before you ever got there."

"But we'd know where they went to," Churicho said to the Cousin. "We can track where they go."

"Which only delays the issue."

Koika pushed through the women surrounding the map and stared at it for a moment. Then a grin spread across her face. "So don't go overland. Go around." Her hand swooped around the map's edge, through the sea and around to Kalistyi.

The suggestion produced a thoughtful, startled silence.

"In winter?" Rin said at last, disbelieving.

"With witches on board?" Koika smirked at her. "Weather manipulation happens to be a specialty of my Ray. The boats won't sink. And I can guarantee they'd make *very* good time."

The debate segued into the logistics of how they would get sufficient ships, during which a few Cousins—casting awed, confused glances at their fellows who had been included in the council—brought up trays of soup, bread, and wine. Satomi nibbled on the bread while she watched the discussion, but pushed her soup aside untouched. Tension made her stomach queasy, and salty fish soup did not appeal.

The others tucked in and kept arguing. Before long she steered them back to the other unaddressed question: What to do about the dissidents as a whole?

"Eliminating the leaders is the key step," Kekkai said around a mouthful of fish. "You'd be amazed how many women are on that side because their Primes are, or their Keys. If there's no one in *their* chain of command telling them to rebel, some of them will come back."

"Not all," Koika pointed out, pessimistically.

"No, but it's a first step. Then you tell them what their leaders have been doing. Few people will be happy to hear about children being murdered, and the ones who don't care about that *will* care that Arinei's sold Starfall out to Kalistyi."

"But once they're back, what do we *do* about them?" Churicho asked hesitantly.

Satomi didn't even have to consider her answer. "We put them on trial."

A few of the women glanced at her. "Trial, Aken?" Churicho said at last.

Satomi nodded. "There are traditions we need to reconsider, even set aside, but that isn't one of them. We must do this openly and correctly—not in secret. We take them prisoner, bring them back here, and put them on trial. Not all of them, the ordinary witches, but the Primes and the Keys. Perhaps a few others. If the decision is for execution, then so be it. But we must make that decision by law."

A knock on the door interrupted her. Naji, who was nearest to it, went and opened it. Ruriko was waiting outside.

"Aken, I'm sorry to disturb you," the secretary said, and bowed to them all. "But the children would like to speak to you."

She could only mean one set of children. "Is it important?" Satomi asked.

"I think so. They're very insistent."

"Go on," Koika said, resigned. "We'll still be chewing this over when you come back."

Satomi put the heel of her bread down and stood. "Bring them to my office, Ruriko."

Arriving there, she lit her lamps and wondered what the girls wanted. They knew by now what had happened with Urishin. Were they all going to demand to be tested as well? If so, Satomi would refuse. One trial of faith was enough; the rest could wait.

A tiny flicker of power behind her—and a *thunk*.

On edge as she was, Satomi whirled around ready to attack whatever had made that noise. It took her a moment to realize the sound was from something landing on her desk. Not the usual message scroll: a ragged wooden board.

"What in the . . ." Satomi murmured, approaching it as if it were a viper about to attack.

It didn't move. But in the warm glow of the lamps, she saw blood on it.

Writing.

> *Shimi dead. Dgs at Silverfire.*
> *Starfall not safe.*

Her heart pounded in her chest as she stared at the words. So terse, telling her so little—"Shimi dead"? How? "Dgs"—doppelgangers—the ones here, or the ones in Kalistyi? If they were at Silverfire, Mirei must have sent them—but why?

Was it a message from Mirei, or some ruse?

Starfall not safe.

A tapping on her office door nearly made her jump out of her skin. Remaining behind her desk, on guard and ready to lash out, Satomi sang the quick spell that would swing the door open.

Ruriko, on the other side, looked startled that Satomi

had not merely told her to come in. Behind her stood four girls, arrayed in pairs: Amas and Hoseki, Lehant and Owairi.

"Where is Mirei?" Satomi demanded, before any of them could speak.

Amas answered her, chin held high with all the conviction and confidence an eleven-year-old could muster. "Aken, she went to Kalistyi. With Urishin. They're rescuing Naspeth. She told me to tell you."

Satomi did not have time to curse the headstrong young witch as she wanted to. *Starfall not safe.* "Have the guards reported anything strange?"

Confused, Ruriko said, "No, Aken—I don't believe so."

"Don't tell me you don't *believe* so. *Find out.*" They scattered out of her way like frightened pigeons as she strode through the door. "Put everyone on alert. There may be something about to happen."

"What, Aken?" Ruriko asked, hurrying along in her wake.

"I don't know. But Mirei sent a warning. And I'm pretty sure it *was* from her." A humorless smile touched Satomi's lips. "Nobody else would send me a message in blood."

Gasps from behind her. She ignored them. "Ruriko, go. The rest of you, with me."

The doppelgangers and witch-students half ran to keep up with her as she swept back to the council room. The corridors were eerily silent; it was late enough that nearly everyone else would be in bed.

Where in the Void was Mirei? Why hadn't she come back?

Arriving at the council room, Satomi flung open the door—and found chaos within.

The women had collapsed on the floor or where they sat at the table. Rin was one of the few on her feet, clinging to a lamp fixture on the far wall, panting and shaking. Kekkai was nearest to the door, staggering toward it one dogged step at a time. Her head came up when Satomi entered, and her pupils were dilated until the irises of her eyes had vanished.

Satomi stared in horror for a few heartbeats. Kekkai's legs gave out; she fell to the floor in a heap. Behind her, she heard the girls gasp again.

"Cover your ears," she said quietly.

Without turning to see if they had obeyed, Satomi sang a spell, and added in the syllables that would magnify its effect as far as she could throw it.

"*ALERT,*" she said, and her voice rang enormously through the halls of Starfall. "*ALERT. THERE HAS BEEN AN ATTACK. ALERT. RURIKO, GET HERE* NOW. *ALL GUARDS OUT. SEARCH STARFALL. TAKE PRISONERS IF YOU CAN; KILL IF YOU HAVE TO. ALERT. WE ARE BEING ATTACKED.*"

The spell ended. In the resounding silence that followed, Amas whispered from behind her. "Poison."

Satomi pivoted sharply to face her. "Are you sure?"

The girl was white, but steady. "Mirei's started teaching us. I don't know much. It's probably a poison."

One that hadn't affected Satomi? She glanced over her shoulder and saw the bowls of soup, most of them drained. *Misetsu and Menukyo. I'm not a healer. What do you do to treat poison?* She tried to remember back to her days as a student, when they'd made her learn everything. *Vomiting. Induce vomiting.*

Footsteps in the hallway, more than a few. Hopefully

some of them would be witches with more experience at healing than she had.

Those who came around the corner, though, were not witches.

At the sight of the Hunters, Satomi knew why it was poison. They had to have witch help—to get past the wards, to find the council room—but the poison was the work of Hunters, designed to cripple them en masse so they could not fight back.

Amas and Lehant stepped in front of Satomi, as if they were going to protect her.

Satomi had not killed anyone since Orezha. She'd rarely been in a position to do so. But now, with these girls in front of her—each doppelganger with her witch, all four together, vulnerable to being killed for good—she didn't hesitate.

She tore one of the lamps from its hanger by the door and threw it straight at the Hunters. It hit the ground well in front of them, but that wasn't the point; the point was the flame itself, all the focus she needed for Fire.

The flames roared up off the floor, filling the corridor completely and rushing away from the council room. The effect was blinding, and for a moment the air was hardly breathable. When the worst of it cleared, the walls and floor were still on fire, threatening to spread—but one of the Hunters was still standing.

He threw himself forward out of the fire, uniform smoldering, and rolled to put it out. When he came to his feet he ran straight at them, sword out, and Satomi didn't have time for another spell.

He didn't make it to her.

She'd never known Mirage. Nor had she gone to the

practices Mirei held; her memories hurt too much for her to watch the girls train. And she'd slipped a knife in Orezha's back, never giving her a chance to fight.

She had never seen a doppelganger *move*.

Amas and Lehant acted in coordinated unison. One went left, one right, both faster than thought; a foot slammed into the back of the Hunter's knees while a pair of hands reached for his sword arm. He was a grown man, stronger than a doppelganger child, but he staggered and lost momentum. Amas hung on to his arm while Lehant pivoted on one foot and kicked him in the kidneys. And Hoseki and Owairi moved, too; they ran past, to where the spell had hit, and together snapped off a piece of floorboard, one end on fire.

The man roared and ripped his arm free of Amas's grip, cutting her along the ribs. She cried out, but kept moving. Lehant kicked him in the stomach even as Amas went for his knees again, this time from the side, and then Owairi threw Lehant the plank; she caught it without looking, as if she knew her double's every move. She went for the Hunter's wrist first, striking hard enough that the wood broke. The blade fell from his fingers, and Amas snatched it up.

"Don't kill him!" Satomi screamed, just in time.

Amas spun in a kick that would have done Mirei proud, knocking the Hunter to his knees, and then clubbed him over the head with the pommel of the sword.

She stared down at the unmoving body, then up at Satomi, wild-eyed with adrenaline. "I only knocked him out," she said, her voice wavering. "I think. I hit him awfully hard. I hope he's not dead."

Then she turned and threw up.

* * *

"INTO THE COUNCIL ROOM," Satomi told the girls. "Close the door. It won't open from the outside, not to anyone less than a Prime." Koika was inside, poisoned. If Rana had betrayed them . . . "I'll be back, or I'll send help. Only open the door if they knock in three sets of three. Do you understand?"

Lehant squared her narrow shoulders. "Aken, we can come with you—"

"Inside." Satomi would brook no argument. The council room was the safest place she could think of for them. She waited until they were in and had closed the door before she turned her attention back to the hall.

The flames from Satomi's attack were spreading, eating through the walls and floor. She sang unsteadily, trying to maintain her pitch, and on the second attempt damped them down until they died out. The remaining patches of floor were too weak to trust, though, and so she had to sing another spell to get across. Without a focus, she couldn't lift her entire body weight, but she could lighten herself enough not to fall through.

At least it made an effective barrier; no one other than a witch was getting past that section. Satomi cast one glance back at the council room door before moving on.

She found Nenikune outside the door to the infirmary hall, frantic with confusion. "Aken, what's going on? Urishin and Mirei vanished—"

"Go to the council room," Satomi said, ignoring her questions. Explanations could wait. "Take help with you. Knock in three sets of three. The women in there have been poisoned; I don't know with what. Once you're inside, close the door again, and don't let in anyone who doesn't knock in three sets of three. Understand?"

Nothing focused Nenikune like word that sick people needed help. She nodded, turned back into the infirmary, and began shouting orders.

Satomi continued on. She could hear noise from outside: the ring of blades and clashing melodies of multiple spells. Witches in various states of wakefulness and dress crowded the hallways, calling out questions. Attack? How could they be under attack? Satomi barked orders for them to all follow her, and most of them did.

Outside, she found chaos.

The courtyards had become battlegrounds. Kalistyin soldiers were locked in combat with the Cousins; Satomi caught a brief glimpse of Nae, bellowing orders to a squadron of armed women. But they were not the ones that tore out her heart.

Witches stood with the Kalistyin soldiers, singing out spells. In the clamor, Satomi could not begin to sort out what they were; she could only guess by the effects. Nae's squadron, moving at the run toward one knot of battle, fell in their tracks, and Satomi could only hope they were unconscious instead of dead. *But they could be doing much worse; they could be singing Fire—*

Behind her, the witches she had summoned stared in horror, unable to understand what was going on.

"The dissidents are here," she said in a carrying voice. *Nevermind how. That question is for later.* "We must defend Starfall."

And she began to sing.

Chapter Twenty-Five

❧——╂——╂——❧

THE DAGGER SLIPPED through Mirei's fingers and fell, hilt-first, onto her knees, then to the floor with a heavy clunk.

She swayed where she knelt, eyes closed, senses reeling. She'd felt pain at first, but then it had ended. Merciful, that.

Except why did she still feel pain from everything *else*?

Strong fingers closed around her wrists, yanking them back far too late. Eyes still closed, Mirei waited for the end.

It didn't come.

Eclipse's voice whispered, almost too soft to hear, *"Goddess."*

Mirei finally had to admit she wasn't dying. The lack of pain from shoving several inches of steel into her brain wasn't shock. There was no blood pouring out of her neck.

She opened her eyes.

Eclipse's blue eyes stared at her from mere inches away, lost between horror and awe. He still held her wrists, and now his grip was bruisingly strong. Mirei didn't even try to pull free. He stared at her, and she stared at him, and then finally he said in a stronger voice, "You

Void-damned *idiot*—what in the Warrior's bloody name did you think you were *doing*?"

Mirei moved her hand at last. Eclipse didn't let go, so she dragged his hand along as she reached up to touch the skin beneath her jaw. It was smooth and unmarked.

"Life for a life," she whispered. Her voice wouldn't manage more. "Rigai said it might work. They used to do it—killing someone else in exchange. But the only life I had the right to offer the Warrior was my own."

"Mirei, the whole damned point of me bleeding out was that I refused to be responsible for you dying!"

She managed a wavering smile. "Both of us trying to trade ourselves in for the other. Looks like *some* part of the Goddess took pity on a pair of fools."

He finally let go of her wrists, then, but only so that he could enfold her in a bone-crunching hug. Mirei gasped in pain. He released her. "Sorry. Crone's teeth. I feel better; you don't look like you do."

Mirei shook her head. "The Warrior didn't heal anything else." She reached for him again, and this time he held her in a gentler embrace. She could feel his heart beating, its pace rapid. Alive. She'd saved him.

Assuming they could escape from here.

Eclipse helped her to her feet. "Can you do that magic thing and get us out of here?"

She fought the urge to crack up at "that magic thing." Shock had made her giddy. She shook her head in response to his question. "I'll fall apart if I do." Maybe literally. She felt like her body was coming apart at the seams.

He grinned down at her, though there was worry in those blue eyes. "Then I guess it's up to me to get us out of the giant mess you made of this place. Has becoming a witch made you forget what subtlety is?"

ECLIPSE'S REFLEXES saved them before they'd gone a hundred paces; when they were about to step out the door of the building, he dragged Mirei back into the shadows as figures rushed by outside. They were indistinct in the darkness: witches or Cousins or soldiers, Mirei didn't know. He waited until the lane was clear, then led her across to the shadows of another building.

"Good diversion," he muttered, peering around a corner at the chaos enveloping much of the town. "A little *too* good—they've stirred the whole place up."

Mirei's tongue felt slow and thick when she spoke. "I asked for a distraction."

He grinned at her, a flash of white teeth in the shadows. "So did I."

It explained the scale. Mirei wanted to ask how he'd gotten help from the Cousins, but she had to focus on keeping her feet in the snow. Eclipse led her from one bit of cover to another, his hand locked in hers. Anyone else, Mirei would not have been able to trust to get her out of there. Eclipse, she let work without interference. Even back when she was a doppelganger, her Warrior-blessed gifts hadn't helped her much with stealth. He'd always been better at it than she was.

She almost cried when they reached the slope of the valley. Eclipse helped her scramble up the broken, icy ground, but the climb took what remained of her energy; by the time they reached the top, she wanted nothing more than to lie down in the snow.

Eclipse growled a curse. She felt his arm wrap around

her hips, and then she was swinging through the air, up and onto his shoulders. *I should argue, but Goddess, I'm so tired. . . .*

But a short time later, he stopped and put her down. "This isn't going to work—I'm leaving a trail a blind man could follow and I'm going to smack your head into a tree if I don't watch out. Come on, Mirei. On your feet."

She mumbled something incoherent even to herself.

There was a brief silence. When he spoke again, it was not with the voice of a friend; he sounded like their training-masters from Silverfire.

"Get *up*. What are you, weak? I'm not asking you to run laps with a pack on; you just have to walk through the snow. On your feet, already. Mother's tits—did you lose all your strength when you turned into Mirei? The Mirage part of you's got to be crying in shame. Move your *ass*. It isn't time to collapse yet. Are you a Hunter or not?"

He got uglier before she got to her feet, and uglier still by the time they were able to stop. Mirei was soon snarling half-articulated death threats back at him. But it worked; it kept her awake and moving. She no longer had a separate half to call on for strength, but she did have stubbornness and pride, and he knew how to wake them both up.

Refuge was a cave where he'd left his pack, and getting down to it was the last straw for Mirei. Her foot slipped on an icy stone and she slid the rest of the way into the ravine where it lay, adding bruises to her other pains. But once there, Eclipse's harsh, goading tone vanished as if it had never been; he spoke soothingly to her while he built up the tiny fire that was all they dared risk.

"I didn't expect to be coming back here," he admitted

while he coaxed the flames to grow. "Rode a horse to death on my way north—we'll have to try and get another one. I just figured to come here, on the off chance that I might be able to find and kill the witch who made me swear the oath."

"Shimi," Mirei whispered; she lacked the energy to speak more loudly.

Her year-mate glanced at her sideways. "The Air Prime?"

"Cast the oath spell on you."

He fed more pine needles into the fire. "You killed her."

"Yeah."

His face was still in the shifting illumination; then he shrugged. "Saves us having to Hunt her."

Might have come to that, Mirei thought sleepily, curling herself around the fire while Eclipse warmed broth from what was left of his supplies. *If they couldn't get her back to Starfall.* He'd lost weight while they were apart, and it made his cheekbones stand out sharply in his face. *What did Shimi mean about Arinei? Why isn't Starfall safe?*

She whispered that last question to Eclipse. He shook his head. "I don't know. Traitors among you?"

"Found one already."

"There might be more. Or some way to get past the defenses." He bit his lip, then looked down at Mirei. "Shimi hated Hunters, right?"

"Hated the Warrior."

"So you don't think she would have hired any."

Shimi, no. But what had she said? *"Arinei has seen to that."*

He must have seen the shift in her expression, because

he grew even more serious. "Mirei—someone hired a whole lot of Wolfstars recently."

Assassins. "Didn't hear about that."

"I got it from Silverfire contacts. And I—" He hesitated, looking unexpectedly guilty. "I didn't pass it along. To be honest . . . the most logical explanation seemed to be that Satomi hired them. She's done it before, and that would be one way to take out the opposition."

Mirei shook her head, feeling her neck muscles creak as she did. "No. Won't do that—won't murder them. But Arinei . . ."

Eclipse swore softly and creatively. "We have to warn them."

"Already did." As much as she could. When was the attack planned for, and what form would it take? Mirei's mind was too slow to work through it in her current state. She would have to wait for the morning, and pray it wouldn't be too late. "Girls are at Silverfire, though. The doppelgangers. And Urishin." She managed a smile. "Guess I was thinking more like Mirage than Miryo, when I sent them." So at least they were safe.

He placed the cup of broth on a stone by her head and sat looking down at her. The right side of his face was lit by the fire, but the left side lay in shadow, turning his expression into an unreadable mask. "Mirei—what you did—"

She had to sit up, though every inch of her body protested when she did. But what she had to say couldn't be mumbled into the fire.

"Eclipse," she said. When had she stopped thinking of him as Kerestel, his old name? When she became Mirei. When she saw him as much with Miryo's eyes as Mirage's. "Everyone keeps treating me like I'm irreplaceable—but

I'm not. Valuable, yes. But they know what to do, now. And I wouldn't be able to look at myself in the mirror—much less accept the responsibilities they want to give me—if I let you bleed out in front of me."

He bit his lip, showing more uncertainty than she'd seen from him in a long time. "But you didn't know it would work."

A variety of painfully serious answers suggested themselves, but she couldn't bring herself to voice any of them. Instead, she gave him a wry smile. "Story of my life. I'm making it up as I go along."

SHE WOKE the next morning feeling like one very large sore muscle with a headache on top.

Eclipse said, "I think this is for you," and placed a message scroll on the ground in front of her face.

Mirei jerked upright, muscles screaming in protest. The blocking spell she'd cast before leaving Starfall must have worn off in the night, for anyone to send her anything—or had they targeted Eclipse? Paranoia made her clear her throat and hum, but there was no spell on the scroll, so she unrolled it and read.

> *THERE YOU ARE. We've been trying to find you since last night. Attack on Starfall—Hunters and Kalistyin soldiers, led by Arinei. They tried to poison us. How did you know? How is Shimi dead? Get back here at once.*

Mirei fetched a charred splinter from the fire and wrote on the back of the scroll in clumsy characters, *Can't come yet, unless you want me dead on the other side. With*

Eclipse. Oath gone. Will return to Silverfire, check on girls, come back when I can.

Eclipse peered over her shoulder as she wrote. "She's not going to like that."

"She can live with it," Mirei said, and dredged up the energy to send the scroll back.

She renewed the blocking spell right afterward, and that was the sum total of the magic she felt up to working that day. "I think we're on our own," Eclipse said when she was done. "I ran afoul of a patrol of Cousins when I got into the area, but turned out they were on the side of Starfall, and recognized me; they're the ones who arranged my diversion. But I don't particularly want to go back to that valley and look for them. Do you?"

They made their way on foot until they reached a farm where, with misgivings, Eclipse stole a horse. He hadn't taken coin with him when he left Silverfire, so it was that or walk the entire distance. Mirei marked the location of the farm in her mind, and vowed to repay the farmer later.

By the time they reached Silverfire, she had more energy, and so she didn't fall over when a patrol from the school descended on them and grilled them extensively at sword point before letting them pass. Mirei learned the reason for the caution when they got inside the compound.

Jaguar stood outside the stable, arms crossed over his chest and an unamused look on his face.

"Sir," Mirei said, and hastily dismounted to salute him.

"As I recall," the Grandmaster said in a cool, level tone, "I told you to bring Amas and Indera back to me. Not to send me a flock of girls I've never seen before."

She winced. "Sir, they—"

"I know who they are. The Void Prime sent a message."

He regarded her for a moment longer. "Are they leaving soon?"

"As soon as I can get them a proper escort."

He nodded. "Good. Keeping up the patrols has interfered with our usual schedule." And with no more statement on the matter, he turned to Eclipse. "You look good, for a dead man."

In her peripheral vision, Mirei saw Eclipse grin. "Thank you, sir."

"However you broke that oath, I don't want to know." Jaguar turned away as Briar came out to take the horse. "My office, five minutes," the Grandmaster called over his shoulder. "You're still half mine, Mirei, and I expect a report."

Epilogue

"You ready?" Eclipse asked from the door of Mirei's office.

She glanced up from a list of reports she'd received that morning from Kimeko. Though her work for the Void Heart Key made her into something of a glorified secretary, she'd settled into it better than she expected to. Helping rebuild Starfall's traditions to be stronger was not a bad way to spend her time.

At least they hadn't made her a Key yet. There had been plenty of vacancies at that rank once Hyoka pieced together the ritual that released the Primes from their positions; Satomi and Koika were reinstated, but Shimi was dead, Arinei was awaiting trial, and Rana had stepped down. Kekkai, despite rumblings, had taken Arinei's place. She was more qualified than Onomita, and her return to Starfall made her a better candidate than Mejiki, who was imprisoned along with Arinei and the two other Keys who had left. Paere of the Water Heart replaced Rana, and Naji replaced Shimi. All told, seven Key positions were vacant at the moment—but none of them in the Void Ray.

Satomi, when asked, made no bones about it. She wanted Mirei in her Ray, but wasn't so eager to get her into an administrative position—yet—that she would force one of her current Keys out. They both agreed that she needed experience first.

But the work Mirei was doing was Void work anyway, and so she didn't mind as much as she might have. Dealing with the Cousins, the Primes had decided, was the responsibility of the Void Ray, and she and Eikyo had been tapped as liaisons. Then there were the children to deal with: the doppelgangers to train in the fledgling school, and the witch-students to prepare for their tests. Only a few now, but there would be more, once the changes really started taking hold. For the time being at least, it seemed best to go on conducting the ritual of connection in infancy, and to let the doppelgangers and witch-halves grow up separately. Mirei was grateful that Eclipse had been allowed to stay at Starfall, to help her with the school, since in a few years they would have quite a lot of children to train.

Including those the Cousins had sent to them. The connection rituals for those five were coming up very, very soon, and Mirei prayed they would go well.

She wasn't the only one praying for it, either, and that was a good sign, too.

Eclipse snapped his fingers. "Message for Mirei. They want you downstairs."

She jerked out of her reverie. "Oh. Right." She rose and went to where he stood in the door, pausing long enough to touch his arm and smile. Their relationship, like so many things at Starfall, was still being sorted out, but she was grateful every day for the chance to do so.

As she went through the halls, Eclipse at her side, Mirei could still feel the uncertainty in the air. Nothing but time would make the new ways feel comfortable;

witches and Cousins alike were walking gingerly, unsure of what the changes would mean. Urishin's experience meant that no more witches would become Cousins, but what of the Cousins already in the world, those descended from the failed witches of the past? So much hinged on the five children they had given to Starfall.

Problems in the future, problems in the present. She wasn't looking forward to Arinei's trial. The Fire Prime had sold her people in multiple directions, spending coin she didn't have in a gamble to take Starfall. If anything saved her from execution, it would be that the poison put in the soup hadn't been intended as lethal; she'd asked the Hunters to prevent the women who ate it from singing. It would have killed them if left untreated, but she *had* intended to heal them.

Still, the fact remained that she'd made extravagant promises to Lady Chaha of Kalistyi, spread damaging rumors about Satomi and Mirei in other domains, arranged for Ice's murder to anger the Thornbloods, and then hired Thornbloods and Wolfstars alike to help her attack Starfall. She'd built a fragile house of political cards, and clearing the wreckage would take awhile.

But that was Kekkai's problem now, not Mirei's. At least until she finished recovering from translocation enough for Satomi to send her out as an emissary to the Hunter schools.

She'd already had an uncomfortable conversation with Jaguar about Amas and Indera.

"No one's sure whether Indera's still . . . well, still a doppelganger," Mirei told him when she was recuperating at Silverfire, waiting to escort the girls south. "In the physical sense. The theory witches are arguing about it."

They'd gotten right back to their intellectual debates before the smoke had even cleared from Starfall, to hear Satomi tell it.

"Can't they tell?" the Grandmaster asked.

"Not by looking at her," Mirei said. "And if she's still strong and fast, she isn't showing it. She won't train anymore. They're trying to decide what to do with her."

He bypassed the unspoken question for the moment. "Amas?"

"She and Hoseki are going to wait until they're older to go through the tests—though Satomi has ideas about how to change those, to make them safer. They might start before they're twenty-five. But Amas wants to go on training while she can."

Jaguar steepled his fingers, face lined with thought. "Given what's happened, I'm not sure she can return here. Or Indera."

Mirei nodded; she'd half-expected that. Too many people knew what the doppelgangers were, now. And, though Jaguar didn't mention it and probably didn't care, Lehant could never go back to Thornblood. Especially once they found out about the Thornblood involvement in the attack.

Today, though, Lehant was not her concern, nor was Amas.

Eclipse left her when they reached the downstairs room where the others waited. Satomi had decided to let him stay at Starfall, and he'd become the theory witches' favorite new object of study since Mirei saved him from the blood-oath, but there were some things they would not let him witness yet.

Satomi was there, along with Koika, Paere, Kekkai,

and Naji. And, a little distance away from the changed circle of Primes, were Urishin and Naspeth.

Together, the eight of them went across the nighttime courtyards and into Star Hall, to conduct a ritual performed only once before.

Beneath the shattered crossing and the eyes of the Goddess, Urishin sang and Naspeth danced, and strands of visible power wove around them, lifting them up. The four Elements of the world, coruscating with light, and only Mirei and the two girls could see the fifth one among them, defining their existence by opposition: the Void.

The light flared beyond Mirei's ability to watch, and then when it cleared a single, trembling figure knelt on the dais.

Smiling through her tears, Mirei went forward to welcome her sister witch into the world.

Glossary

Ai—the honorific used for an unranked witch of the Void Ray.

Air—one of the five Elements. Air is associated with the Bride. Among the witches, the Air Ray is itinerant, and serves anyone in need.

Akara—the honorific used for a Key of the Void Ray.

Aken—the honorific used for the Prime of the Void Ray.

Amas—a Hunter-trainee at Silverfire; eleven years old, and a year-mate of Indera. Doppelganger of Hoseki.

Anness—a child of two years; doppelganger of Chanka.

Arinei—a witch; Prime of the Fire Ray.

Ashin—a witch; the Key of the Air Hand; mother of Indera and Sharyo.

Atami—a witch; Key of the Water Hand.

Avannans—members of a religious sect that honors the Dance as the highest form of adoration to the Goddess.

Bansu—a witch; named interim Key of the Fire Hand.

Barani—a witch who became a Cousin.

Briar—a Hunter of Silverfire; stablemaster at the school.

Bride—the second Aspect of the Goddess, associated with marriage and the Element of Air.

Chaha—the Lady of Kalistyi; adherent of the Nalochkan sect.

Chai—the honorific used for an unranked witch of the Earth Ray.

Chaiban—a witch-student with a doppelganger.

Chakoa—the honorific used for a Key of the Earth Ray.

Chanka—a witch-student; two years old; witch-half of Anness.

Chashi—the honorific used for the Prime of the Earth Ray.

Chime—a division of the clock developed in Insebrar; each lasts three hours. In order, they are Low, Dark, First, Mid, High, Light, Late, and Last.

Churicho—a witch, named interim Key of the Fire Heart.

Cloudhawk—one of the Hunter schools, training bonded spies, who are often employed by Lords or other powerful figures.

Cousin—term used for the servants of the witches, descended from witches who failed their final tests.

Crone—the eldest Aspect of the Goddess, associated with wisdom and the Element of Earth.

Dance—an art practiced in some temples (especially Avannan temples) to honor the Goddess.

Dark—the second chime of the clock, corresponding to 3 A.M.

Domain—the primary political unit. Formerly the fifteen domains were subsets of three large kingdoms, but those realms fractured centuries ago.

Earth—one of the five Elements. Earth is associated with the Crone. Among the witches, the Earth Ray serves the land itself, working to prevent droughts and other natural disasters.

Eclipse—a Hunter of Silverfire; twenty-five years old; year-mate of Mirage.

Edame—a witch of the Fire Hand; serves Lord Iseman and Lady Terica of Haira as the domain adviser.

Eikyo—a witch-student at Starfall; twenty-five years old, and a friend of Miryo's.

Elements—the substances that make up the world. Each has a variety of symbolic associations. The five Elements are Fire, Air, Water, Earth, and Void.

Falya—a child of nine years; doppelganger of Yimoe.

Fire—one of the five Elements. Fire is associated with the Maiden. Among the witches, the Fire Ray serves the rulers of the land as advisers.

First—the third chime of the clock, corresponding to 6 A.M.

Gichara—a witch of the Water Hand; stationed in central Miest.

Goyoi—a witch; Key of the Earth Hand.

Hand—one of the three Paths. Witches of the Hand carry out the work of their Ray, usually in other domains.

Hassei—a witch; Key of the Air Head.

Head—one of the three Paths. Witches of the Head conduct the research and recordkeeping of their Ray, often in Starfall or one of the domain halls.

Heart—one of the three Paths. Witches of the Heart are the organizational and administrative structure of their Ray, and often live in Starfall.

High—the fifth chime of the clock, corresponding to noon.

Hoseki—a witch-student, eleven years old; witch-half of Amas.

Hunter—an individual trained by one of the Hunter schools. Hunters may be trained in a specialty, such as spying, assassination, bodyguarding, or mercenary soldiering, or they may generalize. Some are bonded; others are freelance. All Hunters are highly skilled at individual combat. Their training lasts for ten years, ending at the age of twenty.

Hyoka—a witch; Key of the Void Head.

Ice—a Hunter of Thornblood, twenty-seven years old. A long-standing enemy of Mirage, she sold information on Miryo and Mirage to the Primes.

Indera—a Hunter-trainee at Silverfire; eleven years old, and a year-mate of Amas. Doppelganger of Sharyo, and daughter of Ashin.

Iseman—the Lord of Haira, and husband of Terica; like his wife, a devout Avannan.

Itsumen—a witch; Key of the Void Hand.

Jaguar—the Grandmaster of Silverfire.

Kai—the honorific used for an unranked witch of the Air Ray.

Kane—the honorific used for the Prime of the Air Ray.

Kasane—a witch of the Air Heart; mother of Miryo.

Kasora—the honorific used for a Key of the Air Ray.

Katsu—the honorific used for a witch of unknown or un-decided affiliation.

Kekkai—a witch; Key of the Fire Heart; succeeded Tari after her death.

Key—a witch who leads a Path. A new Prime is selected from among the Keys of the appropriate Ray.

Kimeko—a witch; Key of the Void Heart.

Koika—a witch; Prime of the Earth Ray.

Kyou—the Cousin name given to Eikyo.

Lady—the ruler of a domain, if female; the highest political rank.

Last—the eighth chime of the clock, corresponding to 9 P.M.

Late—the seventh chime of the clock, corresponding to 6 P.M.

Lehant—a Hunter-trainee at Thornblood; twelve years old; doppelganger of Owairi.

Light—the sixth chime of the clock, corresponding to 3 P.M.

Linea—the Lady of Abern.

Lord—the ruler of a domain, if male; the highest political rank.

Low—the first chime of the clock, corresponding to mid-night.

Mai—the honorific used for an unranked witch of the Water Ray.

Maiden—the youngest Aspect of the Goddess, associated with youth and the Element of Fire.

Makiza—the honorific used for a Key of the Water Ray.

Mari—the honorific used for the Prime of the Water Ray.

Mejiki—a witch; Key of the Fire Hand.

Menukyo—a witch; eldest daughter of Monisuko, and granddaughter of Misetsu. She was the first to kill her doppelganger.

Mid—the fourth chime of the clock, corresponding to 9 A.M.

Mirage—a Hunter of Silverfire; the doppelganger-half of the woman now known as Mirei.

Miryo—a witch of Starfall; the witch-half of the woman now known as Mirei.

Misetsu—the first witch; a holy woman who received the gift of magic for her piety. Had three daughters: Monisuko, Machayu, and Maiyaki, all of whom died from uncontrolled magic. Her granddaughter Menukyo was the first to successfully control her gift.

Mother—the third Aspect of the Goddess, associated with family and the Element of Water.

Nae—a Cousin; leader of the Cousins who dwell permanently at Starfall, who takes into custody any witch who fails.

Nai—the honorific used for an unranked witch of the Fire Ray.

Nakana—the honorific used for a Key of the Fire Ray.

Nalochkans—members of a religious sect that denies the Warrior Aspect of the Goddess.

Naji—a witch, Key of the Air Heart.

Naspeth—a Hunter-trainee of Windblade, eleven years old; doppelganger of Urishin.

Nayo—the honorific used for the Prime of the Fire Ray.

Nenikune—a witch in charge of the Starfall infirmary.

Obura—a witch of the Water Head; pregnant with her third daughter.

Ometrice—a doppelganger; age seven.

Onomita—a witch; Key of the Fire Head.

Orezha—Satomi's doppelganger.

Owairi—a witch-student, twelve years old; witch-half of Lehant.

Palend—the former Lord of Abern; predecessor to his daughter Linea.

Path—one of the three divisions of a Ray, each dedicated to a different function. The three Paths are the Hand, the Head, and the Heart. A Path is led by a Key.

Prime—a witch who leads a Ray. Together, the five Primes rule the domain of Starfall, and the witches who serve in other domains.

Rana—a witch; Prime of the Water Ray.

Ranell—a doppelganger; age six.

Ray—one of the five divisions used among the witches, corresponding to the Elements. Each Ray serves a different subset of the world. A Ray is led by a Prime.

Rin—leader of the eastern Cousins.

Rigai—a witch of the Void Head; part of Hyoka's research group of theorists.

Rinshu—a witch; Key of the Water Head.

Ruriko—a witch of the Void Heart; secretary to Satomi.

Satomi—a witch; Prime of the Void Ray; killed her doppelganger, Orezha.

Seniade—the childhood name of Mirage.

Sharyo—a witch-student, eleven years old; witch-half of Indera; daughter of Ashin.

Shimi—a witch; Prime of the Air Ray.

Silverfire—one of the Hunter schools, training freelancers who do a variety of work. Their school is located a short distance away from Elensk in Miest. They have a longstanding rivalry with Thornblood.

Slip—a Hunter of Silverfire, retired from active work; twin of Wisp; Jaguar's secretary.

Snowspear—a Hunter school founded as an offshoot of Wildmoon over a hundred years ago.

Stoneshadow—one of the Hunter schools, training bonded assassins, who are often employed by Lords or other powerful figures.

Tajio—a witch of the Void Head; part of Hyoka's research group of theorists.

Tari—a witch; the Key of the Fire Heart Path; now deceased; assassinated by Wraith on the orders of the Primes, for her part in helping doppelgangers survive.

Terica—the Lady of Haira, and wife of Iseman; like her husband, a devout Avannan.

Thornblood—one of the Hunter schools, training freelancers who do a variety of work. Their school is located north of **Angrim** in Abern. They have a longstanding rivalry with Silverfire.

Tokaga—a witch; Void Prime when Satomi became a witch.

Tserenar—one of the three Old Kingdoms, encompassing land now divided into the domains of Miest, Liak, Askavya, and Kalistyi.

Ueda—a witch; Key of the Earth Heart.

Ukotto—a witch of the Fire Head.

Urishin—a witch-student, eleven years old; witch-half of Naspeth.

Viper—a Hunter of Silverfire.

Void—one of the five Elements. Void is associated with the Warrior. Among the witches, the Void Ray serves the witches themselves, handling the internal affairs of Starfall and its people. Alone among the Elements, Void does not make up a part of the physical world, but rather represents that which is not the world.

Wall—the Grandmaster of Windblade.

Warrior—the fifth Aspect of the Goddess, associated with death, warfare, and the element of the Void. Alone among the Aspects, she does not stand for a stage in the cycle of life, but rather for the end of that life.

Water—one of the five Elements. Water is associated with the Mother. Among the witches, the Water Ray serves the common people of the land, often living in the larger villages and towns to heal diseases and handle other problems.

Wheel—a silver coin used in Abern and neighboring domains.

Wildmoon—a Hunter school, from which Snowspear split off.

Wisp—a Hunter of Silverfire, retired from active work; twin of Slip; stationed as an agent in Angrim.

Yimoe—a witch-student, nine years old; witch-half of Falya.

About the Author

MARIE BRENNAN holds an undergraduate degree in archaeology and folklore from Harvard and is now pursuing a Ph.D. in anthropology and folklore at Indiana University, which means that people keep giving her things like degrees and fellowship money for studying stuff that's useful to her as a fantasy writer. She rather likes this arrangement. Because she's been in school without interruption since she was five, she doesn't have the list of odd jobs that a writer should, although she did work one summer pruning Christmas trees with a very large serrated knife, which ought to count for something.

Warrior and Witch is the sequel to her first novel, *Doppelganger*. More information on the novels and her short stories may be found at http://www.swantower.com.

If you like **Warrior and Witch**

You'll love . . .

Doppelganger

*Turn the page
for a sneak peek.*

CHAPTER ONE

Commission [Mirage]

RAIN PATTERED STEADILY through the leaves of the wood and dripped to the ground below. Two figures slipped between the trees, all but invisible in the darkness, silent under the cover of the rain. The one in the lead moved well, but the one trailing him moved better, ghost-like and undetectable, and he never knew she was there.

Three men waited for him, crouching in a tight clump under an old elm and shivering in the rain. He came up to them and spoke in a low voice. "She's alone. And looks like she'll be bedding down soon enough. If we wait, she should be easy to take."

Hidden in the trees just a short distance away, the woman who had been following him smiled thinly.

"I still don't like this," one of the other men hissed. "What if she's got spells set up or something?"

The woman's jaw hardened, and the amusement faded from her face.

"She ain't a witch," someone else said, with the tone of a man who's said it several times already. "You saw her in the alehouse. She damn near cut that fellow's throat when he called her one. And Tre would have said if she'd been singing when he looked in on her."

"She wasn't," the spy confirmed. "Just talking to her horse, like anybody does. And besides, witches don't carry swords, or play cards in alehouses. She's just a Cousin."

"We're wasting time," the last of the men said. "Heth, you go first. You make friends with the horse so it don't warn her. Then Nessel can knock her out. Tre and I'll be ready in case something goes wrong."

"Some help that'll be if she *is* a witch," the fearful one said. "How else did she manage to get five Primes in one hand?"

The leader spat into the bushes. "She probably cheated. Don't have to be a witch to cheat at cards. Look, there's four of us and one of her. We'll be fine."

Ten of you wouldn't be enough, the woman thought, and her smile returned. *Not against a Hunter. Not against me.*

Mirage didn't object to being accused of cheating at cards, especially not when it was true. She *did* object to being called a witch—or a Cousin, for that matter. And she objected to being driven out to sleep in a rain-drenched wood, when she'd been hoping for a warm, dry inn. Now these idiotic thugs were planning on *jumping* her?

They deserved what they were going to get.

She slipped away from the men and returned to her campsite. Surveying it, she calculated the directions Heth and Nessel were likely to come from, then arranged her bedding so it would look as though she were in it. The illusion was weaker from the other direction, but with the fire in the way, any scouts on the other side shouldn't be able to see anything amiss.

Then she retired to the shadows and waited.

The men took their time in coming, but Mirage was patient. Just as her fire was beginning to burn low, she heard noise; not all of the men were as good at moving through the forest as Tre. Scanning the woods, she saw the spy nearby, already in place. She hadn't heard him get there. Not bad.

Quiet whispers, too muted for her to pick out. Then one man eased up next to her horse.

Ordinarily that would have been a mistake. Mist was trained to take the hand off any stranger who touched her. But Mirage had given her a command before leaving, and so the mare stood stock-still, not reacting to the man trying to quiet the noises she wasn't making.

Mirage smiled, and continued to wait.

Now it was Nessel's turn. The leader, who had slid around to the far side of the fire, gestured for him to move. Nessel came forward on exaggerated tiptoe, club in his hands. Then, with a howl, he brought the weapon crashing down on her bedding.

Tre went down without a sound half a second later. Fixed on the scene in front of him, he never noticed Mirage coming up behind him.

"She's not here!" Nessel yelled in panic.

Mist, responding to Mirage's whistle, kicked Heth in the chest and laid him out flat. Mirage stepped into the firelight next to the horse. "Yes, I am," she said, and smiled again.

Nessel, a credit to his courage if not to his brain, charged her with another yell. Mirage didn't even bother to draw a blade; she sidestepped his wild swipe and kicked him twice, once in the chest and once in the head. He went down like a log. Mirage, pausing only to give Heth a judicious tap with her boot, leapt over the fire in pursuit of the last man.

He fled as soon as she appeared, but it wasn't enough of a head start. Mirage kept to an easy pace until her eyes adjusted once more; then she put on a burst of speed and overtook him. A flying tackle brought him down. She came up before he did and stamped on his knee, ending any further chance of flight.

Then she knelt, relieving him of the dagger he was trying to draw, and pinned him to the ground. "What did you think you were doing?" she growled, holding the dagger ready.

He was trying not to cry from the pain of his injured knee. "Gold," he gasped. "Only that. We weren't going to kill you. I swear!"

"I believe you," Mirage said. "And for that, you live. Provided you learn one little lesson."

He nodded fearfully.

"I," Mirage said, "am not a witch. Nor am I a Cousin. I have *nothing* to do with them. Can you remember that?" He nodded again. "Good. And be sure to tell your friends." She stood and tucked his dagger into her belt. "I don't like people making that kind of mistake."

Then, with a swift kick to his head, she knocked him out.

ECLIPSE SCOWLED as he shouldered his way through the crowds swarming through the streets of Chervie. The newer parts of the city, outside the walls built during the city's heyday as an Old Kingdom capital, were more open in their plan, but here in the central parts even carts couldn't make it down half the lanes. That had never been a problem for him before, but then he'd never been in Chervie this close to the Midsummer Festival. It seemed

that every resident of the city had packed back inside the
Old Kingdom walls, along with all twelve of their country
cousins. The sheer press of people made him twitchy and
irritable. It was a relief to step into the alehouse he was
seeking; the interior was full, but it was nothing compared
to the streets outside.

He scanned the patrons, dressed up for festival in bead-
work and lace, and soon spotted a familiar and distinctive
head. She found him at the same instant, and even across
the room he could see her light up. He sidled his way between the tables and came up to her, grinning. "Sitting
with your back to a door, Seniade? What *would* our teach-
ers say?"

"They'd say I should have picked a different alehouse.
Two doors on opposite walls, and hardly a seat to be
found in the whole room. I decided to watch one and take
my chances with the other."

He snagged a stool out from under a patron who had
just stood to leave and settled himself onto it. "Well, I'll
watch your back and you watch mine. Not all of us have
your reflexes, Sen."

She quirked one eyebrow at him. "You know, you're
the *only* one who still calls me that. Even the rest of our
year-mates call me Mirage."

"And you still call me Kerestel. Old habits die hard, I
guess. Or else we're slow learners."

Mirage grinned. "Can you believe this crowd? I'd forgotten how seriously they take Midsummer in Liak. I
knew Chervie would be full, but this is ridiculous—and
the festival hasn't even really started yet! It's a shock,
after the quiet of the road."

"From what I hear, your trip wasn't what I'd call quiet," Eclipse said pointedly.

Mirage raised her eyebrow again.

"I came here by way of Enden. An alehouse maid there treated me to—well, several things, but two stories in particular. One about how a soldier playing cards was almost knifed in their common room, and another about how four village lads showed up the next morning, bruised, bloody, and stripped of everything but their skins."

"They were lucky to keep those. I figured they owed me their coin for trying to steal mine, and as for the other . . ." She shrugged. "I wouldn't have actually *stabbed* him."

"Your fuse has gotten shorter, I see. Or did he have an extra deck up his sleeve?"

"No," Mirage said, looking down. "In fact, I won the hand."

Eclipse leaned forward. "Void it. That again?"

"Yeah." She sighed. Eclipse noted frustrated fury in her eyes when she lifted her head, but it was soon muted. "Same with the four fools. Except *they* thought I was a Cousin."

"So they're idiots. Not all witches have red hair. And just because you *do* doesn't make you one of them, or one of their servants."

"Tell that to the idiots who panic when I lay down five Primes."

His eyes widened. "You did that? No wonder they were suspicious."

"It didn't take magic," Mirage said, and grinned wickedly. "Just agile fingers."

Eclipse swore a blistering oath that earned him a dark look from a prim-mouthed merchant woman at the next table. "Void it, Sen, you're going to get yourself killed! Cheating at cards is *not* going to improve your reputation!"

She shrugged. "I was bored."

"Bored?" He stared at her in disbelief. "Of all the people I know, you're the *last* one I would expect to court trouble just because you're bored."

Mirage gestured dismissively and looked away.

He caught hold of her arm, worried. "No, don't you brush me off. What's wrong?"

She pulled her wrist free of his grip and sighed. "Nothing. I'm just . . . bored."

"Haven't you had any jobs lately?"

"Plenty. So many, in fact, that I'm taking a rest; Mist and I have been on the road for months. Three hires, all back-to-back. Courier run clear across the land from Insebrar to Abern, for starters, and then they had word that a town farther out in the mountains was having trouble from bandits—ended up being some men they'd turned out of their town for thievery. Then *they* said a village even farther out needed a bloody *mountain cat* hunted down."

Eclipse smiled, hoping to lighten her mood. "Looks like they took the term 'Hunter' in the wrong sense."

Mirage snorted. "The saddest thing is, that bloody cat was the most interesting part of the whole series. It was a damn sight more intelligent than those so-called bandits."

"So that's why you're bored."

"Kerestel, I haven't felt *challenged* since . . . since I got that commission two years ago. Remember, when I was sent to Hunt Kobach?"

"The one who tried to take the rule of Liak from Narevoi?"

"I went through seven domains after him. Finally caught him in Haira, not too long after I left you. That was *tough,* Kerestel. It made me work, made me actually use the skills I've learned. Since then, though . . . nothing. Routine. Boredom."

Eclipse eyed her and tried to gauge her exact mood. He had the answer to her problems tucked in his belt pouch, but right now, with her recent difficulties, might *not* be the time to bring it up. It might help, or it might be more trouble than it was worth.

And speaking of trouble . . .

Distracted as he was by his thoughts, he hadn't even seen the woman come in the door. Eclipse opened his mouth to warn Mirage, but it was too late.

"Well, if it isn't the witch-brat," the newcomer said, stalking up to them. She always stalked; he didn't think he'd ever seen her in a good mood.

Mirage's eyes sparked. She turned in her chair and leaned back with an air of pure, unadulterated arrogance. "Ah, Ice. So good to see your usual frigid self."

Ice's own blue eyes smoldered with a low fury which belied her name. Smoldering was her usual state; eye color was the only conceivable reason she'd ended up being called "Ice." Then she lifted her gaze to meet Eclipse's, and suddenly her expression held a different sort of fire. "Well met, Eclipse."

"Keep your claws off him, Ice," Mirage said, her voice flat. "I just ate lunch, and I wouldn't want to lose it watching you try your tricks on him."

"Taken already, is he?" Ice asked with a malicious smile.

Eclipse stiffened. He considered Mirage a sister; most Hunters of the same school and year did. What Ice was implying was little short of incest. But Mirage, to judge by her own faint smile, had things well in hand. "No, dear. I'm not so desperate that I have to seduce my own year-mate—although from what I've heard about Lion, it seems *your* luck isn't so good."

Eclipse stifled a laugh. He hadn't heard *that* particular rumor. Mirage might be making it up, but Ice's expression suggested she wasn't. Now it was his turn to add fuel to the fire. "Come, ladies, this is no talk for the week before Midsummer. This is a festival! We should be celebrating! Ice, please, join us in a drink. I'm told this place has an excellent stock of silverwine."

He thought he heard a snarl. Silverwine—not a wine at all, but an appallingly strong vodka—was brewed in the Miest Valley, and was the drink of choice for Hunters from Silverfire, Mirage and Eclipse's school of training.

"Now, Eclipse," Mirage said reprovingly before Ice could get any words past her clenched teeth. "This may be a festival, but you know Hunters should try to keep clear heads. Silverwine is hard on those not used to it; we wouldn't want to lead Ice into trouble."

The inarticulate noises Ice was making were quite entertaining. She was such fun to goad; for some reason Hunters from Thornblood all seemed to have short fuses.

"I can drink anything you can," Ice snarled finally. Red mottled her face and neck.

Mirage smiled a touch too sweetly. "I'm sure you can, my dear." Ice could probably drink Mirage under the table; Thornbloods prided themselves on the amount of alcohol they could down. But Ice was too infuriated to think clearly. "I'm afraid, however, that I have important matters to attend to—ones that won't permit me to get drunk with an old friend."

"What 'important' matters?" Ice spat. "You spend your time catching wife-beaters and rescuing kittens from trees."

Eclipse hesitated. He and Mirage had played in these verbal duels before; it was his turn to attack. And he had a very good response to Ice's insult. The problem was, if he brought it out now, he might hurt Mirage more than Ice.

Recovering from his pause, Eclipse made his decision. He slipped one hand into his belt pouch and removed a tiny scroll. Keeping his fingers over the seal, he waved it to get Ice's attention.

Both of the other Hunters froze, looking at it. Eclipse nodded, smiling. "A two-person commission," he said, addressing the Thornblood. "Mirage and I will be handling it together."

The fury on Ice's face was profoundly satisfying. Official commissions were rare enough that receiving one was an honor; as far as he knew, she hadn't been offered one yet, in seven years out of Thornblood. This would be his first as well, but the second for Mirage.

Across the table, Mirage's expression was incredulous. Eclipse was pleased by the delight in her eyes; this was, he well knew, the answer to her complaints of boredom and inactivity. Commissions were always difficult, always a challenge.

He just hoped she wouldn't kill him when she found out who had ordered the job.

Ice was still apoplectic. "Who's it from?" she growled at last.

He pulled the scroll away when she tried to reach for it. "Uh-uh," he admonished her, waving one finger in her face. "Authorized Hunters only. I'm afraid you'll have to wait with everyone else to find out what we're up to." He tucked the scroll back into his pouch. Once he got Mirage alone, he'd tell her more.

Mirage had smoothed her expression by the time Ice looked at her. She smiled at the Thornblood. "Don't worry, Ice," she said. "I'm sure you'll get your turn— some day."

That, coming from a Hunter two years her junior, was too much for the Thornblood. Growling, Ice turned and stormed out of the alehouse.

As soon as she was gone, Mirage leaned forward. "When were you planning on telling me about *this*?"

Eclipse shrugged uncomfortably. "I was about to say something when she showed up. I'm sorry; I didn't mean to trap you into it."

"Trap me? As if I'd turn a commission *down*?"

He stood to hide his discomfort. "Come on. Let's go someplace more private to talk."

MIDSUMMER TRADITION IN CHERVIE meant that no one cooked and ate at home if they could afford not to, which meant that everybody with two coins to rub together was eating somewhere in the city's public quarters. Prices skyrocketed, and space at tables, along counters, and under awnings became harder to come by than fresh fruit in winter. Mirage had to pay through the nose for a small, private dining room in a place called the Garden of

Bells. It was more like a private closet than a whole room, but the Garden's architecture was copied from an eastern style; the fretwork walls would be very cold in Chervie's northern winters, but on this summer day it was pleasantly cool. Besides, there was nowhere for an eavesdropper to hide.

Normally she wouldn't have dreamed of paying the cost, but she was starving, the Garden had good food, and the commission was sure to pay enough that she could indulge a bit. "So, what *will* we be doing?" she asked her year-mate once the maid bringing in the roast pheasant and fruit had departed.

Eclipse looked uneasy.

Mirage put her fork down and gave him a sharp look. "What is it?"

By way of response, he pulled the scroll out again and rolled it across the table to her. Mirage picked it up and froze.

The seal was pressed into black wax flecked with silver—a color only one group of people used. And the sigil itself, a triskele knot intersecting a circle, would be instantly recognizable to even the most illiterate of peasants.

It was the symbol of the witches.

Mirage set the scroll down carefully and looked across at Eclipse. "This is from Starfall."

"Yes," he admitted.

Mirage stood and walked to the fretwork wall, putting her hands against it. Behind her she could hear him shift uncomfortably.

"You don't have to," he said at last. "No matter what we said to Ice. Everyone knows you stay away from witches; everyone would understand if you turned it down. Everyone who matters, anyway."

More silence. Mirage closed her eyes. "What do they want?"

"I don't know," he said. "I haven't opened it yet."

"How did you get it?"

"Jaguar. A Void Hand witch brought the scroll to him; he chose me to take it on."

Jaguar's not stupid, Mirage thought. *He knew Eclipse would pick me as his second.*

What's his motive?

"A Void witch," she said, turning away from the wall at last. "Then it's an internal issue."

Eclipse nodded. "Which might explain why they're hiring Hunters. They may not trust their own people to be impartial."

Mirage returned to the table and picked up the scroll. *A commission from the witches. I wanted a new challenge, but not from them.*

"If you're uncomfortable . . ." Eclipse began again.

Mirage broke the seal with her thumb and unrolled the scroll. Now she was committed; it was a hanging offense for such a message to be read by an unauthorized person. So absorbed was she in fighting down her irrational surge of uneasiness, she almost did not notice Eclipse rising to read over her shoulder.

The message was short, and brutally to the point.

"No wonder they wanted the insurance of two Hunters," Eclipse breathed into her ear. "Although what the Key of the Fire Heart Path was doing out where she could be assassinated escapes me."

"Damn them to *Void,*" Mirage growled, flinging the

scroll across the room. *Surge of uneasiness, my ass.* It had been a spell settling into place. "They've enchanted us against speaking of it."

"Do you blame them?" Eclipse asked.

"No." She sighed and pressed her hands against her eyes.

Her fellow Hunter crossed the floor and picked up the scroll once more. "Blank."

No more than I expected.

"This could mean trouble," he said reluctantly.

"Trouble" didn't come close to describing the possible outcome, and they both knew it. The commission, before it had faded, had commanded them not only to Hunt the assassin, but also to seek out whoever had been behind the task. And only someone very powerful could afford to pay for the death of such a high-ranking witch.

"If we call Hunt on a Lord or Lady . . ."

Mirage would have preferred him to leave it unspoken. "They may not ask for that. The witches may prefer to take care of payback themselves."

"From your lips to the Warrior's heart," Eclipse murmured.

Grim silence followed his prayer, before Mirage rose to her feet. "Well. We're instructed to present ourselves in Corberth before the full moon. We've just enough time to make it. Unless you want to be late?"

"Not on your life," Eclipse said.

"FRESH, HIP, FANTASTIC"* FICTION
by Carrie Vaughn

"I relished this one. Carrie Vaughn's *Kitty and The Midnight Hour* has enough excitement, astonishment, pathos, and victory to satisfy any reader."
> —New York Times bestselling author
> Charlaine Harris, author of *Definitely Dead*

Kitty and the Midnight Hour
(0-446-61641-9)

Kitty Norville is a midnight-shift DJ for a Denver radio station—and a werewolf in the closet. Her new late-night advice show for the supernaturally disadvantaged is a raging success, but it's Kitty who can use some help. With one sexy werewolf-hunter and a few homicidal undead on her tail, Kitty may have bitten off more than she can chew . . .

Kitty Goes To Washington
(0-446-61642-7)

The country's only celebrity werewolf, late-night radio host Kitty Norville is invited to testify at a Senate hearing on behalf of supernaturals. Kitty's been in hot water before, but jumping into the D.C. underworld brings a new set of problems. And a new set of friends and enemies. Kitty quickly learns that in this city of dirty politicians and backstabbing pundits, everyone's itching for a fight.

* "Fresh, hip, fantastic—Don't miss this one, you're in for a real treat!"
> —L.A. Banks, author of
> *The Vampire Huntress Legends* series

AVAILABLE WHEREVER BOOKS ARE SOLD.

When the Devil needs a demon killed, who does he call?

**Dante Valentine,
Necromance-for-hire.**

NOVELS BY LILITH SAINTCROW

"Lilith Saintcrow's *Working for the Devil* is pure fantasy and fun. A take into a different world, a fantastic escape. I enjoyed it tremendously."
—Heather Graham, New York Times
bestselling author on *Working for the Devil*

Working For the Devil
(0-446-61670-2)

The Devil hires Dante to eliminate a rogue demon: Vardimal Santino. In return, he will let her live. It's an offer she can't refuse. But how do you kill something that can't die?

Dead Man Rising
(0-446-61671-0)

Psychics all over the city are being savagely murdered—and a piece of the past Dante thought she'd buried is stalking the night with a vengeance. Now her most horrifying nightmares are gathering to take one kick-ass bounty hunter down for the count.